DEEP CROSSING

Editor:
Frank MacDonald
Contact: SciFiProofreadingDoneRight@gmail.com
Web Site: https://sites.google.com/site/scifiproofreading

ISBN 978-0-692-64995-4

Mase Publishing

Adrian Tarn Series Books by E.R. Mason:

Fatal Boarding

Deep Crossing

Shock Diamonds

Dark Vengeance

Mu Arae

info@freefallamerica.com

Digital Publishing of Florida, Inc.
Book Printing for the Author and Publisher
www.digitaldata-corp.com
2016

Chapter 1

I was surf fishing off the rocks at Port Canaveral when they arrived. You are not allowed to fish off the rocks, so I was gambling I could bring something in before the beach patrol showed up and brought me in.

It was the perfect time of day. The morning's peak tide was just beginning to ease out, encouraging the pompano to gather beyond the breakers where they waited to collect sand fleas before the beach line became too shallow.

They don't like you out on the rocks because it's easy to fall and if you do you will almost certainly be seriously hurt. Then the paramedics must do their least favorite imitation of Laurel and Hardy trying to maneuver a body board out onto the jagged breakwater to bring you in. My six-foot-two frame would be an added disappointment to them if such an incident did occur, and I already have enough scars here and there to commemorate the philosophy of not obeying rules. But, there it is.

So, struggling to balance myself and at the same time set a frozen shrimp on my hook, I was trying to keep an eye out for the shore patrol's ATV when the shuttle suddenly came streaking in above the trees. It was a gaudy entrance, really. They hovered over the parking lot for longer than needed, then settled into the RV parking area having caused everyone on the beach and in the picnic area to stop what they were doing and gawk. There were fifty or sixty others enjoying the ocean so I figured there was a good chance this wasn't about me. Still, the eagle and olive branch seals on the shuttle's polished blue and white surface gave me pause to worry since I recently had more attention from government agencies than any mortal man should have to bear.

It was too good a day to waste. I cast out, teetered a bit, then slowly brought in the slack until I could feel the pyramid sinker. Waiting to feel the quick hard taps on the end of the line, I watched in the direction of the shuttle, hoping its occupants had other business.

Three of them emerged. They were not wearing beachwear. The lead man was short, balding, and wore a light blue Nehru-styled suit with matching sunglasses. He was followed by two in standard black Alfani's with dark sunglasses. I don't know why those guys don't just have the word security embroidered in big letters on their suit backs.

The lead man took a confused path to the edge of the beach, chin up, looking erratically for a particular individual. Too late, I thought to turn my back. The delicate little man's gaze zeroed in and locked on me. He made an obtuse gesture and began tromping through the sand in my direction, dragging his black suits along with him. Beach-goers continued to stop and stare at the three white-skinned, fully dressed invaders intruding on their shore.

He came to the rock-covered beach and began waving one hand as though it had a handkerchief in it. His bodyguards tried to conceal their embarrassment by scanning the beach for aggressors, though everyone had already decided this man was not worth their attention. I was far enough out that he had to yell, something he did not seem accustomed to. "Mr. Tarn… Mr. Tarn, may I interrupt your maritime quest for a word?"

I pointed to the water and yelled back, "My line's already out. Your shoes are getting wet."

He looked down, became alarmed, and tiptoed back away from the foam. "Really Mr. Tarn, despite the importance of your immediate investment, I think it would be wise for you to join me."

"Who are you?"

He looked down in dismay, gathered himself and began again. "My name is Bernard Porre, senior advisor to the Global Space Initiative."

I cursed under my breath. His title commanded more respect than his appearance. "You'd better get out of the sun. I'll be right there."

He stared for a moment, waved in disdain, and headed back toward the parking area.

Begrudgingly I made my way to their shuttle, tapped on the hatch and stood back. It hissed upward, allowing cold air to push by. Bernard sat at a small desk behind the pilot. He motioned me in and pointed at a seat as the door gushed closed.

"Bernard, right up front, if you're here to sell me on something you're setting yourself up for disappointment."

He was not deterred. He picked up a folder, opened it and patted the top page. "I am going to propose a mission to you, Mr. Tarn. You are going to accept, and then I will leave, hopefully forever."

"Well, you're right about one thing."

"You haven't been in trouble recently, have you? No new injuries or illnesses? Anything that would affect your flight status?"

"For God's sake, Bernard. What is this about?"

"Have you heard of the Griffin, Mr. Tarn?"

"It sounds vaguely familiar."

"It is a prototype, designed by a retired transport pilot. It is unique in that it's a spacecraft that can deploy wings and perform atmospheric flight, if necessary. The designer disliked the idea that a re-entering spacecraft that lost thrust and gravity repulsion became rocklike. Because of his reputation, he was able to pull in a few investors, and the prototype was constructed. It's the only one of its kind. Spacecraft systems became so fail-proof by the time it was completed the concept was deemed unnecessary.

"Fail-proof is an oxymoron, I think."

"If I may continue. The Griffin's design and systems work perfectly. It is an interstellar craft that can fly in an atmosphere using wings when necessary. The wings are normally swept back to become part of the superstructure."

"Did you say interstellar?"

"It supports a crew of eight. It has both repulsive and OMS drives, along with one other significant drive system. No habitat gravity generators. Standard captain, first officer cabin arrangement with dual engineering stations behind them. Modest life support system. Quite a few extra amenities have been added."

"You did say interstellar."

"The mission is to take the Griffin to coordinates directly south of the ecliptic, one thousand light years from Earth, retrieve a certain artifact, gather intelligence, and return safely."

"Bernard, you misspoke. You said one thousand light years."

"No, I did not misspeak. I never do."

"Bernard, a trip that long would take years."

"Not for the Griffin."

"What are you talking about?"

"The Griffin has been equipped with two experimental Stellar Drive engines. You will get light beyond the P9 with it."

"You're pulling my leg."

He reached in a waist pocket of his suit and pulled out a small memory module. He pushed it at me. "This will give you everything on the Griffin. You'll need to begin studying right away. Time is constrained on this project. Your sim training is set up at Genesis. You can check in there anytime you like. You're already in the system. Is there anything special you need?"

"Bernard, you're taking way too much for granted here. I'm not going anywhere. In fact, let me outline for you how many items in your plan would make me say no just on their own merit. First, you want me to sign onto a small ship. I don't do that. If I'm going to give away months of my life, I don't intend to spend it in a sardine can. Second, what you're proposing means a really small crew. Too few people confined to too small a space tend to find reasons to dislike each other. Third, you implied it's a weightless habitat module. I don't mind zero G, but I'd prefer not spend months going somewhere floating around in it. The toilets always break down. Four, you're planning to take an experimental vehicle farther than anyone's ever gone before. Sound like a good idea to you? And five, did I understand correctly that you don't even know what the item is you intend to retrieve? No unmanned scout ships have checked that sector, am I right? It's all one big unknown. So there you are. Every aspect of this mission is exactly the kind I do not accept. On top of all that, I just recently survived a first class mission from hell. I'm not looking to tempt fate a second time. Sorry you wasted your time on the beach, Bernard. Is there anything else?"

"Actually there is one other thing, Mr. Tarn. Since you mentioned your previous assignment, I have your classified debriefing from the Electra right here. Let's take a quick look at it, shall we? Ah, Mr. Tarn where do I begin? I've studied your illustrious history until I could bear it no longer. How you achieved command status is well beyond my conception of reality and will remain so until my death I fear, and probably will contribute to the reward of that. In keeping with your infamy, your previous mission aboard the Electra was somewhat aberrant, wouldn't you say? The situation would need to be desperate in the extreme to facilitate your assuming command of a vessel that size. Don't you agree? In any case, beyond the long and sordid story described here, one of the many unexpected consequences of that debacle was your exposure to the emissary."

"You have my full attention now, but you'd better get to it."

"No one was to know about the alien emissaries aboard interstellar ships unless they had months of special preparation. Even now, their presence is a closely guarded secret. Were they not helping us, we would be stooges in space, wreaking havoc everywhere we went, not knowing the rules, customs, or dangers."

"You could give us a little more credit than that, I think."

"It says here you not only interacted with the emissary, but from what I gather this emissary actually physically touched you. That sort of thing has never happened before. Our intercourse with the Nasebian race is not as progressive as we would like it to be. They are a bit standoffish. "

"You don't need to tell me."

"Please, Mr. Tarn. So when an opportunity becomes available to advance our relations with them, there is very little we won't do. We recently had a meeting with their representatives, which lasted longer than all of our previous contacts combined. They have several planets which support them in various ways, societies that are more than happy to do so. We now have a chance to be one of those. The task they have offered us, however, is substantially beyond anything we have ever attempted. Since we understand very little about the Nasebian race, the story they told us was translated down into terms we could comprehend. According to their spokesperson, it's not broadly accurate, but is fundamentally correct. Roughly two thousand years ago, Earth time, a Nasebian repository ship was sent to a sector of deep space to establish a Centre. To them that is like a remote base of some kind. That's all we know. The Centre was successfully set up, but the ship never returned. The Nasebians know that some form of accident or foul play was involved, but they do not know what. The time has come that a component of this Centre must be retrieved. The Nasebians want us to retrieve it and learn what happened to their vessel and its Nasebian occupant."

"Why don't they just go get it themselves?"

"The closer one travels to the dark matter halo beyond the galactic boundary, the more primeval the surrounding space becomes. These coordinates are so deep they represent a sector so primitive it is not conducive to the Nasebians. It would be dangerous for them to venture there. It was something even they had not expected when the first mission was sent."

"Look, that's all fine and good, but it doesn't need to involve me. As you've repeatedly insinuated, there are quite a few others that represent your idea of command level much more than I do. Why are you wasting my time with this?"

"Does the name Mellennia mean anything to you, Mr. Tarn?"

"No."

"Mellennia is the Nasebian who is sponsoring this mission for us. Mellennia is also the Nasebian you interacted with on the Electra. Mellennia stipulated that only you can be the mission commander for this charter."

"Oh, shit."

The little twerp bent his head down and coughed out a quiet laugh, having known all along it was his ace in the hole. He gathered his tablet and tucked it into its holder, then piled it atop his briefcase. He sat back with a look of placid satisfaction. "Apparently the Nasebians have been looking a very long time for just the right person to lead this mission. It had to be someone with just the right amount of intelligence combined with foolhardiness. I made that last part up myself, but it's basically a good translation and it pleases me to say it. Our initial meetings took place six months ago. A month later, the Nasebian representative showed up with some engineers from a species unknown to us. They took possession of the Griffin. It was gone for three months and came back with the new engines and some other accessories. That's how sure they were that you'd accept. They did all that before allowing us to contact you."

"Son of a bitch."

"If it's any consolation to you, we didn't get much of what we wanted, either. We do not get to study the new engines. They will be recovered by the Nasebians' envoy when you return. We will understand how to operate them, but not how to service or construct them. Some of the other accessories they installed have the same restrictions. Also, we get to pick one pilot and one engineer. You choose the rest of your crew. There will be a total of four pilots including you, and four support engineers."

"For Pete's sake..."

"Since we've never flown these new engines, there will be a test flight before the actual mission with just the pilots. Those details will be forwarded to you. There is also a simulator being installed at the Cape. All four pilots will need to log considerable time in it beforehand."

Bernard did not offer me a chance to accept. He knew I could not refuse. Nor did he ask if there were questions. There were too many. He pushed up from his seat and tapped the open button by the shuttle door. With a disingenuous smile, he stood waiting for me to leave.

"Despite my contentious appraisal of you, Mr. Tarn, I am reassured that everything I've said is secure, and let me emphasize, we have given our word to the Nasebians that none of it will ever be released. Can we give you a lift somewhere?"

"No thanks. My corvette is parked out there."

"Ah yes, a man who could be using a PAV, and you cling to that outdated mode of travel from the combustion engine era. I have been told how dedicated you are to it."

"It's something you'll never be able to understand, Bernard."

"Tell me, Mr. Tarn, what do you do if one of those old-fashioned fabric tires deflates?"

"You change it, Bernard. Of course, you get your hands dirty."

"Well, let us hope that does not occur then."

"It doesn't happen often."

"You know, your propensity for demeaning eccentricity is surpassed only by your close associate Mr. R.J. Smith, who maintains that his antique Corvair automobile is still the finest land vehicle ever produced."

"Some of us have a need for speed, Bernard. You're too high up to get much of that in a personal air vehicle."

"Well, you'll be getting all the speed you could ask for on the Nadir mission, Mr. Tarn. Perhaps it will dampen your enthusiasm for it."

"Goodbye, Bernard."

I stepped down as his associates boarded the shuttle. I glanced back to see him wave a dainty salute and tap the hatch close button. To my relief, the shuttle door shut down his smiling, squirrelly little face. They afforded me the least amount of clearance possible, vented pre-thrust and lifted upward, turning one-eighty to face north. As I watched them engage, it occurred to me that Bernard had accomplished everything he said he would. He had outlined a mission, I had accepted it, and he had left smiling. The little twerp.

Chapter 2

The surf fishing was ruined. Thanks to Bernard, I could not get my mind back to it. I packed up, crossed the parking lot, and began to open the door of my Corvette when a pang of anger flared up. Maybe I should have taken a swing at him for the 'demeaning eccentricity' remark. You can screw with me a bit and get away with it, but do not screw with my car. Any Vette owner will tell you the same thing. I paused and wondered just how many of his slanted comments were delayed time bombs waiting to aggravate me.

It is a pristine, black, 1995 Corvette coupe, rebuilt to perfection from the ground up. As required, it's adapted to run biosynthetic fuel, which is okay with me, and the fact that biosyn gives you 2 percent more horsepower has nothing to do with that. Really.

PAV 'driving' is rated for morons. When their popularity began to soar, it didn't take many low-level horrific air crashes in the city to make computer control mandatory except in emergencies. That took the would-be fighter jocks and drunken-party people out of the equation real fast. These days, you get caught running in manual and you'll be grounded for a very long time.

On the road, the Corvette's punch was consoling. I hit the com button on my dash and got an erratic, blurry image of people, bottles, and blue sky until RJ finally got control of his wrist. He looked distracted and amused. "Ah, Kemosabi. Did you catch anything? If not, Cocoa Village appears well-stocked at the moment."

"I caught something, alright. What you doing?"

"We were innocently strolling along the cobblestone, minding our own business when some sort of unjustified celebration broke out. We seem to have become a part of that. There be ale here."

"Want to go flying?"

He stopped all motion and stared down at his communicator. "Don't tease me about such things. I've warned you about that."

"It'll be a really ugly vacation."

"Where?"

"You'll need to stop by. But do not bring any catch with you."

"I understand. Expect me to make my way there at P10."

"Funny you should say that."

"What?"

"See you at my place."

Back in my piece of hex-plex, I moped around in a daze mumbling to myself about suddenly being attached to a project without having made anyone grovel. I plugged Bernard Porre's memory stick into my PC and scrolled through the data on the Griffin. To my surprise, it seemed impressive. Perhaps I was placating myself by being overly optimistic. I closed it out for later, pulled off my fishing apparel, and headed for the shower. Within the embrace of steam, I complained out loud in hopes of restoring some illusion of independence but it only came out sounding like whining. Groping around from behind the shower curtain produced no towels. Naked and dripping, I marched down the hall to the kitchen to get my beach bag. A desperate cry rang out. "Oh lord, my eyes, my eyes! I'm blind!" RJ was sitting at the kitchen table drinking coffee from a paper cup. "Where is my seppuku sword when I need it? I can't live with what I've just seen."

I hustled my way back down the hallway to my bedroom, found something to dry with and pulled on jeans and a Jets T-shirt. Back in the kitchen, he shoved a capped cup of coffee at me. It was rich and dark and still hot.

"Cocoa Village was hopping, eh?"

"Yes, it was. Many voluptuous women in search of many things." RJ stroked his short red-brown beard and stared at the wall in recollection. His hair was a bit askew, as always. It gave him that could-be-crazy look that dogged Einstein, the same cranial aurora associated with people so absent in thought they forget where they are or what they were doing. They can drift off on you in mid-sentence, or in some cases even walk away in that same lost thought. Most of them have RJ's unkempt eyebrows. Too many lines in the face from too frequent and prolonged episodes of perplexed concentration. Dark eyes a little too piercing when they're genuinely focused on you can sometimes make you fear an awakening within that you're not ready to accept. Having known RJ since high school, I would trust him with my life. "How was the beach?" he asked, as he resurfaced and took a sip.

"Beautiful, up to a point."

"Mr. Porre was less than flattering, I take it."

"How'd you know?"

"They called because your com system was blocking them."

"Well, that didn't work."

"Some of his staff like to call him by his directory listing; Porre, Bernard."

"It's not just me then."

"No, it's pretty much a universal standard. Must've been a pretty big deal for him to show up like that."

"The little bastard made me an offer I couldn't refuse."

"I can tell your brain is compiling like a quantum processor. That's why you're wandering around the house naked. What's the scoop?"

"It's pretty ugly. You may not want it."

"Are you at the top of the heap?"

"I am on this one."

"Well then, I'm down. Now tell me how bad it is."

"Crew of eight. No grav. Have I lost you yet?"

"Hmm, that'll be a long first three days. Nope. Still aboard. Go on."

"Untested prototype vehicle. Unexplored deep space. Straight down from the ecliptic."

"Wow! Who the hell dreamed up this one?"

"Well put. That's classified."

"What's the objective?"

"Retrieve unspecified artifact. Gather intelligence."

"So we're taking an untested ship, to an unknown area of space, to pick up an unknown object?"

"Exactly what I said when they told me."

"What's my classification?"

"We'll sell you off as a systems engineer. Hell, you've done so much procedure assurance on that stuff you know more than most of them anyway."

"You sure you really want me on this one?"

"It's a truck load of unknowns. Your brain seems to be at its best with unknowns. Your relentless analytical saved our asses on the last trip. You're a walking think-tank. You see stuff that other people miss. Paradigms are like candy to you. My only fear is if anything happens to you I'll be mentally screwed forever."

"In that case, I shall be careful, Kemosabi. Who else will be entombed with us?"

"It's just you and me so far. The agency gets to pick two. The rest are up to me."

"Is Nira on your list?"

"Get out of jail free card on that one. She's the lead on the Electra data investigation. There's no way they'll let her go."

"You forget how persuasive she can be, or should I say how impossible to refuse. She got to you pretty good, didn't she?"

"She's still got me. That's why she shouldn't go."

"How about Perk Murphy?"

"I'm glad to say he's still not back on flight status from the Electra mission. He's okay but after that severe an injury, they get worried you might freeze up in an emergency. It's really pissing him off as I understand it, but he's in Honolulu recuperating with that blonde he met on Cocoa Beach."

"Ah, that one."

"I think this kind of trip might be too much on him too soon. Too small a spacecraft."

RJ leaned back in his seat and clasped his hands behind his head. "Well, if it's an eight-seater, I guess that rules my books out. I'll have to actually use that blasted reader. But, at least I can still cram an awful lot of crossword puzzle printouts in my case, along with my folding chess set. There's also my magnetic poker set. You have to take care of the important things first, you understand."

"You might consider heading back to the Village to pick up one of those voluptuous women in search of many things. It may be a long trip."

"You are correct, oh great mentor of man's primeval desires. I certainly would not want my last memory of someone naked to be you."

RJ left me to the wilderness of the decision-making I had suddenly inherited. It would have been a depressing executive state of mind except for one thought that kept overtaking all the others.

There was a new flight simulator being set up at Genesis. An accurate flight simulator is one step away from real flying. And, because you can do dangerous things in it without dying, it actually offers some possibilities the real thing does not. Flight Sims are complex machines. They take a variety of engineers and technicians to operate them. I wondered how far along the Griffin's was. I changed into gray flight coveralls, grabbed my keys and headed for the Cape.

Chapter 3

The Space Center is divided into two halves, the Manned Operations side, and the Eastern Range side. Manned Operations takes up part of the beach and a big section of inland. It's where that behemoth known as the space shuttle used to jump off and to this day, many people still call it the Shuttle side of the Cape. The Eastern Range occupies one side of Port Canaveral and its own big section of beach. It's always been considered a testing ground, and in keeping to that sentiment, an awful lot of vehicles never left the pad and even more came flaming down ahead of schedule.

Genesis is a very old facility located near the south gate of the Eastern Range dating way back to when it was called the Eastern Test Range, but some silly admiral decided the word "test" was too scary for the local residents so it was abbreviated down to the Eastern Range instead. The natives of Cape Canaveral have seen errant rocket motors splash down in their river, had a B-27 crash on the beach, heard numerous booms coming from the Center when there should not have been, and endured countless expensive fire works in the sky overhead from boosters that had developed minds of their own and were interrupted by the quick destruct trigger at Range Control. Good thing they took that word "test" out of the name so people won't be worried.

The facility called Genesis was built in an era that is beyond my imagination. It was from a time when vacuum tubes and hand soldered circuit boards put men into space. Today's strangely dominant language called software did not exist at the time, but man was headed for the moon so it needed to. Its time had come. There were plenty of zeros and ones hanging around, so why not organize them into a language for machines? That was the purpose of Genesis; create the first space system software. Invent a new way to talk to machines. Like everything else done during the Mercury and Apollo era, they did that and did it exceptionally well. So well, in fact, that today some of us wonder if someday a HAL 9000 or a Skynet computer system may elect to overrule us all and we'll change places with the machines.

Genesis has served a wide range of purposes since software conception was realized. It has been an administrative think-tank, a records facility, and eventually a solar energy research center for the University of Central Florida, until some of the ship captains coming into Port Canaveral complained that the solar panels were blinding them with reflected sunlight. It continued to support various research projects until private sector space made it too valuable to be anything but spacecraft orientated.

You do not need a badge to get into Genesis. You hang a right turn just before the south gate, as though you're turning into the old Trident Basin, then a quick left and the fenced area to Genesis sits wide open.

On this day, another surprise awaited me. As I pulled into the Genesis gate, a new portable guard shack had been set up. A security officer emerged and stopped me. I dug in the center console, rolled down the passenger's window, and handed him my Space Center badge. He returned to his shack and began typing at a computer screen.

You can always run the gates at the Space Center and make it. You just don't make it far. The system has been tested countless times by angry spouses, would-be assassins, illegal immigrants, protestors of every cause, drunken drivers, impatient tourists, and persons of questionable mental stability. All of these found their way to the back of a security vehicle before being taken to headquarters. Even the right CAT scan will set off a radiation alert. If you spend any time inside the Center, you cannot miss the five hundred foot parachute jumps by men with guns, or the assortment of spent shells around your facility after a weekend of security drills, or the camouflaged, machine gun wielding special forces coming out of the snake and alligator infested woodlands when an intruder has been detected by infrared from a helicopter overhead. If any of these people ever yell "halt" to me, I won't need to think it over.

The guard returned to the passenger's window, a tablet and badge in hand. "All your documentation is already processed Mr. Tarn. I just need a signature there at the bottom."

I scribbled an electronic signature and traded it for the badge. "Have a good day, Sir."

"Thanks."

With nine or ten gray metallic buildings to choose from, I headed for the one with the five-story hanger door. The main entrance opened to a security room and another guard. He looked up from his podium and stood. "It's a badge exchange.

I'll need yours," he said and reached out one hand. He looked at the coding on my new badge, deposited it in a numbered slot and handed me a smaller red badge with that number on it. Without speaking, he keyed in a code on a pad by the door and let me through.

There was a hallway created by stand-up blue dividers on the left that separated a break room area with a scraped-up tan wall on the right. The air conditioning was almost too cool. Halfway down the makeshift corridor, another hallway on the right led to what looked like office areas. Straight ahead was a large double door to a high-bay. It had its own keypad lock. There was a big red buzzer button next to it for those not privileged enough for the key code. It was my intention to push that button, but I was cut off when an attractive middle-aged woman sped around the corner and partially crashed into me. She pulled up startled and stepped back with a half displeased, half questioning stare. Her voice suggested tempered impatience. "Who are you? Can I help you?"

"Adrian Tarn, and you?"

"Oh! Oh, Commander, we've been expecting you, but they couldn't give us any timeline. I'm pleased to finally meet you. I'm Julia Zeller, Resident Director. Have you been in the high-bay yet? Have you seen it?"

Julia was disciplined and self-assured. She had that air of being unquestionably in charge. She was slightly tall, dark hair bundled up behind her head, low eyebrows turned up at the end giving that narrow-eyed, bedroom-dare stare, rosy cheeks and puffy red lips. She wore a dark, printed, silk twill wrap that left an open V that was almost too revealing. An unbuttoned black long sleeve cardigan was draped over it. I had the feeling I would not want to debate Julia or be on her wrong side.

"Just got here."

"Oh good. I'll get to take you in myself. I've never seen a project advance this quickly. It's quite amazing."

"It's a pleasure to meet you, Julia." I held out a hand and she responded with a deceptively timid, reluctant handshake. "How long have you been director?"

She turned and headed for the high-bay doors. Our footsteps echoed down the hallway. "It's usually a five-year stint. Part of the learn-everything tour. I've been overseeing the facility for about two years. Your mission has somewhat thrown us for a loop. It kind of fell out of the sky, if you don't mind the play on words. Our high-bay hasn't been used much. The last program was drop tests of an inter-stage. I've never seen so much equipment transferred so quickly. There must be some high level urgency driving this. Care to fill me in on any of that?"

"What have you got so far?"

"They brought in a pneumatic support structure from the old Constellation program. It was unused, but old. They completely refurbished and adapted it for the new spacecraft mockup. The simulator itself is like nothing I've ever seen. It's bigger and more complete. It's futuristic-looking. Any idea where it was developed?"

"Can I fly it yet?"

"You could on a very limited basis, but that would rob us of three days of twenty-four hour processing to get the thing completely ready for testing."

"Let's not do that, then. I'll wait."

"Commander Tarn, you're evading my questions with the skill of a politician."

"Julia, there's no reason to insult me."

She stopped and laughed. "Oh, for the days of the dumb jet-jockeys. Is there nothing at all you can tell me about all this?"

"I'm going to be spending a lot of time here repeatedly crashing your new simulator, so you probably should start calling me Adrian. Can I see it?"

She offered a conciliatory smile and held one hand up. "This way." She led me past the break room to the heavy metal doors. After a quick look around she said, "Yours is 8376." She tapped it in, waited for the clicks, and pulled the door open.

The massive steel high-bay looked like a clean room, though it was not. Gray acoustic door-size panels lined the walls from floor to ceiling. Big high-pressure sodium lights hung fifty feet overhead. A yellow gantry crane was parked at the far end of the building. The reinforced white tile floor looked like you could eat off it. The place was busy. Half a dozen technicians in white coveralls and hairnets were coming and going, their choreography managed by two or three engineers in white lab smocks. Periodically, some of them were pausing to stare at us.

The item in the middle of the bay was so profound it mesmerized me. Julia picked up on my stun. "Yeah, the platform was ready when they brought the simulator in. It came by barge. They offloaded up by the industrial area onto a kneel-down transporter. I had no idea what to expect. They used a huge, special transfer container. We opened the bay doors and the thing was completely covered in foil. After they raised it on the air pallets, they rolled it forward and let the nose tear through the foil. You remember that very old movie with Charlton Heston where he crashes his spacecraft into a lake? When I first saw the front end I though it was the prop from that movie. That front end is almost identical except bigger."

It was an excellent description of the portion of the Griffin that now sat atop the motion platform. The front end looked like a white, three-blade broad head arrow tip. It could have been a spearhead. The nose came to such a distinct point; it really did look like a weapon. There was something unusual about the surface coating. It was not standard. It looked like a white, metallic substance had somehow been bonded to the craft. The side blades that began near the nose swept back to become the retracted wings. I instinctively looked for the red labels that usually said 'no step' on them but did not find any. Blue-tinted windshields were fit into the top and bottom half of the front end forming almost a cupola of vision. These were three way windows; transparency, video display, or heads up display data. External, retractable blast shields were available around them.

The vehicle was much larger than expected, the body wider than tall. A repulse drive dome was attached to the bottom mid section. Behind that, the simulator was cut off. No reproduction of the habitat module or power plants.

Julia said, "You see the guy in the gray suit and tie with his head in the back of that console against the wall behind the simulator, the only guy not wearing standard issue high-bay gear?"

The man backed out of the console, said something to a technician helping him, and looked over at us. Julia waved him over. "He's your Test Director, Terry Costerly. He came in about a week ago. He's sharp."

Costerly approached us with eyebrows raised. He stuck his hand out and spoke as we shook. "Terry Costerly."

"Adrian Tarn."

"Oh, I see. What do you think?" He waved a hand across the high-bay.

"My kind of toys."

He stifled a laugh, thought about being offended, and then smiled and said, "Yeah, me too."

Julia's cell interrupted. "Zeller... No, no, no, that's not what was promised. I have the invoice on my desk. Give me a minute to get there." The fierce-look returned to her face. She nodded at me and said, "I'll have to turn you over to your drill instructor here, Adrian. Come see me in my office when you get a chance so I can ask some more questions you won't answer." She ducked her head back to the phone and headed off.

Costerly appraised me out of the corner of his eye.

"Can I get a look at the flight deck?"

"It's sealed for pressure testing at the moment. They'll be through in about forty-five minutes. Why don't I show you your office first?"

"Pressure testing? There's a real environmental control system in the thing?"

"Yes, and if I program in a life support failure and any of you hot shots fail to recognize and correct it, I will let you pass out before I flood the cabin."

"Wow! I'm impressed"

He led me to a hallway on the north side of the hanger. My office was the first door on the right. It opened to quite a large open room. Desk in the middle stacked so high with logbooks and systems manuals it was intimidating. Big picture window in front of the desk looking out over the high-bay. Comfortable brown-leather chairs all around. A long wood-grained chart table against one wall with diagrams and flow charts pinned to the wall on a large bulletin board.

"I've been using your office because of all the books. Mine are still arriving piece by piece. Haven't seen this much paper in a long time. It's because of when the Griffin and the motion platform were designed. Paper was still in use quite a bit back then."

He stood at the high-bay observation window staring out at the Griffin mockup. "You realize of course that it's a full flight simulator. Actually, it's a lot more than an FFS, really. The DOF is beyond the six degrees-of-freedom motion that we're accustomed to in most simulators. It was a standard Stewart platform hexapod, but they've pushed it way beyond that. The thing will go completely vertical in either direction, and the acceleration onset cueing is much deeper than normal. You will think you're diving, and there will be nothing you can do to make your mind not believe that."

I took a seat at the desk and tested the chair. "I thought you were a launch director. How do you know so much about simulator platforms?"

"My studies were in aeronautical science even though most of my applied is unmanned aerospace. I wanted it that way. The unmanned payloads don't mind fifteen or twenty G's, so why waste gravity repulse systems on them? That's the only reason we still send payloads up with liquids and solids these days. The atmosphere in the Launch Control Centers is quite a bit more intense for those."

I swiveled my chair back and forth. "So have you ever lost one?"

He looked at me as though it was almost too personal a question. "Why? Are you worried?"

"Not at all."

"We had a small assist motor attached to the side of a Delta Triple X burn through once. There was a metallurgical flaw in the motor casing that somehow didn't get picked up. The vehicle got just above the trees when the burn-through set off the main propellant. The thing was still full of fuel. It went off like a bomb. The blast radius was about a mile. It set fire to a couple dozen cars in the parking lot. They locked down our launch room because we were too close, but we started getting smoke in the ventilation system. We had to use the masks in the emergency storage locker. It was the first time that had ever happened. They kept us in the damn launch room for twelve hours while the fires got put out and the orange cloud headed out to sea. Other than that, all my projects have been smooth or correctable."

"Somebody must really love you to bring you in on this one. Why'd you take it?"

"There were some old debts brought into play, but the truth is I would've signed on anyway. I don't have all the data yet but there's something happening here. Those engines? I haven't heard of any development phases for those. The spec sheets tell you everything they'll do but not how they do it. And where did this vehicle come from? I'd like to know that. My curiosity got the best of me, and that's okay as long as none of this clandestine stuff affects my work. Is there anything you can add to what I already know?"

"That seems to be the question of the day."

"Yeah, yeah. I got it. I'm getting new flight data requirements in, pretty much by the hour. I've got a pretty good picture. About forty-five minutes ago, they started sending me mandates for the first and only test flight. That's damn interesting. Have you seen it?"

"To be honest, everybody seems to know more than me."

"Did you know you're headed for the G1.9 brown dwarf, our sun's companion star? That's just to certify the vehicle and crew for deep space."

"I did not."

"That's what just came in encrypted in my email. That will be the only beyond-orbit test flight we get before initiating the long countdown for the actual mission. Wherever those dream engines came from, they must be damn sure of them. You'll get to test them with a few seconds of engagement, and that's it. Then afterward, the space station Navigation Scanning Verification Group can use the data to certify you for deep space."

"Any other surprises I should know about?"

"Hey, at least I'm glad to have known something you didn't." He laughed. "There's quite a few rocks enslaved to that dwarf. The test mission objective is to locate the correct one. The retrieval portion of the test flight plan may have a mistake in it, though. There's a part that's too strange to be legitimate."

"Like what?"

"It says the objective is to locate and retrieve a simulated artifact that will be placed on one of the dwarf's asteroids by a probe."

"What's funny about that?"

"It says the simulated artifact is the lug nut locking key to a 1995 Corvette."

"No."

"Yes, that's what it says. Do you have any idea why they'd put that in there?"

"It can't be."

"Can't be what?"

Without answering, I got up and stomped out of the room. In the parking lot, I searched the center console of my car. It was missing. While I had been busy talking to Bernard, the little bastard had his people steal the lug nut locking key out of my car. It was Bernard's idea of a joke. My lug nut locking key was likely already on its way to a dwarf star sixty AU's from Earth, where it would sit on a cold desolate rock in space forever unless I could get there and find it. It was such an ingenious ploy it scared me a bit. If I didn't recover that key, I'd be chiseling lug nut locks off hard-to-find Corvette wheels, not a pleasant thought. I decided not to underestimate Bernard in the future. I also vowed to get him back.

Chapter 4

Back in my new office, I paused at the high-bay window and noticed the rear hatch to the Griffin simulator raised and open. The place was even busier than it had been. Terry was out there, waiting next to the air-stairs leading up, smiling at me and pointing upward.

In the high-bay, I stopped alongside him and waited as two technicians came down. "Did you find what you were looking for outside?" he asked.

"Yes. I didn't find what I was looking for."

He stared with a half smile and nodded to the techs as they passed. "It's cold and dark on the flight deck. They don't dare bring up full power until they've finished analyzing each system's power usage. They don't want to crash any optical drives by having console circuit breakers trip from overload," he said.

"Lead the way."

We marched up the steps and ducked into the cabin. Overhead strip lights were on, but nothing else. The first sight of that darkened flight deck filled me with such passion I consciously had to hide it. The layout was standard, but the controls much more futuristic than I had ever seen.

Terry sensed my awe. "Who the hell could do all this?" he asked.

There was a short vestibule of cables and electronics just inside the entrance, not part of the real Griffin. Ignoring Terry, I stepped past and lowered my head into the flight deck as far as I could. The pilot seat on the left had three large dark screens in front of it. The copilot's on the right was the same. The leftmost screen would be spacecraft orientation, speed, and distance measuring along with the many other indicators needed for control. The middle screen would be navigation, flight management computer data, and flight director status. The right screen was for the SSCAS, Spacecraft Systems Crew Alert System showing fuels, electrical systems, physical configuration, environmental control and a myriad of other things needing monitoring from time to time.

Those layouts were as expected, but the rest was mind-blowing. The console that ran between the seats had a variety of thrust levers, some familiar, some not. Forward of the thrust levers was the standard set of flight management computers, one for each pilot, but they were larger and had some keys I did not recognize. There were fuel feed controls, air braking controls, trim, and others items mixed in that were new. The communications system at the end of the console looked overly simplified. Above our heads where I expected to find fire control, environmental, fuel distribution, and general systems controls, there was a collection of a dozen or more dark touch screens that ran from one end of the flight deck to the other and a second row above them.

An engineering station sat behind each pilot seat consisting almost entirely of dozens of display screens. Eventually I noticed the windshields, front, overhead, and forward in the floor. Frosty white displays that would simulate our window views. They followed the lines of the ship and narrowed down to points forward in long, reaching triangles.

"Want me to go get some smelling salts?" joked Terry. "You might need them because if you think this is awesome, wait until you get the tour of the habitat area simulator in the east hanger."

I wanted to sit in the left pilot's seat in the worse way, but there was no real reason to. The cabin was cold and dark, the windscreens misty white. I would only have been checking the seat. The climb in would have betrayed any attempt to hide my exhilaration.

"Okay, let's have it, then." With sheer willpower, I forced myself to turn away.

He led me back down the hanger hallway, past my office, and opened the silver double doors to the east hanger. This high-bay was almost as expansive as the last, but with a lower, thirty-foot ceiling. Once again, techs were busy coming and going, wearing hairnets and white coveralls.

The Griffin habitat module was a large ellipse on its side. There was no exterior spacecraft modeling. Except for various cables and electronic interfaces, it was a bare brown shell created to contain simulated living space and the systems intended to support it, including some of the propulsion service areas. A short span of portable steps near the front led up. We waited for two technicians to clear the stairs and then entered into a shiny, metallic airlock.

"This forward airlock is actually secondary, Adrian. Its main use is for docking and backup for EVA's. When it's sealed for EVAs, it isolates the flight deck, so the rear airlock is the primary. The door we just entered through is a pressure hatch on the real Griffin, and there's one here in the ceiling as well. You can dock in either configuration. There are eight Bell Standard spacesuits. Two against that wall, two against this one, four more in the rear airlock. Do you like the Bell Standards, Adrian?"

"To be honest, I and a friend by the name of Perk owe our lives to Bell Flight suits. I wouldn't use anything else if I didn't have to."

"Perk? You're not talking about Perk Murphy, are you?"

"You know Perk?"

"No, but there's this big rumor out there that he got into a firefight with aliens on an EVA in open space and came out on top. You couldn't be referring to that, could you?" He stared at me wide-eyed.

"Are these the K-version of the EVA suit, or the base model?"

"The rumor was that Perk Murphy was hit in the chest with some kind of plasma weapon, and barely made it back."

"Damn it all. It was a fair question. K-version or base model?"

Terry searched my eyes in earnest. I tried to avoid his gaze. His stare widened even more. "Oh my God, it's true and you were there!" He paused, speechless. He swallowed and continued to gawk. Finally, he answered. "K-version. On this project they've brought in only the best." He put aside the distraction and moved out of the airlock and into the living area.

"Did you notice the two techs coming out had their shoes wrapped in antistatic bags? You see this strange looking white carpet and padding on the floor and walls? It's photosynthetic! This entire interior is photosynthetic! You can set it to display anything you want. You can be in the middle of Sherwood Forest, or out in the middle of the ocean! The entire module is covered in cushioned, carpet-like material for protection from weightless flight, but it's all really a big video display. The sleeper compartments are the same"

The airlock wall on my left had a fake pressure door to the flight deck. On my right, the chamber opened to the striking expanse of living environment. Everything was off-white and new. The width of the cabin was an extraordinary fifteen feet. Two oval viewing windows on either side peered out into the hanger. There was a padded, elliptical table, with eight padded seats around it to my right. Three other seats with smaller dedicated tables were distributed apart from it. Beyond the community area, an open kitchen with duplicate food processors on either side cast metallic reflections of the seating area.

Terry strolled among the seats. "Have you noticed the little depressions in the floors under the furniture? All this stuff unfolds and telescopes down into the floor. The room can be set up with no furniture at all with the press of a button. You can have a wide-open weightless environment if you want to. Take off and landing seating is in the wall. You tap a button and four seats deploy. All of these seats are A.I. The crew flight apparel has metallic fiber woven into the legs and torso. If a seat detects that kind of signature, it becomes magnetic and continuously adjusts to provide just the right amount of gentle restraint so you can remain seated in a weightless environment but still move around in your seat. I've never seen anything like it, have you?"

He did not wait for an answer. He went back to the galley area. "Double and triple redundancy on everything, and it's not all dehydrated crap either. But, look back here," he pointed through a five-foot doorway that led to the back. "These are the sleeper cells."

They were three-foot high, horizontal cubicles built against the wall, one low and one high. Two on the left and two on the right. They were roughly seven feet long, and five feet deep, covered in the same white photo-syn material.

"So you climb in and shut yourself up in one of these and you can switch on any video or still image you like. You can be lying in the grass in a field somewhere, or at home in your bedroom. There's also a feed to the outside cameras, so you can project that against the wall and it's like a big window looking outside. You get one foot of storage space in the ceiling above you. The entertainment display is super-A.I. They call it 5-D. If you're watching a film on a display you can reach out and touch one of the 3-D characters and that character will respond to you and the A.I. changes the story line to compensate."

"There's a relief tube in every cubicle. You do not have to get up to do that. And, forgive me for mentioning it, but it's designed to accommodate sex, if you know what I mean." Terry smirked, coughed uncomfortably, and moved on, passing by the first four private cubicles. "Twin zero-G toilets and showers separate the next four sleeper cubicles. And right through here, just beyond the back four sleepers, brings us to the gym. Dual everything on either side. Two people can work out in here at the same time. The next compartment is the Science and Med lab, and beyond it the aft airlock. There's a bulkhead door on the far wall of the airlock that opens to the service module. The first non-habitat cell is the expendable storage, O2, water, all that stuff. That turns into a hatchway which becomes crawl space until you get to the propulsion systems. Then it weaves you all around as you move farther aft, and it's crowded as hell in

there. I'm sure you'll be climbing around back there to familiar-
ize yourself as you get time."

I nodded appropriate awe. We worked our way back to
the main living area. Terry stopped at the front airlock, leaned
against the wall and folded his arms. "So, as your TD, we're going to be having some very serious private discussions about
your personnel and their performance, as well as the performance of ship systems."

"You got that right."

"I see something going on here. The design of this
spacecraft is pretty suggestive, don't you think?"

I tried a seat at the elliptical table. Terry followed.

"What's on your mind, TD?"

"They've pulled out all the stops on this spacecraft. Obviously, there's stuff in here not from Earth, or at least not from
human technology. I have never seen the agency go this far,
this fast for any single mission. This spacecraft has been refit
with a blank check. So what I'm seeing here is not just an absolute determination that the mission be successful. I'm seeing
more than that."

"I don't think I follow."

"Stress. I believe that this spacecraft was designed to
protect the crew as best as possible through a stressful environment, or stressful circumstances. That's why all the luxury.
This ship is going somewhere that's going to be either very dangerous, very difficult, or both."

"Have you seen a course plan for the actual mission?"

"I've seen the basic block diagram for it, with attach-
ments, and that's another thing. There's to be star charts we
don't have yet. Somebody's helping out with that, if you know
what I mean. And, the nadir trajectory. You get farther from
Earth than anyone's ever been and you hit this patch of space
called the void. The best I could make of it, not being a physicist, is that it's an area of space that contains less than nothing,
whatever that means. And, it's big. You'll be in it for quite a
while. Apparently, you will not be able to see any stars, or anything else. You have to cross that, and it's so far away there will
be nothing good enough to reach you. It will be a deep crossing
you'll have to make on your own; no communications, no visual
navigation. Did you know about that?"

"I'm glad you're here, Terry. And, you're right. We'll be
having many more private talks like this. I want to know every
misgiving you have, no matter how small."

He sat back and folded his hands behind his head. "Well,
I just hope that someday I get to know what this is all about."

Chapter 5

The next morning, marathon-cramming sessions began. I never do well with those. You need a certain amount of fear as motivation and I just didn't have it. I procrastinated briefly by clearing a path to the computer screen and submitting RJ's clearances and team assignment. From there the battle began to group the pile of musty-smelling notebooks and printouts into four meaningful stacks, a half-hearted effort that helped me fool myself into thinking I was doing something. It worked for a while, until wanderlust kicked in and my alter ego began asking questions about the flight simulator in the high-bay just outside the hanger window. Curtains will need to be installed at some point.

Along with the ungodly stacks of ringed notebooks, they had provided three linked tablets, which offered a certain modest amusement. When you called up info on one, the other two automatically displayed supporting data. I ended up tilted back in my chair studying the Griffin's flight deck until a mercifully distracting knock came at the door and it swung open to reveal someone new.

She wore tan cargo pants tight enough that they almost made me laugh. She had high brown leather boots that would have complimented a riding crop nicely. The sky blue blouse had a faint image of a milky-white swirl leading up over the shoulder. Her red exchange badge was clipped to the open V near the neck. Her hair was dark-brown short, her makeup reserved and precisely applied. She had a pert little upturned nose, and green eyes behind an appraising stare. There was no hint of a smile from the small cherry red lips. I guessed her to be mid-thirties. Her self-assured demeanor made the shields kick in.

"Yes?"

"Danica Donoro, Commander. I report under Porre. I wanted to check in and let you know I'm on board."

"I'm sorry. Things are happening so fast they did not send me a file or let me know you were coming. If you'll forgive an awkward question, you're here to fill what position?"

"I'm a pilot, Commander. Really, that's probably the first thing we should clear the air on."

"Come in, Danica. Have a seat. What kind of air-clearing would you like?"

"Female test pilots. Enough women have come back shot up these days that they pretty much don't question us as fighter pilots anymore, but there's still a big matzo ball hanging out there that women aren't cut out for the experimental stuff. I'm hoping you and I are not going to go round and round about that."

She sat back in the seat almost in a slouch, lowered her chin in anticipation, and stared. Many people after having the courage to deliver an ultimatum to their new boss tend to cower a bit immediately afterward, having used up their courage in the delivery. This woman was having none of that. Her intense gaze told me she was locked and loaded. I did my best to hide the fact that I was impressed.

"Have you seen the sim out there?"

"First place I stopped."

"You must know that by the time we finish crashing that thing a few hundred times, everyone is going to know who can fly and who can't. We're going to burn up, break up, and do the lawn dart trick until we know what we can get away with and what we can't. And each time somebody screws up, the simulator playbacks are going to tell on them. It wouldn't matter if you were Chewbacca, ET, or Flash Gordon, those flight profiles are gonna scream to the whole world what kind of pilot you are. There'll be no guesswork involved. As for me, am I prejudiced against women left-seaters? If you're worried about that, you may have come to the right place. My father let me start flying when I was twelve. He took me out to the smallest airport he could find and said if I mastered the short strips, the big ones would be a breeze. The FBO was a tiny wooden shack about the size of a tollbooth. I told them who I was and went and sat on a bench outside to wait. A few minutes later, this old German lady comes out. Had to be in her seventies, at least. She looks at me, says my name, looks at her clipboard and says, "You want to learn to fly, eh?" I nodded my head and to my surprise she says, "Okay, let's go."

"She had an antique Pitts Special. She buckled me in the front and off we went. She made that thing do every aerobatic maneuver known to man until she was sure I was about to puke into the wind, which would not have been good for her in the back seat. On the ground, while I was still choking it back, she said, "Okay Mr. Tarn, if you're here tomorrow at this same time,

I'll know you really want to fly." The next day, I was there early expecting the same torture. Out comes one of the most beautiful women I had ever seen, in a see-through blouse, and she says, "My name is Mary Mackly. I'll be your instructor for the next few weeks. So, Danica, do you think I have any insecurity about women pilots?"

"How about vendettas?"

"You've got to know, I can't afford to cut anybody any slack on this tour. You could say it's a long reach. You'll know I'm not prejudice the first time I have to come down on you for screwing up. Equality works both ways. Something I would like to know, though; what got you into the business of flying?"

"It was all I ever wanted. When I was a kid, I used to hope the aircraft going overhead would crash on our property so maybe they'd let me keep the wreckage and I could pretend in it. Then, I stole my father's Jetstream when I was ten."

"You must be kidding. You soloed a PAV when you were ten?"

"We were camping in the mountains, fortunately. There was no municipal air traffic anywhere. I was so sure I could handle it I thought if I could show my parents they'd let me fly."

"And?"

"I got lost real fast and had to put down in the middle of nowhere. Lions and tigers and bears, oh my. Scared the shit out of myself. When they finally tracked me down, I was grounded for good, in more ways than one. There were no citations because there was nobody around. After the rage settled, my father started taking me to simulator classes and at least I got that out of it. I was the only ten-year-old girl in a class full of older boys. I was arrogant and overconfident, and I thought I could do anything. I ended up beating the pants off all those guys. Made them feel like they'd lost their man-cards. Never gave it a second thought. Flying was never an option. It was always compulsory."

"Why did Porre pick you? No profiling intended."

"I was an assistant to the assistant test engineer on the original Griffin design. Nobody knows more about the Griffin than I do. I can't wait to see her again."

"My report says it's in the Flight Processing Facility near the VAB, being configured for a twelve-month excursion, but we'll have a test flight before actual departure. Do you really know what you're signing on to?"

"Actually, I pulled some strings to get here. I have always kept track of the Griffin, hoping someday it would be pulled out of mothballs. You know how it got its name?"

"Not a clue."

"It's the wings. The Griffin was a mythological creature with the body of a lion and the wings of an eagle. That ship has all the power of a spacecraft, but the wings of an aircraft as well. So they called it the Griffin. I had a friend on the inside and when the Griffin was sent out for refitting, he let me know. It took a lot of calls but I finally locked in on Porre's office. I was lucky, too. He had someone else lined up for the job, and he didn't want to replace him. If I hadn't called in favors from executives above his office, I wouldn't be here right now. And, yeah, by that time I knew enough about the mission to know it was aggressive, but that's the way I like it."

"And you know there have been some significant changes to the Griffin?"

"Just that it has a whole lot of range and a whole lot of P-factor and not the kind you get from a propeller, either. When can we fly the sim?"

"According to our resident director, in a couple days, but it will take a lot longer than that to go through these spec and cert books. I suggest you get started right away. Tell me, since I know nothing about you: are you married?"

"Nope. No self-important stud is going to tell me what to do."

"Wow! Which one of us is the chauvinist?"

"No, no. I'm just saying. A lot of people think they can take over your life if they get too comfortable, if you know what I mean."

"Any kids?"

"Hell no. They can take over your life."

"I'll go through your file when I get it. There's actually just one concern I have. How obligated did you make yourself to Mr. Bernard Porre?"

"I owe him periodic progress reports."

"Has he tried to insert himself into the command structure through you?"

"I see where you're going with this. He's manipulative, but I never promised him anything."

"The deal is, when our butts are hanging out a few hundred light years from here, and he's sitting at home in his den having tea and crumpets, his orders don't mean jack-shit. And before we strap in for the long haul, I'm going to need to know you believe that."

"Fair enough."

"On this ride there is not going to be a standard command structure. There's going to be seven bosses with one boss over them: me. If I begin to sense that anyone is developing a superiority complex over anyone else, it will immediately qualify them for permanent galley and latrine duty and that's just for starters."

She smiled and leaned back in her seat. "I've been looking forward to meeting you, Commander. I did a lot of asking around when your name came up. It seems you're as mysterious as the Griffin. I know you were on the last Electra mission, but try to get anyone to talk about that. There's some stories floating around; stuff has leaked out. People say that ship was too damaged to get back. There are rumors about a battle with aliens. There's one particularly interesting rumor maybe even you haven't heard about. It reminded me of a very old story I once heard in flight school. There was an incident way back in the 1980s. A new passenger airliner had just been put into service. It was sitting on the ramp ready to go with passengers onboard waiting. The thing was so new the fuel indicators weren't working yet, so the ground crew had to climb up and measure the tanks manually. They used a metric fuel stick. The problem was, the system wasn't set up in metric. They told the Captain he was good to go when he actually had half of the fuel he needed. He got halfway to the destination at thirty-thousand feet when fuel pump alarms start popping up. A few minutes later engines begin shutting down. By the time the last engine died, they finally had to accept there was no fuel and they were going down. Even back then it was a glass cockpit, so all their readouts went dark. The APU was not running off course, so they had to crank open a little door on the underside to get a wind turbine turning to get some electrical power back. They called Air Traffic Control and were told the only thing in range was a short, abandoned airstrip and it was at the very edge of their envelope or even beyond it a bit. The Captain went for it. A mile out they see a car show or something taking place on the abandoned runway, people everywhere, and they're silent cause there's no engines running. Finally, a kid on a bike sees this big heavy airplane coming in and starts screaming bloody murder and the car show turns into a mad panic to get out of the way. Although the runway was supposedly a bit out of range, somehow the Captain made it there with a little extra. He's high. He and the copilot stand on the rudder and slip a heavy jumbo jet down and land safely on that overgrown field. At first the flight crew is in a panic to get through the post crash procedures to prevent fire, until the Captain realizes there's not gonna be any fire, cause there isn't any fuel. Anyway, in the following weeks, the airline company programs the same failure into its main simulator system. A bunch of pilots go in there to duplicate what happened, and not one of them gets the plane safely down to that runway. I tell you this story, because the rumors I hear say it's kind of the same thing with the Electra. In the Washington training facility, they set up the same circumstances the Electra had with the same spacecraft systems out of commission. Flight and engineering crews went in repeatedly and tried to get the Electra simulation back to Earth. Nobody's made it yet. I thought you'd like to know that, and I'd sure like to hear that story."

"Where are you staying, Danica?"

"They put me up in an apartment on Merritt Island. The view is fantastic but I don't think I'll be spending much time there."

"Have you started working the spec sheets?"

"A bunch of it downloaded this morning."

"You need to check in with Terry Costerley, our test director. He'll set you up with an office and a schedule."

She pushed herself up to leave, and paused at the door. "Commander, do any kick boxing?"

"Only when I'm forced to, Danica."

She nodded. "It's a hobby. I need to find a sparring partner."

It made me notice how well conditioned she was. "You may be in luck. There might be someone coming on board I think will give you a challenge at that. By the way, do you have any idea who else Porre is sending?"

"I know it's a propulsion engineer, but that's all. He was pretty pissed off about having to appoint me, so I wasn't on the in with him, if you know what I mean."

"Well, welcome aboard. I look forward to having you up front."

"You'd better stay sharp Commander, or I'll have your man-card!" She laughed, and shut the door too hard.

Chapter 6

By midnight, I had made it through the flight basics portion of the mountain. I found that every time the quit-for-the-night light came on in my head, if I looked out at the simulator it flickered and died. As I pushed back my chair to fetch another cup of coffee, Julia Zeller stuck her head in the door.

"Still here, Julia?"

"I could've asked you that."

"This stuff's like candy to me."

"Very funny, but you may be glad you stayed."

"What's up?"

"They're way ahead of schedule. I just got word that inspection will sign off on the master buss panels at 04:00. That means the simulator could be flown to low orbit."

"No kidding? Would the Test Director's staff be here?"

"Doesn't matter. Our orders are to support you twenty-four-seven. Besides, if we call those guys, wild horses couldn't keep them away."

"I'll take a Dramamine, in that case."

"You are the funny one, even at midnight, aren't you?"

"Thanks, Julia."

As she was leaving, a second unexpected face peered in beside her. RJ, in a pewter herringbone shirt, jeans, and work shoes pushed his way in and plunked down in a chair near the door. He bit down on an egg sitter pipe and spoke without removing it. "Got my new badge," he said and held it up proudly.

"RJ, you know there's a smoke detector hovering over us, right?"

"I was an inspector before this job's incarnation, remember? It is not lit, nor am I."

"Couldn't sleep or something?"

"I do not conform to a repetitive twenty-four hour clock. Who made that rule, anyway?"

"Oh no, I've set you off."

"A near miss. No harm done."

"Have you started your homework?"

"It's easy so far. Most of the support systems are standard or updated versions. Old reading for me. I'm cruising on through."

"Have you checked out the Griffin's habitat module? It's got stuff you wouldn't believe."

"Ah yes, technology. The answer to all men's prayers. Let me tell you about our synthesized, freeze-dried, time-compacted society, my friend."

"Oh boy."

"We are going to automate ourselves to the point that we become bulbous beings with stubby little arms and legs, who sit in a holoprogram somewhere living a mental life that is pure fantasy with no connection whatsoever to the outside world. And at some point, we will have finally drained the charge from every last electron in every last molecule of matter, so that suddenly with all of their charge absent all the electrons collapse onto the nuclei, leaving each of us to solidify into a frozen carbonite mass, still alive, staring at one another, wondering what the heck happened."

"Whew. You know, some of that may not be completely plausible."

"What? Which part?"

"RJ, have you read the initial mission briefing I sent out?"

"Yes I have, and to quote one of the greatest philosophers of all time, this is a fine mess you've gotten us into."

"Which one of your obscure gurus was that?"

"A Dr. Hardy. PHD, University of Laurel."

"I don't know that one. But you did read through it?"

"Yes, and then I took a moment to embrace the ground."

"Speaking of ground, want to go flying?"

"Are you kidding?"

"04:00. Nobody else is here. You can have the right seat."

"Kick the tires and light the fires."

All hope of further study abandoned, we escaped the glowering specter of books on my desk and took refuge in the break room where the coffee was still hot and a failing white box on the table contained aging donut fragments.

"Have you met Danica?"

"I have not had the pleasure."

"Better watch yourself. Apparently she collects man-cards."

"Sounds like my kind of woman. Have you made a choice for a second systems engineer?"

"I'm thinking Wilson Mirtos."

"Really? Isn't he the one..."

"Yep."

"What's the infamous phrase that brings sobriety to those having achieved intoxication Zen with him?"

"Now I don't want any trouble."

"That's the one. Legend has it that should you ever hear him say it, you will know that in the next two or three seconds all hell is going to break loose."

As we sipped our coffee, a technician sped by brandishing a bottle of champagne in each hand. He nodded shyly, tucked them in the refrigerator, and headed to the high-bay.

RJ perked up. "Apparently they take the maiden flight of a simulator system quite seriously around here."

"They've really busted their butts on this one. Can you blame them?"

"It is reassuring to see, actually. I love people who care. So tell me, how did old Wilson come to coin that holocaustic phrase anyway?"

"It's the teddy bear syndrome. He's big, but when he's relaxed he kind of looks like a teddy bear. So, all through college and the academy, and to this day really, the jerks out there that have a few drinks and want to show they can take a big guy, all think he's a prime candidate. The trouble is, when they start pushing him, he goes through the hulk metamorphose and all that teddy bear bulk suddenly becomes bulging muscle. By that time, the idiots who picked on him realize they've made a horrible mistake, but it's too late to back down. After one particularly memorable bar-clearing, a judge made him go for counseling, and the stupid psychologist taught him to use that phrase to try to defuse situations that were in their final stage. It doesn't work worth a damn, but since an expensive doctor taught him to use it, he figures it's always worth a try."

"Have you ever joined him in celebration of such a futile antidote?"

"Oh yeah. The last time, I was just entering a bar to meet him when a punk came crashing out the window next to the entrance. It was three guys against just Wilson, but they were all sleeping or elsewhere by the time I got there. I asked him how come he sent the guy through the window and he said he thought the man wouldn't be able to cause any more trouble if he was outside."

RJ sipped and smiled. "Ah, a truly down-to-earth person. I shall enjoy his company and insight. Let us hope we never hear the phrase."

"He's one hell of an engineer, by the way. You'll like his dry sense of humor. He injects it into the most serious of situations, once he knows he has a handle on them, even if you do not."

"Have you tracked him down with the surprise yet?"

I opened my mouth to answer but paused at the sight of Terry Costerly walking briskly by in a suit and tie. He tapped in his code and charged into the high-bay without even a glance in our direction.

RJ smirked. "It's going to be a party. You'd better not crash the damn thing or these people may hold a funeral."

"Don't worry. I crash better than anybody I know."

"Please, don't remind me."

At 03:30, a crowd of a dozen or so engineers, technicians, and inspectors gathered in the simulator Test Control Center affectionately known as the TCC, to witness the buy-off of the final power distribution console. The installation people must have been in a hell of a hurry when they stripped this very large chamber that adjoins both the high-bay and my office. The dingy white walls have shadows of decorations past, and there are scarred floor tiles here and there. My office has a door leading directly into the room though it cannot be used for the stack of equipment piled against it. Observation windows looking out over the high-bay run the full length of the place. Computer console stations, some ill-positioned, line the walls. Stacks of cabling cover the floor behind the consoles and some run directly across the room with floor guards protecting them, a clear sign of how quickly the installation was done. Routing cables under the raised floor had not even been considered. Someone had hung a ten-foot banner against the far wall that read 'TRANQUILITY BASE', a sardonic tribute to the frantic effort required of the team.

Within a small crowd of onlookers, an inspector and technician were bent over a table buying off steps on the last installation procedure. Julia Zeller looked on. An assortment of comical remarks punctuated the event, such as "it took you long enough" and "why don't you just stamp it with our blood," and "does this mean we're all laid off now?" There were handshakes and pats on the back, and to my surprise as the jubilation began to subside the entire assemblage turned and stared at me. RJ broke into laughter so hard he spilled his coffee.

"I'm getting the feeling you guys are ready."

Spontaneous laughter broke out. Terry took a seat at the TD station and motioned others to take their place. He swiveled in his chair and looked at me with his professional face. "We don't have the real star charts yet, so you have to stay orbital. Orbiting targets are all in there, including the agency and private space stations. Where to, Adrian?"

"Let's fall back on that ancient wisdom: keep it simple, stupid. How about we hover at twenty for five or ten minutes to see if everything is as it should be, then go sub orbital for one orbit, and on the way down I'd like to do a manual reentry. I wouldn't want to be known as a Captain Dunsel."

Terry nodded to a programmer, and looked back at me. "Anything else?"

"Yeah, would you go ahead and bring up the flight deck, and the flight management computer. It's a little late to spend time going though the power up and FMC programming. We just want to see if it flies. I'll take RJ in the right seat, so the weight will be for two."

"Got it. And there's one other important thing I have been holding for you." He punched in a key code and opened a drawer at his station. From it, he drew out a palm-sized device made up of three glowing tubes each the size of an AA battery, one red, one green, one blue. The glowing tubes looked like fluid in motion. They were connected at the top by a round display bearing three red lights. He handed it over and said, "Believe it or not, these things contain samples of your DNA. The flight deck will be up and running when you get in there, but the controls will not respond or operate until you insert this into the command bus authorization port in the center console. By the way, it's the key to the real Griffin, too. Yours is the only one with administrator authority. When this key is inserted, the ship will scan for your bio signs continuously. If twenty-four hours pass without seeing your bio signs, the ship will automatically go into standby mode. It will hold its position and current status no matter where it is until it does see your bio signs. You can vary the twenty-four-hour default as necessary. The other pilots will have subordinate keys. If one of those is inserted in place of yours, the pilot will only be allowed to return the ship to the mission start point, nowhere else. If you somehow lose your key, there is an electrode kit in the ship's science lab that will allow you to program a new one, but you'll need to stick yourself with three electrodes in three different spots to do it, so you may want to take care of this one. On your personal training log, you can now check the command authorization briefing off as complete."

RJ stared silently with a somber, curious expression. I tried my best to look reassuring.

In the high-bay, we climbed to the simulator and found it suddenly alive with active displays and the subtle sound of ventilation. The cabin was filled with such a complete veil of colored lights it felt like we were inside a Christmas tree. Outside in the real world, the sun was not up, but our simulator windows glowed brightly with sunshine and a view of Space Center buildings. The cockpit air felt cool and electric, and had that new-vehicle smell. We pushed the white, imitation leather seats aside and squeezed into our places. I pulled the glowing keys from my fight suit pocket, slid open the authorization port and inserted them. Immediately the SICAS screen displayed the message, 'Tarn, A., Commander, Administrative'. The controls on the center console flashed a green greeting and quickly returned to subdued yellow.

RJ folded down his armrests. "I've got just one word for this thing; WOW!"

"RJ, you've got to buckle in or the computer will scold us."

"Isn't that what I'm always saying? Who's in charge here?" He buckled in, pulled his headset on and adjusted the mike. "Major Tom to Ground Control."

"For Pete's sake."

"Who is Pete, anyway, and how did he become a timeless reference? God, the view through these windows really does look like the launch apron outside the SPF building."

"I believe the Pete thing is a reference to St. Peter."

"Well, let us hope we will not need him."

"Your checklist is by your right knee. We do need to go through a few things. Start with environmental and by the way, Terry says if we screw that one up, he will let us pass out before he pumps air into the compartment."

"Let us also not incur his wrath, then. Doors are sealed; therefore, no one should fall out. Three air packs are running. Pressure coming up to 8,000, at 4.5 PSI differential."

I called up the control surface imagery readout on the SICAS display and did a quick check of the side stick and the rudder pedals. It was a very smooth implementation. Switching to space systems, my side stick fired simulated thrusters on the SICAS display, just as it should.

"Griffin to TD, all flight deck systems appear active and functional, all SICAS readouts are nominal. It's great to be back in the office."

"TD to Griffin, copy. We concur. There are no flags."

"Collision avoidance system is on and set to forward view."

"Ah, glad to see you remembered, Adrian. I would intentionally not have reminded you of that one."

"No, we are using the checklist, TD."

"Oh, okay. I see."

"Keying a twenty foot ascent and hover into the gravity repulse system. Radio altimeter online. Space flight management computer has accepted the input. Are you ready, TD?"

"TD to Griffin, please proceed."

"Engaged."

We shook briefly in our seats, heard a low-pitched whine, and watched the ground fall away through the window displays in the floor. We climbed upward against the buildings in front of us and felt the simulator pitch and yaw slightly as she went. At twenty feet, the ship paused, but continued to adjust underneath us as it steadied itself at the assigned altitude.

"Griffin to TD, we have visual in all view ports; thrusters are firing to maintain station-keeping. We have appropriate simulator motion."

"TD to Griffin, please hold while we monitor power usage."

"Griffin in the hold."

RJ reached out and pushed up on the landing gear lever. "Gear up so that we do not melt our tires on the way back down."

"Griffin, all nominal in the TCC, you may proceed."

"Keying in a GRS apogee of 200 miles and Mach 25 to the orbital maneuvering system with a 2-G constraint."

"TD to Griffin, understand you have passengers."

RJ took issue. "Hey! I don't mind positive Gs! It's only the negative ones that make my damn eyeballs pop out! Besides, how much acceleration can you get out of a simulator, anyway?"

I watched the blue flight path lines appear on the navigation display as the TD again squelched in over the headset.

"TD to Griffin, set your Nav display to the M50 coordinate selection. We input a flight path that should put you - 5708531 X, 18914656 Y, and 10185790 Z, at main engine cutoff. You'll be looking for Dakar on the coast of Africa. You are cleared for departure."

"Griffin copies. Autothrust engaged. Autopilot C assigned. Flight program ...engaged."

With the first burst of simulated thrust, we were jerked back in our seats more than I expected as the Griffin nosed up and jumped skyward. The ground below raced by to become Atlantic Ocean, our forward windshields filled with blue sky dotted by patches of clouds.

RJ marveled at the realism. "Wow. I'm still feeling acceleration."

"It's the simulator nosing straight up but using the window displays to fool us into thinking we're only at a sixty-degree angle. I'll be damned if I can make my mind not believe it, either."

The blue sky began to gray, then morphed into blackness. Stars began to appear as the nose of the spacecraft settled into an orbital attitude. Miles below us, we could see the familiar cloudbanks obscuring the ocean. Ahead, the continent of Africa began to take form in the distant haze.

"Griffin to TD, the visual is stunning and accurate. Coming up to top of climb."

"TD to Griffin, we see you're TOC here as well. Expect a main engine cutoff in seventeen seconds."

We watched the atmosphere pass by below us, and felt a shudder as the main OMS engines cut off. The Griffin's acceleration gently eased up and an orbital insertion indication appeared on the Nav screen along with an orbit tracking display.

"Griffin to TD. We are on orbit. All visuals and readouts as expected."

"Roger, Griffin, enjoy the ride while we review systems."

"It's quite spectacular, Adrian. The realism, I mean. My brain keeps thinking I must be weightless."

"You're not gonna start puking, are you?"

"Very funny."

"I don't recall ever having windows in the floor in a spacecraft flight deck before. We'll get to see Dakar pass by down there. This thing is a luxury vehicle."

"We may not think so after the first six months."

"Yeah. Are you starting to get your head around that?"

"I'm still in the excited-to-be-going mode. After a couple weeks I'll be wondering what the heck I was thinking."

"The dirty trick of long space flight."

"So is Danica pretty hot, I hope?"

"You'd better watch yourself around her. She's a pistol."

"All the better. We'll need some challenge if we're to retain what sanity we have left."

I had seen Earth from the same altitude countless times, yet I could not tell this was a simulation. Scattered stars dimly decorated the haze-lined curvature of the horizon, giving way to the profoundly deep blackness of space and the dense blanket of lights that dwelled there. Above the umbra, the constellations are not so easy to pick out. There are just too many stars competing for the sky. You have to find a couple that are bright enough to be seen from the ground, and then piece them into their named pattern, but it is such a overwhelming sight, you can lose yourself in the effort.

RJ broke the spell. "Dakar, dead ahead."

"Tarn to TD, good displays of the African continent."

'We see that, Griffin. We're enjoying it on the monitors."

"Coming up on the terminator. We have city lights."

"Copy, Griffin. It all looks per spec."

RJ and I sat back, relaxed, and let the Griffin sim give us a ride. The time passed so quickly, the call from TD surprised me.

"Griffin, TD. You can come about anytime you please. Deorbit burn in five minutes for a long manual descent."

On the console by my stick control, I punched in the Y-axis, yaw only key and tapped the control stick to the right. The Griffin responded by shifting us in our seats as she turned to face backward. On the attitude screen, I watched the little silhouette of our spacecraft turn on a point, as the turn rate digits scrolled next to it.

"Wow. It handles like a dream. TD, we are configured for the burn."

"Griffin, TD, roger. Your burn will be approximately three minutes with a coast to entry interface. As usual, there is too much space junk on your orbit decay for a vertical descent. You'll need to maintain three miles per second to stay clear until FL 40K before going to full gravity repulse."

"Understand TD. Are there any orbits left that do not have space garbage?" I glanced over at RJ. "We're seated backwards going roughly 17,000 miles per hour."

"Something unsettling about that. Don't tell me any more."

"Yeah, the Mercury and Apollo guys did this in a ball of fire all the way down."

"Which proves the early days of space travel were forged, and perhaps that's not the best word, by crazy people."

"Griffin, TD. We've sent you up a flight path with top of descent over the mid-Pacific that brings you down to shuttle runway 15. Crosswinds 8 knots from three-one-five degrees. You should not need additional OMS provided energy management is maintained to your onscreen display."

"Tarn to TD, Copy. TOD mid-Pacific with a friendly crosswind on the surface."

"So you don't want to pop the wings out and see how she glides?"

"Not this time, RJ. It's been a long day. I'd like to be a little more clear-headed for that. Don't want to embarrass myself. We'll manually follow the Nav display and glide slope, though. That'll be enough for this trip."

"Okay, and don't forget to put the gear down."

"GUMP."

"What?"

"It's an ancient acronym. It means fuel pumps on, undercarriages down, mixture rich, and propeller full forward. It's an old pre landing memory check, probably created by pilots who forgot to put the landing gear down. It's evolved over the years to be gravity repulse on, undercarriage armed, monitors to reentry, and programming accepted."

"Forgetting the landing gear? Could anything be more embarrassing?"

"Agreed."

"TD to Griffin, you should see a sixty second countdown clock for the burn on your Nav display."

"We have that, TD. Standing by for the burn."

We watched the numbers tick down to zero and felt the Griffin vibrate and push us back in our seats, and for nearly three minutes it felt like we were accelerating. At the end of the burn, the spacecraft settled back, though the world passing below our feet did not appear to have slowed.

"Griffin, TD, we show a nominal burn. You are cleared for spacecraft reorientation."

"Griffin copies." I tapped at my control stick and jetted her back around to face orbit. The Nav and attitude displays showed a descent rate of 9680 feet per minute.

RJ shook his head in awe. "Coming up on the west coast. I remain completely impressed by this machine."

"Tarn to TD, Attitude display shows gravity repulse coming on line."

RJ leaned forward in his seat. "Wow, Adrian. We're getting a little re-entry glow in the bottom windows."

"We are hauling ass, my friend."

"TD to Tarn, we show air braking spoilers have deployed."

"Griffin copies."

"Looks like a beautiful simulated day on that big beach down there," said RJ.

As the gravity repulse system came online, a small readout on the SICAS display cautioned, 'reaction control system manual'. I lightly held the control stick and focused on the flight path and descent map, stealing occasional glances out the window. We burned in over Texas and pushed out over the Gulf of Mexico, setting up for the one hundred and eighty-degree turn that would line us up with runway 15. The descent could have been halted in midair with the OMS engines, and the Griffin lowered to the runway with only the GRS, but translating altitude to airspeed and coming in like an airplane was far more fuel efficient, not to mention a lot more enjoyable.

We began our turn, banking as though wings were supporting us rather than the gravity repulse system.

Terry's voice squelched in, "On at the one-eighty."

"On at the one-eighty."

"Griffin, TD, how about full stop midway on the runway, hover at twenty, and set down?"

"Tarn, to TD, will comply."

Using the RCS thrusters, we came in over the threshold and slowed to a stop above the runway, then tapped in the descent and park command and watched the hardened black surface come up to meet us. There was a jostling of sorts, and the whining down of gyros and power systems as the ship settled and went to standby.

"Tarn to TD, we'll leave the shut down to you. We'll meet you in the TCC."

We could hear the celebration in the background as Terry acknowledged. We smiled at each other, unstrapped, and headed for the party.

The scene in the Test Control Center was comical. A white lab smock was going round and round in one of the ceiling fans. The sound of champagne corks popping echoed from the hallway. People were milling around the room with cake and drinks, laughing and shaking hands. Terry and a few of his people were still at the consoles checking data. An office assistant in a very short tan skirt and a brown silk shirt unbuttoned too low handed us plastic cups filled with champagne. Not paying attention to the correct cup, RJ fumbled and nearly spilled his. As the celebration continued, first-shift people began showing up and joining in. Julia Zeller appeared next to me for a moment, complete with her own drink. She raised it and smiled, and was summarily dragged off by two of her subordinates. Speeches were made, marked by frequent applause, tributes and jokes, and no one seemed to be in any hurry at all to wrap things up. RJ and I gradually made our way to the doors and slipped out.

"I was supposed to begin systems training in the habitat simulator this morning. Will you give me a note to be excused, Dad?" he said in a hoarse voice as we headed for our rides.

"I'll let them know, and I wouldn't worry. I doubt there's going to be much training today."

Chapter 7

I awoke in my clothes on a bed still made. Getting all the way to consciousness proved a very slow ascent. Flying, even simulated flying, is so surreal and satisfying it makes you sleep as though life is complete.

There was light glowing behind the curtains, but my mind still refused to spin up. There was a fragmented memory of a phone call in the middle of unconsciousness, an irate woman complaining about not having been called in. There may have been a question or request at some point about approving the use of the simulator for another test flight, and it may have been approved just to end the call. I achieved a sitting position on the edge of the bed and wondered if it had actually happened, or had been just a nuisance dream.

Three eggs over easy, nearly burnt toast, black coffee. Sitting at the kitchen table staring out the window I began to ponder the true nature of the universe but caught myself and regained sobriety in realizing I needed to get back to work. That in turn pissed me off—the fact that I now had work.

The Test Control Center was as busy when I arrived as it had been the night before. The simulator was twisting and turning. The room was humming with power and dampened sounds from the motion platform. Techs and engineers were at their stations communicating on the intercom and making adjustments to a flight profile. Terry was at his position, sitting back casually watching it all. He saw me leaning against the door and came over.

"Hey, it's been pretty amazing."

"What's that?"

"Danica. You gave her permission to fly and she's been up ever since. It's given us a good chance to tweak the calibrations and take a hard look at the data rates. The equipment is operating like a dream."

"Funny, I used those exact words last night."

"That's not all. It looks like you got yourself one hell of a deal with this pilot. She's been doing 360-degree turns around each spacecraft axis using an imaginary point in space. Smooth as silk. She's been doing it in low orbit, too. Everyone here is impressed. Where did you find her, anyway?"

"I didn't. She found us."

"Wow. A lucky turn. You may want to get in a poker game somewhere."

"For God's sake, don't tempt me."

"Anyway, that's the good news."

"Uh-oh."

"Yeah, there's someone waiting in your office. He says he was sent by the agency. Might be an auditor or something. I'm pretty good at first impressions. I didn't get such a good one from him."

"Thanks for the warning. Guess I'll go do the annoying part of this job."

The man waiting in my office wore an unbuttoned black Herringbone suit and a striped red tie hanging out to one side against a light-blue oxford shirt. His receding black hair was cut short leaving a sharp V at the forehead. His beard was kept back and narrowed to meet his sideburns. His well-trimmed mustache joined it just beyond the edges of his mouth. He had the look of a man with a practiced shell, a force field that forbid others from seeing through to his true nature. I placed him in his forties, with a few extra lines in the face possibly from failures that should not have happened. There was the aura of a man with secret allegiances to others, but I couldn't be sure about that. He sat studying a book that had been taken from my desk, which immediately pissed me off again. My initial impressions of people have almost invariably been incorrect. People I have felt immediate acclimation to have on occasion stabbed me in the back and twisted the blade. Others I have found to be completely reprehensible have saved my neck on more than one occasion. It is a painfully slow process learning not to judge someone too quickly. Some of us never learn it. Others take so long the final awakening brings a benefit too late to be of service. A few have the enviable ability not to cast judgment at all. They invariably do better than the rest of us.

I stopped alongside and looked down at him. "You'd better let me take that." He handed the ringed notebook over. I placed it back on the desk, took a seat on one corner and folded my arms. Through the observation window behind me, the simulator twisted and turned as Danica continued to put it through its paces.

He rose and offered me his hand. It was a limp handshake. "Good afternoon, Mr. Tarn. Paris Denard, Propulsion Systems. Mr. Porre suggested I check in with you before looking over the arrangements."

Strike one; he had not used my title to address me initially, a clear gesture of disrespect. Strike two; He was acting on Porre's orders as though he were an independent agent. Strike three; Propulsion engineers do not oversee arrangements.

"Mr. Denard, clarify something for me. Are you here as an outside observer for Mr. Porre?"

"Actually, I've been consigned to accompany you on this mission."

"Well, that would make it sound as though you are a team member. Are you a team member?"

"I was expecting to fill the position of propulsion engineer."

"Sounds like a team member to me, Mr. Denard. I'm really not one to beat around the bush. Don't have the patience for it, and I don't think adults should need to be supervised. Are you familiar with the standard chain of command on a starship?"

"Obviously there are several divisions of hierarchy. I believe I'm familiar with most of the inherencies in each."

"Mr. Denard, who would you report to on this mission?"

"Well, ultimately that would be Bernard Porre. I believe we all do."

He was playing the game. It would have been all too easy just to give me the answers I wanted, along with a casual insincerity. But, that wasn't enough for Denard. He was making it known that his only obligation to me was to accept the least possible amount of authority he could get by with. I had already made up my mind. He would not be taking a seat on the Griffin.

"The crew roster has not been finalized, Mr. Denard. We'll see how you do, and I'll let you know."

"It was my understanding from Mr. Porre that this was an approved assignment."

"Mr. Porre won't be coming along on this flight, Mr. Denard."

There was just a glimpse of concern through the well-practiced stone-face. It vanished as quickly as it appeared. "If you'll excuse me, Mr. Denard. I have quite a workload. I'll go over your file as soon as it comes in and probably have some questions after that. You can report to Terry Costerly and he'll set you up with your training schedule. Good luck."

I did not offer to shake his hand. I gathered items on my desk and let him leave with my back turned. He did not speak. He closed the door quietly as though no offense had been taken. I wondered just how thick the steel skin was.

A vivacious Ms. Mary Walski, Julia Zeller's assistant, came trotting in behind Denard, waving the number for Wilson Mirtos she had been kind enough to track down for me. She wore a beige skirt even shorter than the one she had handed out champagne in, and she had the legs for it. The well-fit white silk blouse, again too open, suggested the rest of her was equally well proportioned. She slid the paper down on my desk, gave me a big wide lipstick smile, and dashed off without saying a word.

After the lingering appreciative stare, I punched Wilson's number into my flip phone and sat back. He answered in the middle of the first ring.

"Wilson here. Whadda ya want?"

"Hey buddy, it's Adrian."

"No shit! It's good to hear your voice, compadre."

"Wilson, where the hell are you?"

"Orlando, Adrian. I'm in Orlando."

"What? You're kidding! You're in Florida?"

"None other."

"Why don't I have video?"

"My phone got crushed a little bit this morning."

"You're in Florida, why didn't you give me a call?"

"Well, there was some trouble."

"No."

"Yeah, I'm on probation."

"How's that?"

"Well, I thought it was a fair fight, but the judge didn't."

"How much probation you got?"

"Twelve months because of the time before. I kept tryin' to tell 'em I didn't want any trouble..."

"I know. I know."

"Adrian, that shit don't work."

"What kind of work do they have you doing?"

"I'm on the Journey Into Space, and a couple other ones."

"Disney World? You're working at Disney World?"

"I'm telling you, their stuff has gotten so advanced nobody here understands it. I'm kind of popular here."

"You're a spacecraft systems engineer and you're working at Disney World?"

"The judge says I got to stay in his jurisdiction so he will know if there's any more trouble."

"Well listen, I want you to come fly with me."

"Jesus Adrian, are you kidding?"

"Can you handle a long one in a zero-G vehicle?"

"Hell, I don't care what it is. I'm down, but you'd have to get me released from the judge."

"No problem. Give your notice this afternoon, pack it up, and report in at Genesis as soon as you can. Go to the south gate of the space center, but don't go in. It's Genesis, on the right, just before you get there."

"No shit? For real? Man, I owe you one, Adrian. A big one."

"I got a cute little hot shot pilot here who loves kick boxing and wants to take you on."

"Now I don't want no more trouble..."

"Friendly fighting, Wilson. Sparring."

"Oh, okay, I guess."

"Your badge will be waiting at the guard shack."

"Thanks, Adrian. Thanks. I'm on my way."

It had been the right call at the right time. I prided myself on getting a grade A systems engineer to agree to the mission and even be happy about it. A few calls from the right agency brass and Wilson's probation would quickly disappear forever. I felt like whooping it up but was interrupted when RJ barged in. He had a smug look on his face and was laughing under his breath. He plunked down in a chair and looked at me with a smirk.

"They tried to catch me with the ECS but I got 'em good."

"You made it in! I thought you were taking the day off?"

"I told you. I do not conform to a prescribed daily rotation. I listen to the body. It tells me what it needs and what it doesn't." He laughed under his breath again. "They tried to pop-the-top on me."

"A hull breach? They tried to get you with a rapid depress?"

"Yep, but I knew it was coming. My ears are really sensitive. They starting popping even before any of the alarms went off, so I was over at the environmental control panel in the B-airlock before anything really happened. They programmed the leak in the science lab so I sealed it just as the first alarm bell rang. It was so fast they thought the habitat simulator was not working correctly. Instead of checking what I had done, they all went into diagnostic mode. It was funny."

"Gee... I'm impressed, RJ."

"Yeah. You should have seen their faces trying to figure out why there was no decompression. The joke was on them."

"You know they're going to try harder now next time, right?"

RJ lost his smirk and thought about it. "Hmm, I may have outsmarted myself on this. I'd better bring donuts tomorrow morning. How's it going on your end?"

"Up and down. Wilson's on board."

"Wow, that was fast. I wish I could have heard the sales pitch."

"Wasn't necessary. He was looking for something."

"You said up and down. What's the down?"

"Have you run into Paris Denard?"

"Nope."

"He's the agency's choice for propulsion engineer. When you get a chance, bump into him and introduce yourself. Let me know what you think. I've already formed an opinion."

"Sounds contentious."

"He thinks he's going. I think he's not."

"Well I know who's gonna win that one."

I leaned back, swiveled in my chair, and noticed that the flight simulator had settled into its inert state. "Mmm, I'd better go check in with the TD."

"Oh good. I'll join you and pretend I'm not smug."

In the Test Control Center, Terry and Danica were standing in the center of the room talking as the techs and engineers milled about their stations resetting things and reviewing data. As we approached, Danica stopped talking and looked over at me.

"Well, did you get it out of your system?"

"Never. By the way, sorry about the phone call, Commander."

"Oh. So that really happened, huh?"

"Hell hath no fury like a woman scorned."

"No kidding? What do we have tomorrow, Terry?"

"Rendezvous and docking, with manual."

"Danica, you want the left seat first?"

"Are you kidding now?"

"I'll get to see how an expert does it."

She eyed me with distrust. "Yes. Yes, you will."

"Terry, have you set Paris Denard up?"

"Yes. We'll throw some OMS engine failures at him to start with, see how he does crawling around in the service corridor. I'd really like to reserve the pool over at KSC and see how he handles removing panels in a spacesuit. He says he's done it, but I'd like to see it."

"Don't spend too much resource on him just yet."

"Oh, okay."

"Well folks, if anyone needs me, I'll be in my office. If you don't see me just dig through the pile of books. I'll be under there somewhere."

Terry raised his hand. "Adrian, we need our other two pilots."

"You're right. That's the top of my list, with everything else."

Terry turned to RJ, "We need to talk to you about that last habitat emergency. Got a minute?"

RJ followed Terry and looked back with a smirk on his face as they headed for the habitat simulator.

Chapter 8

Thursday morning began with delusion. I had the idea I would face the day with careful planning. I slid open my closet to grab a pair of flight coveralls and for some reason realized my wardrobe was a pathetic representation of the unsophisticated. There was the one black Stafford suit that needed dry cleaning, half a dozen collared work shirts, jeans, and fifteen flight suits of every color available. At the end, next to the neglected dress suit, my fishing waders showed much more use. I grabbed a Nomex olive-green flight jumpsuit and consoled myself that my lack of style and grace wouldn't matter for a year.

I managed to arrive at Genesis at a respectable 08:00A.M. to find the day already waiting for me with its own plans. The door to the Test Control Center was blocked open and as usual, the place was busy. Technicians were booting up for the day's practice drills and Terry was talking energetically to Danica. As I passed by on my way to the break room, she spotted me and I became a lock on her radar. I managed to grab a cup and the coffee pot and pour before she came banking around the corner.

She wore a black, one-piece hipster flight suit with the legs rolled up to the knee and tall, black, lace-up military flight boots. It met the criteria for regulation wear if not exactly the prescribed presentation, and it made it amply clear she was an independent woman. I braced. She came to me, took the cup from my hand and began sipping with a discerning stare. "You'll be ready to go quick, right?"

"I get the feeling I will be."

"I have another pilot for you, if you're interested."

"Really? What's it going to cost me?"

"Just that it's another... WOMAN!"

"There's a joke in there somewhere, but I think I'll let it pass."

"She drives a Harley Davidson."

"Well, knowing your standards I guess I don't have to ask if she's qualified."

"Gosh, was that a compliment?"

"Whoops."

"So should I tell her to come?"

"Is she flying?"

"Heavy cargo on a fixed run, based out of Atlanta. She's bored to death."

"Will we screw up somebody's delivery schedule?"

"Bullshit."

"I beg your pardon?"

"I'm sorry. I should have said cow manure. She delivers compressed tons of it to the bio-fuel processing centers."

"Wow! There's actually quite a few jokes in there."

"She's heard them all."

"Has she been in space?"

"Two tours, intersystem."

"Hmm, that's a little bit green, don't you think? How about weightlessness?"

"She pukes as good as anyone."

"Point taken. What's her name so I can run it?"

"Shelly Savoie. So can I call her?"

"How do you know she'll accept?"

"Cause I already called her."

It made me laugh out loud. Danica stared, unsure if that was good or bad.

"So she's already on her way?"

"Sort of."

"What if I had refused?"

"Then she would have shown up and begged in person."

"Danica, I have to tell you. I think I'm starting to like you whether I want to or not."

"We haven't flown together yet."

"That will change this morning."

"You'll be ready quick, right?"

"Yes, ma'am."

She dashed off toward her office to make the call, and for a moment it bothered me that there was someone who seemed to love flying as much as I did. I managed to beat her to the simulator, took the copilot seat, and went through power up and the flight management computer set up. A short time later, she came hurrying through the door, stopped in surprise to find me there, and then continued her climb into the pilot seat without speaking.

I flipped up the toggles for the auxiliary power systems and tried to sound coy. "What took you so long?"

"Very funny." She pulled out her checklist and went about the left seat setups.

When the lights were lit and the power levels nominal, we launched off the apron into an orbit that brought us below and behind the One-World Space Station, the largest assemblage on orbit, a big wheel that turned endlessly to give its civilian squatters time away from weightlessness when not working in the center hub laboratories. Rumors are that the new artificial gravity systems soon to come will be so power-efficient the big passive gravity wheels will no longer be needed. There will no longer be rotational linking of a spacecraft with a docking port or hanger bay. It will be the end of a space era. As we approached, I heard Danica singing Proud Mary under her breath, "big wheel keep on turning, proud Mary keep on burnin," the adopted theme song of the place. The lights were on, the docking port open. The spokes of the big silver wheel turned with us as we closed in to the brightly lit center port.

Danica was in her element. She flew the Griffin as if it was an extension of her body. I could only sit back in the copilot seat and be impressed. But as we closed in to dock, something happened. The spacecraft began a slow roll to the left. Instinctively, Danica tapped at her control stick to bring in opposite thrusters. For a moment the roll slowed, but then resumed. Increased opposite thruster brought the same result.

"Hold on, something's happening," she said in a raised voice and she leaned forward tapping through different displays on the SICAS. As we rolled, I brought up the reaction control system diagram on my SICAS display. It showed the two starboard thrusters stuck open. I said nothing and waited for her to pick it up.

"Starboard thrusters all locked open. There can't be multiple failures, that doesn't happen. Adrian, bring up the fly-by-wire schematic."

Our roll continued to speed up. We were sitting in a barrel that was rotating faster and faster. The world outside the windows was becoming a blurry swirl. The G-meter on my attitude display was flashing a big red 7. I did as she asked.

"There it is, failure in the thrust command distributor. Adrian, pull the breaker on that thing."

By then the shiny metallic station outside our windows was rolling by so fast the view had become a solid eddy of gray. Danica was making her first mistake. I had seen this problem before. I quickly leaned back to the engineering panel behind my seat and snapped out the breaker for the malfunctioning thruster controller. Nothing happened. We were still spinning like a top.

"Shit! They didn't close! Adrian, kill the fuel cutoff valve to all A-system thrusters."

I smiled to myself. That was the right move. I reached back and tripped off the pressure valve. Our wild spin continued, but without the acceleration.

"Switching to Bs." Danica jerked at her side stick. The swirl outside regained motion then became a blurred portion of the space station until finally we slowed to a stop. She glanced at me for a terse moment, tiny beads of sweat on her forehead, and then reoriented the spacecraft to the docking port. We had drifted well to port and below. There was silence on the headsets. The TD wasn't commenting.

"Nice one, Terry. Remind me not to forget you're down there," she said when we were back in position.

"You are cleared to dock, Griffin."

We docked, separated, and made our way down toward simulated Earth. As we dropped into atmosphere, she glanced over, "Did he get me?" she asked.

"I'm not sure. I didn't see how bad the spin got."

"Fuck," she said.

When TDs do a debriefing, they always do it in the debriefing room. It is a place decorated in the most positive ways possible. There are murals of the sky from orbit, live flowers in large vases, subdued lighting, a big screen built into the wall for playbacks, along with soda, coffee and refreshments, and soft reclining chairs. You never do debriefings in anyone's office. Sometimes difficult things must be said at debriefings that cause stressful emotions within those being debriefed, and those memories must not be associated with any particular support staff or their place of business. Terry was waiting for us when we arrived.

Danica was beside herself. "Okay, let's have it. How many Gs in the spin?"

Terry looked sympathetic but still impressed. "Twelve to thirteen. You may have taken too long. You may have lost consciousness."

"No, I would have been awake."

"How high have you rated in the centrifuge?"

Danica did not answer. We all waited.

"It's not the same in real life. You can take more in an emergency than you can in the skin-stretcher."

"That's often true. More adrenaline pumping. Adrian, would you have gotten it?"

"I can't say."

"Well, Danica, this is why we do this. Next time you'll go right for the feed shutoff. Actually, everything you did was correct. You isolated the problem and followed it right down to the cause. Beautiful troubleshooting, done very quickly. The only problem was you did not have time to do that. Once you knew it was thrusters, you should've killed the primary thruster system immediately. Nevertheless, the application of your knowledge of the system was very impressive. Just one little procedural refreshment here, that's all."

The rest of the debriefing felt unimportant. The atmosphere remained discordant. When it was over, we left Terry and headed down the hall toward our offices.

"You going to be okay with this?"

"Shit," was all she said as she turned into her office.

In the break room, someone had ordered sub sandwiches for the entire staff. The place was abuzz with people coming and going, some talking in low tones about the morning's flight. I grabbed the nearest sub and made it back to my office without getting waylaid.

Turkey, provolone, shredded lettuce, and the brightest red tomato slices I'd ever seen. Both mayo, and oil and vinegar. The damn thing tasted so good I sat back at my desk and gave it my full attention. Someone had left a new bottle of water on my desk. My guess was, the short skirted, open bloused Mary Walski. I washed the delicacy down, stared at the pile on my desk, and quickly lost the culinary contentment. I pushed some stuff aside and, using the space agency search engine, called up everything I could find on Shelly Savoie. Danica's recommendation was not quite enough.

Savoie's education history had a curious diversion within it. There was an associate's degree in biology, then suddenly it all changed to aerospace engineering. There had to be a story there. The next thing that came up was a photo. Danica had not mentioned the large burn scar on the left side of Shelly's face. She was attractive, even with it. In the photo, she was wearing a green flight suit, parachute still strapped on, helmet in the left hand. Her dark hair well past the shoulders, tangled from having been under the helmet. Deep brown eyes gave her slightly long face a kind of sullen look, the look you see in fighter pilots who are insistent in the idea that they will never allow anyone to shoot them down. She had rosy-red cheeks and precisely applied makeup, even though she had obviously just gotten out of an aircraft. The caption below the picture read 'Tactical Electronic Warfare, Squadron 34.'

I backed up to the search listing, scrolled down and found one that said 'Pilot Exonerated In Tanker Crash'. That set me back. Not many refueling tankers crash and no crewmembers survive when they do. The NTSB report read like science fiction. It was a high altitude refueling. The first part of the incident was captured on cameras attached to the aircraft being refueled. Something came out of the sky so fast you couldn't see it. It cut the tanker in half in mid-flight. It went up in a blossoming fireball. The aircraft being refueled suffered damage but by some miracle was blown clear from the debris, spun down, recovered, and continued flying. The two pilots and two engineers on board the tanker all had ejection seats. They continued forward from momentum in a crew compartment without an airplane attached. The pilot in command initiated eject for all four seats as they went down. It must have looked like a bunch of roman candles popping out the top of a flight simulator. All of the seats came out okay, but Savoie got a patch of plastic explosive from someone else's seat stuck to her oxygen mask. There wasn't much air at that altitude, but that stuff doesn't need it. It burned all the way down. All four crewmembers survived, with injuries. They never figured out what hit the tanker. A freak meteorite or space debris was suspected. After extensive reconstruction surgery, Savoie was transferred to Tactical Electronic Warfare. I sat back in my seat and rubbed my forehead. I couldn't read anymore, nor did I need to.

Outside my high-bay picture window, the Griffin simulator rose up from its position at rest and then sat back down. It meant the system had been reset and was ready to fly.

I headed for the Test Control Center and stopped off at Danica's office on the way.

"Ready?"

She dropped her half-eaten sub on a paper plate, took a quick gulp of her coffee and followed me down the hall. As we stuck our heads through the TCC doorway, Terry looked up and asked, "Ready?"

In the simulator, I took the pilot seat and strapped in. Danica followed and gave me a flat smile as she adjusted her seat. She remained sullen but tried to use the checklist steps to conceal it. Secretly, it made me admire her even more. Her absolute dedication to perfection was the most reassuring trait I could ask for. I knew that on the Nadir mission, when she was manning the pilot's seat, I would sleep well.

This time our ascent to orbit was smooth and pleasant with no anomalies during docking or separation. We backed away from the hub of the big turning wheel and as I expected, a master alarm lit up and pulsed its annoying buzzer sound. I canceled the buzzer but the alarm light and SICAS display continued to flash.

It was a landing gear malfunction in space. The nose gear had deployed seemingly of its own accord. I had never seen such a thing happen and doubted I ever would. It was Terry trying to find something unexpected. Commands to retract were ignored. The only option was to deorbit in that configuration without allowing too much reentry heat to enter the wheel well.

You cannot actually slow down in orbit very much. It's not just you streaking along at sixteen or seventeen thousand miles per hour, it's also everything behind you. Bullets travel anywhere from 700 to 3000 miles per hour. It doesn't take a Steven Hawking to figure out that if you slow your spacecraft down to say 1000 mph, some of the stuff coming up from behind will strike you at speeds five times faster than a bullet. At those velocities, that kind of energy disbursement from something as small as a penny becomes an explosion.

There are so many kinds of space debris, and so many dead satellites on orbit, there is nowhere safe anymore. My friend Perk Murphy once did a stint in low orbit gathering the big stuff up onto a tug and sending it to the sun. When he completed his tour, they had not even made a dent in the mess. They took the biggest stuff because when it collides with other stuff, it explodes into a million smaller pieces. There's no way to collect those. There's no fishing net that will capture metallic parts traveling at thousands of miles per hour. You have to wait for them to sink in orbit and burn.

So, we went down the hard way. We turned the spacecraft around backward to orbit, set the Collision Avoidance System to look forward for crap coming at us, waited for what appeared to be a clear spot, and made tiny deorbit burns to lower, slower altitudes. We were playing real live Pac Man with a spacecraft. Had the CAS been mistaken, or had we missed something on the screen, we would have seen the speeding debris coming straight at us but only for an instant.

After ten small deorbit burns, we began to pick up atmosphere. We cut in the air brakes and let the gravity repulsion system lower us back down to the space center. It was a very time-consuming and meticulous use of simulator, and in real life, the truth is I would not have risked it. I would have come down as quickly as possible with an open wheel well, let the gear burn, and set down a damaged spacecraft using the GRS.

As we left the simulator, Danica gave me an annoyed look and said, "You got off easy."

Chapter 9

I was ground-bound the following day. While Danica worked the simulator alone, I badgered the computer for one more pilot and one more propulsion engineer. It is an unenviable task trying to find someone with just the right qualifications who can be persuaded to accept a mission that will take them away from everyone and everything. People with immediate family are unlikely to make that commitment. Those trying to advance their career or continue postgraduate education do not wish to be out of sight and out of mind for that long. Beyond that, the arrest records and personality profiles sometimes set off other types of warning bells. When you are light years away in open space, you can't call the men in white coats to come get them.

What I really needed was a medical doctor with piloting skills. Even though background checks and DNA evaluations make the threat of unexpected illness almost nonexistent, and the medical programming used onboard spacecraft these days being quite incredible, it's still not a substitute for a real EMT or doctor. The person we needed didn't have to be current with their practitioner certificates. We just wanted someone with the touch. There was one name on my list that seemed to be too good to be true. Reeves Walker, call sign 'Doc'. He was a non-practicing MD who had worked with the Blue Angels. Strangely, he had no history of combat flying or combat training, and yet they had accepted him. He had an extensive background in aerobatics. Unfortunately for me, he was married. I put off calling him thinking there was no way. He was married, retiring from the drill team life, probably wanted to lie back on the beach. Come to think of it, that's what I had been doing, damn it!

I bit the bullet and dialed him. The number was in Texas. It took six rings before he picked up.

"Walker."

"Mr. Walker, my name's Adrian Tarn. I'm with the space agency. Have you got a minute?"

"Let me take a table away from the bar. Hold on a second. What did you say your name was?"

"Tarn. Adrian Tarn." I looked at my watch. It was 10:00A.M. Texas time. This wasn't starting out so good.

"Okay. Oh damn, I spilled my beer. Wait a second. Okay, go ahead."

"You are in Texas, right?"

"I was the last time I looked out the window."

"Well, I'll get right down to it. I need a pilot."

There was a long pause. "Reeves?"

"What kind of pilot you need?"

"Space."

Another long pause. "Space? You need a space pilot?"

"They are sometimes called astronauts, Mr. Reeves."

"I know what the hell they're called. You just don't get someone ringing your damned phone asking for one too often. You know what I mean?"

"I might as well tell you right up front, it's a twelve-month mission, approximately."

"How'd you get my number? You sure this isn't a joke? Did Dean put you up to this?"

"Have you ever heard of the Griffin, Mr. Reeves?"

Another pause. "Hell, I do remember that. It was Sam Hudson trying to make a spacecraft into a damn airplane. That all fell through on him."

"The prototype was built and it's been refitted. That's what you'd be flying. Is there any chance you could come to Florida and work in the simulator a little bit and see if you're interested?" I leaned back in my seat and suddenly realized I wasn't sure if I was interested.

"This is a serious offer?"

"Twelve months worth of serious."

"This is got to be a sign from God. I got separated from my wife of twenty years a couple months ago. I still don't know what I did wrong. I was gone a lot, sure, but she knew all that. She just kind of decided she wanted to go a different airway. She's made it clear there isn't going to be any reconcile, so I can't think of anything I rather do than get as far away from here as I can. It's gotta be a sign from God."

"So you'll come in and give it a shot?"

"Where you at?"

"The south gate at KSC. The Genesis facility."

"What the hell. Gimme a couple days. I'll be there."

I hung up extremely worried that I had reached the wrong Reeves Walker. I raced over to Mary Walski's desk, handed her his picture and asked her to double check and make sure

I had signed on the right person. I wondered how to handle it if the wrong guy showed up at the gate. Back at my desk, I sat nervously drumming my fingers, promising myself I'd be more careful with the propulsion engineer.

RJ barged in and plopped down in a seat. "I get a break while they set up the next program. By the way, I've now worked with and briefly spoken with... Mr. Paris Denard."

"Oh yeah? What do you think?"

"You've got a problem."

"Damn straight."

"The man does not bond well."

"I wish it was only that."

"He is sincere and forthcoming in that you cannot trust him."

"Just what we need."

"How's the crew roster coming along?"

"Other than that, you mean?"

"Any new candidates?"

"Yes. I just called in a guy who's supposed to be an MD and a stunt pilot and it sounds like he's going to show up in an old pickup truck with a beer in one hand and a hound dog in the back."

"Why'd you do that?"

"Would you please shoot me and put me out of my misery?"

"Hey, some have already tried that and are now the worse for it. Don't look at me. Has this guy got any space in him?"

"I don't really know. I wanted a doctor so bad I thought if I could just get someone who was a real flyer we could nursemaid them through the orbital stuff."

"Hmm. They're going to be calling us the Vomit Comet 2."

"Not too worried about that. Stunt guys spend their lives going from eleven positive Gs to five negative Gs and back again. Plus, he's in his fifties so he's middle-aged. Your blood vessels start getting stiffened up around then so G's and weightlessness don't mean as much."

"How about a propulsion engineer since the one we just got appears to be a loony-tune?"

"The stunt pilot shook me up so bad I haven't been able to get going on it. I'm glad you stopped in."

"Dr. Smith prescribes lunch with beer."

I laughed. "God, I didn't need a doctor, after all."

"Don't be too sure. I prescribe beer for everything."

We took the Vette to Marlin's on the Pier. A server in a tiny short pink skirt with an overfull blouse took our orders without writing anything down. She was so well endowed I could not remember what I had ordered as soon as I had given it. She had a thick southern drawl in her voice that was intoxicatingly sexual. It forced me to keep looking up at her cherry red lips, which was a good thing, otherwise RJ and I would have both been staring at her blouse, though she did not seem to mind.

"Why have I never been in here before?" RJ asked, when she had left.

"When she comes back, should I tell her you're interested?"

"She knows. She has us both on the tip of her little finger. She could make us roll over and beg with a single wink."

"Speak for yourself. She wouldn't need the wink for me."

"When she comes back, should I tell her you're interested?"

"You know better. There's a data analysis woman out there somewhere who holds my leash."

"That's right. Does she know about this trip yet?"

"Shit."

"Well, that answers that."

After lunch, we left a preposterously large tip and headed back to Genesis. I came up on the guard shack too fast and got chewed out by the guard. He knew who I was but had no reservations about dishing it out, and told me he'd write me up right there in his shack if I ever did it again. I was impressed and humbled. RJ laughed all the way inside. As I opened the door to my office, I heard RJ call out from the TCC, "Hey Terry, Adrian got bawled out by the guard."

At the computer, I pulled up what was left of the list of current propulsion engineers and suddenly realized I had been subconsciously skipping over the female names. Men always have this image of delicate little fingers decorated with long nails, attached to elegant, dainty arms not made for wrenching things. Maybe Danica was right.

There was a name on the list that sounded familiar. Erin Duan. Where had I heard that? I called it up and scanned down the search list results. One in particular stood out. 'Stealth 2 Uses JATO Power To Set New Hybrid Land Speed Record at Bonneville.' I sped-read the article. They hadn't actually used JATO-assist rockets to supplement the power of the vehicle. The motors attached to it were real solid rocket boost motors. Once lit, there was no turning back. At the end of the article, the three propulsion engineers who had dared to let someone drive something like that were listed. The last name was Erin Duan.

I sipped coffee and mulled it over. The rest of her dossier was superb, solids, liquids, turbine, jet turbine, amp-light, and tachyon. They were all there. The land speed record thing had just been a hobby. I called up a photo. It was a bit disappointing. Maid of honor at her friend's wedding. Long white gown with a lot of shiny clear stones. Ivory blonde hair past the shoulders. She could have been modeling the outfit. Tiny lips, pert nose, bedroom blue eyes. This could not be a propulsion engineer. The marital status line said 'single'. How could someone who looked like that hold a PHD and still be single? She had to be in her late twenties. After the Reeves 'Doc' Walker fiasco, I didn't want to set myself up again. But, why was I worrying? There was no way she'd accept. Looking like that, single, young, advanced in her field. No way. I could call her and cross her off the list real quick, maybe exchange a sports car story or two and clear my mind of her. I leaned back, flipped my phone open and punched in the number. Probably wouldn't get her anyway.

She answered on the third ring.

"Ms. Duan, my name is Adrian Tarn. I'm with the space agency. I'm calling because I'm looking for a propulsion engineer for an upcoming mission."

"Okay. I'm in. Where do I report?"

I nearly fell out of my chair. It left me speechless. I did not have a prepared response. I had just won the Publisher's Clearing House giant bonanza. The cameras were rolling. The world was waiting for a response. The spotlight was on me.

"What?"

"I said okay. Count me in. Where do I check in?"

"But you don't know what the mission is, or how long even."

"Hang on a second. Let me tell my boyfriend before he leaves." She yelled with her hand over the phone. "Hey Brad, I'm going into space."

An irate voice cut in from the background. "What the hell are you talking about now?"

"I'm going into space. I just signed on."

"For Christ's sake, Eri. If you do this, that's it. I'm not taking any more of your shit. I'm out of here."

"Well, okay then,"

"Well, okay. I'm leaving right now. Good-bye"

She yelled, "Good-bye! Good riddance!"

A door slammed.

She came back. "Sorry about that. I've been trying to get rid of him. It was perfect timing. So where do you want me?"

"Are you okay, really?"

"Just fine. I'll pack up and head your way and you can explain everything when I get there. If there's a problem, we'll see."

"Have you heard of the Genesis facility?"

"Yep. Between KSC and the Port Canaveral inlet. I've spent so much time at the space center; I even know all the tunnels."

"When can you be here?"

"Take my cat to my parents. Let them know. Maybe leave tomorrow. What kind of engines? I can't wait to know that."

"Stellar Drive."

There was silence for moment. "This isn't a joke is it? There's no such thing."

"There is now."

Silence again. "Oh my God. If I can be there today somehow, I will."

"See you soon, Erin."

"Count on it."

I hung up the phone and sat up straight with a big grin on my face. That was it. I now had a full crew complement with the exception of Bernard's Denard. All I had to do was wait for him to crash and burn, or abandon him somewhere and go with seven.

Or so I thought.

Chapter 10

Saturday began with the doldrums. The flight sim was shut down so they could load and align the new star charts that would give us beyond-orbit simulations. Danica took the day off, saying she had not had a chance to see any of the sights yet. I sat memorizing the procedures for wing extension and aerodynamic flight in the Griffin, maneuvers that promised to be challenging and enjoyable. The V-speeds were atrocious. In atmospheric flight mode with the wings fully deployed, the spacecraft would stall and fall out of the sky at one hundred and eighty knots. Recommended final approach speed was two-ten. It only made me love her more.

As I pored over the flap, air brakes, and gear speeds, a call came in; Mary Walski, letting me know that there was a courier-secure delivery at the front gate. The courier could not be allowed in. I would need to go out there and sign for it. It seems a stark irony that printed material has become more secure than electronic documentation these days. If a text exists only in printed form, it can never be easily hidden, easily copied, or illegally transmitted. If there is only a single copy made, it can be controlled much more closely, and tracked much more carefully. Maybe RJ is right in his aversion to technology.

I gladly dropped my studies and headed for the guard shack. The courier was arguing football with the guard, something about the Jets being overdue. He stopped as I approached, went to his van, and came back with a fancy clipboard and strange-looking pen. I took a hard look at it. The damn pen took my fingerprint as I signed. The courier handed me a small black briefcase with digital combination locks on either side of the handle, and security seals on the locks.

Back in my office, I tore off the seals and sat looking at the combination locks. Five digits each. Was I supposed to know these? As I wondered, my computer beeped incoming message.

It was from the agency's human resource division. The message read:

Commander Tarn,

The employee numbers you requested are as follows:

L.L. Cummings, 73841   R.L. Anders, 62915

I dialed up 73841 on the left and the lock popped open. 62915 in the right lock, same result.

As I opened the case, the first sheet made me laugh. Orange plastic with 'TOP SECRET' emblazoned across it. Under that, a cover sheet followed by brief instructions;

**TOP SECRET
EYES ONLY**

**DO NOT RETAIN FOR FILES. DESTROY
EXTRANEOUS MATERIAL AFTER READING**

COMMAND BRIEFING DOCUMENT

MATERIAL CLASSIFICATION: ATS

DESIGNATED RECIPIENT: TARN, ADRIAN, COMMANDER

YOUR EYES ONLY

PREPARED BY THE OFFICE OF EXTRAGLOBAL RELATIONS

WARNING!

**This is an official intelligence transmission pertaining to
classified information and material not intended for general distribution. Dissemination of its contents to unau-
thorized personnel not cleared by the appropriate security office is strictly prohibited and punishable by law.**

**TOP SECRET
EYES ONLY**

Commander Tarn,

You are directed to disseminate the enclosed information or portions thereof only as is absolutely necessary to accomplish your mission and to only those individuals who have a verifiable need. Please understand, this is our agreement with those who were responsible for providing these resources. No copies are to be made, and upon completion of your mission, these original materials must be returned in completeness to this office for return to the proper custodians.

Lecia Townsend
Director
Office of Extraglobal Affairs
Washington D.C.

So, it was easy to guess. This had to be information on the Stellar Drives. I looked out at the simulator high-bay. There was still no curtain on my observation window, but there was no one in the high-bay. I lifted a thin foam cover off the contents of the case.

It was two, very thick manuals embedded in black foam. Both covers were blank. One was dull green, the other a light gray. I carefully wiggled the green one out and opened it to the first page. The title read, 'Folded Membrane Communications'.

It set me back. Not at all what I expected. The next page contained an overview. It talked about long distance communication using a membrane between two adjacent dimensions. Bewildered, I flipped ahead through the pages and found diagrams of a new communications panel on the Griffin that did not exist in the simulator. My impression had been that when we were far enough away from Earth, there would no longer be practical communication. This manual was contradicting that. According to the description, communications data could be transmitted to a Nasebian support planet and relayed to them. The more space we traversed, the greater the transmission time, but at least messages could be sent. It was a one-way system. We could transmit, but not receive.

Checking the high-bay once more, I pulled the second book from its place. Inside the cover the title read, 'Multiharmonic Reactive Shielding'. I sped-read the overview. It was talking about protective shields. Farther in, there was a diagram of yet another control panel that did not exist in the simulator.

The Griffin had shields, and from the description, they appeared to be extremely powerful.

I sat back stunned. This was starting to sound like a combat mission. Had there been a weapons manual in the briefcase I would really have been beside myself. As it stood, the Griffin carried no weapons other than the hand-held type locked in the armory closet, but I was left feeling uneasy. Was all of this just to make the crew as safe as possible, or was someone, somewhere, expecting trouble? This wasn't human technology. What did they know? What weren't we being told?

Glancing over my shoulder, a janitor had entered the high-bay. I put everything back, snapped the case shut and committed the lock codes to memory. With the message from HR deleted, the case fit neatly into a bottom desk drawer with a key lock. I leaned forward on the desk with my chin resting in my palm and continued to be perplexed.

There were other matters that needed attention. More crewmembers would be showing up today. Wilson had been the closest. I wondered where he was. Almost in answer to the question, there was suddenly the faint sound of glass shattering. I sat up and thought, "It can't be." Curiosity quickly overcame doubt. I headed for the break room.

He was on one knee with a tray in one hand picking up jagged pieces of glass scattered on the break room floor. In keeping with his irreverence for fashion, he had on black dress slacks and a yellow New York Yankee's tank top. Mary Walski stood over him, wringing her hands and shaking her head. I leaned against the divider and folded my arms.

"That was my favorite mug, too."

"I'm so sorry. I bumped the tray. It was an accident."

"It's irreplaceable, you know."

"I'll replace it. I promise."

"How can you? It came from the space station."

"I'll get you one even better."

"How could you do that?"

"He will, Mary. I'll vouch for him." They both stopped and looked over at me. Wilson let out a short yelp and stood up. "Adrian!"

"Mary Walski, Wilson Mirtos."

Wilson charged awkwardly over and gave me a hug. He stepped back and shook my hand for too long. "By God, it's good to see you, buddy. It's double good this time."

I put one arm around his shoulder and smiled at Mary. "He's a member of the flight team, Mary. I promise you, he'll make up for it. We have a stop at the station, so we'll hit the gift shop before we leave."

Mary relaxed and reappraised him. "I haven't seen a transfer request on you yet; otherwise I would have known who you were."

"It's coming. I just put the paperwork in a couple days ago," I said.

"I guess the tray was kind of sticking out over the edge. I'm glad to meet you, Wilson." She stepped forward and shook his hand. "But just the same, I'll leave the mess to you two." She shrugged and headed back toward her office.

Wilson had changed little since I had last seen him. The big upper body was there, supported by legs that looked like they belonged to a boxer. His short dark brown hair was slightly receding in the front, making him look like a muscular scientific-type. Women loved Wilson, partly because his size made them feel safe, and partly because, contrary to popular myth, size does matter. Wilson has always worn his heart on his sleeve, but at the same time his watchful stare suggests he is ready for and unafraid of the unexpected. The hazel red eyes befit someone who had seen most everything at least once. There was no sense in ever playing games with this man. Seeing him again gave me that same old feeling. It was always good to have Wilson around, especially if there might be hazard involved. Together he and I cleaned up the remnants of Mary's mug and carefully returned the brooms and dustpans to the janitor's closet so the janitorial staff would not come looking for us. We poured coffee, and took refuge in my office.

"So that's it, eh?" said Wilson standing in front of the high-bay window.

"The front half, anyway."

"It reminds me of the ship in that movie about the apes."

"You're not the first to make that comparison."

"I'm still a movie hoe, you know."

"You'll have plenty of time to watch some."

"Twelve months, you said?"

"That's a rough guess. You never know on a search and recover mission. You still play chess occasionally?"

"Oh hell yes. Even though I don't win a lot."

"RJ is on this cruise. My money says you can beat him."

"Smith? You dragged Smith into this?"

"I doubt I could have kept him away with a big stick."

"Well, how is that self-proclaimed philosopher these days, anyway?"

"The same. He's in the next hanger bay, in training on the habitat simulator. You should go track him down and let him know you've arrived. He'll introduce you to our TD."

"I'm looking forward to that. Can't wait to see the tin can we're getting."

"Hold on to your hat. It's something special. You still play the bass?"

"You bet. The electric for the blues. The standup for bluegrass."

"Don't try to bring that along, okay?"

"Damn. I bet there's no smoking, either."

"Very funny. Here's a tablet with all our personnel and resources. That'll get you started. The TD will take over from there. When you get settled in, I know a good place with friendly barmaids. We'll go get some beers."

"Damn, it's good to be here. I owe you a big one, Adrian. The sky started looking different after you called. To be honest, I can't wait to get past it."

He stood and took the tablet, went to the door and looked back with a nod, then closed the door so hard that the glass shook. Same old Wilson. No sooner had the shaking settled than someone began tapping. The door pulled back open and a technician pushing a cart full of video monitors worked his way through and turned the corner in front of my desk.

"I have a service order to install these and set up your video feed, Mr. Tarn. Can I do this now, or should I come back?"

"What am I getting?"

"This will give you video feeds from both hangers," he said. "You'll be able to monitor what's going on in both places."

"Wow! Great. Please proceed."

"Won't take very long. All the hook ups are already here."

"You know, what I really need is a curtain for this high-bay window."

"I have that too. The stuff just came in today. It's been on order. The big screen fits up against the window. It's clear unless you want privacy, then you just select an image and it blocks the view both ways. It'll run video, of course, as well."

"Wow!"

"Yeah, if it's not too much of an interruption, I'll hang that one right after these."

"Please do. Great. I'll go get a refill."

I amused myself by wandering around, wiping up the table in the break room, and standing in the doorway of the TCC watching monitors of the ongoing training exercise. Wilson was leaning on a station counter beside Terry, looking on and asking questions. RJ's image was on the main monitor in the habitat simulator, near the hatchway to the rear service crawlway, handing tools to someone lying on their side in an EVA suit. It had to be Denard.

When the exercise began to wrap up, I left and went to the deserted flight simulator hanger and climbed up to the flight deck. The cabin was cold and dark. I found the locations of the hidden communications and shield panels. There was nothing but blank plating. Climbing back down, I could still see into my office, although there was a new, clear video panel mounted against the glass. The other video panels against the wall were all up and running. One was set to monitor the hallway, another the TCC, and a third the habitat simulator. None was set to the Griffin high-bay. As I approached the door to the hallway something caught my eye, something out of place. Through the window, the technician was bent over my desk. It looked like he was fooling with the locked drawer. As I watched, the new screen morphed into a white raster blocking my view. I hurried to the hallway and entered my office with as little warning as possible.

His head popped up from behind the desk. He did not look startled, but he did look prepared. "Just tucking in a few cables. I'm about finished here." He wrestled briefly with something beneath the desk, and stood.

"Your selector control is right here on the side of your desk. You can call up any monitor and then assign any camera to it. The big screen over the window has its own controls right on the base here. This is the operator's manual for it on your desk. On the back cover is our contact info. Just give us a call if you have any questions or problems. Anything else I can do for you?"

"That should do it. Thanks."

"My pleasure."

He gathered up his tools and dropped his tool bag on the pushcart. I held the door for him as he maneuvered out. As soon as the coast was clear, I went to my desk and inspected the locked drawer. There was no sign of tampering. I unlocked it. The briefcase was still there and had not been repositioned. I pulled it out, unlocked it, and flipped through the classified books. It was all there. Nothing seemed amiss.

Was I imagining things now? Had I become so paranoid that a video technician now looked like a threat? But, was it a coincidence that he showed up right after delivery of the documents? Was it chance that he seemed to be working at the only locked drawer in my desk? Were both of those things just happenstance and I was becoming neurotic? I sat down, rubbed my forehead, and decided it was time to knock off.

Chapter 11

Coming in late the following afternoon, I tried cruising past the gate guard at idle, offering a conciliatory wave. He gave me a stolid nod and went back to his tablet. Someone new was shuffling luggage around in the parking lot. She had a briefcase on the ground and a bag slung over her shoulder. She wore jeans with short, brown leather lace-up boots, and an amber red, three quarter sleeve print blouse with a pearl necklace hanging out of it. Her long ivory-blonde hair was tied behind her head. The gentle lines of her face had an oriental tone. Dark eyes, deep set and knowing. She had a tiny nose and thin lips without lipstick. She was shorter than I had expected. My guess was five-feet-five. She stopped and stared as I got out.

"Erin, you made it!"

"The guard was very nice. He didn't have my paperwork but he called around and had it brought out."

"The guard was nice to you?"

"He was very nice. I haven't checked in yet. I've just arrived. But, I have many questions. Is this a bad time?"

"The sooner the better. Let me take that briefcase."

We made the obligatory stop in Julia's office, paused at the door to the TCC and waved, got lustful stares, and escaped to my office. My new screen was blocking the view of the highbay with a photo of the Pantheon at sunset. I fumbled around pushing buttons and finally got it to clear. We stood staring at the Griffin simulator, idle on its platform.

"So were you serious? Stellar drive engines?"

"We haven't been able to see them. The real Griffin is at the Spacecraft Processing Facility on the KSC side. They won't let us in yet."

"How much sub light velocity do you need before they take over?"

"None. As I understand it, the Stellar Drives take you from sub light, up to light, and then through it all on their own."

She gasped. "A single set of engines takes you directly to P-factors of light? There are no Amplight drives at all?"

"That's what we've been doing in the sim."

"What is the intake and what are the emissions?"

"We don't know."

"Who designed these?"

"Non-human engineers."

"Oh, I see. Can I see the design specs?"

"We have all the sensor and control interface schematics, and all the interface circuitry. We have not been allowed anything on the engine cores."

"What if one fails?"

"We are told they will not."

"Gee... Will engine schematics be coming?"

"No. This is a special circumstance. A one-time undertaking. Much of it is classified, even from us. Our mission is to locate an artifact, retrieve it, and bring it back. The rough estimate is twelve months."

"Just how fast can we go?"

"We don't know yet. But we will."

"How many people?"

"Seven or eight, but you'll find the crew quarters quite extraordinary."

"I see. So despite the blank spots, we stand to learn a whole bunch, don't we?"

"We will be going farther and faster than anyone ever has. Is any of this a showstopper for you?"

"No way. I'll bet I'll know a lot about those engines before we're done."

"I'm sure you will. Here's your check-in tablet. It has most of what we know. Our TD is Terry Costerly. They've set up an office for you. Actually, you have your pick of three. Come on, I'll take you there and you can pick one out and start getting settled in."

We took the hallway to the adjoining offices where Erin stacked her belongings in the one nearest the habitat high-bay. I paused in the doorway as she began to open her pack.

"When you get set up, wander around and get your bearings, then go see Terry and he'll work out a familiarization schedule with you. I'm still going over your file. I'll probably have some questions when I'm done."

"A mission with an advanced engine never before seen. I'm glad I took your call, Commander."

"Me too, Erin."

RJ was waiting in my office. His gray flight suit had a streak of grease on one shoulder.

"Escaped again, I see, or did they let you off the leash?"

"I saw you in the hall with an attractive blonde. Thought I should make sure she's okay."

"Erin Duan, our second propulsion expert."

"Wow! Much nicer than the other one."

"How is the other one doing?"

"As you would expect. Terry threw an O2 leak in the service crawlway at him. He went in and installed a pressure seal and fixed it, but then complained endlessly that it was too easy and a waste of his time."

"How is Terry holding up to that crap?"

"Oh yeah. After the last barrage of complaints, Terry went back in and programmed the same failure in a decompressed service module and made old Paris do it in a pressurized spacesuit. Not so easy. It seemed to shut him up a bit. If he considered you to be important at all, he would already have been here to complain."

"Well, I guess insignificance has its benefits, then."

"Enjoy it while you can. It won't last."

As RJ spoke, my phone chimed. It was the KSC visitor's center personnel office. Someone by the name of Shelly Savoie had come to their office by mistake. Could we please send someone over because an escort would be required.

"RJ, want to take a ride?"

"Gladly; let us depart before Paris shows up to explain things to you."

As we left the parking lot, I coasted cautiously by the gate guard. This time he did not even look up. We looped around to the CCAFS entrance, held up our badges, and picked up speed on Phillips Parkway

"Hey, let's take the back route that goes by the lighthouse."

"Great. I'd love to see the old lighthouse again. Now that's what technology should be."

We turned down Pier Road and watched the beach come up on our right. Past the old Delta launch pads, the security exercise yard and shooting range, we came up on Pad 46. I slowed, stopped, and pointed at a crumbling structure on our right.

"See that big cement ramp coming out of that broken down building pointing toward the ocean?"

"Yeah, what's left of it."

"Way back in the fifties, before guidance was developed, they used to launch a vehicle off that ramp called a Snark. Most of them crashed and sunk in the ocean. I hear some old timers say that this part of the beach is still called Snark infested waters."

RJ laughed and stared as though he was trying to imagine one coming off the ramp.

"On the left, just past those trees is a runway most people have never heard of even though it's still used all the time. Everybody thinks the shuttle runway is the only one. This one's called the skid-strip, because way back when it was built an awful lot of experimental didn't actually land here, it skidded in."

"They still use it?"

"Oh yeah. There's a control tower. It's used quite a bit for touch and gos. And, you see this fence and gate straight ahead of us?"

"It's abandoned."

"It is now. Way, way back they used to have a blimp here called Fat Albert. It was used for security radar coverage before radar improved. The thing was nearly the size of the Goodyear blimp and it was anchored by a special tether even though it had its own radio controlled steering and motors. The story is that there was one just like it used down in the Florida Keys. Supposedly, during a storm, the one in the Keys broke loose from its mooring and drifted out over the Atlantic. As the temperature cooled, it came down until it was dragging the tether across the water. Before the agency could get a handle on it, a guy in a small fishing boat came along and thought he had found himself a free blimp. He tied the tether off to his boat and decided he'd tow it back home. Problem was, as soon as he got going, the forward motion produced a whole lot of lift and up went the blimp, the boat, and the guy. The guy grabbed his life preserver and jumped, and the blimp flew away with a boat hanging off it. Neither the agency nor the military could figure out how to bring the thing back safely, so they dispatched a fighter jet and shot it down. That night, the ground crew snuck into the hanger and painted a blimp symbol on the side of the fighter to show it had bagged one blimp. That's how I got the story. The fighter is in an air museum and still has the blimp silhouette on the side of it."

"Now that, my friend, is a good story."

We made our way through the industrial area and headed west over the river. The NASA causeway was alive with traffic and people. We scanned the distant facilities, soaking up the history that surrounded us, passing the launch areas where long, long ago, the first space shuttles had jumped off their pads to construct the first real space station, the circling harbor that had given us a foothold to build bigger, better islands in orbit. Huge domes now covered those areas, but the sentiments from time were still glowing all around us. In the distance, the VAB still commanded the skyline, and the viewing stands stood waiting for the next big event.

Shelly Savoie was sitting on the steps of the HR office. The burn on her face was more apparent than I expected. We introduced ourselves, got her a temporary badge from the office, and watched as she threw her leg over a humongous cherry-red, abundantly chromed Harley Davidson and cranked it to life.

"My kind of woman," remarked RJ.

Chapter 12

The last and possibly the best of us arrived the next day. Reeves 'Doc' Walker strolled into my office as I sat going over personnel records. His handshake was special. There was a current of experience and knowledge within the grasp that was new to me. His irreverent attitude on the phone had been misleading. There was deepness about him. His demeanor was self-assured, but at the same time, there was a humbleness beneath it. He wasn't shy about his success, but he seemed not to be waving any banners, either.

I noticed too many lines for a fifty-year-old face. His complexion seemed permanently wind-burned. He had deep wood-brown eyes and low eyebrows, a sharp chin and a quick, genuine smile. He looked a lot more like a jet-jockey than a medical doctor. I noticed his hands. They looked like hands that had a lot of hours holding a control stick in the left and thrust levers in the right.

I asked him to sit, went out and came back with two black coffees. "Cream and sugar on my desk there, Reeves."

"Doc would probably be more appropriate for we two, Adrian. I've read up a bit on you. Black is good. So that's it?" He pointed at the window to the hanger.

"That's the flight deck of the Griffin. We'll be going faster and farther than anyone ever has."

"Mmm. I've heard stories of the spacecraft that can fly like an airplane. Never thought I'd actually see it."

"It can, but it's a barnburner. You did a stint with the Blue Angels, as I understand it."

"Not really. I was doin' a lot of the same air shows as they were, demonstrating personal family jets for the Avaron Corporation. Supposed to show how crash proof they were. But the truth is, there are people who can crash anything. At one show, two of the Angels came looking for me. The team leader had a migraine that was ten on the Richter scale. It was too painful for him to fly. It was a pinched nerve from playin' touch football behind the hanger. I cortisoned it and he was okay. After that, they kept stopping by at air shows, or when they needed something. They use chase planes when they're developing new patterns. Eventually they invited me to fly chase with them and later, when they were short a fifth, they'd let me fly outside man during practice sessions. But I never went in any shows with them. My name was never on the flight list."

"Those guys are a tight group."

"Tight as it gets. You've got quite a bit of time under your belt yourself."

"I have managed to recover from stupid mistakes on quite a few occasions."

"As have we all, Adrian. As have we all."

"It wakes you up at night sometimes."

He smiled and sipped his coffee. "That's the trick, isn't it? Trying not to think about it."

"What scares you the most? The world of medicine, or plummeting through the sky?"

"People, Adrian. People scare me the most. The ones who have no conscience. The ones who care only about themselves."

"Want to go take a look at the flight deck?"

"Lead the way."

In the hanger, we climbed the air stairs and stood looking into the darkened cabin. He said nothing but stood appraising it with a veteran's eye.

"How much space time you got, Doc?"

"Not much, but it's just a matter of missing stars, right?" He looked at me with a dead serious expression on his face and then burst into laughter. I couldn't help but join in.

"Actually that's true, but you don't really do any stick time en route. Everything is programmed into the Spacecraft Management System before you go light, and the Nav computer and Flight Management Computer have to approve what you've requested before they'll allow you to engage. It's pretty much the same as the heavies you've flown, except the scale on the Nav display is in light years or AU's instead of nautical miles. All the orbital stuff is joystick and Nav display. What about EVA time? Ever done any of that?"

"I've logged a bunch of weightless time doin' zero-G rides, but never in a spacesuit."

"I'll want to schedule a little EVA sim time for you in the water tank over at KSC. Would you be alright with that?"

"Hell yes. Better than Disney."

"Let me show you the habitat simulator. You might find it interesting."

On the way, we stopped by the TCC where RJ and Terry were hanging over a station display looking at replays of a recent procedure. The appropriate introductions and handshakes were made. Danica and Shelly were away getting Shelly settled into her apartment. No one knew where Paris was.

Doc was duly impressed with the interior of the habitat module. Someone had set the living quarter's wall display to reflect a cow pasture with cows. I had a strong suspicion who. Like the rest of us, the luxury of it was far more than Doc was accustomed to. Most professional pilots spend their free time sleeping in lounges, back offices, and sometimes their vehicle. Back in the TCC I gave Doc his study material, directions to his temporary housing, and begged off when he got into a long discussion with Terry. Doc was already intent on getting flying time in the Griffin.

Paris Denard was waiting in my office. No work apparel. Instead, a silly-looking green cashmere sweater and gray dress slacks with black penny-loafers. He was poking around but keeping his hands in his pockets so as to look innocent. It wasn't working. It made me decide to start locking the office. He stopped and looked up as I entered, and reset himself for the task at hand.

"Enjoying the view," he commented and pointed to the new monitors set to display the habitat training.

"They were just installed yesterday, but yes I am."

"Getting a kick out of people jumping through hoops?"

"Paris, what's up?"

"Forgive me for being blunt, but this training itinerary is bullshit."

"Well, I'm flattered that you would consider bringing this to my attention." I sat on the corner of the desk and folded my arms.

He sat back in a chair by the wall. "I know what's going on here. It's pathetically obvious. You know, of course."

"Okay, back up a bit. To what are you referring, exactly?"

"You have the Test Director harassing me with trivia because you are offended by my stature here."

I had to keep myself from laughing. "Paris, I have not said one word to the Test Director about your training or testing, and I'm not sure what you mean by stature. Everyone on this team is at the top of their field. No one is subordinate."

"Your Test Director buddy is assigning me tasks that are below my level of expertise. You are trying to demean me and make me look like an amateur, and you're making a mistake, because I will not accept it."

"Paris, let me be blunt. What you've just said shows that your level of expertise, as you call it, is not quite up to what it should be. If it were, you would know that TDs are completely independent entities. They are the policemen of mission hardware and crew. They are outside of the jurisdiction of any management, and any mission hierarchy. It is done that way to prevent people who aren't qualified from being slipped into operations where they might be a danger to the mission or its crew. Any attempt to influence a Test Director, or modify his test plan, sets off alarms in the organization that brings more internal investigation than you can imagine. I would caution you against trying to pull any strings on Terry Costerly. You'll get a lot more blowback than you'd be expecting."

He stood, looking slightly disarmed. He wrinkled his brow and pursed his lips. He had the disposition of a man who had taken a wrong turn in a crowded city, and did not know where to go next.

"Paris, are you sure you want to give up a year for this project?"

He regained his composure. "I've made the commitment."

"To whom or what?"

"I'll discuss this with Mr. Costerly and see where it takes me."

"Paris, we know you think you're good. Now we need to think you're good."

He made a 'humph' sound and walked out. RJ was waiting outside the door and came in behind him, pausing to watch him storm by.

"Bet that was fun," he said when the coast was clear.

"The man is a legend in his own mind."

"He really does know his stuff, Adrian. When TD gives us something, he knows where to go and the correct procedure. Sometimes he seems a little awkward at implementing it, but he does know his field."

"You mean like someone who had taught a class in something, but has not had a lot of practical experience doing it?"

"Exactly."

"Hmm. I just wish he could put the harness on and pull with the team."

"What a wonderful metaphor."

"How are you doing back there, anyway?"

"It's a breeze. I'm going deeper into the systems than is actually necessary. By the way, I get the afternoon off tomorrow. They need the sim time to let the newbies catch up a little. I want to hit the surf at high tide. Can I borrow your waders? Spike shredded one leg of mine."

"Sounds like your cat is sending you a message."

"There's no doubt."

"You know, our new propulsion engineer Erin has a cat. Maybe you could compare notes on feline training."

"No training necessary. The cat has completed the training itinerary. I'm completely trained. The cat's in charge. I'm his butler."

"My waders are hanging up in my bedroom closet, right next to the suit I don't wear. You have a key."

"Thanks. I promise to keep your waders away from Spike."

He smiled and left me to my misgivings about Paris Denard. The man had received too many accolades for too little suffering and now wore them like medals of valor everywhere he went. A little more notoriety and his ego would bring him one short step away from the ugly little snare that waits and watches for those too fond of themselves. It is the same nasty little trap that lures the nouveau rich or puerile famous. As fame and notoriety take hold, suddenly you are surrounded with an ample variety of overindulgences available to you most any time. Innocently you begin sampling the ones that do not offend your morals or ethics while secretly eyeing those that do. After a while, the lines become blurred and they all become indulgences that you rightly deserve, a normal part of the avant-garde life style you lead. The compromises become greater and greater until you are so possessed by overindulgence that you are a person owned by indiscretions, and those who provide them. That is the trap. You lose your self, one sin at a time, until those who specialize in sin can make you serve them and do most anything they require you to do to further their own aims. It is at that point many wealthy or famous individuals decide there is no going back, though they are unwilling to continue. They help fill the news and star magazines with the regretful obituaries of people who gave so much, and who were so dearly loved it seemed unthinkable that they took their own lives. They will always be remembered. There will always be gratitude.

Lingering on, are those smart enough to realize early what has happened. They too have found the bridges behind burned or collapsed. There is no way back. Yet to go forward is to delve deep into lonely or deluded darkness. The only option is to try to cut back on the excesses. To give them up completely would be to become a normal person, a fearful and consequential debasement. So they try to mold the high roller's lifestyle back to a less soul-depleting existence, but it only makes for a longer, slower crash. It is an ugly little story that has happened to so many wonderful, gifted people you would think there would be an agenda to remedy it, but the lights are too blinding, and the praise too ingratiating. No drugs can compare to it, they can only pay homage and provide continuity to the illusion. Paris

Denard had enough illusions to go around. One was that he was accompanying us on the Nadir mission.

Chapter 13

The new week began with a wonderful simulated day. The prospect of departure to points unknown was becoming more a reality, and our crew was formed and beginning to bond. I rode right seat for Doc and then Shelly. To my surprise, Terry allowed Doc a docking procedure with the One-World space station and the man greased it in as if he had been doing it all his life. "Just like a video game," was his only remark.

Shelly was also the consummate professional. Where Danica was usually aggressive, Shelly was patient and precise. Watching two gifted pilots work a new spacecraft was something I would have paid to see. It was a privilege to admire their skills from the right seat and I never had a single word to offer. They could have cared less that I was there, and seemed to consider me an unnecessary distraction. Afterward, in the TCC, I found Terry just as silently jubilant as I, and we both acted a bit stiff trying to conceal it.

Someone ordered pizza. We milled around the break room trading jokes and upbeat conversation when my phone interrupted. Balancing a sagging piece of pepperoni and mushroom, I managed to flip it and answer. It was RJ.

"Hey, Kemosabi, I'm here at your place getting your waders."

"We just had a couple text book flights, RJ. Life is good."

"Couple of things. Did you forget to lock the side door?"

"I don't think so. Was it unlocked?"

"Yeah, but I'll lock it when I go."

"Okay. Thanks."

"You've got a steady drip in your kitchen sink faucet and I can't get it to stop. You might want to get that fixed before departure."

"Okay. Anything else?"

"Just one thing. There's someone sleeping in your bed."

"What?"

"At first I thought the blankets were just piled up but then I saw the dark hair underneath the pillow."

"Long dark hair?"

"Familiar-looking long dark hair."

"Uh-oh."

"Uh-huh."

"I'd better get home."

"Remember not to speed past the guard."

I hurried down the hall to let Terry know I was going, and then sprinted to the Vette. The guard took notice and stood ready. Clutching the wheel for tension relief, I gave a forced smile and wave as I went slowly by, but as soon as he was out of sight, I brought it up to float level, just short of the legendary Dale Earnhart Sr. loose front end. If any municipal satellites were monitoring my stretch of 528 I would be assured a summons in the mail. By the grace of the slowness of government, I probably would not be at home when it arrived.

Creeping into my own house I found her still asleep, her head covered by pillows. Without waking her, I sat gently on the side, and ever so slowly lifted a pillow away. Her deep dark hair was splayed across her face. I carefully pushed it aside and stroked it. Without opening her eyes, she moaned and the right hand came up in an uncoordinated seeking until it found my chest and pressed against it, clinging to me for security.

Some light years ago, Nira Prnca and I had bonded by chance in the vacuum of space in a few frightening moments where life had become an uncertain prospect. We had clutched at each other like fierce lovers, separated by layers and layers of pressurized life support, droplets of her blood tinting her damaged armor, the redness squeezing through my fingers as I fought furiously to heal the carnage. We had shared life from my backpack, exchanged breath through an umbilical cord of cold plastic, and stared at each other though the glass in our helmets, hoping for reassurance that each was still there and that nothing else was more important. And, when life had regained its composure and the threat of timelessness past, we both discovered something had been left behind. Somehow, we had revealed more of ourselves to each other than people should. Secrets had been compromised. There needed to be an understanding that those unintended exposés were safe. There needed to be intimate trust.

She understood what had happened better than I, and had explained it to me soon after in such a primeval way that even I came to the realization something extraordinary had changed us. Inside, a tiny fusion-reaction had taken place leaving new starlight where there had been only darkness, a perpetual light that graced our minds and hearts.

I brushed the strong chin line with the back of my fingers. The hand clutching me pulled me down. Without opening her eyes, she turned and hooked the other arm around my neck, murmuring in half sleep. I touched my lips to hers, and was pulled in harder. The blankets covering her naked form were pedaled away. The left hand wrenched at my flight suit accompanied by an annoyed moan. With all barriers resolved, we locked into each other, turning and twisting, gasping from the effort, pausing only to collect on the exchanges of sensuality and lust. Each time the desire faded, it returned with a greater vengeance. Too much time had been missed, but nothing had been forgotten. The star was still burning, the pact of intimacy still in place. Sunlight from the curtained window turned golden and faded. The islands of sleep that crept in between lovemaking grew longer. Finally, we lay wrapped in each other in corporal exhaustion.

When new sunlight began beaming in through the curtains, I opened my eyes to find her lying on her side staring at me, her hand pushing down on the pillow to see.

"What did I do to deserve this?"

Her voice was dry and sultry. "Someone has to look in on you from time to time."

"How'd you get here?"

"You would think a flight from D.C. to Orlando would be quick and easy. Got stuck in Atlanta for three hours. Ended being up all night and getting here late in the morning."

"Aren't you going to be missed?"

"Oh yeah."

"Why'd you do it?"

"Rumors and clues."

"What?"

"One of us has signed on for something off-world without telling the other."

"Uh-oh."

"So what has my six-foot-two knight in dented armor got himself into this time?"

"It all just happened. I was trying to find the right time."

"Mmm, I see your dilemma. There would not have been a right time."

"I didn't have a choice. I had to take it."

"I didn't have a choice, Mommy. I had to eat the candy."

"There's some very serious issues involved. Debts to be paid. Allegiances to maintain."

"Aren't there always, dear? How long?"

"The consignment is for twelve months, but from what I've seen it will probably be less."

She sat up on one elbow. "A year? A whole fucking year? Are you shitting me?"

"It could be as little as six months. I don't have all the details yet. It's so damn classified we only know half of it."

She flopped over onto her back and threw her arms up in disgust.

"I had no choice, please believe me."

She looked at me with a sullen, narrowed stare. "Let's make a pact that for now on, we only sign on to long missions that we both can take."

"Okay, but we need to modify that slightly. It needs to be, we will try to accept only missions that we can both be on. I do not want to be in a situation where I am forced to break a promise to you or you to me."

"Okay. I guess."

"You know there is the M-word. It gives people more leverage in those situations. But the concept has always scared the hell out of me."

"No way. I don't want the married stigma again. When you show up in my stateroom, I want to know it's because you want to be there, nothing else."

"I can't imagine anything else."

"Remember I told you about my ex-husband, the diplomat, and how he was always going back and forth while I was in space systems going up and down, so that we hardly ever got together?"

"I'm not so good at relationship counseling. Why are you asking?"

"We'll I'm sort of stuck in group data analysis for a while, and now you're going vertical again. I don't want that same thing happening here."

"Nira, there's no way you could go along on this trip."

"But why are you going? I know this must be one fucking dangerous mission 'cause the agency picked you for it. It must be something really important to them and so fucking dangerous that they think you're the only one who might have a chance of pulling it off, right? I know them. That's what they do. Am I right? Why the fuck did you accept it, anyway? You're set up. Wasn't the Electra close enough to dying for you? Why would you get in another crap game, and believe me that's a good play on words. Why did you take this?"

"Doll, sometimes you are too smart for your own damn good. I'll tell you what; enlighten me about the extraterrestrial we brought back sedated from the last trip."

She hesitated and stammered, "I can't go into that. It's above top secret."

"I'm classified above top secret."

"But I still can't talk about it. You know that, for God's sake."

"That's my point. I have to go on this mission, and I can't talk about why. Did I get you?"

"You're a tricky bastard, Adrian. Yes, you got me."

I pushed her back on the bed and kissed her, then spoke an inch from her lips. "You couldn't go anyway because I couldn't bear the thought of anything happening to you. It would screw up my command structure. Here on the ground, I'll know you're safe. That'll help me get through the mission and back to you."

She made a "humph" sound and hit me with a pillow.

I made her scrambled eggs with cheddar. She attacked them with the ferocity of a tiger. We sat with coffee and stared at each other, riding a train of emotions that were in constant conflict. She had to get right back. Her flight was a little past five. We squeezed lawn chairs into the back of the Vette and went to her favorite place on the beach, just south of the Pier. We set up where the incoming tide could run up under our chairs and tried to find meaningful things to say. We would plan something special for when I got back. A trip where no one could find us. We'd stay as long as we felt like it and the hell with whatever was going on back home. She was fiercely serious, and for once, so was I.

I took her to OIA and went as far as security would allow. The place was packed but in our minds we were the only two there. We held on for a long time until boarding calls threatened. She did not wave. We just stared each other down until she disappeared into the concourse.

The day became morose. I thought to push her to take a leave of absence and stay in Florida until T-0 day, but that would have made the parting even more painful. Too many hours of preparation were being invested to ask her to wait around for my free time--what there was of it. Back at Genesis, my work was suddenly not inviting. I wandered around the place watching the intense discussions going on, the drama of simulated failures and mitigations. Even through gloom, the Genesis teams were so exceptional in their work it forced an uplifting. Julia's staff would show up periodically with questions. The break room was a mess since everything else going on was too important for anyone to care. People were upbeat and enthusiastic. All except for me.

Chapter 14

Genesis began running at full capacity. Each day marked a new level of efficiency. In the habitat service module, engineers learned where everything was without having to think. They worked on maintenance, troubleshooting, and correcting problems. Personnel rotations were used in such a way that each member could develop a working relationship with the others. Most were good at that, one not so good.

Four pilots worked the flight sim in rotation, one team at a time, team substitutions used to make sure everyone was on the same page. Flight-testing became more aggressive. Although the star charts were now in the system, orbital and atmospheric flight remained the primary test bed since it demanded the most from a flight crew. Programming light speed travel began with simulated trips outside the solar system. To the TD's relief, no one tried to fly through any stars.

When there were breaks in the schedule, engineers and pilots would sometimes be switched to the other simulator. Pilots learned the habitat module system while engineers practiced with flight deck controls and interstellar navigation. Everyone was required to be certified on the Nav system. That standard was set by two very embarrassing incidents from way back in the early days of light travel when navigators became incapacitated and their pilots did not understand the Nav equipment well enough to get back home.

The performances we were seeing from our crews were more than encouraging. They were all so good it was like watching a blockbuster movie. All the unexpected failures initiated by the TD were systematically analyzed and mitigated. There were few instances where missions would not have been allowed to continue. The flight crew was doing so well it worried me. I would sit at my desk and watch them beat almost everything thrown at them. Pilots and copilots were anticipating each other's needs so well they were effecting inputs before each could finish speaking.

Overconfidence. I could not let them adopt overconfidence.

On a particularly successful day, I waited for Terry to come to my office to drop off daily performance cert records. I made a point of not calling him in. These people were too sharp. If he were summoned to my office, one or two would notice and wonder. Word would spread. So I waited. Midmorning Terry strolled in and smiled at me like a man who was acing his job.

"They are good, Adrian. Really good. I don't know where you found these people, but your luck is running."

"I have a concern."

"What could that possibly be?"

"Too good."

"Oh. You don't want it going to their head."

"Exactly."

"What do you want?"

"I want them to crash and burn badly at least once, to wake them up to reality. In real life, you don't always win."

"You have a point. What do you want me to program?"

"I want a standard deorbit burn, then electrical fire. They lose gravity repulse, and all thrust. They have to deploy wings, come in dead stick with no power at all. The only place to put down is right at the edge of the envelope. The Flight Management Computer says they can reach it, but they have to clear obstacles to do it. When they get there, a temperature inversion drags them down too low to make it."

"Adrian, that is pure sadism. I didn't think you had it in you."

"I'll be the first to fly it. That way, they'll all know what's coming, but they won't know the details. They'll only know that I crashed and burned. They'll be anxious to top me. They'll be sucked right in. That'll get their attention. We'll all fly it solo. I don't want the other hot shots getting a look at this before it's their turn."

"Well, I must say, you make life interesting. I'm looking forward to this. Putting the best I've ever seen up against a no-win situation. I can't imagine what we'll get."

"What will we see on the windshields?"

"At impact, you'll get a big fireball on all screens. The motion platform will jerk about and shudder. That'll last for ten or fifteen seconds, then you'll see the video system reboot."

"Perfect. Can we run it this afternoon?"

"Absolutely. I'll just need to make sure the programmers keep their mouths shut. Most of our test team members and crew members have gotten too friendly."

"I'll be standing by. Just let me know the scheduled time of my death and I'll be sure to be there."

He laughed and headed out the door with software already compiling in his head.

The TCC and flight sim were scheduled immediately after lunch. The condemned man ate a hearty meal. Simulated death on a full stomach. Being strapped in alone in the active cockpit had a slightly eerie feeling to it, but I enjoyed the ascent to orbit, and took extra time to watch the simulated world go by below me. On the way back down, I hit the top of the last mountain at one hundred and eighty-four knots. The sim made an initial "oomph" sound on impact, then an explosive roar as the fireball dissipated and the cockpit settled.

Word spread like wildfire. Subdued, inappropriate conversations here and there just couldn't be resisted. Shelly was up next, but she was almost too smart. She seemed to wonder about the single pilot requirement. During her descent, the simulated electrical fire did not seem to faze her. Even with the emergency, her reactions in the deorbit were smooth and precise, and despite meticulous flight management she exploded exactly the same way I had. In the TCC, I smiled and gave her a shrug. There was anger behind her eyes, but she controlled it with the skill of a diplomat.

Next was Doc. I changed my mind and rode in the copilot seat, not wanting to miss a master trying to coax a dead airship over a mountain range. Even with symphonic artistry in searching for additional lift, he went up in a ball of flame like the rest of us. Afterward, he came into the TCC sipping a fresh cup of coffee and gave me an expressionless look that said volumes. He knew. He understood what I was doing. He had not been fooled for a second. I cursed to myself and he smiled.

I waited in the copilot seat for reset and Danica. As I waited, a call came in. It was Julia Zeller and Mary Walski on a speakerphone.

"Adrian, you need to come to my office right now."

"Kind of busy at the moment. It'll have to wait."

"No, Adrian. You will want to stop whatever you're doing, and come here right now."

I sighed and shook my head. I trusted Julia. She wouldn't insist unless it was necessary. I could watch Danica's path to destruction from the replay monitors. I unbuckled, found Doc and asked him to ride copilot and warned him not to give her any help, then headed for Julia's.

They were on the phone with someone. Julia pointed at the conference caller and then me. "It's Richard Allen from the Spacecraft Processing Facility. Richard, Adrian Tarn just walked in."

"Good afternoon, Commander. I was to call you as soon as we had approval from upper management. We're just about ready to turn your ship over."

I stood by the side of the desk and the adrenaline began to pump. "I can't tell you how much I appreciate the call, Richard. When can we see her?"

"They are installing the last of the inspection seals as we speak. When would you like to come for an initial walk-though?"

"Could it be this evening? We should be burning up the rest of our simulator time in just a few minutes."

"That would be fine. I'll meet you at the hanger entrance. Julia has my contact info. Just text me when you're on your way."

"My sincere thanks, Richard. We'll see you there."

He clicked off and the three of us stared at each other in anticipation. Julia asked sheepishly, "Can we come?"

I nodded as she handed me a pen and pointed to an electronic folder of documents that needed my signature. My look of injury did not sway her. She smiled and tried to look sympathetic.

In a daze, I headed back to my office. RJ caught me in the hall. "Adrian, I just died."

"You too? Must be something going around."

"I was trapped outside the ship and couldn't get back in because of you-know-who."

"Oh crap."

"Oh yeah."

"Well there is some good news."

He raised his eyebrows and waited.

"We get to go see the Griffin tonight unless there's a memorial or something."

"Wow! Does anyone else know?"

"Not yet."

RJ dashed off like Paul Revere. I laughed to myself and marched on. In my office, Terry was waiting. He looked disheveled and confused, something I had not seen before.

"How'd it go, maestro?"

"She made it."

"Who made what?"

"Danica made it. She brought the Griffin in safely."

"But how is that possible? It was supposed to be a no-win situation."

"It was. I'm sorry. We even programmed the simulation to adjust the level of temperature inversion to the Griffin's energy management curve so that no matter how it was done there would be too much pressure differential to allow enough lift to get a powerless spacecraft over those mountains."

"So how'd she do it?"

"She was way ahead of it. She saw the one to two hundred foot clearance over the mountains on the glide slope indicator and didn't like it. Everybody else thought it was enough. When she hit atmosphere, she restarted the main APU and when the temperature inversion began to pull her down, she kicked in the restart system for the OMS engines. They wouldn't start of course, but she got just enough thrust from spinning those engines to clear the peaks. The radio altimeter showed her clearing the highest one by two feet. She even got some bounce from ground effect. She glided in the rest of the way, no spoilers, no flaps, and put the gear down one hundred feet from the runway. She couldn't have known the gravity release would get them down in time, but she waited that long to avoid drag from the gears. Didn't even scratch the paint, damn it."

"Let me get this straight. She's about to hit the mountain peaks like rest of us, and she commands the engines to restart at just the right moment, and gets enough lift from the dead engines to make it over?"

"That's it. Like I said, the readouts say she cleared the last peak by two feet."

"That's just unbelievable."

"It's incredible. What are you going to do about this? She was supposed to get humbled."

"Is there any chance she saw the program beforehand? Did Doc say anything? Could she have known what was coming and figured all this out ahead of time? Did she talk to Shelly?"

"No. No one said a word. Doc was as amazed as the rest of us. This was just flying by the seat of her pants. I am dumbfounded. She's always aggressive. She's always way ahead of the spacecraft. I told you before; you got one hell of deal on this pilot. I've never seen anything like it."

"What did she come over the runway threshold at?"

"One hundred and eight-two knots. Two knots slower and she would have dropped out of the sky. She was supposed to fail. What are you going to do about this?"

"I know what I'm going to do. I'm going to make everybody do it again, with her in the copilot seat, and she's going to teach us this. Damn. We're gonna have a kid teaching us. She said she'd get our man cards if we didn't watch out. I guess she just did."

As Terry and I spoke, people began to gather outside my door. The word that the real Griffin was being readied for inspection was spreading at light speeds. Paris Denard pushed his way through the others and did not bother knocking. He opened the door and leaned in.

"Do we need anything special to head over there?"

"Just me, Paris."

"I'll wait in the break room."

"That would be good."

Terry and I exchanged annoyed stares. Terry asked, "Head over where?"

"They're letting us into the Griffin's hanger."

"Oh jeez! Let me go shut down."

No one wanted to wait for transport. Everyone took their own vehicle or rode with friends. RJ and I led in the Vette. It looked like a cross between a parade and a circus. The guards at the south gate were at first alarmed, then amused. Everyone had the correct badge. Everyone was allowed through.

Our entourage caused people to stop and stare in the VAB and SPC parking lots. We filled up most of the spots near the chain link fence gate. Director Richard Allen came out and waited by the entrance. He broke into laughter as the army of Griffin lovers followed me en mass toward him.

"Good thing it's a large hanger, Commander," he commented as I approached with my hand out.

"Wild horses couldn't have kept them away."

He glanced over the group. "This way, please." He led us to the heavy double metal doors and with a second, questioning glance back, keyed in his pass code and pushed one open.

The Griffin sat like a trophy, polished to a white mirror finish. It seemed larger than the specs or the simulator. She was sitting on short, stubby landing gear assemblies intended to take up as little space as needed when retracted. There were no sharp edges anywhere. Everything was unibody construction that flowed as though it had been poured in a mold. My attention turned quickly to the stellar drives. They were mounted near the fuselage. The intakes formed two ellipses, one large and one a quarter the size of the first, side by side. They were fused together like a single unit. The smaller elliptical body was on the outside. There were covers concealing the intakes. Someone had hung 'Remove Before Flight' ribbons on them as a joke.

A voice from behind me cut in. It was Paris Denard. "See that? There are two engines. The smaller one is the sub light, the larger the super light." He went beneath the nearest one and stood looking up at it.

Richard Allen was guarding the open stairway to the forward airlock. He raised one hand and called out. "Everyone, one moment please. The only thing we ask is that if you enter the cabin please first put the antistatic bags over your shoes. They're right here alongside the stair ramp. Thank you."

When the crowd at the stairs began to dwindle, I bagged my shoes and noticed my pulse rate quicken a bit. At the top of the stairs, the airlock seemed different somehow. As expected the flight deck was cold and dark, yet there was a striking sense of life there. Some of the controls and switches on the Genesis simulator were nonfunctional representations, but here everything was real, along with some extras. I looked where the hidden controls for shields and communications were located. There were access panels in those spots that did not exist in the Sim. Once again, the impulse to sit in the left seat crept in, but I held it at bay.

The habitat and aft areas were virtually identical to the simulator, although you could tell everything in this vehicle was functional. There was an intense feeling of complexity all around. I stood just inside the forward airlock, looking into the spacious white interior of the living area and tried to imagine months of suspended life there. It was another slap of reality. In the sleeper section, I touched the upper compartment assigned to mission commanders. I could visualize myself inside, but could not guess at how it would feel. In the gym, everything had inspection seal stickers. The equipment stood waiting to be needed. Farther back in the science-med lab the place was pristine and more kept than the simulator. It smelled like a hospital room. The silver surfaces cast brighter glints of reflected light. Within the aft airlock, the hatch to the service module was closed with a seal on the latch. The rear airlock external door was open with stairs for the walkthrough exit. I turned and looked back at the deserted ship. Home for a year. What would exist just outside this shell six months from now? What would this ship bring back from the unknown? Who would we be then?

Back at Genesis, another secure courier was waiting at the gate talking to my favorite guard. I was flagged over and asked to sign for yet another briefcase. I pushed it through the passenger's window and plunked it down on RJ's lap. We pulled in and parked, and he looked at me hoping for an explanation but let it pass when I did not offer one.

In my office I locked the damn door and set the window screen to frost. I knew this briefcase had to be for the Stellar Drives. The same pass codes from the other case worked. I opened it, pushed the security messages aside and was surprised to find two more blank-cover books. I pulled out the one on the left, flipped open the cover, and sat stunned. The title read,

Particle Accumulative Beam Weaponry.

Chapter 15

The smaller intake Paris Denard had declared to be part of a sub light drive was not an intake at all. It was the barrel of a gun. There were guns on both wings of the Griffin. The Griffin had weapons and shields more advanced than anything on Earth, beam weapons generated from the engine core, whatever the hell that was.

I heard a thump and looked up in time to see RJ flattened against the window of the door. He backed off and raised both hands with an expression of puzzlement. I plunked the book back in its slot, closed the case, and went over and unlocked it. He pushed the door open and paused.

"Do you want to be alone with your book? It's not a romance novel, is it?"

"Hardly."

He came in, sat down and crossed his legs. "I was about to order Chinese. Just wanted to know if you wanted anything."

"Sweet and sour, please."

"Chicken or shrimp?"

"Better make it chicken. I was baiting a shrimp when this whole thing started. Maybe shrimp's unlucky."

"By the way, you commander-types are sometimes so busy you forget the important little things. Everybody's collecting their favorite videos and images for the Griffin deck displays and the sleeper compartment displays. You do any of that yet?"

"I hadn't thought of that. Thanks."

"I heard Danica robbed you guys of your alleged manhood."

"We have been put in our place. What about you? You never got around to telling me how you lost your life yesterday."

"Mmm. That's an ugly little story about how someone's elevated opinion of themselves caused them to fuck up."

"You were pretending to be outside the ship on an EVA repair?"

"Yeah. I used the aft airlock and was outside replacing an antenna interface. After I climbed back in, a heater in the airlock pressure door failed. The door would not seal properly. I hung in the airlock waiting against the wall in my suit fixture using up my remaining air while Mr. Denard fidgeted with the thing. What Mr. Denard should have done was immediately go to the forward airlock and depressurize it so I could come in through the front. But, Mr. Denard did not want to have both airlocks sealed off, isolating both the flight deck and the service module. He thought he could force an override on the rear airlock door and pressurize that way. While he was messing around trying to do that my O2 regulator froze up. The emergency umbilical uses that, so emergency air was not available either. Suddenly all I had was suit air. Mr. Denard was smart enough to know it was then too late to depressurize the forward airlock and open a door, so he continued to try to override the aft airlock lockout. I died while he was trying. I was actually sitting in a chair in the TCC of course, watching the monitors and talking my part to the ship while all of this was going on, but in the habitat windows and video displays I was outside or in the airlock in a spacesuit."

"What was Mr. Denard's reaction to all this?"

"Unfair test. Dual failures never happen. Airlock lockout could have been bypassed more easily in real life. Everybody's fault but his."

"Is it pick up or delivery?"

"What?"

"My sweet and sour chicken."

"Delivery to the guard shack."

"Hey, would you add an order of egg rolls to that and give it to the guard from me? I saw him eating them one day. I gotta get on better terms with that guy."

"Will do, Kemosabi. Diplomacy through Chinese cuisine. How quaint. I'll be back with yours."

RJ disappeared out the door, waving as he went. I began to reopen the security case to resume my weapons study when two more faces suddenly appeared: Terry Costerly and Julia Zeller. A TD and a Resident Director, all at once. Something was up.

They took seats and stared. Terry leaned back and crossed his legs. Julia folded her hands in her lap. They looked at each other for a moment and silently agreed Julia would speak.

"Things are firing up, Adrian."

"You guys don't know the half of it."

"Did you get word already, or something?"

"To which firing are you referring?"

"We've received dates for the test mission and your Nadir mission departure. We're told they are not flexible."

"Well, that switches on the adrenaline a bit. When's the test mission?"

"Next week."

"Wow, that's ambitious."

Terry answered. "They are recommending pilots only for a two-orbit test flight. Two orbits to check the spacecraft out then return to point of origin. The Spacecraft Processing Facility team then gets twenty-four hours to go over the vehicle with a fine-toothed comb. If everything looks okay, you and the rest of your crew are off to the brown dwarf."

I sat back and tried to look relaxed. "Well, I can't say I disagree with any of that."

Terry continued. "Best planetary alignment for the Nadir mission is in three weeks. Not much window with it if you want to get the best first leg."

"I see. We should let everyone know immediately so they can begin taking care of personal business. How is everyone doing with the scanning arrays? I haven't had time to check on that."

Terry said, "It's been okay. They should all be able to scan, decode and analyze to find the practice target. We'll put in some more time before you go. I'll give them some really weak signatures blended in with pulsar noise. That should sharpen them up a bit. You'll probably be searching for a needle in a haystack, but I'd bet it'll be alright. I can't imagine this team coming back from the practice mission without locating the item."

"Thanks. Let me know if there are any problems."

Julia asked, "What about you, Adrian? Have you assembled all the personal items you'll need? Are you taking care of the comfort stuff?"

"Thanks for asking. RJ reminded me about that. I need to get my butt in gear. The launch dates will help that."

"Anything else we need to do for you?" she asked.

"You've both been exceptional. I can't thank you enough. Hope I can return the favors someday."

They stood and headed for the door. As he was leaving, Terry looked back. "So technically, we've started the countdown."

"At zero. On your mark." I watched him nod and close the door.

The spec books on the Griffin's weaponry and stellar drives suddenly had even more meaning. The beam weapons would normally fire in two-second bursts, but that could be varied as necessary. They were not lasers. They did not burn holes. They delivered energy in explosive quantities. They used the matter being targeted as part of the fuel for the explosion. The more target matter, the larger the boom, the greater the destruction. It was a hell of a power to put in the hands of humans. They had even included a simulation program in the software so that users could practice shooting at things while en route. I committed the firing sequence to memory, along with the controls and firing path schematics, and went on to the stellar drives.

The power cores were not explained. I had the feeling the physics was just too far beyond comprehension. As best I could derive from the overview, each engine had a small sun burning within it. The recommended maximum output worked out to be a P-factor of X, the speed of light to the standard power of X, the same standard used on all earthborn engines. There was a footnote indicating PX was not the maximum the engines were capable of, whatever that meant.

There was also a stark warning in the intro to the stellar drive book that set me back a bit. Information on the drives, shields, communications, and weapons was not to be revealed to the crew until the Griffin was underway on the Nadir trajectory. Nor was the dissemination of such information to any ground personnel permitted. The Griffin's secrets would remain contained within her superstructure, and me.

With a couple hours of study under my belt, I went back to the shields and communications manuals, pausing periodically to watch as the flight simulator jerked around into unusual flight attitudes. In the back of my mind, I was working on a plan to ditch Pairs Denard. I could not contact Bernard Porre and ask him what the hell he was thinking. I suspected he had ulterior motives and would not be accepting compromise. I could not request psychiatric evaluation for dismissal, Denard would be able to talk his way through those sessions and then be the worse for them. I could not, as commander of the mission, invoke my authority to disqualify him since there would need to be documented evidence for my reasoning and a review board to approve it. Killing RJ in the airlock was not enough. He had not failed enough other simulations for Terry to recommend disqualification. There was no way to depart on our scheduled T-0 and accidentally leave him behind. As classified as we were, there would be too much attention. We'd be in orbit and get the "whoops, you almost forgot Denard," alert from the agency.

But, there was the space station. We were scheduled to stop there briefly to double check long range scanning and navigation outside of the Earth's atmosphere, standard operating procedures for long duration trips. All I needed was to have everyone on board and Denard somewhere on the main wheel of the station. Once I ordered the hatch sealed the crew would all know what was going on. It was a dirty trick. It was the best dirty trick I could come up with. We would separate, maneuver to the jump coordinates, and be light years away before Paris realized he had missed his ride. How could I do such a despicable thing? I have never been one to play strictly by the rules. It has brought me a lot of trouble over the years and there are a few scars in various places that are memoirs from that philosophy. On the other side of the coin, there were a number of instances where I, and those around me, would not have survived had the rules not been put aside. Those are the wildcards that remind you to trust your own mind and not someone else's.

Would there be consequences for dumping Denard? Hell yes. Big ones. There would be nasty little meetings and fancy hearings and many harsh things would be said, rule books quoted, sayings by wise men invoked, breaks for lunch followed by a matinee of injured feelings proffered by indignant participants. On occasion, they would ramble off subject and need to be redirected to the matter at hand. It is the infamous spaghetti navigation of the committee, usually a diverse group of uninvolved people who know very little of why they are there or what the subject is. But, they have been deemed experts so their testimony, no matter how irrelevant, must be taken. And when the smoke clears and the dust settles, the sentence that was already determined before the circus began is handed down.

I am usually on the beach with a fishing pole when that part happens.

Chapter 16

We began receiving special deliveries for crewmembers. Flight suits and other flight apparel with the mag-sensitive weave incorporated into the fabric. There were even mission patches on the flight suits, an image of the Milky Way galaxy with the word 'Nadir' written vertically in the middle of it. With full access to Griffin, people began packing personal items for storage in their sleeper cells, using the overhead and side compartments until they were bursting. My sleeper had a security safe for classified material, built-in under the bedding.

The day before our two-orbit test flight the Genesis simulators were shut down to make sure everyone took a day off. When test launch morning finally came, we donned our official light-blue flight suits and met at Genesis, taking a single crew transport to the SPF followed by an excited herd. Once again, no one wanted to be left behind. All the way there, we listened to muted complaints and comic sarcasm from crewmembers in the back who were not allowed to fly the two orbits.

We descended from the transport to find the Griffin already positioned on the launch apron. She sat shimmering in the morning sun, her smooth white surface glowing a subdued orange. The fire-hose-sized ground connection cables were still attached under retracted wings. We could see cabin lights illuminated within. The forward airlock side pressure door was open and the air-stairs moved into place. Covers had been removed from the OMS and stellar drives. The front openings in the stellar drives had a faint orange glow from deep within. A much larger crowd than expected was scattered around, joined by our own Genesis test team.

Terry Costerly came up beside me and held out a hand. I shook it, smiled, and nodded.

"They assigned the Auxiliary Operations Control Center for us. I'll have all telemetry and outside orbital references. I'm heading over there now. I'll meet you on the headset."

"Hover at twenty feet and see how she feels?"

"I'd like to check the station keeping and gyro profiles. It may take a few minutes."

"We'll hold until the word is given."

"Who's your right seat?"

"Danica."

He nodded and headed for the OCC. A large group of his staff broke away from the crowd and followed after him.

The noise from the onlookers faded as we approached the stairs. All eight members of my team followed, making me wonder if some were going to try to force their way on. To my relief, RJ, Wilson, Erin, and even Paris remained at the bottom of the stairs as we ascended.

RJ couldn't restrain himself. "Be quick about it, okay?" he called out and a murmur of laughter broke out around him.

"Yeah, don't make us come looking for you," added Wilson.

As Doc and Shelly sealed the pressure door, Danica and I went forward. Danica waited as I climbed in and then worked her way in beside me. Behind me, Doc strapped into the engineer's position. Shelly took her place next to him. They rotated their seats to the forward position and tapped at keys at their stations to set monitors and controls in the preferred mode.

Danica began the power up. As she read and I acknowledged, more and more lights and displays came to life around us until the Griffin's flight deck looked like an eccentric's Christmas display. On the power systems display we saw an alert that the ground support cables had been disconnected. Out my window crewmen were dragging them away. After the emergency oxygen mask and system tests, the checklist called for headsets. We pulled them on, looked at each other and made sure everyone was online.

At last came engine systems and the inevitable awareness that we were sitting in front of a whole lot of explosive power. As the OMS spooled up we could hear pressure valves clicking and feel the hum of power welling up through the ship. This was not a simulator. This ship was alive. The vehicle had awakened and was waiting. Danica looked down at the next step on the checklist which called for stellar drive activation. She glanced over at me and squelched in over my headset. "Should I?"

"Please proceed."

It was two red switches under clear switch guards. She lifted the covers and toggled both switches up simultaneously. We both turned our heads and listened. Even through the headsets, there was a gentle 'thud' sound from both sides, and then an unmistakable whine that rose in pitch. It reminded me of fan turbines spinning up, but it lasted longer and went higher in pitch. After what seemed like a very long, very high squeal, it dropped out suddenly and left a faint rumble in the background. Danica and I stared at each other in a moment of awe and watched the bar graphs on our status displays climb to green line.

Terry's voice cut in over the headset. "Griffin, this is your Flight Director Terry Costerly and friends; how do you read us?"

"Five by five, Terry. How be we?"

"Loud and clear, Griffin. Com checks all around, please. Doc?"

"Loud and clear."

"Danica?"

"Loud and clear."

"Shelly?"

"Loud and clear."

"Griffin, we see your systems on or coming up. I've already gone around the room and have all gos. Give us two more minutes to monitor gyro profiles, then expect clearance for hover. Griffin standby."

"Standing by."

With the checklist complete we sat within the hum of the real Griffin beneath us, living a favorite life fantasy, waiting to be turned loose to space in the most maneuverable, capable spacecraft I had ever had the privilege to fly. The feeling of freedom was overwhelming. The four of us silently traded stares of anticipation and jubilation. Blue sky filled the windshield above us.

Terry's voice squelched in over the comm. "You look good, Adrian. Cleared to ascend and hover."

With a last look around, I tapped on the repulse drive enable button and on the mode control panel engaged the flight director. The Griffin reacted immediately by raising up from the steady-state horizontal plane of earth to a slightly shifting ascent above it. It felt like the floor was moving beneath us because it was. I was surprised there was no vibration, just a completely smooth lift with tiny X, Y, and Z-axis corrections to hold attitude while rising. At twenty feet the attitude and navigation displays showed her switch to station keeping. We floated above the tarmac, watching onlookers in the distance below applauding.

"FD, Griffin, level at twenty."

"Griffin, FD, it looks very good. Give us a couple minutes."

"Griffin in the hold."

Danica reached out for the landing gear lever. "Gear up?"

"Gear up."

"She pulled the lever out and up and watched the SICAS display. "Gear coming up. And, it's good."

We had already programmed our ascent and orbit insertion. On the Nav display the little blue lines showed our path over the continents and oceans. Next to that other blue lines displayed our vertical components and top of climb. Speed vectors were written in along the way, along with feet per second climb markers. The collision avoidance system was set to forward and above and would warn us of unexpected encounters. All that was left was to set the thrust levers to auto and hit the Flight Director button to engage, and then watch the autopilot follow those lines up. If there was a problem the slight touch of my control stick would bring us back to manual, and I'd take over. We had done it all dozens of times in the sim, but this was the real world with real dangers and real exhilaration.

An offshore breeze began to push at us, causing the thrusters to work harder to hold position. Danica's excitement slipped out. "My God, we're gonna get to go. If there was a problem he would've said something by now."

She had barely finished speaking when Terry's voice cut in. "Griffin, FD, You are good. Have a safe trip. Cleared to launch."

"FD, Griffin. All our thanks. Departing the hold in T minus five, four, three, two, one, engage..."

I tapped the engage button. The Griffin's nose jerked up in front of us. The inertia dampening was a tad late kicking in. We were snapped forcefully back in our seats and compressed deeply into them until the counter force eased in and allowed us to inflate back to normal. I wondered if it was a glitch or that was to be expected on every acceleration phase. No one commented, but I sensed some contained surprise. My pilots were too professional to allow any hint of anxiety.

We had nothing but blue sky in the upper windows, but the feeling of speed was intense. There was vibration, such a smooth steady hum that it was reassuring. The world raced by below. The windows began to fog, then the moisture began to condense into thin streams running across the glass. Below us the ocean became obscured by wisps of cloud. The sky ahead began to gray. She nosed down slightly as we began to lose the blue. The thrust levers moved back and forth of their own accord as the windshields faded to black and the first stars became bright enough to penetrate the corona haze. The Griffin's nose leveled, bringing the Earth's curvature up into our windows against a star-studded black background. There was a slight push forward and a lessening of vibration as our status displays showed the OMS engines shutting down. On our Nav display the orbit information and speed vectors began to flash yellow, signaling we were approaching the assigned targets. Bell tones in our headsets told us we had inserted properly.

"FD, Griffin, we have main OMS cut-off."

"FD, Griffin, we see that. Insertion nominal. Have a good ride."

I looked around at everyone. They were all smiling. Shelly spun a weightless pen at us. Doc grabbed it and spun it back. "Permission to disengage, Commander," he said and placed one hand on the buckle of his seatbelts.

I pulled one earpiece back, smiled and shook my head. "You are free to move about the cabin."

Danica broke out laughing at Shelly as she unbuckled and her butt came around and bumped the back of our seats. Doc clung to the frame of the door and pulled himself back into the living area, turning near the ceiling to wave.

I forced myself back to the Nav display. Griffin was tracking the assigned flight path perfectly. On the SICAS display, life support was exactly on the numbers. Switching to the engine displays, all pressures and temperatures were stable and correct. It appeared we had a very solid spacecraft. I looked over at Danica to find her switching her displays to check the same items.

Shelly began laughing behind us. We looked to see Doc doing somersaults in the back. Shelly pushed off and went into vertical spins next to him like an ice dancer closing her routine. Danica called out, "nine-point-five," and the three of them laughed together.

"The view of the northern hemisphere is great out the side windows," said Doc.

Shelly added, "It's the same on this side. The southern curvature is solid white."

We had roughly three hours to enjoy the spacecraft and weightlessness. I was surprised when Doc poked his head in with a half-eaten candy bar in his hand. Not one of the four had the slightest nausea. At the one-hour mark we switched flight crews with Shelly in the pilot's seat and Doc riding copilot. Danica and I coasted our way through the rest of the habitat module and even opened the pressure door to the service module crawlway. Everything was tight. Everything worked.

The ride was a dream. For both orbits, Griffin tracked perfectly and left us nothing to do but monitor systems and enjoy the views. As deorbit time approached, Danica and I reclaimed our seats and programmed an autopilot flight profile. It would have been nice to do a manual, but the spacecraft's flight director and autopilot system needed to be tested to the max. Even so, the ride down was as exhilarating as the ascent. A fresh cloud layer blinded us for ten thousand feet but the Griffin's navigation remained precise. We held at one hundred feet above the launch apron and kept the gear up until we reached the twenty-foot hover. The crowd had reformed to watch the victorious Griffin settle back to the tarmac. She touched ever so lightly and bounced just a little as the weight came to bear on the struts. They had the air-stairs in place at the side door while we were still doing the shutdown, and as soon as the pressures equalized we heard the clunk and hiss of the door being opened. As we left the spacecraft there was some sporadic, undeserved applause, and at the bottom of the steps a preponderance of handshaking broke out. The ground crew had the tug already running. They looked like they couldn't wait to tow her back in.

We were dragged into the hanger observation room where cake and other calorie-costly indulgences were being distributed. Through the big windows we watched the Griffin proudly roll back in, the ground crew fussing over her as if she was a newborn which in a way she was. So we ate cake and celebrated the telemetry data, and watched a proud Terry Costerly sign off the flight certification documentation.

As we celebrated, somewhere far over our heads there was a brown dwarf dragging a whole bunch of rock satellites around with it and we needed to get there. Tomorrow was that day.

Chapter 17

On the morning of the brown dwarf a cold front moved in over the Cape, leaving the ground warmer than the air. It summoned a ten-foot tall fog bank, making the drive to Genesis treacherous and slow. Somehow, everyone arrived early.

We left our vehicles and took an equally slow, escorted transport to the SPC where the Griffin waited within the fog. Smaller crowds had gathered, looking like ghosts looming in the haze. Above the fog the sky was a stark blue, but the lack of wind left the haze swirling and lingering as we headed for the stairs. It made for a spooky, surreal boarding.

Inside the Griffin, four habitat module seats had already been extended and set to the forward position. Danica, Doc, Shelly, and I assumed our launch positions up front as Erin, RJ, Wilson, and Paris took refuge in the back. A ground crew member on the tarmac signaled detached and clear as I began calling out checklist steps. With the sounds of power and engine systems coming to life, the fog became turbulent and withdrew from around the ship. Com checks with the crew in the back were good, although Paris was slow to respond.

When the checklists were complete and our Flight Director satisfied, we applied gravity repulse and rose up and above the fog layer to the twenty-foot hover. I could feel the tension in the back but their consternation was brief. The all-go signal came quickly. We raised the gear, rotated her nose, keyed in the engage command, and were jolted back in our seats to the OMS whine as Griffin jumped like a stallion and headed for orbit. I heard one joyous yelp from behind us. I suspect it was Wilson.

The climb to orbit, as quiet and smooth as it had been on the test flight, carried us over a choppy Atlantic. Blue ocean whitecaps raced by the lower windows. The vibration and hum of engines captured and held our senses as we listened for anything ominous. On orbit she shifted into the correct attitude and settled down to a gentle ride, leaving us with black sky and stars above and a hazy, golden curvature ahead. Post insertion checklists began as a few errant floating items were corralled and tucked away. We traded smiles and pulled off our headsets, switching ground control to the overhead.

Doc broke the euphoria. "Well, ladies and gentleman, I did not have a chance to go wee on the ground, so with your permission Commander I am going to head back for a moment and try out one of the cock-suckers."

Shelly burst into hysterical laughter. Danica tried to look offended and turned her head to hide a choked laugh.

I tapped the intercom. "Welcome to orbit, everyone. Everything looks good up here. You have two orbits before we set up for the jump. You are clear to unbuckle."

Whooping and hollering broke out.

"Gear system power off, Adrian."

"I see that. You show two amps on navigation redundancy?"

"Two amps."

RJ floated into the cabin and hung near the ceiling, looking no worse for wear. I gave him a thumb up. "Everybody okay back there?"

"I think Paris may be feeling it. The rest are fine."

"How about you?"

"It never gets me until about an hour. Maybe it won't this time. Hey, that was quite a little kick when we left the launch area. Took my breath away for a second."

"I didn't hear any screaming."

"Yeah, but they were pretty stone-faced for a few minutes."

Shelly continued working. "Power systems are all within less than a volt, less than ten milliamps, Adrian. I'm checking that off."

"Very good."

"RJ, soon as we all finish our post launch logs we'll give you back your engineering stations."

"I shall await your word with weightless apprehension, Kemosabi. We are looking forward to checkout of the real scanning arrays. Better keep your fingers crossed, my friends. That's about the only showstopper left."

Doc returned and floated in beneath RJ.

"How'd that go for you, Doc?" asked Shelly.

"It reminded me of a girl I knew in high school. There was a poem about her. Her nickname was Bambi. Let's see... How did that go? There was a girl named Bambi from Nantucket. She arrived wearing only a bucket. A longshoreman stared, and finally declared, if you pulled out the tap you could..."

"That's quite enough, Doctor," said Danica.

"Sorry, it's just part of the psych evaluation I was asked to make on the crew."

Danica looked at me. I shook my head. Shelly broke out laughing again.

"My dear Shelly, you are a wonderful sentiment to have onboard. Ah'm glad you are here. We will be friends. You know, it's lucky they set up two restrooms on this ship because I believe Mr. Denard may be living in one of them."

"RJ, would you go back and make sure Paris is alright?"

RJ pushed backwards and disappeared to the habitat area.

Shelly called out, "Cabin leak checks complete, Adrian. Containment pressures stable."

"Verified. Thank you."

"Primary APU shut down. Auxiliary APU's online," added Danica.

"I concur."

"Avionic and flight controls all nominal," said Doc. "That's all I have. Engineering Station A is complete."

A few seconds later RJ appeared back at the flight deck door, upside-down and smiling. "Paris will be alright if we've brought enough barf bags. Hey! And look at me. No problem at all this time. I think I've got it."

"How is Erin?"

"She's hanging out by herself back in the science lab. I think she doesn't want anyone to know she's sick."

"Would you go check on her again then, please?"

"Will do, Commander. Third star on the right and straight on 'til morning."

Danica stopped and laughed. We continued our systems checks and in a few minutes Erin visited us in the doorway, her long ivory blonde hair splayed out in the zero G. I looked back and tried to appear sympathetic. "Erin, are you okay?"

"I'm fine, Commander. If anyone said I was sick, they were mistaken. I'm fine."

"Everything stowed okay back in the lab?"

"Yes, it's, whooommp!" She clutched one hand over her mouth, stared wide-eyed for a moment, and disappeared toward the back. RJ's face took her place. He looked back and then at us. "Oh boy, now both restrooms are occupied."

I tried to look back through the floating tangle of people behind us. "Has anyone seen Wilson?"

RJ pulled himself upright. "He's back there re-stowing the seats. I don't think anyone's told him we're in space."

"Remind him we have just a little over one hour before trans-system injection and you'll all need to be strapped back in those seats before then."

"Okie-dokie."

Danica gave me an amused look. "Is he always that jovial?"

"He is unless you mention how important technology is."

"Did you notice the stellar drive display has changed to pre-jump status?"

"Pretty impressive, don't you agree?"

"If our two propulsion engineers weren't puking their breakfasts up they'd probably be in here hanging over us in awe."

"Perhaps we should not tell them about it right now."

"Agreed."

Danica tapped her checklist tablet. "Spacecraft configuration is complete, Adrian."

"I agree. Let's go on to personal log entries."

With the challenge and response phase of our checklist complete, there was a moment to listen to, and feel the Griffin. She spoke to us through her displays and audio tones, an obedient spacecraft reporting systems status to its keepers. It felt like there was a gladness about her. She seemed alive, and happy to be aloft. Perhaps it was our own emotions impressed upon the thousands of circuits and controls, systems so complex they deserved the title of artificial intelligence. It made me wonder if there were other attributes in there invoked by the Nasebians that I was not aware of. It also made me realize in agreeing to take this mission I had, by default, agreed to trust them quite a great deal.

Doc and Shelly finally gave up their engineering positions to RJ and Wilson, and after forty-five minutes of monitoring it was becoming apparent nothing would prohibit us from pushing away to make a light speed jump to the G1.9 brown dwarf sector. A single short burst of energy from our stellar drives would put us well past the Kuiper Belt, a favorite expendable resource area for many ships. It would drop us out short of the Oort Cloud, shallow enough that cometary material would not be a threat. From that point our radiological Easter egg hunt could begin. It was likely if we found the correct signature a second short jump might be needed to get within maneuvering distance of the target.

We came around Mother Earth to the orbit withdrawal point. The boards remained reassuringly green. There was applause from mission control over the speakers as we fired the OMS and coasted to a point outside Earth's stronger influence. With window blast shields closed and forward camera views selected, it was time.

I twisted around and looked through the airlock to the habitat module. They were all strapped in leaning over in their seats staring back. Paris still had a sick bag in his hand. Erin looked okay. There was a tense, silent air of anticipation. It made me smile.

"Okay, flight director and Nav computer are happy with our coordinates. Anybody have any doubts?"

Wilson answered first. "Go."

RJ, "Go."

I looked at Danica. She just smiled.

"Okay back there, get ready. Jump in five, four, three, two, one, engage."

The view screens blurred stars together in a spray of light. It was the smoothest acceleration I had ever felt, a rush of speed with no sensation of physical duress at all. I expected a jolt passing through the quantum tunnel, but there was only a strange feeling of resistance being overcome by energy, like an ocean liner pushing through a deep wave. There seemed to be no physiological or psychological effects of any kind.

Transition to superlight was just as easy. It felt like the weightlessness you get in a roller coaster at the top of a climb. The ride seemed so brief I did not have time to relax. Dropout was the same, a strange impetus wanting to pull us forward in our seats being overcome by an invisible opposing force. As we fell to sublight, the familiar effects from the deceleration compensators took over. The coordinates on the Nav display flashed green. The stellar drive bar graphs fell to idle. Our blurry forward-looking displays cleared to a fresh blanket of stars. We were there.

"It's our coordinates, Adrian. We're parked correctly."

"Open the blast shields and switch to transparency. Let's see what we see."

As the panels slid open, the real stellar portrait began to appear. The black backdrop seemed even more densely decorated than the displays had suggested. It was such a crowded carpet of light it almost looked like a radiant barrier in the distance. The faint aura from a red nova glowed near the bottom of the windshield on the right. The hum and clicks from our avionics made the reality of it even more surreal.

One of my overhead left-hand monitors displayed the star field from before the jump. The display next to it reflected the current forward view. The two looked so different it seemed impossible we had traveled in a straight line for just a few brief moments.

"Adrian, Nav is showing the dwarf at our three o'clock. Can I bring her around?"

"Good idea. You have the spacecraft."

"I have the spacecraft." Danica switched thrusters to manual and began gently edging her control stick to the right. The Griffin obliged by turning in place. The stars moved slowly to the left, bringing new constellations into view as we turned.

Gradually a large red sun dominated the distance. It glowed a very steady state radiance with no clearly defined edge. Instead, it was bordered by a blurry corona of red and purple, back dropped by the inky blackness.

"Oh gosh," she said, and we stared in awe.

I hit the button to open the habitat portals. "Why don't you bring us back around so they can get a look back there?" Danica tapped at her control and brought the spacecraft back so that the side view faced the dwarf.

"You guys can unbuckle back there. We'll be here for a while." I looked back at RJ and Wilson. "You two may want to take a good look before you begin scanning."

We listened to oohs and aahs as we went through the remaining systems checks. The Griffin looked clean. The position displays reaffirmed we were right on target.

I looked back to see RJ glide back to his engineering station behind me. We exchanged a smile and nodded. "Would you let mission control know we've arrived, all systems go, proceeding with radiographics?"

"Got it."

"Danica, I'm satisfied here. I want to do a float around. You'll see the service module hatch open. I'll be right back. You have the spacecraft."

"I have the spacecraft."

I unstrapped and pushed myself up and back. With a half roll I pulled through the B-airlock and into the habitat module. They were all gathered against the portals looking at the dwarf. Erin smiled.

"Commander, it's incredible. Have you seen one before?"

"No, not like that."

"The satellites look like diamonds all around."

"One of those is probably the one we're looking for."

"Amazing." She returned to dwarf gazing.

The feel in the habitat module gave impressions of absolute tightness and integrity. Past the galley, in the sleeping compartment corridor, the hum of the equipment picked up a bit. The sleepers were all closed. I tapped the button for my unit and waited while the door opened. It looked secure. Integrity seemed the same in the gym and the science lab. Past the aft airlock I entered my key code and pulled the service module pressure door open. For a moment I thought I detected an odor, but quickly decided it was just new vehicle smell. Everything looked fine. I sealed it up and headed back.

Back in the habitat module, they were still at the portals staring into space.

"It's probably going to take several hours of scanning to get a lead on what we're looking for. RJ's already at it. Who wants the B-station?"

Wilson jumped in, "I get bored easily. I'll take it."

Paris looked sickly glad. Erin remained stuck to the window.

I pulled my way back to the flight deck. Danica glanced back and smiled. "What do you say we bring up the other flight crew and take a break?" I asked.

"Sounds good. Is there a restroom open yet?"

"Both, last I looked." Without taking my seat, I pushed in and tapped the intercom. "Doc and Shelly, you guys are up."

Doc coasted in almost immediately, grabbed my shoulders to get by, and worked himself into my seat.

Danica smiled at him. "You have the spacecraft."

"I have the spacecraft."

She unbuckled and floated by me, passing Shelly on her way in. We drifted back to the habitat area and took our turn at the windows. The brown dwarf looked like a big red eye in space, staring back at us as though we were newly arrived intruders.

Doc and Shelly had already retracted the launch seats and brought up the oval table and its seats. I went to the galley, found my premixed coffee squeeze bottle, and stuck it in the warmer. Fifteen seconds later it binged and I had a hot coffee dispenser with straw and check valve in hand. Steam came out of the straw in fair warning. The mix seemed to taste better than it ever had. I moved over to an empty seat at the table, maneuvered my butt over it and felt the mag unit sense me, switch on, and suck me down into the seat. I sat sipping hot coffee, feeling quite pleased with my ship, my crew, and myself. Paris gave a disturbed glance as he disappeared back into a restroom. Erin remained stuck at the window. Danica pulled herself into the other restroom and tapped the sliding door shut.

There was nothing to do now but sit back and enjoy the wait. With luck Engineering would find us a radio signature from our target, the Nav system would show us a course and what type of drive was needed, and we'd wrap up this practice mission in record time. I sat, a man enjoying good fortune in pristine white surroundings with circular portals of infinite blackness.

Danica emerged and hung in mid air for a moment as though undecided. She saw me sipping, decided it was a good idea, and after a galley stop joined me, sucking on hot chicken noodle.

"Can you believe we're here?"

"It's still sinking in."

"I'm usually the stone-faced type, but I admit, I'm feeling pretty giddy."

"Most of the time this point in the flight is where people are dashing around fixing things that didn't get done right before flight, or finding things that didn't operate through departure like they should have. So I confess, I'm not used to this perfection in a spacecraft. It's quite gratifying."

"A toast to the Griffin and her crew, then."

"To the Griffin and her noble crew." We tapped our plastic bottles and sucked at the straws.

Paris emerged from the restroom. I sat up straight. "Paris, you okay? Can I get you anything?"

He shook his head and grabbed onto the ceiling but a sudden look of distress returned and he waved off and reentered the restroom. The door slid shut.

"What's your guess on the scan time?" asked Danica.

"Your guess is as good as mine. If they hid it in on one of the big ones, then it'll be quick. I'm guessing they didn't. I'll bet they put it on something too small to land on. That damn Bernard Porre is going to make us rendezvous and EVA for it."

"Well, you wouldn't want life to get dull..."

"Hell, I bet they made the package's signature so close to the natural radiations around here we'll have trouble isolating it."

"What is a lug nut locking key, anyway?"

"There's one lug nut on each wheel of my Corvette that can only be removed with a special lug nut key. It's so no one can take hard to find wheels off your car."

"You can't get another one?"

"It's a one of a kind key."

"Well, that was kind of risqué of him to do that wasn't it?" As we spoke Erin left the window, went to the galley and began rummaging around. We watched as she pulled out a blueberry muffin, allowed it to float away, laughed, and grabbed her own premixed coffee bottle and heated it. The muffin drifted behind Danica, who twisted around and captured it. Erin took a seat next to her and accepted it with a smirk.

"You sure you want to do that?" I asked, as she unwrapped the muffin.

"Hungry as a bear. Just watch me." She stuck her coffee to the table and took a healthy bite.

"Should we check on Paris again?" asked Danica.

"Are you volunteering?" I replied."

"Maybe a few more minutes."

I turned in my seat and hit the intercom button on the wall. "Hey, you guys up front want any coffee or anything?"

Shelly's voice came back. "We're okay. Thanks."

Wilson floated by headed for the galley.

"Anything?" I asked.

"Lots of it," he replied. "The sorting will be way harder than the scanning."

He foraged through the squeeze bottles, found his and headed back to his engineering station.

Erin spoke with her mouth half full. "Hey, maybe we should start a pool on how long it will take."

Danica laughed. "What are we going to bet? There's no place to shop."

Before Erin could reply, RJ called out. "Adrian, you need to come look at this. There's something strange."

I pushed out of my seat, went forward and floated in behind him. "What've you got?"

"There's something out there. It's artificial."

"Our package? You've found it already?"

"No. This is in the other direction."

"Why are you scanning in the other direction?"

"There was a strange frequency interrupting one of our sectors. It puzzled me. I followed it back to the source. It's way the heck out there, but there's something not right about it."

"Should we care, really?"

A crowd began to gather behind me.

"I've got a funny feeling about this."

"Okay. Target it and see what you get."

"I just did. I'm waiting for the reflection."

Danica bumped against my shoulder, trying to see. Wilson turned his seat to face us.

"There it is. Gee, it's big, and it is artificial."

"What do we have on the charts and schedules, anything?"

"No. That's the thing. I already checked that. There's not supposed to be anything out there."

"Wow, RJ. There you go again. Let's run it for telemetry and com. Maybe it's just a derelict something."

"Nope. Too big. Here comes more. No telemetry data. No com data. No, wait... There is telemetry. A single signal. I almost missed it. Wow! It's a weak transponder code!"

"A ship? It's a ship?"

"It is. Let me run the code through the library. There it is! The Akuma. The Akuma is out there!"

"And you're sure it's not supposed to be there?"

"Not according to published schedules."

"Okay. Open a channel and send a standard greeting."

RJ rotated over to the com section, typed in a greeting and transmitted it. We waited. After a few minutes of silence, he spun around and looked up at me. "There's something wrong. No telemetry. No response to our hail. What are you going to do?"

"Contact Ground Control. Ask them to find out what the Akuma is doing there."

"You know there's a thirty minute delay."

"We'll wait."

Chapter 18

There is such a thing as an astronaut's Communication's Scale of Concern (CSC). When response to radio communications takes 1.25 times longer than the inherent delay in transmission time, something is amiss. Mission control has always prided itself on having already worked out the answer to every possible question before the mission begins, so when reply to an important question does not come back instantly with a touch of indignation attached, awkward surprise is indicated. When the answer to a question is not known, veiled alarm arises in the minds of those seated at Capcom. There are usually a few moments of fear and disbelief that the answer is not immediately in hand, followed by some tentative exchanged stares in which everyone is hoping someone else will pop out with the answer, each pretending they already know the answer but are waiting to see who else does. At 1.5 on the scale, it can be assumed higher authorities are reluctantly being contacted in a deceptively casual comportment which suggests the matter is a simple formality and certainly nothing that reflects incompetence on the part of anyone.

The higher authorities never have the answers. They make good guesses about whom to ask next. At 2.0 those aboard the spacecraft who posed the question in the first place now know higher authorities have contacted other higher authorities and the answers have still not been forthcoming. Never a good sign. Usually at that point Mission Control has established that this particular unknown is not any fault of theirs, and a great flow of relief travels backward down the flow chart to Capcom. The standard message is then sent, "we're trying to get some answers for you on that."

Our two and a half hour wait finally brought the recorded image of an agency executive I did not know: Walter Provose. The knot of his black, violet-stripped tie was too large, keeping him consistent with the don't-quite-understand-style demeanor most agency upper echelons seem prone to suffer. The collar of his black dress jacket was too shallow against the high blue collar of his dress shirt. His graying-brown hair was well cut but stuck out on one side, making a somewhat loveable overall appearance any pandering grandmother would quickly embrace. The man probably had an IQ higher than Einstein but had now achieved such a high level position in management that it would seldom ever be called upon again.

"Commander Tarn, the Japanese Aerospace Exo Agency and their Resource Ministry have finally responded to our inquiries about the Akuma. It seems you and your crew have caused quite a stir over at JSA. Apparently you have stumbled upon something that is a complete surprise to them. The Akuma was on a resource survey mission and was not due back for another two months. If the lack of Akuma emissions is as complete as you say, it would explain why none of the outpost grid stations have detected its presence. Needless to say, they are very upset by this and requesting our assistance. There are no appropriate vessels immediately available to investigate. We have advised our JSA friends that you are on a test flight and are not certified at this time for any other extra-system travel, but the Akuma has a crew of eighty so there is a very serious human issue here. Washington has advised us that they are willing to authorize a deviation of your mission to allow you to make visual contact with the Akuma and establish its condition. The deviation will only be granted on the basis of your recommendation, however. Very sorry about this, Commander. We understand your flight had enough unknowns already. Didn't mean to put you on the spot. Advise us of your decision and we will support whatever that is. Provose out."

Before I could speak, Doc shouted from up front. "For God's sake, let's go!"

JR agreed, "Go."

Danica nodded, "Damn right, go."

The rest in rapid fire, "Go; Go."

All except Paris. Even through the red-face nausea, "Absolutely not. We will not be improvising a new mission. It's not even an American spacecraft. I did not sign on for rescue duty. Let a trained rescue ship come do the rescuing. They might not be in trouble, anyway. Stupid, going on a wild goose chase. We are here to evaluate this ship and nothing more. We should head back now, anyway. That's all been accomplished. We don't need to recover a stupid car part. We're done. We're going back. I insist."

Danica became terse. "There are lives at stake here, Paris."

"Yes. Our lives. Let's preserve them by returning immediately. This is not our job and not our problem."

I hadn't noticed Shelly leaving the copilot seat. As she brushed past me, it occurred to me the burn scar on her face was a much brighter red. I did not understand what she was doing until she grabbed Paris by the collar of his flight suit and got in his face.

"Listen you selfish little asshole. I've heard enough from you over the past few weeks. Go sit your self-important ass down in the back and turn up the mag level so it keeps your ass there or I'll take you back myself and super glue you to the fucking seat."

Wilson and I looked at each other with raised eyebrows. He mouthed the word, "Wow." We both silently agreed no further instructions were necessary. It was one of those moments where you wonder if the idiot is going to break out swinging or be exposed for the spoiled child that he is. In Denard's case, the wimp factor kicked right in. He made his practiced 'humph' sound, pushed away from her grasp, and turned and floated back to his chosen restroom as though his departure would hurt everyone's feelings.

Shelly gave me an incensed look and returned to her copilot position. I did not like the fact she had left it, but decided this was not the time to discuss it. I looked back at the deflated form of Paris Denard hanging sickly to the door. "Paris. I'm sorry but this is not your decision. We're going to see if those people need help."

He would not look at me. He gripped the cloth in his hand, stared at the restroom door and punched at the button to open it. Without another look in our direction he disappeared inside.

"Danica, would you please relieve Doc and ask him to come back here? Pull up RJ's coordinates and program a jump to the Akuma that drops us out in visual range but not too close. Let me know as soon as you're set up. We'll get ready back here."

With a touch of hesitation she nodded and headed up front. A few moments later Doc coasted back alongside me.

"You know why I pulled you back here, right?"

"Not my first rodeo, Adrian. I guess the water tank training was a good idea, eh?"

"We may not need that."

"You realize of course if there is no communication from that ship you must not dock with it or make physical contact with the hull in any way until the situation is understood."

"I have some experience with this sort of thing."

"As Chief Medical Officer on this spacecraft, that would be my recommendation."

"You're not going to turn into a Paris Denard on me, are you?"

"There are medications which could help that man."

I left him and pushed myself through the forward airlock up to the flight deck door. The four of them turned back to face me.

"RJ and Wilson, strap in and stay at your stations. Keep trying to make contact. Continue looking for telemetry, and let Ground know we are proceeding to investigate. Danica and Shelly, after dropout keep us orientated to forward view. We'll see what we can get out of viewscreen scanning." I turned to speak to the others and found Erin bumping up against my shoulder. Doc was already deploying jump seats.

We had to knock on the restroom door to get Paris out. His red face seemed a bit more puffed up than it had been. He appeared in no condition to speak, much less protest further. We strapped him in so he could continue to clutch the fresh white towel against his mouth. We buckled up around him and waited. Out the right hand portals the brown dwarf seemed to wink goodbye. It did not take Danica long. She came over the intercom in her most reassuringly professional voice. "Ready, Commander."

"Proceed, Danica."

"View ports closing. In five, four, three, two, one, engage."

The jump lasted less than five seconds, but that was longer than the time it had taken us to reach the dwarf. The slight press against our harnesses signaled final deceleration. Danica's voice switched back on. "Jump successful. Station keeping at six hundred meters."

I had a short tinge of irritation. That was closer than I had wanted. We all hurriedly unbuckled and pulled our way to the front. The Akuma was a lonely silhouette in the empty distance. She was precisely in the center of our view screen. I had to admit a flush of admiration for Danica's piloting.

RJ wasted no time. "She is drifting, Adrian."

"Magnify to 100 percent."

The big ship came plainly into view in our window displays. Gray, dish-shaped hull, the shape of a standard gravity field generator envelope. An aft array of engines cascaded behind it.

RJ continued, "There doesn't seem to be any obvious exterior damage. I don't see any venting anywhere, but there is an open airlock outer door forward and to starboard."

Wilson said, "There are power signatures within her, Adrian. Temperature and O2."

"Do either of you see any other ships in the vicinity or any other unusual signatures?"

"There's nothing, Adrian. I've been tracking that since the start," replied RJ.

"Send a message to Ground that we have rendezvoused with the Akuma and have visual. Outer hull appears intact. Standby for additional data. Danica, take us in halfway, then hold."

"Thrusting forward."

We held on as Griffin pushed ahead.

"There's an awful lot of darkened portals on that ship," commented Shelly. "It's like nobody's home."

RJ added, "There's a small object that's fallen into orbit around her. Amazing how fast that can happen. It's gone behind. It'll come back around to visual in a just a minute."

"Hold position."

Danica said, "The antenna arrays all look intact. They should be able to communicate."

Shelly added, "There's no external damage at all that I see. Sure seems strange. Something is definitely wrong."

RJ's voice rose in anticipation. "Here comes the orbiting debris. Looks like it might be ice with some organics."

"Full magnification."

RJ suddenly sounded anxious, "Wait, wait a second."

His warning came too late. The screen zoomed in and tracked the Akuma's small, adopted satellite. We stared silently at the full screen image of a frozen man turning slowly in space as he made his way along the ship's superstructure. He was frosted over from head to foot, but somehow held the posture of rich man who could have been posing for an oil painting, chin slightly up, blank white eyes staring off into providence, full head of Jack Frost hair, flat smile of superiority. He wore a frosty black vested tuxedo, modern cut, with an icy bow tie on the high collar of a white dress shirt. There were no shoes, just frozen stocking feet. His arms were locked slightly outward from the waist, hands baring large rings with an icy bracelet on the right.

The silence in the cabin was deafening. Someone pulled the camera view magnification back to normal so that the image once again became a small satellite orbiting a mystery ship, but the tiny spec of light flying along the superstructure was now too clearly defined in our minds.

Doc spoke. "I'd say we have definitively established something is very wrong."

I looked down at Danica. "Keep the nose pointed at her midsection and do a 360-degree orbit above and below so we can see all of her."

It took a moment for everyone to overcome the shock. Danica could have done the maneuver with one hand tied behind her back, but she had to shake it off to refocus. She brought us in closer and then thrust into a large X-axis circle above the Akuma. As we passed over the top, everything continued to look intact and undamaged. I expected to find something on the underside but as we circled beneath the ship continued to look unscathed. We came around and back to our starting point with nothing out of place.

"Okay, let's do the same thing Y-axis front to back."

Danica moved us to a point in front of the ship. With the nose fixed, she began a slow thrust toward the back end. Maybe there was damage in the engine section. Maybe we would find something there.

We completed the orbit and sat facing the Akuma without a clue. I looked at Doc. He raised one eyebrow and lowered his chin, but said nothing. I waved him to follow me back. The others knew enough not to come along. Paris stared, still strapped in his seat, as we made our way back to the aft airlock.

In the airlock, I held to a pressure door for stability. Doc braced himself against the wall.

"What do you think?" I asked.

"What do you think?" he replied.

"Do we try to get in, or wait for someone else to come out here?"

"As a medical professional I am trained never to wait for a patient to get worse, but can we get in?"

"There's an open airlock outer door. The airlocks have a key code. These suits are the K-version. We can have them on and decompressed in an hour. By that time, we should be able to get the access codes from Earth. We might not need them."

"You know the moment we put a hand on that ship even without going inside, we cannot return to the Griffin."

"Is there a decontamination procedure for this sort of thing?"

"There's really no such thing as decontamination in space. There are so many new substances and life forms out here that no decontamination process can account for them all. We visit other worlds and expose ourselves every day and that's a big risk, but it's only when there's a sign of trouble that the quarantine rules kick in."

"So if I tap in an access code and it doesn't work, we're screwed."

"Your space suit is. Yes."

"So you will hang back, and if the airlock door fails to open you can still return."

"Oh, I don't like that."

"And if we do get inside, we are there to stay until we establish that no contamination exists, or until we can prove we have not been infected by it."

"Yes."

I tapped the intercom button on the wall. "RJ, please send a message to Ground Control requesting the entry codes for the Akuma airlocks and authorization to board her."

There was a long pause, followed by an annoyed response. "Roger."

"Danica, take us to within three hundred yards of the open airlock, and then station keeping."

"Understood, Commander."

"Erin and Wilson, please report back to the aft airlock."

Doc and I began suit-up, a procedure I had done more times than I could count. We were pulling on our white, veined suit liners by the time Erin and Wilson arrived. They worked silently to get us the rest of the way there. They were business-like but I could tell they did not like what was happening.

When the sagging white outer trousers and rigid torsos were locked in place, Doc and I faced each other from opposite sides of the airlock and worked the sleeve and inside collar procedures. These were top of the line Bell Standard K-series EVA suits, the best you could ask for. On my last, very memorable space walk, I had been forced to use a pilot's flight suit, a lightweight that left me feeling naked and unprotected. These suits were a blessing, less agile than flight suits but packed with bells and whistles. Bell Standard EVAs were considered to be miniature spacecraft. A man alone could get into one, but not easily, and once the airlock bled out if you found you hadn't tightened something correctly, getting things set right could be a fear-provoking episode. Having suit personnel to help get it right was a welcome luxury.

We hung against the wall without our helmets, waiting impatiently for the readouts on our sleeves to show suit electrical checks complete. When the displays came up all green, Wilson gave me a last look, adjusted my microphone, and pulled the helmet over my head. He twisted it in place and tapped on the visor. Suit arms and legs began to inflate.

When suit pressure had stabilized and we had successfully become balloon-boys, the countdown timer on my sleeve automatically began clicking down, the gas mixture bar graphs slowly increased, and the suit-pressure bar graphs slowly began to fall. It would be a forty-minute wait for our blood chemistry to adapt. If we made it into the Akuma it would take the same amount of time to get back out. Since our suits were now sealed in theory we could go right out the door, but lessons of the past have taught us working in the suit and human body is best not done until both have stabilized.

When we were fifteen minutes from ready Wilson and Erin withdrew and set the airlock to depressurize. Five minutes later RJ's voice cut in over the headset. "We've got authorization to enter the Akuma, Adrian. I'm transmitting the airlock codes to your suit display. The JSA is bringing the Akuma ground station back online and linking it to ours. They'll be assisting every step of the way but the time lag will be slightly longer."

Our suit status lights turned green at the same instant the airlock doors clicked to unlocked. I pushed the side door open as Doc gathered up the satchel Erin and Wilson had brought for us. We paused at the door. Wilson's voice came on. "By the way, Commander, there are weapons in that satchel. I'd suggest you both strap them on when you get there."

"Yes, mother."

I never get used to how much nothingness awaits you outside the airlock door. Even though you're already floating, it feels like you will fall over the edge. As the door swung open, the cold began to chill our suits and our visors tried to fog. I felt the veins in my suit liner pump up as the environmental control system reacted to keep me warm. Air jets around my visor gushed air and the haze quickly cleared. We pushed out into the grand light show of stars and became smaller than nothing, feeling the brief compulsory fear of absolute loneliness. Once Doc was clear we closed and sealed the outer door. In the distance, the gray ghost of the Akuma waited. The small, dark silhouette of the frozen man patrolling her coasted out of sight behind her.

"Let's jet over and look through a couple of the lighted portholes."

"Okay. I'd suggest caution, Commander. If anyone is in there we'll scare the hell out of them."

"Let's take the nearest one. Follow me, but you stay clear of the bulkhead."

We pulled down our backpack handles and jetted over the bottomless expanse toward the closest lighted window on the Akuma. It was three quarters of the way up the side, just starboard of the ship's forward section. It was a small round window. The light coming from it had a yellowish tint. My approach was a bit too aggressive. Extra braking was needed to park. With my thrust controls in micro, I maneuvered next to and below the portal.

It was a small conference room; one long table with chairs alongside, one chair tipped over. The room was deserted.

"There's gravity in there. But I do not see anyone."

I backed away and propelled to a window lower down and more forward. With careful jetting I got within inches and steadied myself with one hand on the bulkhead. It was the office of a high-ranking officer. A cluttered desk, overturned cabinet, broken display case with a model ship in it. Once again, no one there. I backed away and rotated around to face Doc.

"Can't tell what's going on in there. No one around and the place is a mess. Let's check out the airlock."

As we headed in that direction, frozen man came speeding back around from behind the Akuma, approaching us like a macabre guard dog making rounds. We paused to let him pass and I noticed a frozen carnation attached to his lapel. He coasted by, his cold stare seeming to evaluate potential intruders, then turned away as though regarding us as unimportant. Leaning slightly forward, he headed out on another endless orbit.

The open airlock glowed yellow-orange from emergency lights. I pulled myself in and suddenly became weighted in the Akuma's gravity. I shuffled and rocked my way across the grated floor to the inner door. Spacesuits hung against the walls, control panels marked in Japanese surrounded them, a few umbilical cables dangled near the floor. The inner door was closed, but the keypad panel beside it had three illuminated green buttons. No key code required. My guess was that frozen man had departed here and left no one behind to secure the airlock.

"Doc. This airlock looks ready to be recycled. Last chance to change your mind and return to Griffin."

I heard a scoff over the intercom and watched Doc jet through the outer door, pulling our satchel in behind him. He sank to the floor, bent at the knees, and signed off on his commitment by grabbing a handhold on the wall.

I shuffled aside to the outer door controls and suddenly the Griffin came into view. It was a striking image. Griffin's white fuselage had a golden tint. It was the first time I had seen her hanging in space, back dropped by a thick wall of stars. She was more than beautiful. She had become a guardian. It gave me a streak of fear. Closing this hatch might mean never returning. How did we get to this point again? Was there another option I missed? She was only a short backpack distance away, but already out of reach. We had touched the Akuma. We now belonged to the Akuma. We could change our minds, break the rules, and re-board the Griffin. This was probably the last chance to do that. Endanger my own ship and crew? Never. Nor would the man beside me.

"RJ, I'm closing up. The keypad is active and still waiting for the close command."

"Copy, Adrian. Standing by."

The door mechanism had a large lever. I pulled it down and silently the oval door swung shut and rotated its latches. In the middle of the airlock, there was a big red button on the wall with big red exclamatory Japanese underneath it. Emergency Airlock Control. You didn't need to read Japanese to understand. I slapped it with the heel of my palm and a rotating light began to flash. Vented pressure vapor came out of ports around the outer door. Valves in the floor and ceiling began to open and emit similar vapor streams, precursors to emergency pressurization. Doc leaned against the crowded wall across from me but said nothing.

"What do you think?"

"Spacesuits need to stay on for the time being. Isolate us if there's really a pathogen in there."

"Understood. Depending on what's on the other side of that door when it opens, where do you think we should head first?"

"We need to know what's going on as quickly as possible."

"Yeah. I'm thinking the bridge or somewhere we can get to the Captain's log."

"If at any point it looks like an epidemic, we should change up and get to sickbay, try to find out what we're up against."

"You'd better pull those weapons out of the satchel. It's kind of late to be asking but, you ever handle one?"

"I'm from Texas."

"Sorry; I forgot. Let's set them to wide beam, half second pulse, the stun-1 setting."

He dug in the satchel and drew out the pulse-beam guns. He leaned forward and handed me one. It was hard to imagine firing one in an EVA suit, even though it would not be a first. I secured it to my waist and sat back. The screen on my wrist showed outside pressure rising rapidly. We both looked at the inner door, knowing it would slide open at any moment. The question was, what was on the other side?

Chapter 19

The inner door snapped open so quickly it took us by surprise. We braced and stared out into an airlock ready room. The place was a mess. The lights were out except a single overhead spot flickering like a strobe in a Halloween haunted house. It cast ghostly reflections on my visor. All the tools of the EVA trade were there scattered about. No one was present. The access way beyond was open but dark.

I looked down at my sleeve display and called up com system control. "Doc, you need to add Com External in case we run into somebody to talk to."

"Copy."

"And we need to ditch the maneuvering units and the utility belt or we'll be too heavy."

"Yeah, I got it."

We disconnected our backpacks and escaped the shoulder straps. I rolled over to one side, found a handhold on the wall and pulled myself up to become Robby the Robot. Doc had a bit more trouble getting to his feet. From his hands and knees, he paddled up the wall and inched himself around to face me.

I gave him a thumb up and we started for the ready room, our rocking, rigid, movements adding to the macabre atmosphere of the place. Stepping over the inner airlock door proved to be a test of gravity walk in a space suit. Somehow, we both made it. At the opposite end of the ready room a wide hallway waited. I peered into the darkness but could not see more than a few feet in either direction.

"Headlamps, Doc."

"Copy."

"Tarn to Griffin."

"Go ahead, Adrian."

"Let Ground know we have gained access and are proceeding inside Akuma. No crew contact yet. Advise them of the casualty outside."

"Griffin Copies."

With the lamp atop my helmet switched on, the beam showed a disrupted walkway in both directions. There was a cooking pot on the grated floor to my left and a push broom leaning against the wall beyond it. To the right, women's clothes were strewn along the way near two chairs turned upside down, blocking the passage. The control bridge had to be somewhere to the right on a higher level. I waddled out into the corridor and pushed along through the trail of clothes, dragging a few along with me. The chairs gave way. My helmet beam bounced along the walls and curved ceiling. Doc grabbed me by one arm and stopped me.

He was looking down at the floor. There was a dark amber stain running down the wall forming a dried puddle. I wanted to ask him what it was, but I already knew. He looked up at me and he knew I knew.

"Did you set your weapon?" I asked.

"Yeah, and the safety's off. All of this seems irrational. We could be seeing the results of a virus that affects the central nervous system."

"Or intruders."

"Has that ever happened?"

"Yes."

"It could also just be some sort of accident."

"The least likely of the three."

"Agreed. What should we do?"

"As a friend of mine is fond of saying, only two choices: go back, or continue on, and we can't go back."

"Maybe sickbay is a better first choice."

"If we find it on the way we'll stop in and see what there is to see. I'm expecting Ground to send us the Akuma's layout anytime now. RJ will forward that when he gets it, then we'll know where we're going. Our hand scanners will translate Japanese if we meet anyone. Right now I'm thinking we're walking around in deep shit here."

"I concur."

Suddenly a bloodcurdling howl echoed in over our coms. It was from within the ship. We froze and listened. Silence returned. There was only the sound of air conditioners.

"That was human. One point against the intruder theory," said Doc in a half whisper.

"The good news is, it may be a virus. The bad news is, it may be a virus."

We moved along in the direction of the sound, trying to be stealthy inside our heavy, pressurized balloons. My beam showed the corridor ahead branching off in three different directions. I was hoping for an elevator though the thought of using one was unsettling.

At the intersection, we quickly searched. There was still no sign of life. On the left an access way led to a large hanger. On the right it looked like door after door of refrigerated storage. Straight ahead was our best option. The passage was deeper than our beams could reach. We could see equipment alcoves and storage compartments leading to more darkness. Occasionally there were noises that sounded like metal banging on metal, but it was impossible to tell from which direction they came. Not far ahead there was a fat brown rope on the floor that led the way into more blackness. I paused at the end of it, kneeled and picked it up. A tug proved that it was attached to something we could not see. We worked our way forward, following it along the darkened hall. As our beams scoured the passage, other light finally appeared in the distance, a flickering yellow glow near the ceiling, still quite far ahead.

We scanned apprehensively with our beams and came to the end of the rope. A dark form on the floor slowly focused into a crumpled body. The rope was a noose around the neck. As we neared it, I searched the distance but saw no one, just more garbage-strewn corridor. Doc knelt beside the motionless figure. He pushed it onto its back. It was a man in an officer's uniform, a high rank. He had on a deep blue, high-collared jacket with gold trim and large buttons down the front, silk stripes down the sides of the pants. His eyes were fixed wide open as though he were recalling some horrid sight. Doc got down on both knees and repositioned the face. He leaned in close and after a moment sat back up. He pushed up to his feet and looked at me.

"This one's gone."

"How can you be sure through the suit?"

"No breath on my visor."

I had forgotten about our helmet cams. RJ's voice cut in over the com.

"Adrian?"

"RJ, we need to keep recording all this, but make display of our helmet cams exclusive to your station. Notify Ground that the ship appears in disarray, and we have located a second victim. Cause of death unknown. Violence is indicated."

There was an extended pause. Finally, he came back. "Griffin copies."

Doc turned in place and looked at me with a somber stare. "They'll just all be hanging over his shoulder."

"Yeah, but it's the best I can do, and at least if some of them don't want to watch this they won't have to. One of us needs to keep a weapon drawn at all times. That'll be me for now. We may come across other victims." I drew my pulse gun, rechecked the setting and removed the safety.

The way ahead began to reflect our beams. We found what we'd been looking for. The corridor ended at an open, lighted elevator. At that point, it was a comfort to find any light at all. I was becoming more and more conscious of the weight of the suit. It made me wonder how long Doc could hold up. The elevator had something orange and brown splashed on the aluminum walls. At least it wasn't blood. As we took turns entering, a brief, shrill scream came from somewhere behind. We stopped and listened. There was nothing further. I wondered if we were being followed at a distance.

There were five buttons on the panel, the numbers one through three, then a Japanese symbol, and above that a five. It was a customary way of denoting bridge level. I tapped it and the doors slid shut. We braced at the back, weapons raised. The doors popped open a moment later to the port side of the Akuma's bridge.

Four large display screens were mounted to the curved front wall on our left. They were switched on, all showing stars except for the far right. It had an image of Griffin. I suspected the ship had automatically locked on and displayed us when we arrived. There was no one on the bridge to have called up that view.

The bridge was smaller than expected, with a low ceiling. To our right at the rear of the room were command stations; three very comfortable looking raised black seats, the arm rests offering an array of displays and controls. In front of them were the engineering stations and consoles, their readouts fully on, scrolling data, and stepping through ship functions. There was a lot of flashing red and yellow on the displays. On the opposite side of the room a large, open double door revealed a meeting room with a long elliptical table, the one I had seen through the overhead portal. There were several other closed doors at various points around the room.

Suddenly there was a clatter from behind the command seats. To our astonishment one of the doors slid open and someone dressed as a cowboy riding a broomstick horse, galloped in. He wore cowboy boots, chaps, a vest, and a wide-brimmed hat. He carried what I hoped was a plastic six-shooter in a holster hung low on his waist. The outfit looked too small for him, as though it was child's clothing he had forced to fit. The horse head on his broomstick looked like it had been cut out of mattress foam, and most disturbing of all, it appeared the horse had real human eyes imbedded in the foam. The man's own eyes were circled in Bela Lugosi black. His lips were bright blue. There appeared to be a run of blood from one nostril.

He noticed the two spacesuit men standing rigidly in shock by the elevator. He did not hesitate. He let out a fearful "Yeehaw," drew his pistol and fired. There was a loud crack and the sound of a display screen shattering along side Doc. I jerked my weapon over and fired. The beam knocked cowboy back against the wall. He slid down dazed, but looked around, regained his feet and horse, and galloped back out the way he had come.

"Oh my God," murmured Doc.

"Adrian!" RJ yelled over the com.

"Standby, Griffin. We're alright."

"Well, yes and no," commented Doc.

"That sews it up, wouldn't you say?"

"Absolutely. There is massive infection here, something that affects higher reasoning, a neurological pathogen of some type. By maritime law this vessel is now officially quarantined. We need to get to sickbay and see how much they learned before it took over."

"RJ, report to Ground that a ship wide infection has been confirmed. There is still crew alive. The Akuma must be designated a quarantined vessel immediately. We need those layouts as soon as possible. Specifically, we need access to sickbay."

"Griffin copies."

"There's something else bothering me," added Doc.

"So many things," I replied.

"There's supposed to be a crew of eighty. Where are they all?"

"Let's try to get some more answers before we find out. You think the suits are protecting us?"

"There's a good chance. If it's air-born or passed on though physical contact, we're isolated. It would have to be really, really exotic to get through these suits. The problem is, we can't stay in them forever."

"We don't have many options at this point, do we?"

"The trick is how to get out of a contaminated suit."

"You had to bring that up. We need to figure out how to lock out the bridge in case that guy comes back with a posse."

"Lock out sounds like a great idea to me. Remember the Alamo."

"We need to find a terminal that was maybe left open. Something we can get into without a command code."

We began searching the stations nearby. I worked myself into position and sat at the first one. As soon as my weight was in the seat, the outline of a face appeared on the display screen. I moved over to the next one with the same result.

"Doc, they're using facial recognition. Keep trying. I'll be right back." I paused to look in his direction. "Keep that weapon handy."

He turned and looked back at me annoyed.

"I didn't have to tell you that."

I headed for the elevator, shuffled in and hit the 1 button. On the first level the doors slid open to the lifeless body still lying prone on the floor. I struggled on one knee, got the loop off the neck and coiled the rope in the elevator. With the agility of a drunk, I dragged the body inside.

Back on bridge level when the doors slid open I pulled my prize out and dragged it to the first station with Doc casting a somber stare. I sat the body in the seat. The facial outline came up, disappeared, and a tiny flashing red X took its place. Wrong station. This guy was not approved for it.

The third position worked. I used the rope to tie him to the seat then studied my new display of Japanese options.

"RJ, are you getting this?"

"Yes, Adrian, we are getting it all."

"Translate for me. I don't want to have to fumble around with a hand scanner in this suit. Is there one that says 'set up' or something like that? We need English."

"Standby. Okay, got it. Bottom of the right hand list. It's 'Setup'."

There were buttons running down both sides of the monitor screen. I pressed the button next to the lower right hand item and to my relief a new list appeared. A small column of words near the bottom of the display included the word 'English'. I quickly punched it and a moment later had readouts on the screen that flickered and turned to English.

"Doc, we're in."

Doc made his way beside me and took a place on the other side of our seated officer.

"Careful not to bump him. If the weight comes off the seat the system will lock us out again."

There was a button labeled 'Home'. I hit it. A new options list appeared still in English. One item was 'Security'. A quick tap and the top choice was 'Bridge'. The Bridge list contained one choice that was 'close all external doors'. I tapped the key and two bridge doors that were still open slid shut. A prompt came up asking, 'secure all?'. I tapped the 'yes' button, and we heard the snapping of locks throughout the room. I stood up and took a deep breath.

Doc cut in over the com. "Well that temporarily puts things in a better perspective. Now if we can get into the Captain's logs."

"We'd better see if we can look at ship's systems first. See if anything really bad is happening."

"Good idea."

I switched back to the main menu. The third item down was Propulsion. I tapped the button and a flow chart with block diagrams appeared. Three of the five main blocks were flashing red. I tapped the one labeled 'Core'. A schematic appeared with flashing red symbols all over it.

"Oh Jesus," said Doc.

Coolant was not flowing. A bar graph beside the core symbol was already in the red and slowly climbing. Valves needed to deliver coolant were all flashing red and in the off position. Near the bottom of the display, a clock was counting down from 9 minutes. Next to it, 'containment will be compromised in:'.

"Danica, stand by to move the Griffin to a safe distance."

There was tense silence on the com.

"What?"

"Stand by to move the Griffin to a safe distance. Do you copy?"

"Why?"

"Do I need to explain it to you, Danica?"

Another tense pause.

"N...no. Griffin copies."

I tapped at the first coolant control valve, hoping to open it. A prompt appeared on the screen, 'Not an engineering station. Do you wish to transfer this station?' I hit 'yes' and after an excruciatingly long moment the core display returned with extra options. I tapped at the first coolant valve. A message appeared beside it, 'valve inoperative'. I tried the next one and got the same error message. There were six paths. The very last one had a small auxiliary valve intended for something other than primary coolant control. I took a breath and tapped on its symbol. To my relief, it turned green and slowly rotated. The flow chart showed a small line of coolant beginning to flow. I straightened up and hung my head inside my helmet.

"Good but not great," said Doc.

"Anything different than what we had is good."

On the screen, the coolant was flowing, but not enough. The countdown clock had reset itself to 90 minutes and was still counting down.

"We bought a little time. We'd better chance a look at power." I backed out of the propulsion section and called up the power systems display. Once again, more than half of the blocks were flashing red. One level deeper and the schematic showed coolant flowing intermittently to the smaller power system core. Valves were clicking open and shut in irregular intervals. Coolant would flow from one area then be cut off for a period then other routes would open and the flow would resume. The temperature level in the core was holding right at the redline.

"How can there be so many failures?" I asked.

"People," Doc replied. "My greatest fear, remember?"

Wilson broke in over the com. "I'm seeing this, Adrian. I'm coming over there right now."

"Hold your position, Wilson. Let us get more of a handle on things. Nobody else needs to be checking in."

"Erin will help me suit up."

Erin's voice burst in. "I'm coming with him. You need a Prop engineer, and right now."

"Erin, it's the Hotel California over here. No one is to transfer. You hear me?"

"You're breaking up, Commander. We're not reading you."

"Oh don't start that, shit. You guys heard me. No one is to transfer over."

Doc looked at me with a wrinkled brow. "Do you think they'll come?"

"Yep."

"Commander, I think your crew is lacking discipline."

"Yep. They're too much like me."

Chapter 20

"We've bought ourselves some time, but not much. We need to take a look at the logs and see what we're up against before we do any more traipsing around out there. The cores are the critical problem. If we don't get them stabilized, the epidemic won't matter. If the other two show up like I expect them to, maybe we can drop you off at sickbay and lock you in while the rest of us try to save the ship."

"A 90 minute cure, Commander?"

"Either that or the patient spontaneously combusts."

RJ's voice came in. "Adrian, we've received ship layout and command codes. Transmitting to you now."

RJ's timing was impeccable. From the Main menu we went into Library. There were four pages in alphabetical order. On page two, there was a choice titled 'Captain's'. I tapped it and a prompt came up, 'Command code required'. The corpse helping us had authorization to make propulsion system changes but did not have authorization to read the Captain's personal log. From my wrist display I entered the highest command code relayed by RJ and a series of dates flashed on the screen. Above them was something that gave me pause.

Captain's Logs
Captain Mako Hayashi
JSA Authorization CD84973Z
Commanding The Akuma

The name was more than familiar. Captain Mako Hayashi was too young to be a legend. More time on the bridges of starships than many officers twice her age. Youngest woman ever to be awarded a master's class license for heavy drafts. Youngest woman ever to have been awarded command of a Fuso-class starship. First woman captain of the starship Yamashiro. A legend she was. I had seen her picture in a dozen different publications. I tried to put it aside, and without thinking chose the most recent log date.

More intraflex needed. Passive administration with preventable funding. Overflow of deterrents. Xxpsj llojjjj aaaaaa.

Meaningless jumble. I went farther down the list and selected a date from four weeks ago. We sped read the readout and found a passage that seemed important.

The unexplained EM pulse was more than our systems could handle. We have damaged systems all over the ship. Communications and Telemetry are down completely. We do not have command of Engineering from the Bridge. Still, I believe we will be able to repair systems though it will take some time. The most serious issue may be the water. Check and feed valves burned out in the open state and fresh water dumped overboard and has been mixed into the emergency coolant tanks. We will try to recollect the frozen water outside and begin the separation process for all available water. It won't be fun around here after a few days with no showers.

The next three entries were about the same. The fourth changed in tone slightly for the worse.

Damage to the Communications, Telemetry, and Navigation appears to be worse than expected. Engineering unable to give me an estimate of when propulsion will be back online. Valves have been rigged so that they can be set manually, and we have rotations operating them hourly to meet systems requirements. We must now consider water to be our most critical problem since we will not be underway any time soon. The navigation group and astrophysics believe we are close enough to the Oort Cloud to harvest water ice using scout craft equipped with tractor beam generators. Those modifications are in progress and should be completed tomorrow provided damage to the various support equipment is repaired.

Two days later the Captain's outlook improved.

The plan to harvest water ice from the Oort Cloud material appears to be working. Two scouts are returning with large sections in tow. This development means we are out of danger. All other expendables remain in adequate supply. Best estimates for repairs to ship's systems continues to be several weeks. We are concentrating as much time as possible on communications in hopes of signaling Earth outposts with modified probe launches. One replacement transponder has been found undamaged and will be installed soon.

Over the next several days, they processed their water ice and refilled their tanks. Repairs continued to go painfully slow. As I scrolled down, Doc stopped me and pointed to something, a single line at the end of one report.

One crewman has fallen ill and has been admitted to sickbay for observation.

Doc shook his head. "There it is. He's almost certainly the index case. The first one to become ill. If it's an airborne or physical contact delivery system, those around him will be next."

Doc's hypothesis quickly played out. As we continued through the log entries, more and more crew became incapacitated. A week into the epidemic the doctors were frantic. In a desperate attempt to understand, they eliminated the airborne option by experimenting on their own crew. They did the same with physical contact. The log entries kept mentioning 'Common Source Outbreak'. Eventually, with half the crew infected, they finally solved the riddle.

It was the new water. It had been tested and retested before use and found to be pure. It had gone through all of the filtration and processing procedures, and then retested again. But even after human testing had proven the water was the source of the outbreak they could not identify a pathogen. It was something beyond the existing test matrix.

From that point on the log entries became a true horror story. Many who were not yet sick had already drunk the water. Even more macabre, those who had not knew that after a few days' time they too would be forced to drink it or die of dehydration.

We scrolled down through a few more entries, and just as the story had become as bad as we thought it could get, it took another turn for the worse.

Most of the crew is now infected, including the doctors. I'm surprised I've held out this long but I had to begin drinking the water last night. It was that or lose consciousness. To make matters worse, if that's possible, the symptoms of the infection have changed. No one is dying except in those cases where there have been accidents or violence. After the initial symptoms run their course, the victims regain their mobility and energy but not their rationality. Some remain semi-comatose, others appear intoxicated, and some seem to regress to childlike personalities or sometimes adopt the personalities of famous people they have admired or studied. Crewman Naoko Sato thinks he is Jesse James, the infamous cowboy-outlaw. Crewman Sora Takahashi is now acting out Empress Suiko. We are

*unable to detain the more dangerous people who are under this
type of influence as I have no one to assign to such a task. I will
use as little water as possible in hopes of delaying the effects.
We have just a single transponder operating. Our only hope now
is for rescue, but we are not expected back to the Terran System for several weeks. I do not see how we will last that long.*

There were two more daily entries and then a gap. To
my surprise, they resumed but contained confusion and absurdi-
ties. In one passage, she was complaining that negotiations with
Genghis Khan were not going well. His trade demands were un-
reasonable. In another, a section of the crew quarters had been
redesigned as a temple palace and it was done without approval
from the Emperor. In still another, her helmsman Sulu had tak-
en a Samurai sword to storm Engineering and regain control of
'Enterprise'. As I read, Wilson's voice came over the intercom.

"Adrian, we're in the airlock."

"Stand by, you two. Do not open that inner door until we
get there. Are you armed?"

"For heaven's sake, Adrian, of course we're armed."

I turned to say something to Doc just in time to see him
twist his helmet and lift it off.

"What the hell are you doing?"

"I switched to decompression as soon as I saw the reference to Common Source Outbreak, Commander."

"Isn't anybody around here going to do what I tell
them?"

"Adrian, it's hardly a surprise you would assemble a
crew of people who think for themselves. It's your own calling
card, for Christ's sake. Don't worry, there's no decision-making
required here. We can't go back to the Griffin unless we prove
we're clean. We can't stay in the suits forever. There's no biology left on this ship to test with, except for us, so, I'm it. You
guys have to stay suited up because you've got to get to that
engine core. We can't risk you becoming Disney characters before that happens. I'm the only one who can pick up the work on
the epidemic and I can't do that too good in a spacesuit. So it's
all very logical, my friend. We'll go secure sickbay and you can
lock me up so I can start my work, then you guys go stop this
ship from becoming a fireworks display."

"Doc..."

"You want me to put my helmet back on?"

"No, I just..."

"For God's sake, don't go getting mushy just when I was
just starting to admire you. How about helping me with the torso? The kids are waiting down in the airlock."

Completely disarmed, I helped him out of the shell and
watched him dig through the satchel for his gray flight suit. We

removed his com unit from the Bell Standard and he worked the earpiece and mike into position around his ear. There was a reasonably safe place for everything by the elevator. With great trepidation, we unlocked the bridge. Weapons ready, we stood at the elevator and waited for the doors to open. The carriage came up empty. With our corpse-assistant left on the bridge still tied to his seat, we headed back to level 1. I tried to sneak occasional glances at Doc, looking for unusual behavior even though we both knew it was far too soon for that.

We found the level one corridor clear. Strange sounds continued all around, but there was no sign of Jesse James or Genghis Kahn. Without the burden of the Bell Standard spacesuit, Doc had to keep waiting for me to catch up. He scanned ahead and behind with his palm beacon, weapon held ready in the other hand.

In the ready room at the airlock door, the pressure panel read 14.2. I tapped the open key and the door slid aside to reveal two space-suited people standing like robots.

Erin exclaimed, "Oh my God, Doc!"

Doc raised one eyebrow and forgot to click his transmit button. "You really think you're any better off?"

Erin saw his lips move but heard nothing of it.

"Coms to external, guys," I said.

They both tapped at their sleeve controls.

Erin turned her body to face me. "What was the propulsion core temperature the last time you saw it?"

"Barely holding at redline, but it won't last. It was still counting down to containment failure," I replied.

"Let's get going. There is nuclear momentum to a core breach. It won't reverse easily."

"Getting there may not be easy, either. There may be interference. Carry your weapons up. Wide beam, stun one should be enough. We need to drop Doc off at sickbay on the way."

"It's level three, halfway to the core," said Wilson. "I've been memorizing the floor plan. We brought four tablets that are setup with floor plan and ship system layouts. They're set to suit frequency. They'll double as com units, if necessary."

They had already dropped their maneuvering units and belt packs. I went to the ready room door and looked in both directions. The way seemed clear. The others gathered awkwardly behind me. I looked back at them to be sure they were ready.

"Shoot first, ask questions later?" They stared back as though more explanation was needed. There were no humorous quips or comebacks. No joviality remained; the dire circumstance we now found ourselves trapped within explicitly written on each of their faces. It was one of those somber moments when com systems are almost unnecessary. Communication takes place on a higher level. Imminent death will do that sometimes.

Chapter 21

The elevator doors slid open to a shadowy level three corridor with dirty green carpet and Japanese graffiti spray-painted on the wall. Wilson held up a hand scanner, squeezed a button with his gloved thumb and proclaimed, "Keep out."

Weapon raised, Doc pushed out first and scanned the area as we awkwardly took turns rocking our way through the door. The ever-changing mixture of dark and light kept casting bizarre reflections on our visors. Overhead, a row of tubular lights on either side had only every other tube partially lit. There were many more white conduit runs along the walls on this level. It was a much wider passage than the level one and the doors along the way were all open and large. In the distance to our right the hall branched off into three more corridors.

"It's to the right," said Wilson.

Doc led the way, weapon first. The three of us trundled along and tried to keep up. We came to the first open door. It was a staging area full of transfer containers and silver sacks of equipment and supplies. The next door ahead on the left was brightly lit. There was a faint musical humming coming from within. Inside, we found only the second living person we had seen. The score was now two to two.

It was a laboratory of some sort test equipment scattered around the gray metallic room, a small forest of flexible lights attached to workbenches with meters and scopes. Coiled power lines hung from the ceiling providing test probes and accessories to the workbenches. In the center of the room, one industrious young crew woman had used the coiled lines to make a swing. She had attached a broken broom handle to them and sat atop it swinging and singing something that sounded like a nursery rhyme. She wore striped bobby socks with no shoes, and a very short pink ruffled skirt with no top. Her lipstick was applied so poorly it could have been clown makeup. Her dark hair was tied back in a failed attempt at a ponytail.

We stood in the doorway gawking, and she smiled at us and continued to sing and swing.

"We can't leave her like this," said Erin and she looked at me in fear and dismay.

"Yes, yes we can. There are dozens more somewhere. Our main concern is that reactor core. Let's get going."

The next three adjoining chambers were empty offices or laboratories. The fourth was a large meeting room with many chairs parted at a central isle. As we looked in, movement stopped us. It took a moment to focus on the eerie setting. A bride in a full, white wedding gown holding a bouquet stood before an alter waiting to be married. Her husband to-be was seated in a chair beside her, his back to us. As we paused in the doorway, she looked back, gave us a sheepish smile, and turned back to the altar waiting for the ceremony to begin. There was no one else in the room. The setting would almost have been believable except for the knife handle protruding from the groom's back. That made it three to three.

Erin gasped and grasped one hand over her visor as though to cover her mouth.

"This place is a fucking house of horrors," said Wilson.

We began to head on when more movement ahead again startled us. Something had darted across the hall from one chamber to the next. It was so fast it was a blur. I held up a hand.

"You see that, Doc?"

"Yes. Too fast."

"Wilson, take the right wall and cover us. Erin, stay behind on this side and watch. Doc, I'll take the right, you can have the left."

Wilson protested, "But..."

"You're in a spacesuit, Wilson. Doc's not. Cover us. Let's go."

Doc and I moved cautiously along, weapons ready. As we neared the next door I held back while Doc pressed his back against the wall. He slid along until he was alongside the door, and gave me a ready-sign. I took careful aim.

He leaned in as little as possible but it was enough. A ball of fur came bursting out of the room into the corridor, jumping and spinning in front of us. It was all I could do not to fire.

A dog dragging a leash. He was medium haired, tan and white, medium sized. Looked like some sort of wolf breed. He went to Doc and sat wagging his tail, looking up hopefully. Doc glanced back in relief.

"Do I look any older? Because I just aged a few years."

"Erin, Wilson; you guys can move up."

Doc knelt and stroked the dog's head. The animal seemed overjoyed that there were humans who cared. Erin came up and pushed by me. She knelt beside Doc and looked at the dog's collar.

"His name is Areno. He's an Akita. They're wonderful pets, very loving."

The dog took an immediate like to her and did not seem fazed by space suits. It put a paw on her knee and barked.

"Erin, you must not do that. Do not take chances with your suit integrity. You understand what I'm saying?" said Doc.

Erin grabbed the dog's leash and held it.

"We can't take him along, Erin. We've got to move out."

Doc interrupted. "Adrian, this dog does not appear to be affected. He must have been drinking the water. I'll take him with me."

Doc reached out and Erin gave up the leash. I looked ahead. We had almost reached the three-way intersection. I looked back at the team. It struck me as another moment of life's highlights in lunacy. Our group, a doctor, three characters in spacesuits, and a dog had just passed the farmer's daughter on a swing, along with an expectant bride with fiancé deceased. We were approaching a point where the road forked off in three different directions. It was straight out of The Wizard of Oz. I almost expected to see a scarecrow up ahead. I tried to shake off the fear that things were really out of control, but quickly realized it was the truth. The Wicked Witch of the West was waiting for us in Engineering. Reality was a bad dream with a countdown timer ticking down.

Wilson held up his tablet. "That center corridor leads to Engineering and the core. The right-hand corridor goes to the science section and sickbay. What do you want to do, Adrian?"

I thought for a moment, opened my mouth and stupid came out. "RJ, are you still monitoring?"

"For God's sake, are you kidding? We're all here following all three cams."

"We're going to need to split up. Wilson and Erin will head for Engineering. I'll take Doc to sickbay and then catch up. Keep your recorders running. If anything goes wrong, we'll want them to know what happened."

"You think?"

"I looked over the team. "Everybody okay with that?"

No objections. Wilson said, "By the way, Adrian, as Erin and I were leaving Denard tried to declare that if we went he would be ranking officer and would assume command."

"Oh, Jesus, that's all we need."

"Shelly asked him how he would command if he was unconscious, and he shut right up."

"Well, that puts my mind at ease. Let's get to it, guys. Erin, follow Wilson's lead. He's an expert in all kinds of trouble."

Wilson scoffed and handed me two tablets from his case. I packed them and watched as the two engineers headed down the middle corridor. They looked back with a half wave, and disappeared into the shadows.

Holding to Areno's leash, Doc led the way to the right. The passageway changed in nature as we progressed. There was a bit more light coming from behind soft green acoustic panels on the walls. Conduit trails ran between them. The floor was still scattered with occasional chairs and debris, but the graffiti was becoming less frequent. Adjoining rooms bore more research equipment or discussion areas.

My spacesuit had become heavy. I was sweating a touch and the suit temperature controller was whining too often trying to compensate. Batteries were holding, but were down. As we approached more open doors, Doc raised his hand and stopped to listen. Just ahead, the next adjoining room was locked open. Flickering colored light came from within. There was a strange kind of crowd noise. Something was discordant about it. There was music playing and someone singing completely out of key.

Bell Standards come with small mirrors Velcro'd to the sleeves to help with angles not accessible in a spacesuit helmet. I peeled one off and handed it to Doc. Next to the doorway, he held it out just enough to see. After a few seconds he looked at me, rolled his eyes, and handed me the mirror, shifting out of the way so I could look.

It was an absurd karaoke party. They were all in costumes, but did not seem to be pretending. There was a Batman standing atop crates in one corner, his fists firmly planted against his hips. Jesse James was parked at a makeshift bar with a glass of something in one hand, watching a Geisha girl making all the motions of singing, yet not achieving that by any true definition. There were at least twenty or thirty of them, not one in a duty uniform or flight suit. Two were dancing near the middle of the room completely naked. Another, in a rough-looking Star Trek uniform, was leaning against his samurai sword, swaying as though intoxicated.

I turned back to Doc. It was understood we did not want the attention of these people. Doc pointed to himself and the dog and motioned that he was going to dash past the open door. I nodded. He gathered up the loose leash, made sure Areno understood, and jumped-stepped by. I looked with the mirror. No one had noticed.

The maneuver was not so easy in a spacesuit. I wondered if they might just think I was one of them. I gathered myself and tried to lurch my way across. Out of the corner of my eye, I could tell at least a couple of them had seen me and stopped what they were doing. On the other side, I took another look with the mirror. There was no reaction. They had shrugged it off, unimpressed by someone as conspicuous and unoriginal as a spaceman. With a sigh of relief, Doc nodded and as briskly as possible we left there.

It was easy to tell we were getting close. Ahead, a Gurney was turned on its side, trailing sheets. Beyond it, more sheets and blankets. There began to be broken test tubes and vials, medicines scattered everywhere, resources that were probably badly needed. By the time the open doors to Sickbay appeared, we had to work our way around too much clutter. Areno jumped most of it.

At the Med-Lab entrance, the sight was atrocious. One body on the floor in a Johnny-type robe, another passed away on a Gurney in a corner. There was another that looked as though he could still be alive, held to a bed by restrains, starving in place, an empty IV bag hanging from the stand next to him. Most of the computer and medical terminals had their service doors open with circuit cards missing or hanging out, a testimony to the crew's efforts to repair the EMI pulse damage. Two or three stations appeared to be intact.

"God, I hope there's at least a medical hand scanner," mumbled Doc. He looked at me like a man assigned a kamikaze mission. "I'll need to set up a link to the Griffin's medical computer, and I may need them to shove some equipment out the airlock for us."

"Whatever you need, Doc."

"The biggest thing will be their logs, if I can get into them. It's for sure they were doing DNA testing and brain scans to see which part of the brain was most affected. If any of them died they'd have done biopsies. I need to know what they knew and then pick up where they left off."

"Tarn to Wilson."

Erin responded. "He's moving a console out of the way, Adrian. Hang on."

"Where are you?"

"We've reached the entrance to Engineering. It's been deliberately blocked. We should be in momentarily."

"How much trouble have you had?"

"Not a soul. Just garbage."

"Keep going. I'll be headed your way in just a minute."

"Copy."

"Doc, I'll help you set up and make sure we can lock you in, then I'm out of here."

"I think you should."

There were IV supplies in a cooler closet. Doc replaced the empty one next to his only living patient. Together we dragged the other body out into the hall and covered it with a sheet. When the remaining corpse was wheeled out and the medical lab reasonably back in order, I waited outside the door while he closed and locked it. Satisfied it was secure, I headed for Engineering.

"Tarn to Wilson"

"We're in, Adrian. What a fucking mess."

"What do you see?"

"They were operating the valve transfer system manually. I guess they all became sick and eventually just stopped doing it. We do have one tiny problem. Some of the key valves are in service crawlways and they're not big enough to get into with a spacesuit. What do you want to do?"

"Can you wait until I get there?"

"Oh yeah, I see where this is going. How is Doc?"

"Unaffected. Hold on a second. I have to sneak by a door."

The party was still in full swing. Batman had apparently tried to fly down from his perch above the crowd. He was lying on the floor face down, spread-eagled, his cape draped out in full glory. No one seemed to mind. I stepped deliberately past and stopped to check. Once again, I was of no interest.

"Okay, listen up. You guys are the engineers. I am not. It would be stupid to chance you getting infected. I'm beginning repress right now. I'll be the one to get unsuited and do the work in the crawlways. Can you wait until I get there?"

Erin answered. "We can wait, but not long."

"I'm on my way. I've been in this damn suit too long anyway. What about power? We need it to stay up."

Wilson answered. "It's the same situation. It's a smaller containment vessel. It would make a lot smaller hole in the hull."

"Wilson, you're such a comfort."

"There are people down here, Adrian, but we haven't seen them," said Erin.

"How do you know?"

"Tools are getting moved around or disappear when we're not looking. We never see it happen, but we know it does. I have the feeling whoever they are they're not dangerous; more like timid."

"Damn it. You guys keep your guard up. Someone always has a weapon in his hand, right?"

I reached the corridor junction and turned down the center pathway. My suit pressure was already up to 10.7. Ahead, I could see the equipment Wilson had moved to clear the way. It was a just few dozen more feet of traversing dark and light and I could escape the burden of spacesuit. My helmet beam was set on automatic, so it kept switching on and off with the changes in ambient glow. Conduit and beam guides became

dense along the walls, supplying data transfer and energy translation to and from the heart of the ship. The collage of tubing
and panel finally opened up to an expanded exit with a widening
gray carpeted ramp that led down to the open expanse of Main
Engineering and its radiant central engine core and surrounding
control consoles. The chamber was at least three stories high.
The semitransparent containment vessel was the familiar circu-
lar-shaped tube dropping from the ceiling into a recess in the
floor. Most of the monitoring view ports at various points up and
down it were closed, but two or three were open and through
the lenses, sparkling explosions of light continuously erupted
within. The two space-suited figures of Erin and Wilson were on
the opposite side of the room, bent over a rectangular table display of engine and power components. I came up alongside and
traded stares. Each of us looked like we were hoping for good
news. There was none.

"I began recompression as soon as you mentioned the
service crawlways. It'll be another ten minutes. How are we doing on time?"

Erin pointed a gloved finger at a main coolant line on the
lighted table display. "If we can get this line open, the danger
will be past. But it's two valves at two different junctions. If you
get to them and we get the coolant flowing, then we'll just need
to work out a new rotation plan so each of the three independent systems has enough re-cool time. That's not how it was designed to work, of course, but that's the way it will work from
now on."

"Any sign of your ghosts?"

"No, but someone is watching us, that's for sure."

"Tarn to Griffin."

"Go ahead."

"Danica, it's time for you and Shelly to switch off to single pilot, twelve hour shifts. We can't keep both of you up front.
We don't know when or if we'll get back to Griffin. Do you copy
that?"

Danica's voice came back. "Griffin copies."

"RJ, you're about to drop to two helmet cams. Have we
gotten anything else from Ground?"

RJ sounded unsettled. "They have acknowledged everything we sent. There seems to be some hold up with the JSA
link. JSA is with us, but the company operating the Akuma
seems to be holding back information. There is some kind of
confusion going on there."

"Okay. Keep us posted. Tarn out. Okay, you guys. My
suit's coming up. Help me out."

They both came around to help when a little alarm bell
went off in my head. I held up one hand. "Wilson, stand watch
with your weapon. Erin will help me de-suit."

Through the glass of his visor, I could see a look of agreement. He nodded as I began the unlocking procedure for my helmet.

We just had the torso up and over when a clinking, crashing sound made us jump and freeze. Something from overhead clanked and rang its way down the conduit and walkways as it fell. It bounced on a portion of metal floor grating and came to rest still ringing. We looked everywhere, but saw no one. There, on the floor on the south side of the room, lay a shiny silver, closed-ended wrench.

Erin looked at me. "See what I mean? And, you know what? See where that came from up near the highest gangway? That's where your first crawlway is located. I'd hate to think that's the wrench that was being used to operate the valve we need."

I sat on the floor and pushed at the suit pants. "I'll let you know shortly."

Chapter 22

With my suit off at last, I peeled away the sweaty white suit liner and stuffed it into the torso. I stood in only my stretch shorts not caring that Erin was standing a foot away staring. She made an "Ooo" sound and touched a scar on my shoulder. "How did you get this one? It's kind of close to the throat."

"A small piece of shrapnel from an explosive."

"Don't you know you're supposed to be elsewhere when those things go off?"

"Yeah, but the bad guy who was holding it wouldn't let me."

She dipped her chin in disbelief, opened her mouth to ask, then decided against it. Instead, she knelt and dug into the satchel, found my gray flight suit and handed it over. As I pulled it on, she held out my stretch boots.

We piled my suit by the console and pulled out my com unit. With a stolid expression of disapproval, Wilson came around the table holding a tablet. I straightened my flight suit and tried to look optimistic. "Man, what a relief. Bell Standards aren't made for walkin'. RJ, you still with us?"

"Griffin standing by."

"We're gonna need you guys to ship us over some water at some point. It'll need to be a heated transfer container so it doesn't freeze on the way. You should pack in some food, too. We can't chance the food here."

"Got it. Anything else?"

"Just stage it in the aft airlock. When we're ready to come get it we'll let you know and you can depressurize and open the outer."

"Griffin copies."

I turned back to the others. "Did you guys bring anything with you?"

Erin answered. "We were in a hurry. Just the water and candy bars in our suit packs."

"Good idea." I bent down, dug in my suit, and pulled out a candy bar. As I unwrapped it, Wilson handed me the tablet.

"This one's set up with a map of the service ways, the ones you need."

I took the tablet and a bite, and studied the map. "How bad are we on time?"

"We need to get going, right now," said Erin. She handed me a shiny silver tool. "This is the self adjusting wrench that fits all the transfer valves. There's a lift over there to the upper levels. No climbing required. I'll take you over."

She adjusted a setting on her spacesuit sleeve and waved me to follow. On the way to the caged service elevator, she stopped and picked up the mysterious tool that had fallen. It was the same type. "See what I mean?" she said. I nodded and took it from her and zipped it in a pants leg pocket.

The lift was made for a single person. She pointed upward at the third level catwalk, where a small, oval opening waited. I rode up, keeping it in sight, watching for anything out of place. At the top the dark, narrow grated walkway had good handrails and guards. I paused at the crawlway entrance, left my half-eaten candy bar on a shelf by the catwalk, and looked down. Erin waved.

Service crawlways are okay as long as you don't have to go too far in or too far up. They are a bit eerie because you cannot back out very easily or very quickly. If you are lucky you are on your hands and knees, but you must keep your head down to avoid banging it on cables or boxes. The lighting only comes on as you progress and automatically shuts off behind you. It leaves you looking at darkness ahead and darkness behind. There is an absolute loss of sense of direction and unless you leave breadcrumbs, no way to recognize where you have been. People have been known to get caught in rectangular loops in service access-ways, spending hours figuring out how to break out. There are always noises, and since darkness both follows you and awaits you, the sounds always come from one darkness or the other. The best of ghost stories have never gotten to me. Deep within the service crawlways, I sometimes get edgy.

I crawled along and made my first left hand turn, then a right, and already began to get the creeped-out feeling. Then it got worse. As I made the next turn at a T-intersection there must have been moisture coming from somewhere, or some kind of temperature differential, because a shallow hang of fog began to form near the floor. It was only six inches deep, but the floor was no longer visible. It made the passageway seem smaller than it already was, and in places there were little hypnotic swirls where air vents were bleeding airflow.

A loud bang from equipment cycling somewhere made me jump. I laughed out loud. Erin heard me over the com.

"You okay up there, Commander?"

"A London fog bank has moved in. All I need now is Jack the Ripper."

As I rounded the corner to the first of the valve junctions, the fog deepened and took on a slightly violet hue. There was now a fire-hose-sized pipeline running along the wall to my right, a clear indication of coolant routing. Out of the darkness the valve assembly station finally appeared, a concave indentation in the wall with its own yellowish light and large automatic valve sitting at eye level. There was no wrench fastened to it. I pulled out the one Erin had given me, fixed it in place on the turn-bolt head, and pushed. It wouldn't budge. "This thing's frozen. It won't move an inch."

I heard Wilson under his breath say, "Shit."

"Let me try a different position, hold on."

I repositioned myself as best I could, gave a silent three count and shoved on the handle with all my strength. "Crap. It's a bastard."

Erin tried to sound supportive. "There's no other way, Adrian. You've got to cycle it somehow."

"Hang on. I'll try something else."

It's not easy to change direction in a crawlway. People frequently get stuck trying. You have to fold up your legs, then position your face so that it's looking at your knees, then slither like a snake past them. At six-foot-two, it's risky business for guys like me. I have the agility, but not the extra inches. As I wiggled through the maneuver, it made me wonder what being stuck in a fog-covered tube would be like with almost no one to come to the rescue. The thought provided extra motivation. Somehow, I made the switch.

I positioned myself with one foot on the handle, holding on to conduit in the ceiling for leverage. With all my might, I stomped on the wrench handle, praying. The wrench went flying off into the darkness, clanking and bouncing away. I sank back against the floor but the fog covered my face, forcing me to sit back up.

The second wrench fit much more tightly. I had inadvertently kicked the first one with an upward angle. It needed to be a straight shot. I braced myself took my best aim and stomped once more.

Nothing happened. The wrench stayed, but the valve held. Two more poundings and it seemed like there was some give. On the third try, I mustered up something extra and to my delight, the wrench handle spun around and smacked against the wall. I hurried back through the one-eighty maneuver, ratcheted the wrench and opened the valve to full.

Erin's voice yelped over the com. "That's it! You did it. Coolant is flowing."

Wilson added, "One more and we get to live, Adrian."

"Have I mentioned what a comfort you are, Wilson?"

I dragged along toward the darkness, and on the way recovered the first valve wrench. There were four more intersections with turns at three of them. The fog continued. As I reached the next intersection the lights were slow to come on. The valve was somewhere to my right. I happened to glance in the other direction and froze.

In the distant darkness, there were eyes. Nothing else, just two yellow eyes staring back from the blackness. They were there for only a second and then disappeared. I listened, but heard nothing. Some kind of optical illusion, maybe. Why would anyone hang out in these godforsaken crawlways? It bothered me but there was no time to dwell on it. I felt my way into the next tube and crawled along.

As I crossed into a set of working lights, for some reason the entire tunnel lit up all the way to the farthest intersection. It was a good ten or twelve yards to the end of it, and the violet-toned fog made it look like a pathway leading to another dimension. As I focused ahead, something absurd happened. A moving shadow from an adjacent corridor was projected on the wall of the intersection. It was far enough away that I couldn't be sure, but there seemed to be something moving within the fog as well.

It was more than I dared risk. I fumbled around and drew my weapon. With the tablet in one hand, and shooter in the other, I began to crawl, but again stopped abruptly.

At the end of the crawlway, a large white rabbit suddenly hopped in from the adjacent corridor and sat in plain view above the fog rubbing its paws. I let go of the tablet, rubbed my eyes, and when I opened them it was gone. A pang of fear raced though me. I fumbled around in the fog, squeezed my communicator button, and switched to a private channel with Doc.

"Adrian to Doc."

It took a few seconds for him to answer. "Go ahead."

"Doc, I think I'm infected. I'm hallucinating."

"No, Adrian. You are not."

"Why do you say that?"

"The doctors here were very good. They did not have time to create a cure or an inoculation, but they did develop a method to detect the disease. It's done with a brain scan. They documented the incubation period as two hours or less. I have been scanning myself every thirty minutes. I am not affected. If I am not affected, you are not affected. I have not been monitoring the three of you. Are you out of your suit?"

"Yes. It was necessary."

"You are not infected."

"Doc, I'm on the third level in Engineering, deep in a service crawlway. I just saw a white rabbit. If I wait, I'll bet Alice will be along any time now."

"Did it have a watch?"

"This is no time to be funny, Doc."

"I'm not. Did it have a watch?"

"No."

"Then I put it to you, you did see a rabbit."

"Oh for God's sake."

"Do you feel sick?"

"No."

"If you were infected, that's the first stage. How do you feel?"

"Like an idiot?"

"I'm in a hurry here, Commander. We both need to get back to our duties."

"You're sure?"

"You are not infected. I'll explain more later."

"Tarn out."

I switched back to the others. "I'm approaching the last intersection."

"Hurry, Adrian. There's no more time buffer on this," answered Erin.

I inched around the corner. The valve junction came into view just a few feet away. A wrench was already mounted atop it. I crawled up, shifted onto my side and tugged at it. It turned easily.

Erin's voice came over the com. "Thank God. We see that, Adrian. Fresh coolant is on its way to the core. We're stable here. Come on out of there."

"With pleasure."

I have never crawled quite that fast, even with a drill sergeant standing over me with a twitch. When my head accidentally met an equipment box on the ceiling and the box won, my cursing echoed off into the distance but did not slow me. Main Engineering finally came into view. I scrambled out and shook off the eeriness of it. For reward and comfort, I looked for my half-eaten candy bar, but it was gone. The service lift brought me down to floor level where Erin and Wilson were tapping though different schematics on the table display.

Wilson looked up with a discerning appraisal. "Good job. Piece of cake, eh?"

"Thought I saw a rabbit."

He burst out a laugh and then stared to see if I was serious. He decided I might be and wrinkled his brow.

"Don't worry. Doc says I'm fine. Which of you guys took my half-eaten candy bar?"

They both looked on with a questioning stare.

"My half-eaten candy bar. I left it on the catwalk up there. It was gone when I got back."

Erin answered, "Adrian, we've been at this station since you left. Maybe it fell off."

While they worked through their flow displays I went and searched. There was nothing.

"Maybe it's partway up the wall, stuck in a cable track or something," said Wilson.

"I told you stuff has been going on. I have an idea," said Erin. She opened the pocket on her spacesuit leg, pushed aside the glow sticks, and drew out a fresh candy bar. She peeled it halfway open and then left us and went into a hallway and disappeared around a corner. A moment later, she returned.

"I put it on a shelf back there. Bait. Let's see what happens."

Wilson tapped at the schematics display and spoke without looking up. "Boy, we got to those valves just in time. The last time the system was cycled was two days ago. If that core had lost containment it would've meant a cascade failure; multiple detonations. We've got plenty of time now. We just need to take care of the power systems generator. It's the same thing, Adrian, only no service crawlways. You just have to climb down below the floor and there should be a big distribution network of valves and switches down there. We'll have to monitor the cross-flows and talk you through the switch-overs as they happen."

"Where's the access point?"

"It should be over by the lift you used, a large panel entrance in the floor. It opens from this console." He tapped at an icon on his panel and a rotating yellow light came to life on the wall near the lift. A large floor panel rose up on four sides and light appeared from below.

The power system stabilization proved easy compared to the crawlway work. I was in and out in less than thirty minutes. Back at the console display the mood had changed from apprehension to maintenance. Erin tried to fold her inflated arms, gave up and leaned against the console. "Well, that's it. If there are no other failures we can maintain systems safety margins until help arrives and the sooner the better."

Wilson agreed. "We cut it too close. If RJ hadn't picked up on this, the Akuma would not have made it through the day. Once they stopped cycling the damaged valves the end was inevitable."

Wilson's commentary stuck in my mind for a moment. "That's kind of funny, isn't it?"

"What's that?"

"When did you say they last cycled the valves?"

"Two days ago."

I rubbed my forehead and tried to remember. "The Captain's log said she was one of the last to become sick. Then her reports turned to gibberish."

"What's funny about that?"

"I thought it was two weeks. Two weeks ago."

They looked at me with uncertainty. Erin said, "So you're saying some of them must've remained well until a few days ago."

"Doc, we've stabilized the core. The danger is past for the time being. We have a question."

"Thank God. Go ahead."

"Doc, could any of the crew who were infected still have been able to perform valve rotations on the ship's systems?"

"Absolutely not. The pathogen shuts down areas of higher reasoning. There is no logic in the actions of the victim. It is all completely arbitrary and impulsive."

"Someone cycled these valves as recently as a few days ago, Doc. So you're saying some of them held out that long then, right?"

"No way, Adrian. You drink the water and the blood accumulation is simple math. Drink enough to live and you drink enough to be infected. There's no getting around that. If valves were reset, it had to be done some other way."

"Thanks, Doc. Tarn out."

We stared at each other in bewilderment. A loud crash from the nearby hallway shattered the silence. Erin took off in a dash toward the sound.

I yelled, "Wait. Be careful."

She ignored me and charged around the corner. Wilson and I started after her and met her in the alcove.

"Candy bar's gone. Shelf is tipped over."

"So if you've become a Looney tune you like candy bars, so what?" suggested Wilson.

"For someone without higher reasoning, they sure are doing a good job of staying out of sight," said Erin.

"And a good job of cycling valves?"

"You think some of them are immune and are just afraid to come out, Adrian?" said Wilson.

"Why would adults hoping for rescue be afraid to come out?"

We stared at each other for a long moment. Pieces began to fit.

"This can't be what I'm thinking," I said.

Erin took the leap. "Children?"

Wilson joined in. "Oh my God, I get it! The adults knew they had to drink the water and were going to be sick, so they trained the children to cycle the valves. The kids are afraid of them and have been hiding ever since but still doing their job."

Erin added, "Until that valve froze up. So one of them threw the wrench down hoping we'd help."

I considered it. "But that would mean..."

Erin cut me off. "Yes, the children were immune." She grabbed her tablet and began typing furiously. I watched the message.

'*We are not sick. We are visitors here to help you. We have more candy bars. Please come out.*'

With the tablet set to translate to Japanese, she set the audio, held it up and began walking around, playing her message at the loudest setting. Wilson and I stood gawking.

A minute or two passed with no result. Erin persisted. Suddenly there was movement on the second level catwalk, a disturbance in the shadows. Ever so slowly, a young face peered out from the darkness. He was seven or eight years old. He held onto the guardrail with one hand, ready to run, and looked down at Erin in her spacesuit.

"Kichigai," he yelled.

Quickly Erin repeated the word into her tablet and read the translation. She typed in a reply and played it back in Japanese. The boy hesitated and slowly withdrew into the shadows. Wilson and I set our tablets to translate.

The boy returned to the catwalk with a friend. The friend yelled down "Kichigai?" but this time it was a question, not an accusation. Wilson and I read our tablets. The translated word was '*insane, crazy*'.

Erin played back her message once more. Our tablets translated for us.

'*Not sick. Friends sent to help you. Come out. We won't hurt you.*'

There was noise behind me. I turned to see a young girl holding a doll in the corridor where the candy bar had been hidden. As I looked back up other children were emerging onto the catwalks. On the third level, a young girl stood tightly holding her pet white rabbit.

To my dismay, Erin placed her tablet on the floor, reached up and twisted off her helmet. She put it down, and with her tablet back in hand, turned in a circle, waving to the children.

I looked at Wilson in dismay. "When the hell did she start recompression without telling me?"

Wilson shrugged. "So can I take mine off too?"

Chapter 23

There were twelve of them, all ten years old or less. They were the smartest kids I had ever met. With the greatest of caution they gathered around us, one by one. Their clothes were dirty and ragged. Their hands and faces needed washing. Erin conducted the dialog. Wilson and I tried to look friendly. They understood everything. They knew it was the water. They knew their parents were sick. They knew to be afraid. They had been told to watch for rescuers.

They told us the adults were gathered in various groups around the ship. The adults were unable to speak coherently. They migrated about but returned to their group unless they were excommunicated. Sometimes they were violent. Most of the time they were just afraid of things. There was plenty of food. You just had to sneak around to get it.

News of our newly made friends astounded and excited the doctor. There had been no reference to children in the Med Lab documentation. He theorized that the discovery of the children's immunity came after the medical staff had succumbed to the infection. He badly wanted blood samples, but we begged off saying "not yet."

The children were the best support we could have had. They knew the ship. They knew the disease. They knew the victims. Most of all, they knew the cooling systems crisis matrix. There were several instances as Erin and Wilson laid out their cyclic plan one of the particularly adept nine year olds would point and shake his head, causing all of us to stare at each other in wonder.

With that one frozen valve now resolved, we suddenly had an army of little engineers ready to launch into the tunnels to effect our cooling plan. These were not only the smartest children I had ever seen, they were also the bravest. The setup allowed the three of us to stand guard and coordinate in Engineering, though no visits from the infected were forthcoming.

When things had settled, I finally had a chance to talk to Erin. "Erin, that was a nice job you did bringing out the kids."

"But that's not what you wanted to talk to me about."

"Erin, you repressed your suit without telling me."

"You were going into those crawlways alone, Adrian. If you had gotten into trouble or needed an extra set of hands, someone had to be available. Wilson's kind of too much of a hulk for that, don't you agree? It had to be me. If there had been trouble with no one to go in after you, we all would have gone up in the cascade. I started recomp as soon as you headed for the lift. I didn't mention it because it didn't seem to matter much at that point."

"Okay, but you've got to let me have the illusion that I'm in charge. It just blows the fantasy all to hell when crew does that kind of stuff."

"Yes, Commander."

"You've got to be careful about taking matters into your own hands without thinking, like running into a dark corridor alone. You can't cover your back when you're by yourself. That's why the rule is secured area, or teams of at least two."

"You're right. That was stupid. I'll be more careful. But you came from sickbay alone."

"It was the only way. Besides, I have certain experience."

"Like the scar on your shoulder?"

"It makes for elevated instincts."

Wilson came over hoping to provide interference. "May I finally de-suit now, Adrian?"

"Since at least one of us is still suited, we can make a quick trip to Griffin. They'll have water and some light food for us. I'll go with you and wait outside the airlock. That is, now that I know Erin is going to be more careful. You'll need help carrying that stuff once you're back in gravity. We'll lock down Engineering before we go."

The crew on Griffin gathered up every candy bar in every spacesuit and locker and packed them up with food. Wilson made the EVA alone, though I never let him out of my sight. When he returned with the supplies in tow we divided it up in the airlock and made a stop at sickbay to stock up the Doctor. On the way back to Engineering we turned a corner and ran into a line of Akuma adults walking in single file to nowhere. We froze and readied ourselves only to watch them casually march by, glazed eyes forward, no interest in us at all. The leader was calling out a marching chant. Not one follower was in step.

In engineering the candy bars went fast. I never expected to see young ladies drawing chalk squares on the metal floor of a spacecraft's most critical area, but there it was. It was some form of hopping game, which they delighted in playing under the protection of non-infected adults. The boys had some form of sandbag pitching game. Wilson and I were hastily shown the rules, attempted to compete, and got our clocks cleaned. Areno was brought down from sickbay and reunited with his owner, resulting in a celebration so moving it caught me off guard and choked me up for a few seconds. At some point during the evening, RJ finished establishing an uplink from sickbay and began relaying all the medical information to Earth, where it was quickly relayed to JSA and from there to the medical rescue ship coming to take control of Akuma.

The first security rescue ship was scheduled to drop of out of light at 07:00 for rendezvous. Somewhere around 05:00, I began to worry. I took a seat away from the others and made a call.

"Hey, Doc."

"What's up, Adrian?"

"What happens when the first security vessel gets here?"

"Well, they'll take charge of the Akuma until the medical ship arrives."

"They'll decide who comes and who goes?"

"Not really. They'll decide nobody comes and nobody goes."

"That's not good."

"I see where you're going with this."

"We're officially quarantined right now, correct?"

"Correct."

"But at this time, you are the ranking medical officer, correct?"

"Yes."

"Are we contagious?"

"No. None of us are even infected."

"Are you sure?"

"Yes."

"You see what I'm thinking, right?"

"Yes."

"How much trouble could you get into if we weren't here when they arrived?"

"Boy, that's a tough one. I'd either have to declare the quarantine lifted, or certify our crew members as not exposed."

"That second one sounds better. Have any of us been exposed?"

"Technically, no. In this case you can only be exposed if you ingest the water. An argument could be made however, that we have been exposed to simple water vapor in the air and are therefore suspect. The purpose of quarantine is to contain anyone and everything that may have come in contact with the virus."

"Until they have been certified as uncontaminated?"

"You actually make a good case, Adrian. If we remain here until the security vessel boards, we will not be allowed to leave probably until well after the Akuma is back in Earth orbit."

"That will blow our Nadir launch date."

"Yes, almost certainly."

"I'm thinking that gives us no choice, do you agree?"

No answer.

I persisted. "We will be long gone on Nadir before any inquiries can be arranged."

"Yes, but they'll be waiting for us when we return."

"We had no choice in coming here."

"No. No choice."

"This ship would no longer exist if we hadn't come."

"No one can argue that."

"What if I told you I had some pull which would guarantee you no repercussions of any kind when we got back?"

"That would help greatly with the ugly questions I'll get when we return just from this trip. The real bureaucracy will probably not have had time to kick in yet, though."

"Let's do it. Let's get out of here as soon as the security vessel docks."

"We'll need to dot every 'I' and cross every 'T'. Make it look like every examination and decontamination procedure was followed to the letter. They'll know every step in the manual was covered, but they'll also know the spirit of the off-world quarantine rules were not adhered to."

"What do we need to do?"

"Bring each one up here, one at a time."

"You've got it."

And that was what we did. It was our only ticket off the ship. We could not leave the children alone, so a plan was devised for two of us to remain behind until security officers arrived and entered the airlock. We had preplanned escape routes on both sides of the Akuma, and would use the side opposite their docking. We explained our situation in simplified terms to our new young friends and, at 06:00 suited Wilson and Doc up and sent them to the Griffin. When the first rescue security ship appeared off Akuma's starboard side, Erin and I disappeared out the opposite airlock and jetted back, keeping our departure masked by Akuma's superstructure. Because of the Doctor's work, the officers arriving knew they could dock and enter without suits. But it still took a bit of time with the airlock, and then a bit more to realize we were not on board. That occurred after Griffin had bid a private, symbolic farewell and jumped silently away. Erin and I made the jump still inside our pressurized suits, locked in the spacesuit docking stations in the aft airlock. Danica dropped us out at the brown dwarf near a particularly large pyramid-shaped asteroid that looked like a huge fishing weight. At least, that's what it looked like to me.

When things had settled down and everyone had drifted off in the wonderment of everything we had just been through, I found Doc mag'd into a seat in the science lab, his feet up and crossed as if there were a hassock supporting them though nothing was. He had an amber beer bottle in his hand and as I entered, he suspended another in midair and shoved it at me. "Weird goin' back into zero-G, isn't it?" he said, and drank. There was a touch of slur in his speech.

I looked around and tapped the door closed and locked.

"A parting gift from the Akuma," he said.

"I guess there's no danger of Akuma water."

"Red Moon, a product from Terra Firma. They say it only takes one with these. I've not found that to be true."

I unscrewed the cap, flipped it like a coin and watched it bounce off the walls and keep going. "Here's to unsung heroes."

He took a drink. "Here's to prosecuted heroes."

"Not going to happen."

"Somehow I believe you."

We both drank.

"There's some shit you don't know," he said, "and I do not use the term lightly." He took another drink as though he needed it.

"Hold on. Let me check my shit meter. Uh-oh, it's already almost on full from Denard's shit."

He laughed. "You'd better make more room."

"Yeah, the man's taking up everybody else's space."

"Don't worry. What I'm talking about is somebody else's shit and it makes Denard look like a saint." He took another drink and his expression began to worry me.

"Seriously?"

He gave me a cold stare that almost made me shiver. "The Akuma virus did not come from the water."

"But you said..."

"I said it was in the water, but it didn't get there from the Oort Cloud. It was put there by a crewman."

"That can't be true."

"He was supposed to inject it in the water if the Akuma did not find a mother load. When the pulse damaged the ship, the mission was abandoned. They were going to come back empty handed. The accident dumped all their water so the saboteur couldn't plant the virus. Then, when they dragged the ice in, it became the perfect opportunity to make it look like the ice was contaminated. The bastard had been told he had been given an immunization, and that he would secretly be picked up after a rescue ship came too late to help the others. The truth was he was not immune at all. They expected him to die along with the crew, and the truth with him."

Doc paused for another drink. "It was a designer virus. What really twists me up is that they knew it wouldn't kill its victims. They knew what would happen. They knew the ship could not be maintained, and would eventually destruct and it would look like a shipboard accident. No way to ever figure out what really happened. Easy to explain. No loose strings. Their patsy figured out too late that he'd been screwed. He'd already been drinking the water and he flips into this personality thing where he thinks he's a secret agent. Finds himself a tuxedo and begins searching for the secret way out. Found it, too. He puts the whole story in a personal log and labels it top secret, with no password or protection at all, just before becoming too incoherent to write. His final entries were garbage. I'm in there searching files with key words on the virus and his pops up. That's how I know the whole story."

"But who?"

A conglomerate called Omega. An international group of investors. They went in deep on this mission. They expected gold deposits along Akuma's field search route, but they gambled too much. They couldn't chance failure. You can't insure a mission in space so that if it comes back empty handed you recover your losses, but you can insure the spacecraft and crew.

"You're not serious."

"If the Akuma came back with anything less than big-time finds, the Omega group was decimated. If the Akuma was destroyed, however, they'd lose nothing. That is why information has not been so forthcoming from the company. They are in a tizzy, you might say." He tipped his bottle at me, and took a drink.

"Who knows?"

"I transmitted it all through RJ's link. It's been sent to all the various agencies. There will be no covering it up."

"What about the people? Can they be cured?"

"A good chance. It will take a team of specialists mapping the new DNA mutations, but there was no actual damage to the brain. So there's a good chance with maybe a year's worth of work they will bring them back from the brink. The ones still alive, anyway."

"So, we found a doomed ship, rescued it, and solved a murder mystery, all in one shot. I believe you've outdone yourself, Holmes."

"It doesn't abdicate my fear of man, my dear Watson."

"How many of those have you had?"

"Not enough, I think."

Chapter 24

The big red eye of the brown dwarf seemed to be watching us once more. Our position was just right so that out of the side portals we could see the distant silver specks of its satellites. We gathered in the forward airlock near the flight deck for a crew meeting. Too much had happened to assume the mission would simply continue.

"So, here we are back where we started. Personally, I'd like to go find my lug nut key, despite everything that's happened. Does anyone see any reason why we should not continue?"

Paris Denard would not be denied. He seemed to be getting past space sickness. "Absurd. Totally absurd. Every standard of discipline there is has been violated, along with a variety of international laws. It is time to abort this fiasco and return to Earth. There is no decision to be made. After everything we've been through, are we now to risk my life in search of some idiotic used car part? That's it. It's over."

We all looked at each other. No one seemed moved.

RJ turned in his engineering station seat and spoke, "Adrian, I just got a message from that security ship asking where the Doctor is and why the Griffin has left the area. They've sent it to us and Ground Control. How should I reply?"

"All Griffin personnel certified as uncontaminated and released from quarantine. Griffin and crew have resumed their assigned mission."

RJ hesitated as though there might be more, then sent the message.

Denard burst forth. "See? See!"

Shelly was in the pilot's seat. She leaned back and eyed Denard. He stiffened and pointed with one bouncing finger. "You don't intimidate me. I have international law on my side."

"Sweetheart, we haven't had any time alone together. I get off in an hour."

He opened his mouth to protest but discovered there was nothing he dared say. For once, he seemed at a loss for words.

I attempted civility. "Does anyone else have anything constructive to offer?"

No one did.

"Then if no one else objects, we are already here. Let's resume scanning and find the Easter egg, and then go home. Has anyone gotten any sleep?"

No one answered.

"Danica, you guys up front, no sleep?"

"We traded off some rest periods, Adrian. No one could sleep."

"We'll all need to get some before we head back. Let's go find the package, then we'll hang for a while and try to catch up some."

Denard growled and pushed off toward the back of the ship. Everyone resumed their positions or headed for the habitat module. I floated over RJ as he set up his scans.

"We've already done most of the scanning, Adrian. It won't take long. All we need to do is catch our grid pattern up to the new position. We already have distinct signatures."

"Let me know when you hear back from Ground."

"You sure you want to know?"

"Whenever we transmit, just try to sound innocent."

"Well, aren't we?"

"Good start."

He leaned into the scanning console and began synchronizing previous data with current changes, while Erin, Wilson, Doc, and I coasted back and raided the galley, bumping each other out of the way, and squeezing tube food out into the air to capture it in our mouths. A faux pas occurred when Wilson squeezed a coffee creamer too hard and sprayed Erin square in the eye. Unwilling to allow the indignation, Erin responded by pasting her full applesauce cup on his nose. There were exclamations and giggling. Before the conflict could escalate, RJ called out. "Adrian, I think we have it. Wow! It's close."

We hovered over RJ as he forwarded the coordinates to Shelly and Danica. Shelly looked back. "It's in the red zone, Adrian, too close to use stellar, but a bit of a haul with OMS."

"You have my permission to get underway, Shelly."

She smiled and tapped the intercom. "All personnel, brace for acceleration."

Denard had disappeared into his sleeper cell. The rest of us found something to hang on to. After a minute of setup, we felt the OMS drives kick the ship forward and come up to speed.

Shelly's voice came back. "It'll be twenty minutes of thrust, an hour and fifteen minutes of coast, then twenty of breaking."

So for twenty minutes we had gravity against the back walls, which Wilson used to pretend he was doing knee bends, causing Erin to giggle and point.

RJ turned and looked up from his seat. "It looks cluttered where we're going, Adrian, kind of like a piece of an asteroid belt. There's big stuff and little stuff, and a lot of it. I'm guessing there won't be a landing anywhere."

"Okay."

"I want to be wingman on this one. I need to get out and stretch my legs."

"Well, no one else has thought to ask, so I guess you're it."

He raised one hand to protest, but realized I had agreed. He shook his head in approval. "Okay. Okay, then. Great."

"Get some rest first. I am."

I checked around to make sure all things looked as they should, then released my handhold and let the acceleration drop me back to the habitat module and into the sleeper cell section. I tapped open my cell and pulled in. The white, photo-synth door mercifully rolled down and shut out the world. My compartment seemed larger than I remembered. I tapped the control on the wall and set the display at my feet to the ship's forward view. The stars made it look like we weren't moving. The press of the wall against my feet assured me we were. Mag sensors in the bed helped hold my body comfortably in place. The water tube fed cold water. My small refrigerator had absolutely nothing in it. I rubbed my eyes, pinched the bridge of my nose, and decided not to let my mind start replaying everything that had happened.

Five minutes later, vibration from the OMS engines kicked off and zero-G seeped back in. Sleeping in zero-G is a very different kind of rest. Though many people do not realize it, we all do a subconscious version of yoga when we climb into bed at night. We use gravity to stretch out the muscles and relax them. We spend time on one side or the other, changing positions, using contact with the bed as pressure points. We rotate from back to front, side to side, subconsciously employing the technique to unwind everything that is contracted or misaligned, and even after we're asleep this treatment continues, part of nature's way of resetting physical elasticity.

It's not like that in weightlessness. You do not have gravity contact to put pressure on muscles and tendons. No matter which way you lay, it's the same. The closest comparison would be sleeping in a dead-man's float in a swimming pool.

But, though your usual nightly relationship with gravity massage is not available, your heart no longer has the extra work of overcoming gravity's pull. Your veins and arteries do not need to resist that earthly drag with each pulse. Your circulatory system tends to relax and disengage because all weight has quite literally been removed. Your toes and fingers often tingle, and sleep becomes a pleasant sensory deprivation of its own.

A voice echoing down from a deep tunnel pulled me up to consciousness. "...for deceleration." Shelly, notifying us that braking was about to begin.

I squinted, shocked that I had fallen asleep. The braking cut in, gently dragging my feet down against the sleeper cell wall so that I had to push back against it as we slowed. She had turned us around and I had not even sensed it. I touched my forehead where there was a sore spot from bumping an equipment box in the Akuma's service crawlway.

In the habitat module, Erin and Paris were in seats staring out portals on opposite sides of the spacecraft. Wilson was up front with Shelly and Danica. I stood with my arms folded and my back pressed against the habitat module back wall, and waited for the braking to ease. Shelly's voice came over the intercom, "Ten minutes."

RJ pulled himself into the room, and took a place against the wall on the other side. He rubbed his face with both hands and then squinted as he took in the surroundings. He looked at me with raised eyebrows and a half smile. "Can't wait to see this place. It will be very, very interesting."

"Bunch a' rocks?"

"Yeah. Interesting rocks."

"A forest of floating fragments?"

"A veritable banquet of boulders."

"Were there chunks at all big enough to land on?"

"Only if you want things banging into you while you're there."

"We have shields."

"What? Who said?"

"Can't tell you."

"Or you'd have to kill me."

"Yep. But, you'll find out soon enough."

"That's okay. I have a theory. I'm betting there won't be any reason for a landing."

"Why not?"

"I think originally they meant to put our target down on a large enough body so that we would be forced to land and get out to find it. I think they screwed up. I think in their hurry to place the item, they didn't take the time to map the target. They didn't realize how populated the area was. They used a standard probe delivery system, assigned it to crash or land on the chosen body, but it wasn't smart enough to navigate through the garbage. It was determined enough, though. It smashed into, or was hit by something. I think we're going to be looking for a smashed up probe that didn't make it to its assigned destination."

"Boy. There you go again. Analyzing crap that nobody else would. You are a seer, Sir."

Shelly's voice interrupted. "Thirty seconds. Brace."

Seconds later, the engine cutoff gave us a slight bounce back into weightlessness. Shelly came over the intercom once more. "It's a jungle out there, folks. This is as close as we're gonna get."

We all floated to the side windows. Someone exclaimed, "Wow!" Outside, a glorious field of large and small animated rock shapes decorated the blackness. Many were as big as a car, many more the size of medicine balls. Smaller stones drifted among them. Occasionally I could make out chunks the size of an airliner, and there were two in the far distance as large as small moons. The rock field went above us and below us as far as I could see. We were one hundred yards outside it. It was an incredible choreography of slow motion going on everywhere. Large stones turning in place, others rotating away, smaller pieces tumbling gradually by them. There was enough separation within the tumbling, turning mass for a man in a spacesuit, but the heads-up attitude display in the spacesuit helmet would be needed to avoid disorientation and conflict.

I pushed myself up to the flight deck and hung over Wilson as he worked the scanners.

"What'da you got?"

"We're in the right place. There's definitely composite metal out there, not naturally occurring. But I can't pinpoint it. It's a foggy footprint. I can feed it to the suit-navs, though, and you will be able to track it and find it, whatever or wherever it is."

"How far?"

"Two hundred-eighty to three hundred and fifteen meters. It's a debris field. That's its volume. That will be your search radius."

I looked back to find RJ in my face. He smiled a big smile.

RJ had not yet fit a suit so it took some extra time. Wilson had to shorten the arms and legs slightly to keep his head up in the helmet. When it was done we sealed in and engaged our depressurization cycles. We sat waiting with the inner and outer doors still sealed. RJ had a wide grin on his face the whole time. I got the feeling he couldn't stop it. Finally, with suit permissions, the airlock depressurized.

The outer door opened to a glorious collage of motion. The Nav display on my visor showed a blue line leading to our target, and next to it the cross hairs that would keep us headed in the right direction no matter how we were oriented. On the sides of my visor a few small outlines flashed yellow, showing they were within caution range. Outside the airlock, we lowered the backpack handles and jetted slowly toward the mass.

We paused at the border and checked everything. There was a small amount of ambient light from the dwarf, but our helmet lamps were staying on just the same. It made for a shadowy environment. Griffin was tracking all transiting objects, so there would be no chance of getting clobbered by something. We cautiously entered the field and the visuals became mesmerizing enough to make you want to stop and watch, a temptation we resisted. We coasted beneath behemoths the size of elephants, and circled around shapes that looked like rock carvings of giant diamonds and pendulums. We passed over a few so closely we could have walked along the tops. I heard RJ laughing under his breath over the com. It pleased me. Deep into the forest, there was a particularly large stone with a naturally formed face that had an uncanny resemblance to a high school French teacher who had flunked me. It glared at me as I passed, and made me realize I had never used the French language even once.

RJ came over the com. "Uh-oh."

I maneuvered around to look. He was holding a gold-plated bar in one glove. He pointed ahead with his other.

It was the debris field. Golden pieces of a small probe scattered everywhere.

"You are indeed a prophet, RJ."

"I now predict this will be quite a job."

"Maybe it's not even the right spacecraft."

"It is."

"How do you know?"

"It's new. It hasn't been out here long. It's still pretty much all in one place. It hasn't scattered yet."

"See why I brought you along?"

"We will have to pick through the pieces for the containment vessel and hope we get lucky."

"We could just beg off. We've accomplished the mission."

"I'm not in hurry to get back. I don't have a date for tonight. It's kind of nice out here."

So that's what we did. It was a playful task not often enjoyed by man. One for the family photo album. Piece by piece we searched. We pushed off nearby boulders, and swam carefully through clouds of golden probe debris, looking for something that might be a container. Some parts had loosely adhered to chunks of stone. Others seemed to be trying to orbit the larger rocks. The endeavor was not work at all. It was a treasure hunt in a celestial rock garden. It was fun. It took three hours. RJ won. He found a brass-colored artifact that looked like a tooth-brush tube. He pulled it apart and my frozen, silver lug nut key floated out. It meant enough to me that I thought to grab it from him, but he pulled it away and zipped it into a torso pocket. He pointed at me as though it was bragging rights. We jetted back like victorious hunters, and sat smiling at each other in the airlock feeling as though we had just gotten the best of Bernard Porre.

I ordered four hours in sleeper cell rotations for everyone before heading back. No one minded, except Paris. He milled about, having already slept. We took shifts up front, and when everyone had filled their rest requirement made a smooth jump back to a parking orbit above Earth. Doc took the pilot seat for the descent. I rode shotgun. To our surprise, they did not hold us in orbit because of the Akuma incident. We set down on the Space Center apron as the rising Florida sun began turning distant storm clouds orange. A variety of dignitaries were there to greet us.

Some friendly. Some not.

Chapter 25

My first duty aground was to put my corvette's lug nut locking key back where it belonged. That shiny, little silver key would never look the same. Each time I picked it up I had to look up at the sky and marvel at the thought of where it had been.

The atmosphere at Genesis was made litigious by the comings and goings of new, important people trying to understand what had happened aboard the Akuma. An accident in space would have been bad enough. An accident followed by a ship-wide virus was almost too much for them to conceptualize. An accident, followed by a ship-wide virus, followed by evidence of sabotage was just too much.

They just did not know what to do with us. They weren't even sure what to do with themselves. Had we not found her the Akuma would have ended up a brief star in the sky, followed by a debris cloud searching for the nearest gravity field. Remote radio telescopes would have picked up the pulse. Sleepless astronomers would have thought they'd discovered something new. Eventually, the dots would have connected. Two or three of the legal-types wanted to skin us alive, but the rescue of the Akuma's crew held them at bay. It reminded me of one of those invisible dog fences. They had to complete their depositions. Statements had to be taken. By what authority did we board a sovereign star-class space cruiser? –By the authority provided from the Japanese Space Agency. How did we know it was safe to board her? –We did not. Why did we disembark without notifying the proper authorities? –At the time, we were the proper authorities. They went on and on until they had become their own source of frustration. It was a big deal. They should have been able to draw some blood. It was a terrible opportunity to waste. But in the end, we wasted them.

The WHO medical attorney's group had such a dilemma with the whole thing I wondered if some of them might eventually need physiological help of their own. They were dying to declare us potential carriers of the Akuma virus, but it was too late for that. Plus, as Doc had directed, we had dotted every 'I' and crossed every 'T' so there wasn't even anything left for them to test. They spent the most time with Doc, but his seasoned experience with the medical profession made him quite a dull and boring fellow. Some of them kept visiting Julia Zeller's office, spending long hours in discussion and then leaving in the same near-catatonic state they had arrived in. Julia had absolutely nothing to do with any of it, but the empty-handed investigators had nowhere else to go so Julia had become something of a comfort to them.

Layered within the chaos, were visits and communications from those whose loved ones from the Akuma would be coming home, along with representatives of the organization that owned the Akuma. They wanted information and to express their deepest gratitude. In one short test flight we had managed to become the greatest of heroes and the worst of villains, and those stark contrasts were not the only irony. I watched grateful, high-level visitors shake Paris Denard's hand and thank him as he nodded his bony little head in acceptance.

They interrogated us and re-interrogated us, but since we had nothing to hide, our stories kept coming out the same. That seemed to annoy some of them to no end. It made others simply give up. We were questioned apart and together, but it made no difference. Paris seemed to be enjoying the notoriety enough that he became a passive play-along. The only updates we could get from the authorities were that there were rising hopes the remaining Akuma crew would make a full recovery. Captain Mako Hayashi had been found in a cold storage hanger unconscious but alive. She had kept the temperature as low as humanly possible in an attempt to slow the virus. The children were fine. Over a few days the onslaught began to diminish and eventually became occasional phone calls. Final determinations would be made later on. They would let us know.

We had better things to do. Two weeks to do everything that needed to be done. Two weeks to get our heads around the idea of being away for up to a year in something resembling a large toothpaste tube with a pointy nose and windows.

I found myself calling Nira daily. Sometimes it was her, sometimes the service. We seemed to be in agreement in our lament. But the train was rolling along and there would be no stopping it. There was no way to get off.

The crew went into separation anxiety, the need to be away from each other. We would occasionally bump into one another at Genesis, but the salutations and interpersonal relations were kept to a minimum. It was part of the instinctive preparation for being bottled up together for too long. Everyone understood. No one complained. Flight training was done only at the request of the pilot. Habitat training was all but inactive. We were ready, at least professionally.

Nira managed another escape from her lab and stayed for two days. It was a very good two days. We did not go anywhere. We just hung together. Spent some time at the beach, and some time shopping. At the airport, she was better than I at holding it in. "Keep the cards and letters coming" was all she said. I choked it back and nodded. Two guys waiting nearby smirked at me.

Two days before departure we decided on a small celebration at Heidi's. RJ and Wilson had become regulars there, and despite RJ's overtures our favorite server, Jeannie had become enamored with Wilson. They set up a big table in the corner for us. The crew came rolling in one by one. Each appearance was a boisterous celebration of standing, toasting, and roasting. It seemed they had all tuned their minds to the light years ahead. There was an undercurrent of resolve behind the jokes and jabs.

When the rumble of motorcycles suddenly bled through the front door, we thought nothing of it. Nowadays there are so many charity rides and club events to raise money for those in need, bikers have become a new kind of standard in community responsibility and caring.

But when the group banged in through the door, none of them was that type. There were seven. I knew it was too many. The nerve of the big shots always increases exponentially based on how many cohorts are along to impress. They had already been drinking. The place quieted a bit. They wore standard black leather, not having been gifted with a talent for creative originality. The one I guessed to be second in command had on a black hat with a short black visor, exactly like Brando had worn in that ancient black and white classic, The Wild One. I came close to guffawing but wisely held back. Our table was already trading too many of the wrong kind of silent stares. We stood out like a sore thumb. The patron who worried me the most was our own Danica. She kept looking past Shelly as though she was wondering how many she could take.

The real problem was Wilson. Jeannie had been pampering him since we'd arrived. She kept bending over in his face so much that the lust had become thick enough to cut with a knife. I was glad there were none around. Normally all of it would have been just fine, except for one thing. Apparently, the leader of the men in black considered himself to have some sort of arrangement with Jeannie. What that was I could not be sure, since she was not the least bit interested in his grand entrance, a slight that seemed to be holding his attention in our direction for too long.

RJ and I exchanged knowing stares. The gang leader yelled out, "Jeannie, get your ass over here!"

Jeannie pretended not to hear. The gang leader left the bar and headed our way. "What you lookin' at?" he said, and this time it was directed at Wilson.

Wilson pretended not to hear.

He came up to the table, leaned against a nearby chair, and persisted. "Hey! You. What you lookin' at?"

Jeannie did not turn around. Wilson leaned slightly sideways, and gave him a you're-not-serious-are-you stare.

"I said what you lookin' at little man?"

Wrong description.

Then he went too far. He clutched Jeannie by one arm, pulled her away, and shoved her toward the bar. "I said get your ass over there."

And that was it. You can insult Wilson all day long and he's okay with it. You could steal his pie off his plate and he'd give it to you. But the moment you pick on one of his friends, all bets are off. You'd better have a pretty good reason, because you are going to justify it one way or another, usually another.

Wilson sat back in his chair and locked his hands behind his head. "Hey, you know why doctors prefer biker-gang brains for transplants? Cause they've hardly been used."

The gang leader snarled, stiffened, and took his first step. Normally I would have grabbed Wilson and prevented him from using his standard catch phrase. This time it didn't matter. It was already too late.

As the leader approached, Wilson's instincts kicked in. The transformation began. His big arms suddenly became rippled as he stood and held up one hand. "Now I don't want no trouble."

RJ cast a glance my way and waved one hand in resignation.

I stood. One by one the others at our table stood, like a chorus line in a Fred Astaire movie. The only real difference was that there would be no dancing.

I was surprised the idiot was not more adept. It seemed only logical someone of his base line intelligence would have been involved in enough skirmishes to have developed some instinct for self-defense. He came in too close and too fast, was jolted back red-faced by Wilson's outstretched hand on his throat, tried to throw a kick with one motorcycle boot, but his body remained behind his feet, sending him crashing to the floor on his back.

With that, the rest of the gang came.

In keeping with his eternal optimism, RJ held up one hand in desperation. "Gentlemen please! We're all civilized men here!" At which point someone who had gotten behind us smashed a framed poster over his head. Fortunately it was only paper so he was not injured, but it left him with a framed, torn paper collar and a wide-eyed expression showing disappointment that diplomacy was no longer a viable option.

The same guy tried to follow up with me but was not big enough. He made a two-step charge but aborted three feet away, realizing he had not planned ahead what he would do upon arrival. He finally settled on an all out charge, followed by a leap that was supposed to end in a straddled bear hug. I caught him in the crotch as he went airborne, sidestepped, and provided enough extra thrust that he cleared the next table and landed on the one beyond it. There was a lot of pushing back of chairs and crashing and rolling.

My next concern was for the somewhat fragile Erin. I looked away long enough to find Shelly holding her back in the corner. To my surprise, it looked like the debutante wanted to get into it, but thank God Shelly wouldn't let her.

On my left, Danica had suddenly changed from hotshot pilot to Bruce Lee. A gang member raised a pool cue to whap Wilson over the head but Danica stepped around and delivered a beautifully placed sidekick to the back of his knee. The guy went down over backwards, looked around for who had kicked him, saw Danica and decided it must have been someone else. When realization quickly took hold, he growled and climbed to his hands and knees intending to go after her, only to meet the loud smack of her round kick on the side of his chin as he stood. He stared in a fractured moment of indignation, teetered a bit, and was asleep before he hit the floor. To my dismay, Danica did not celebrate the moment. Instead, she began looking for more.

You never see Wilson with less than two. In most cases, they charge in and are captured by one big hand, almost like a fly to flypaper. Once there, they discover they are not strong enough to overcome his grasp, so they begin flailing and kicking, like a skydiver on his first jump. I have seen assailants sprain their wrist hitting Wilson in the arm.

Wilson struggled to keep two of the would-be assassins at bay by banging them together at irregular intervals. The disheveled gang leader regained his feet, brushed himself off to look good for the fight, and again charged with a silent-movie kind of exaggerated stare. RJ, holding his newly acquired poster, smacked it over the idiot's head and shoved him head first into a table, where he whacked his head and disappeared beneath it. RJ wiped his hands and gave a flat smile as though he were Stan Laurel. "How chagrin," he declared, and took cover behind me.

I looked for Doc and in the process took a solid whack on the upper left arm. The table crasher had returned with a piece of a chair leg and was in the process of taking his second swing, this time for my head. RJ and I ducked in unison and let it pass. As I came back up, I slapped my hand over the thug's face and dragged him down to the floor. He raised his head up and as carefully as possible with my palm heel, I tapped it back down just enough to make his eyelids flutter and close.

In yet another of life's strange ironies, Doc was a few tables away kneeling on the floor by a gang member who had apparently smashed a bottle on the bar for use as a weapon, and then somehow in the mayhem fallen upon the pointed end of it. It was another testament that this gang was not up to the standards prescribed by Brando's hat. A nasty laceration ran from his chin down across the side of his neck. Doc had applied pressure and was setting up some kind of pressure bandage to keep him from bleeding to death before the ambulance could arrive. One of the man's comrades seemed to be especially concerned and was standing over them trying to help.

The two Wilson had been treating like Marionette puppets were so battered and exhausted he finally set them in chairs where they remained hunched over, holding their bruised heads, and gasping for breath. The others around the room were in various states of disarray, and not yet organized enough to launch a counterstrike.

Handing the pressure bandage off to the man's partner, Doc rose and returned. Before I could find something appropriate to say, Jeannie came up and motioned us to follow. She led us to a back door and held onto Wilson so that he could not leave.

I went to her and held out all the credit slips I had left in my wallet. "Please give this to the owner. Tell him if it's not enough I'll be back in twelve months to settle up."

She got a distressed look. "Twelve months?" She looked at Wilson. She climbed up him and planted one hell of a kiss. "Midnight. I'll meet you at the convenience store on the corner."

We ducked out and made our way through the unlit parking lot, driving past the police and ambulance vehicles as they arrived.

Chapter 26

I had expected the day before launch to be somber. To my surprise, it became comical. A notable black and blue decorated my left arm just below the shoulder, making long sleeves desirable. My home front was battened down for the long haul. Cleaned out the refrigerator, got rid of perishables that wouldn't last, and did all the maintenance that needed doing. In the garage, I lovingly set a trickle charger to the Vette's battery, took care of all the other long term requirements, and covered her over. A shuttle was available to all of us, as needed, for the next two days.

RJ was waiting in my office with his feet up and coffee in hand. There was a second cup sitting on my desk, steam still rising. We looked at each other and laughed for no reason. I sat and sipped. The mix was perfect.

"See? This is why I gave you a key."

"A sad testimony that you must lock your lair."

"Uh-oh. Are you in one of those moods?"

"Not at all. I found last evening to be somewhat refreshing, actually."

"Gentlemen, we're all civilized men here?"

"I believe I may have underestimated the tenacity of souls less evolved."

"Learned something new about you last night."

"Pray tell."

"You are not above going after the gang leader when pressed."

"I was afraid you'd hurt him."

I sipped. It tasted so good it made me wince. "Anyone else in?"

"Wilson showed up wearing a long-sleeved flight suit, purportedly to hide a big bite mark on his left arm bequeathed him by one of the motorcycle men desperate to make any impression at all."

I had to spit out some coffee to laugh.

"Wilson also has quite a large red spot on his neck. I did not recall any attackers having accomplished that, and despite showing up so late he seems surprisingly refreshed and in a good mood."

"Hmm."

"I was told he did not require a ride home."

"Anyone else in?"

"There is one thing I need to warn you about."

A tap at the door interrupted.

"This is it," he whispered.

Julia Zeller slowly opened the door. She leaned inside and looked back and forth at the two of us. "Did you guys get in a fight at Heidi's last night?"

I tried to look like I was searching memory. "No. No, nothing I can recall."

She persisted. "RJ, you weren't in a bar fight with some motorcycle gang?"

"No, no really. Nothing to speak of." RJ attempted to appear casual. I have never seen anyone look so guilty.

"Because if you had, it would mean we went from an off-world police investigation to an on-world police investigation in just a matter of a few days. You know, like it was getting to be a pattern."

I tried to reinforce our lame performance. "No, actually we made some new friends last night."

"At Heidi's?"

I looked at RJ. "We did stop at Heidi's, didn't we?"

"Yes, yes I do recall that. I had a root beer."

"Well, I don't see any black eyes or bruises, so if you two are not being perfectly honest with me, at least I know you must have represented the agency well."

RJ tried again to help. "That is always our intention."

She gave him a disbelieving glance. "Although Wilson does have a big red spot on his neck."

"I believe he got that shaving," I said, completing our pathetic attempt at cover-up.

"Well, the police have called here twice. I don't know how they got this number. You should expect they are going to want to talk to you."

I perked up. "If they call again, would you please ask them if we can schedule that for tomorrow afternoon?"

She gave me a sarcastic half-smile. She paused and looked back over my office. The collar of the blue dress she was wearing seemed to part open more than usual. There was the posture of someone concerned about her figure's presentation. I suddenly had that feeling of a closed, private door being unexpectedly left slightly open. It caught me off guard. I made an awkward wave and began shuffling items on my desk with no particular goal in mind. She left and closed the door behind her.

Sometimes the nervous response will turn them off for good. It offers enough doubt that they return to self-evaluation with a dose of insecurity, which makes them cancel out any further daring. But with others it has no effect at all, or they decide the prey is timid enough that they are already in control. Julia was very attractive and very intelligent, but I already had my going away present with someone too special to compromise.

JR picked up on it immediately. "Uh-oh."

"So, there's talk the Colts may change their offensive coaching staff."

"Funny how things can change overnight."

"Not gonna happen."

"Why not?"

"They'll be on the road, and they'd be crazy to lose who they have."

The door suddenly pushed open and Terry Costerly stuck his head in. "Did you guys get in a fight at Heidi's last night?"

I tried to look surprised. "Why? Did someone say we were in a fight at Heidi's last night?"

"Hey, I'm your Test and Flight Director. That's one step higher than a priest. You can tell me."

"There may have been an exchange of ideas at Heidi's last night."

RJ added, "It was all in the spirit of giving."

"Well, there's steak and cake in the break room. You'd better get out there, though. Wilson has seen it."

"On our way."

Terry began to leave and then paused. "You know they say steak is good for bruising." He looked at us both for a reaction, waved off, and disappeared out the door.

On the way back from the break room I realized there had been no sign of Paris Denard. It was too much to hope he would call in sick and stay behind. As I passed by the door to his office I opened it and leaned in. No one home. There were some eight-by-ten photographs half out of a folder on his desk that caught my eye. Feeling slightly guilty, I went in and stood by the desk. The photos were alarming. They were of the stellar drive engines, front, back, underneath, and a few partials of the top side from a portal. I did not touch them. I looked around and left.

It was a fringe violation of our agreement with the Nasebians. I had not seen him take them. It would be easy for him to claim that as a propulsion engineer he was simply curious about a completely new drive system and wanted to know as much as he could. It was also possible he was collecting information for someone else. I wondered if this could be turned into enough of a violation of the Nasebian contract to expel him from the program. Back in my office, I leaned back in my chair and thought it over.

On my desk was my own set of eight-by-ten glossies, one for each crewmember with a career summary attached. I looked through them one by one with great affection, and stopped at the photo of Paris Denard. What kind of impression would his prying make on Nasebian dignity? They were tough beings to understand.

The Nasebians were so far ahead of us in evolution there was no hope of getting to know them. Their life expectancy of two thousand years or more seemed to make their perception of things far too broad for us to empathize. It was only necessity that finally elicited an Earth visit from a Nasebian representative. A single equation for light speed travel made in chalk on an antique blackboard in the messy one-room dormitory of a kid too young to drive had triggered the end of an age. The age of innocence was over. The age of cosmic puberty had begun. With the advent of light speeds something more than long reach had changed for human beings. The term 'humankind' became a designation specifically for Homo sapiens, the most populous species on Earth, while the expression 'mankind' suddenly embodied all of the biped, intelligent races resident to our galaxy. The word sapien, Latin for 'wise', was no longer the sole property of homo, our all-inclusive ape-evolved genus. Earth's secret non-disclosure pacts quickly evaporated into thin air. UFOs were no longer required to hide unless their presence was disruptive or inappropriate. We had gone from the fallacy of believing we were the most intelligent race in the galaxy to being elementaries on a campus too large to imagine. And to this day many people refuse to accept the idea other intelligent species exist, causing concerned world governments to do their limited best not to force that mind-expanding awareness upon them.

What very few people are told is that now, when a long-range spacecraft ventures out into uncharted space, it secretly takes along a Nasebian emissary to help us avoid being bulls in a china shop. Only the captain and first officer are aware, and even they undergo months of special training before being informed. There are social constraints involved with the Nasebian race. Apparently the Nasebians abhor being in close physical contact with humans. Offensive to them is the particulate matter we exhale with each breath and the olfactory elements our bodies exude wherever we go. There is also the undesirable epidermal and follicle debris. I learned of the Nasebians and their insulting repulsions on my previous mission, only because the first officer became incapacitated and his job dropped into my lap. Not having been prepared in advance that an alien emissary was onboard to prevent us from becoming stooges in space my

Captain, a man of respectable wisdom, did his best to induct me. That was just before he disappeared and left me with a stranded ship and crew being harvested by rogues.

So that last mission had been to hell and back. We had won, but we came limping back, licking our wounds, and there were quite a few. There was no real celebration in surviving. There were too many sadistic memories, images that haunted sleep and sometimes invoked themselves during the day; flashbacks brought on by the wrong combination of words, or a familiar physical object that normally would have triggered a pleasant recollection until the full memory came crashing down around it.

Had there not been a Nasebian emissary on that voyage it is doubtful we would have survived. I would visit her periodically and stand there enamored and awed in her presence, her long silver gown covering most of the luminous form beneath it, her dark eyes too penetrating to look at for more than a moment. I would think questions and before they could be vocalized, she would impress answers directly into my mind. Sometimes a brief flash of understanding would yield pages of information. Unexpectedly, she came to accept my primitiveness, but she had a constraint that could only be described as a compulsory caring for all living creatures, both good and bad. To her, the bad ones were simply less developed souls still in an elementary learning stage.

She helped us barely enough to avoid being destroyed. At one point, I returned to her broken and barely alive. She had touched me and healed me and left an imprint of something beyond love, something I knew would always be there. That alliance had left me no choice but to accept the Nadir mission. She knew she could trust me. She knew more about me than I did.

In the end I had come away with the friendship of a creature so advanced I had no way of understanding what that meant. And to commemorate that, she left me a parting gift. When I checked her secret quarters at mission's end she was gone, but there sitting on a pedestal in her sparsely decorated stateroom was a strange crystal the size of a walnut, a keepsake I still visit often. Color slowly flows and ebbs within it, and if you hold it in your hand it evokes images in your mind. There have been messages from within it. It is a perplexing and unsettling thing to behold.

I dug in my pocket and drew out the cotton satchel. There would be no emissary with us on this mission, but the crystal would be coming along. I took it out, sat it on the desk, and watched it glow and fade through the colors of the spectrum. I lifted the picture of Paris Denard. My plan was solid. At the space station, if I did not get an adequate time-window to leave him behind, I would have him paged to the other end of

176 | E.R. Mason

the station. That would give enough time. When I ordered the hatches sealed, the others would know. There would probably be silent celebrations. I leaned back and stared at Paris' picture, wondering that I did not feel more guilt. Suddenly movement out of the corner of my eye caught my attention. The crystal had begun a slow turn on the desktop. I dropped the photo and stared. It picked up speed, faster and faster. It became a spinning blur like an airplane propeller. To my astonishment, it lifted off the desk and hovered six inches above it, spinning and glowing in place. It did not stop or slow. Finally, I reached out an open hand beneath it; afraid it might fly away and be lost. The spin slowed and it settled into my palm. I closed my hand and held it with my eyes shut. There was a message. It was clear. 'You need Paris Denard.'

I opened my hand. The crystal had returned to its passive state. Swirling blue-green flowed within. A gentle vibration of calm filled my hand. I sat back stunned and bewildered.

Chapter 27

T-minus zero day. In the SPF ready room, we drew straws to see who would take left seat to the space station. I made sure I did not get the short straw so that someone else would have the honor. Doc won. A fitting tribute.

There were few people on the tarmac as we walked to the spacecraft. A misty morning with a big red ball rising. Most of the Genesis team was there, including Julia Zeller. The ground support guys stayed back out of the way, their launch preps complete. Everything that needed to be said had been. We quietly boarded and strapped in. Shelly took the right seat. Wilson and RJ at the engineering stations. Danica and I in the back with Erin and Paris behind us.

Doc gave us a very smooth ride up and parked in an orbit where we could chase down the station fairly quickly. Docking maneuvers require all personnel to be strapped in, so we remained in our seats. Personally, I enjoyed the ride up, but as soon as we hit zero-G Paris looked sick again.

We caught up to the Wheel and with permission from Station Approach Control, mated to a docking port in the center hub, so gently that you could barely feel contact. Danica and I applauded. There was a mad rush to unbuckle and look out windows. When the pressure had equalized enough to open up, everyone except the two pilots coasted into the station receiving area to sign in and explore the sections open to them. Passive artificial gravity was available just beyond the spoke tunnels. Doc and Shelly remained behind, taking their time with the shutdown procedures. Technicians from the station were already waiting outside the airlock so they could enter and begin the final checks on Griffin's Nav system. The numbers had added up perfectly on our run to the brown dwarf, but the trip we were about to attempt required calibration standards beyond imagination.

Long ago my heart had been affianced in a serious relationship with a woman who held a pending lease on one of the
station's laboratories, an orbiting parcel quite valuable. It was
located in the nine-zero sector on the second level. When the
PHD occupying the lab was suddenly charged with ethics viola-
tions, my heart's desire found her lease unexpectedly activated.
She immediately rid herself of me in a less than congenial way.

I wondered if she was still there. I did a quick soul
search and decided not to go find out. As I pulled myself along
the station's padded spoke tube, public service posters marked
the way. 'In case of sudden depressurization, report immediately to the nearest designated security area'. 'Always know where
the nearest designated security area is located'. 'Visitors must
remain within public access areas.' Several other signs reminded
us of materials not allowed on station. The last one was the
best. It was scrawled in large letters on poster paper and taped
to the wall; 'To stop station rotation, run in the opposite direction'.

Gravity began to have influence, coercing me to hold to
the mini ladders along the wall. Soon it became an all out climb
down. A pressure hatch to the outer wheel opened automatically
as I descended toward it. I stepped down into the luxurious carpeted public area where a restaurant, bookstore, and coffee
shop mall made me feel as though I had somehow ended up in
an airport mezzanine. I spotted Wilson in the coffee shop buying
two mugs. He saw me and waved.

This would be our last taste of gravity for a while. Passive artificial gravity is a strange commodity. The world outside
the windows whirls slowly around as the big wheel turns, but to
you the station is parked perfectly still. They say that in the next
few years active electronic gravity field generators will become
so efficient that it will be the end of rotating space stations,
spacecraft, and water-tank training facilities. They say it will
also eventually be the end of zero-G travel altogether, which will
be a blow to the motion sickness pill makers.

The Station keeps Eastern Standard Time. We had come
in a bit early. The concourse was sparsely populated but that
was changing. People were beginning to commute. Wilson and I
sat with our backs to the windows, drank coffee and waited.

"Did you have a good time at Heidi's?"

"I'm sorry about that, Adrian. I would've been okay if he
hadn't shoved her. You can't let a thing like that go."

"I agree."

"Did we get in much trouble about that?"

"If we did, they'll have problems bringing us in."

"I guess we're wanted men, off-world and on."

"A regular James gang."

"Hee, hee."

An attractive woman in a short, amber-red skirt with a high-collared amber blouse strolled by, distracting us.

"You see Danica while all that was goin' on?" he said.

"Yes, grasshopper."

"I think she saved the back of my head. Where the hell did she learn that stuff?"

"Her parents made her study the arts from age six. Now she seems to have developed an addiction for the sparring ring. You'd better watch it."

"That's a dangerous talent, you know."

"I know."

"Too much clean fighting makes you vulnerable when things get down and dirty."

"I know."

"You get surprised when the real punishment starts. Subconsciously you're not expecting to get cut, and when it happens you lose some focus."

"I have a few of those."

"Me too."

He sipped his coffee and got that far away look in his eye. A page came over a nearby loudspeaker. "Commander Tarn, please report to the Griffin."

It was a surprisingly short visit. We returned to the Griffin to a chorus of praise and awe at how well the ship's navigation system was set up. They had never seen programming of such cyclomatic complexity. The tolerances were beyond what they had expected. They wanted to know what group did the initial setups. What equipment was used for the final alignments? I had to plead innocence to it all. They gathered up their equipment and headed off in a bunch, rambling on about the artistry of the A.I. just experienced, something to add to the 'remember when' list for natural born geniuses who live in a mindset of zeros and ones.

One by one, I called the crew back. They were all brisk about it, except for Paris Denard. He had to be persuaded to return no less than three times. Ironically, my original plan of abandoning him would have been a piece of cake.

Danica asked for the helm. Everyone approved. I took the copilot seat. At physical separation she swung us around and outside to a position above the South Pole, far enough away to be adequately clear of Earth's influence, a synchronous orbit and spacecraft alignment that made us an arrowhead at Earth's South Pole. In the back they set the main view screens to the rear-looking cameras for last looks at Earth. On the flight deck we all chose a personal monitor and did the same. This time there were no ecliptic bodies to be concerned with. We would be literally diving away from Earth, straight down. After a forty-five minute wait for the proper trajectory, Danica tapped in the pre-launch sequence and the Griffin automatically thrust its nose to precisely the right direction and tracked it there.

She pressed the intercom, "Is everyone ready?"

RJ responded. "Wait, I think I left the water running."

There were moans and groans.

With a five-second countdown, she punched the engage button. We were pressed back into our seats and watched Earth's blue quickly fade to become a small star. Just as quickly it disappeared from view, leaving only our sun shrinking in the distance behind us.

Chapter 28

The Griffin became our world. Cold, empty vacuum waited just outside its thin shell. It did not take long for someone to set the habitat module's walls, ceiling, and floor to display a portion of Yellowstone, with open portals of distant stars interrupting the illusion. At light speeds, the stars always seem to look different. There is no distortion or phase-shifted coloring, but there is the feeling of being inside a cosmic bubble looking out. The fact the stars pass so slowly, even as you travel at speeds that are powers of light, makes you realize your greatest concept of distance remains wanting.

We began our pilot and engineering rotations. Pilot teams of two on twelve-hour shifts, with each pilot required to log six hours as pilot in command. We could switch off and take breaks as desired as long as we put in our six. Danica and Shelly asked to be a team. That left Doc and me. Only one engineer needed to maintain station on the engineering consoles, so for them it was rotating six-hour shifts, with a designated backup for breaks.

We settled into a smooth daily pattern of keeping busy. On the flight deck some of the digital readouts were spinning like tops, so fast you could not read them, but outside the forward windows it always looked as though the ship was barely moving. The pilots had their overhead monitors set to display the external cameras all around so they could see the stars in every direction. In the habitat module there was always someone mag-locked in a chair at the oval table, reading or writing on a tablet. RJ had a particular seat he used to play solitaire with his slightly magnetic deck of cards. Occasionally a card would get away and he would snatch it out of the air and pat it back down. Poker games and other pastimes fell into a schedule of sorts with varying participants, some experienced, some not. The table became a place for the meeting of minds. Paris had been resident in the bathroom for the first three days, just as he had on the brown dwarf mission. We slated him for engineering shifts, but for those first three days he was a no-show. He set a new standard for someone incompatible with space travel.

Griffin was large enough that we weren't in each other's face. Since there were usually two or three people manning the flight deck, the remaining five tended to spread out in the gym, the science lab, the aft airlock, the sleeper compartments, and the habitat area. There seemed to be enough privacy. The wall displays changed often and were sometimes exotic. I once passed by RJ with his sleeper cell open. He was lying in a boat on a river, with tangerine trees and marmalade skies, as he described it. He claimed it was something from an ancient music album.

When the time seemed right, I held an impromptu meeting using the forward airlock and flight deck and blew everyone's mind by revealing that the Griffin had long-range communications, shields, and weapons. With the concealed panels opened they got a crash course in the use of those and a stern lecture of when it would be appropriate and when not. The weapons were off-limits to everyone except pilots since spacecraft maneuvering was a part of the operation. Copilots could run the sim program for practice at their convenience.

That discussion on special attributes set me up nicely to go into our mission objectives and mission sponsors. I did my best to explain how unexplainable the Nasebian race was, and went into as much detail as I had on the lost Nasebian spacecraft, its purpose, and the artifact we were to locate and recover. I must have done a pretty good job, because afterward they all seemed somewhat dumbfounded and unable to find any questions to ask. They had all read the mission briefing documents. They were probably hoping I would clarify the portions that skimmed over the advanced cultural and scientific differences of the Nasebian race, attributes which were actually beyond human understanding. Our impromptu meeting broke up with many looks of consternation and no discussion at all.

The conclusion of our first leg eventually would be marked by a rendezvous with an unexplored celestial body designated as ZY627a, detected some time ago by a deep space probe but never visited by an Earth ship. It was farther away than anyone had ever been. Probe data indicated the presence of water and possibly vegetation. The agency considered it a win-win place for us to make a stop. It would signal our entry into unexplored space and provide a good location for a relay station. For the first time, data originating in deep south polar ecliptic space would be sent back from what might possibly be an Earth-like planet capable of supporting human outposts on future flights. We were to park in orbit, evaluate a landing, and if feasible put down and set up the relay station. If the environment was hospitable we could take a brief shore leave and collect specimens. It would take us eight weeks to get there, a five hundred light year plunge.

Doc turned out to be one hell of a card player. The man could bluff a psychic. He claimed it was from years of lying to his patients. I sat with two fives showing and a pair of aces in my hand. He had two fours on the table, kept raising, and every time I caught him looking at his hand, I'd swear I saw the reflection of the third four in his eye. It was so persuasive I had to fold, and then of course as the bastard raked in the magnetic pot he wouldn't tell me if he had it or not.

Erin was a card shark in her own right as well. She tried to play the distraction game. She kept asking him about his past and his MD status. She pressed him on the subject, wanting to know how a medical man could end up spending most of his time in a cockpit. Doc was not shy about it.

"Actually, I don't mind telling that story cause there's some stuff people ought to know about doctoring. I was the gifted child growing up. Went into college pre-med when I was sixteen. I had a good take on things. Figured healing people had to be the most beneficial thing a person could do. Breezed through college in three but then the intern crap started. It's when you learn there's something wrong with a whole bunch of the residents you're following around. You don't realize the system has driven them batty until it's too late. You're already strapped in and going along on the same ride. If you survive the breakneck pace of internship and the frequent pummeling that goes along with it, they find you guilty of being ready and throw you into triage. They don't believe in letting you hone your newly applied skills at a reasonable rate. They cast you into a nonstop mess of every illness and injury imaginable where you only get seconds to diagnose, and when you're wrong sometimes somebody dies. They consider that an important part of the training. By the time you get your license to practice you are not the same dude you were, and you are not the dude you intended to be. And so the practitioner becomes licensed to be as eccentric as he wants to allow him to put aside all the hell he didn't expect to go through to get there. For me, I needed something intense to get away from it. I started drinking, only on off-hours, mind you. Didn't want any more nightmares added to the ones I was already keeping. All that, and I was only 27 years old. Lucky for me there was a big air show outside of Dallas one year. I took a ride in an old P38 trainer. The guy scared the hell outa' me so bad it made me realize I had forgotten everything while I was up there. And that was it. I started flying weekends and seeing patients during the week. Then it became three-day weekends. Then one day I sat up in bed and realized I was flying more days than I was being a practitioner. I did a stint in the National Guard as a med-vac pilot. Started doing air shows on weekends. Kept up with my medical certs, but only did volunteer work at local clinics. And so, there you have it, kiddies: the real true nature of medicine and the practice thereof."

"Amazing," replied Erin.

"Ah, but not so much more than your own story, I'm betting," said Doc.

"What do you mean?"

"Well, a darling young thing perfectly sculpted for some fashion designer's fancy, and yet you chose to be a greasemonkey, my dear; a member of my own club if you think about it. How could such an unlikely pairing as that be possible?"

Erin laughed. "I was my father's daughter, as they say. It began with the handing of tools when I was six or seven. My parents noticed I had an affection for powered vehicles so they got me a plastic, motorized racer. I ran it inside too fast so I was evicted to the back yard. I couldn't get it to go fast enough out there, so one day I taped ten of my brothers model rockets to it and hooked the igniters to the battery with a switch in the driver's compartment. I got the thing up to full speed outside on the sidewalk, where I was not allowed to go, and then fired off the rockets. It only gave me another couple miles per hour, but my parents happened to step outside just as I went by and it scared the crap out of them. From that time on they kept a closer eye on what I was doing, and they accepted that my vocation was all but chosen."

Erin looked at me. "What about you, Adrian? What's your story?"

"Oh no. I have a past but I choose not to account for it."

RJ shuffled and laughed under his breath. "It's just as well, my fellow tube stuffers. Anything he might say would need parental guidance."

Erin persisted. She twisted around and called to the flight deck. "Hey, Wilson, is Adrian's secret past really that bad?"

Wilson leaned back and looked out from his engineering station. "If you're talking about that time in Delaware, it was blown all out of proportion. Nobody had a flamethrower. That was all a lie."

RJ dealt. "I rest my case."

We made it through the next four weeks with few problems. Paris Denard's sullenness gave everyone the creeps, but other than that the ride was enjoyable. The company I had chosen to keep turned out to be solid, reliable people who knew how to make the best of any situation. The fact that we were closing in on ZY627a perked everyone's interest. There were frequent guests on the flight deck. RJ began asking, "Are we there yet?"

I was stretched out in my sleeper watching a very old video called Apollo 13 when I got a call. I had just about decided it was the wrong thing to be watching when you're several hundred light years from Earth in an untested spacecraft.

'Commander, report to the flight deck' was an unusual way of calling me after so many weeks together. I shut down the movie, opened up, and pushed out.

There were six of them squeezed into the flight deck; Danica and Shelly up front, RJ and Wilson at Engineering, Erin and Doc suspended between them. They had to maneuver out of the way for me to enter.

RJ spoke. "It's the secondary high gain scanning antenna; suddenly went completely dead. No collision avoidance systems warnings, but maybe something small hit it. Or, maybe it just died."

"And the primary?"

"Just fine. All the other systems are just fine."

Wilson, added, "We can live without it, Adrian, but standard procedure is to go out and fix it."

"Mmm. So the options are, hold light and wait until we're parked in orbit, or drop out now, fix it, and go back to light. That's an iffy little choice, isn't it? Anyone have an opinion?"

Erin piped up. "Fix it."

I nodded. "You know what? I'd like to get in a good inspection of Griffin before we drop into anybody's gravity field. So let's do it. Danica set it up and shut us down. Who's got the most background on scanning arrays?"

Before anyone else could answer, Erin barged in, "Me!"

We all knew it was Wilson. Nobody said anything. I looked at Wilson. He nodded.

"Okay, you'd better go set up a suit then. RJ, want to be her suit tech? As soon as you're done, we'll all strap in for decel."

Erin threw herself happily toward the back. RJ pushed out and followed.

"So Danica and Shelly, program us to resume as soon as we're back inside. Wilson, if we have any problems we will call you."

"If I'm not here, leave a message."

"Funny, Wilson. Really funny."

We strapped in for deceleration, and as the stellar drives wound down to station keeping Erin and I unbuckled and headed back. In the airlock, I secretly marveled at her. We sat, waiting for the pressures in our suits to drop to green, watching RJ seal us in. The long ivory-blonde hair was tied back and bundled under her white stretch cap, but it only made her look more childlike. She had that pink aura about her face surrounding the delicate, fine lines of a newborn. I had to steal glances so she would not catch me looking. Her beauty was a complete contrast to the techno-rigidity of the spacesuit helmet and visor. Her face behind the clear glass did not seem real. When the suits gave us the ready signal, I hit the door control and was finally distracted by distant stars coming into view.

That familiar feeling of first-step-outside returned. Each time your mind searches for new ways to define it. A feeling of emptiness and vulnerability as if you don't have a suit on at all, always so overwhelming it takes something away. You notice Mother Earth's absence even though it does not come as a surprise. The curtain of stars all around are too far away to be surrogate companions.

A pang of fear hit me as I turned to look at Griffin. With no other ships nearby she suddenly looked tiny. It was another stark, familiar reminder that we were delicate human forms kept alive in a vacuum by only this man-made eggshell. Even with all the EVA hours I had spent embraced by this special brand of cold, there was apparently still some fear left. I turned and looked for Erin. She was parked too close over my right shoulder. Through her clear visor I realized the newness of that same fear had gripped her much more tightly. I tapped the private com button on my spacesuit sleeve. "Just like the simulations, Erin."

She was gutsy. Many people with that same look on their face would not have been able to speak. She stared into the emptiness and without looking away said, "No, not the same. It's God out here."

I had never heard it put quite that way. Perhaps it was the only title you could put on something so inconceivably enormous and yet at the same time expanding all around you. Perhaps, with everything else removed, that really was what you were suspended within.

"You ready to head up?"

She fumbled with her backpack arms and jetted slightly the wrong way, but quickly corrected. "Ready."

We thrusted above the retracted wing toward the back of the ship, then up the side to the tail section where the scanning arrays were located. There were service rings to clip to and the access panels were topside and in our faces, easy to remove. I folded back my control arms and with Erin clipped next to me, pulled out the fastener remover and began opening the twelve-inch service panel for the secondary array antenna amplifier. Even through the suit I could feel cold on the panel and fasteners. This would be an easy-level repair. Pull out the black box, shove in its replacement, close up the patient and you're done. The exterior service lighting was doing a good job. Sometimes the fasteners bind, but this time they did not. The package came out so smoothly it surprised me and the new one went in just as nicely. I called in. "How's that look, guys?"

Wilson's voice came over the com. "Hold there a minute."

I held the compartment cover in place but waited before securing it. Finally, Wilson came back. "Wow! That's it, you guys. You're good."

Erin helped with the plate as I got the fasteners started, then torqued everything down. When it was done, I held up one glove. It took her a minute to understand, but she finally high-fived me. Her first high-five in space. We stowed our stuff, pulled down our thrust controls and unhooked. If it had been Wilson we would have separated and each taken a side of the ship to inspect, but Erin still had that look on her face. So we stayed together. We jetted over the top of the tail, and down around to the underside. Griffin's skin still looked new. Erin held too close, occasionally bumping me. I tried not to notice.

We coasted along the underside and came up around the nose. They had set the windows to transparent and four of them were in there waving at us. Erin forgot herself for the moment and began waving back wildly. I had to pause for her to catch up.

Griffin looked great. She was ready for another five hundred light years. We sealed in the airlock and sat waiting for our suits to come up to pressure and our air mix to bleed down to cabin air. When the time came, Erin twisted off her helmet and there was a smile from ear to ear that she could not hide. We did not waste time. We strapped back in and made the jump. Next stop, ZY627a.

Chapter 29

ZY627a was a wonder to see. Big yellow guardian sun in the distance, about the size of our own. Danica parked us in a fairly low orbit, roughly two hundred miles up. From there the view below was spectacular. The blues were bluer and the greens greener, although it is said weeks of dark space will do that to you. We did not see desert anywhere. The planet was rich with nature.

Wilson and RJ worked the scans. The rest of us hung at the windows with binocs for when interesting terrain demanded a closer look. The first thing I began to notice was that the vegetation appeared to be super-sized. The preliminary reports from the engineering stations suggested a lower planetary mass and lower gravity. We were too far up to spot any bio forms, but no one doubted there were some down there.

When the first computer analysis came in, everyone was overjoyed. Oxygen rich, slightly less ambient pressure, tropical temperatures. It was looking like shore leave was a good bet. Personally, I had too many scars to bet on it. I wanted trace element readings and a complete atmospheric composition before we'd even consider going down. I also wanted life form scans and analysis. Doc was already certain we'd be making a landing. He was in charge of the Earth relay station and headed back to the science lab to set it up. After two hours on orbit there were some strange scan reflections but nothing to prevent a landing. Animal bio signatures showed groups within the denser forests but never in the open. There were occasional shadowy imprints on the bio scanners so large the engineer's best guess was bio-atmospheric interference, possibly concentrated flocks of birds.

The vegetation was dense enough that it left few obvious places to put down. We spent another hour doing surface mapping and finally came up with an area mixed with large rocks and flora where quite a few clearings existed. I could feel the anticipation building.

Our descent plan was designed around the possibility of having to leave quickly if a problem arose. Doc and I would set up the relay station. Wilson would stand by in the door of the forward airlock with a weapon. Erin had some horticulture training so she would come outside with us to take some quick specimens. Once the ground station was set up, if there were no problems, two-man teams would secure the area and begin rotations off the ship. Both airlocks would be left open so that fresh air could circulate.

When the FMC was properly programmed with coordinates we came around on orbit, drank down our re-G mind-numbing medicine regimen, and strapped in. The ride down was smooth, suggesting a very stable upper atmosphere. Everyone was beaming when braking cut in and we felt the slight bounce of ground beneath our wheels. In the forward airlock Wilson popped the door open and a warm rush of garden air flowed past us.

The place was beyond beautiful. A picture of Eden. A land of untouched color and vibrancy. There was a wide clearing just outside the airlock door. Large green and yellow leaf vegetation bordered both sides, with short, bright blue needle-covered trees here and there. Twenty yards away a black, house-sized boulder glistened in the light. Even with the pull of gravity dragging at us it was still an uplifting sight.

I forced myself to leave the view and hauled my heavy body back to the science lab where Doc, looking a bit haggard, was bent over the relay station making some final adjustments. It was a brass-colored circular station, chest-high, with four adjustable legs meant to keep it in place until we drilled stanchions into the soil to anchor it. As I entered, he stood and grabbed the handle on his side and waited. I picked up the porta-drill by the door, slung it over my shoulder, and found my handle. Together we lifted the relay station, tried not to look labored, and jockeyed our way down the airlock ramp into fresh air. Erin was already out, collecting plant life and exploring. Wilson was on one knee just inside the forward airlock with a short-barreled pulse rifle raised and ready.

The earth felt strange beneath our feet: rich black dirt with patches of a strange triangular-bladed grass. We quickly picked a spot, put the station package down, and set up the lightweight drill. It burrowed into the soil with ease. When we had four good holes, we set the station in place and deployed the stanchions, then covered them in and packed the dirt down. Doc opened the top and began powering up the station and raising antennae.

My part of the relay station work was done. I backed up, wiped my hands, and took a look around. It was the last real look I got. We had all relaxed. Safe landing. Beautiful paradise to explore. Relay station almost ready to transmit. That's when it usually happens. Just when you think the danger has passed.

The thing appeared overhead so quickly there was no chance to anticipate. It was the size of an airliner and looked like some kind of giant praying mantis. Two little front legs rubbing together twenty feet above my head. Two large insect eyes staring down, interested only in us.

I yelled, looked for Erin and made a dash in her direction. Doc went for the airlock. I pulled my weapon and fired on the run. My beam intersected Wilson's. Both shots went through the creature's main body and had no effect. As we fired a column of rings fell from the creature's mouth and captured Doc halfway to the Griffin. In the same motion, a green liquid gushed down and filled the rings, engulfing him. In a fraction of a second, the whole thing was sucked backed up into the mouth. Doc was gone.

With our beams still passing through it, the thing disappeared back the way it had come. I yanked Erin by the arm and with her in tow made it to the Griffin and dove into the forward airlock. Wilson's voice called "clear' and a split second later we were in a vertical ascent that had to be nine Gs. I wanted to yell 'Hold at ten thousand' but the air was crushed out of my lungs and my face was plastered to the airlock floor. At eight thousand, the airlock doors closed automatically. A moment later, I felt forward thrust as the G-force eased. As soon as I could I pushed myself up. Erin's eyes were open. I grabbed her arm. "Are you hurt?" She shook her head.

I pulled myself up past Wilson and into the flight deck. RJ was still at his engineering console, his face snow white. "RJ, can we track it?"

It took him several excruciating moments to gather himself. He shook his head. "None of the scanners picked it up. Not even the optics saw it until it was right on top of us. If I hadn't been looking at the monitor I wouldn't even have known it was there. I think the thing was translucent. It was invisible right up until it attacked. If we went back down there'd be nothing to track or search for."

"We know the general direction it took. Have you looked for any kind of trail? Temperature, pressures, trace bio signs, anything?"

"I did that before we pancaked up, Adrian. There's nothing to track. That's why they weren't seen before landing."

I cursed under my breath and looked back into the habitat module. Paris was floating face down and out cold. "Is anyone hurt?"

No answer. Stunned silence.

Danica spoke. "We're parked back in our original orbit, Adrian. What are your orders?"

"Hold orbit for further instructions." I pulled myself back through the airlock, glancing at Wilson and Erin who were still pulling themselves together after the nine-G ride.

In the habitat module I grabbed the unconscious Paris and strapped him in a seat. His arms floated outward like a ghost.

I tried to think. It wasn't working. I needed to go over what had just happened, but my mind was refusing. I held to the ceiling and watched as a small string of drool floated out of Paris' mouth. His glazed eyes opened and searched for reality. He looked up at me and his psyche came quickly up to speed.

"Well, I hope you're satisfied now, Tarn. It was inevitable that something like this would happen. I'm surprised only one of us is dead. The loose way you operate, it could have been more. It probably will be."

"Cap it, Denard. This isn't the time. I need to think."

He unbuckled and pushed himself up. "I wonder how much time we have left with you around, you incompetent idiot. I'm surprised I'm not dead. Now you've killed Doc. Doesn't that mean anything to you?"

He kept on for too long. Something in my head snapped. He awkwardly stuck his face in too close. His lips were still moving but I couldn't hear. Out of nowhere, my right hand suddenly appeared in a hook and caught him just on the left jawbone. His eyes popped open wide and in slow motion he tumbled over backwards toward the sleeper cell compartments. A single droplet of blood escaped the corner of his mouth as he went. Erin had come back and was hanging there. She grabbed the unconscious form and worked her way back toward the science lab with it.

Wilson came up alongside me. "Nice one. Two more seconds and it would have been another one on my permanent record."

RJ floated by. "Thank you. The man was out of control. Now if you two will excuse me, I'm going to the restroom and throw my guts up."

Wilson looked more distressed than I had ever seen him. "What are your orders, Adrian?"

I tried to snap myself out of it. "What?"

"What are your orders?"

"Oh, ah, ask Danica and Shelly to park us on orbit and hold for further instruction."

"I'll pass it on, but you've already said that." He pushed off toward the flight deck.

I looked around for a place to escape to and found there was none, then realized what had happened on the planet's surface was actually the thing I was trying to flee. There was nowhere to hide. I had those ugly, desperate little feelings you get when someone close dies, the feeling that maybe something will reset and everything will be okay with just a big scare engram left over. Then I searched for a way to go back in time so it could all be fixed. Every possibility had to be considered.

There was no way out. I had just lost a friend. A good one. As I admitted helplessness to myself, Danica came back from the flight deck.

"Anything I can do?"

"Yes. Would you work out a three pilot shift schedule? One pilot up front for eight hours with a designated backup. You and Shelly were supposed to be off in a few minutes, so I'll take the first shift. It'll give me some time to sort out where we go from here. Does that sound okay?"

"Shelly's been in the left seat the past six. I can ride up front with you for a while if you want."

"Thanks, but the three of us need to make sure we get enough rest since the shifts will be longer. I'll be okay. Will you be okay?"

"I'll be as okay as anyone can be."

"We'll have a full crew meeting as soon as everyone has had a little time to come to terms. Keep an eye on everyone for me, would you?"

"I'll do my best."

I went forward to the flight deck and put my hand on Wilson's shoulder as I passed him. He stopped me. "You know I burned that thing good right where the heart should've been. It took the beam for a good twenty seconds. Your beam came in a split second after mine. Neither one did a damn thing. Didn't bother it a bit."

"I know."

"Your shot cut through the head, too. Two beams, no effect. What the hell else could we have done?"

"If you think of anything, let me know. It's a bitch."

"Shit!"

I tapped Shelly on the shoulder. She looked up sympathetically and pushed out of her seat. I squeezed by and lowered myself in. She handed me the pilot's log and headed back. Wilson watched from behind as I went through the checklist. Neither of us had anything else to say, because there was nothing else to say.

Chapter 30

Desperate scanning found no additional traces of the creature. It was a new kind of nightmare. I had lost people before but never that quickly and never that unexpectedly. And, it was a cheat. It had happened so fast there was very little memory to replay in search of understanding. We had set up the relay station, then twenty seconds later Doc was gone. Should I have reacted differently? How? There had been no time to react at all. Could I have tried to make myself the creature's target so the others could escape? How could I have done that? If I can't figure it out now, how could I have in those twenty seconds?

I speed-read the pilot's checklist, lost my temper, and threw it at the floor. It had very little mass. It rushed downward, bounced off, and floated away. As if in response to the emotional outburst a power alarm popped up on the system's monitor and began chirping. I looked back at Wilson who had taken a seat at RJ's engineering station. He shrugged. It was an easy problem to correct. For me, it was a good problem to have. It forced the analytical portion of my mind to kick back in and focus. We reset the phase balance for the system and the master alarm chirped a last time and cleared.

There could be no time for soul searching or mourning. We were in orbit around a strange planet many light years from home, and we still had a long way to go. Command does not allow the luxury of sentimental self-abuse, or perhaps command has the greatest excuse of all to put that off until later. Any commander would be negligent to give himself to the lost, rather than being responsible to the living. Mine were scattered about the ship, trying to get a handle on the unthinkable. By ducking out to the flight deck, I was not helping. I tapped the intercom. "Danica, please come up."

It took her less than a minute. She started to climb into the copilot seat, but I held up a hand. "Would you take the spacecraft and call everyone up here?"

I pushed out and let her slip into the seat. She switched on the intercom. "All personnel, please report to the flight deck."

I hung by the empty engineering station next to Wilson and watched them gather in the forward airlock. Last to arrive was Shelly and Paris. She was helping him along, talking all the way. He still looked a little dazed as though he was unsure exactly what had happened. To my surprise, there was no pang of guilt associated with seeing him.

When I had their attention, I did my best to sound consoling. "Here's where we are. All ship systems are online and nominal. We're parked in a stable orbit. Obviously there will be no further landings on ZY627a. RJ, did Doc finish activating the relay station before we lost him?"

"Yes, Adrian. It is scanning and transmitting."

"Would you or Wilson please download a repeating warning to its send folder, something that will go out regularly to warn other ships of the danger down there?"

"No problem."

"Okay, I know how you all feel, but we need to continue on. We would not gain anything by returning to Earth at this point. We would have spent months in space and not accomplished what we came to do. So if anybody knows of any reason that would prevent us from breaking orbit and continuing, now's the time."

Silence.

"We'll set up and make the jump as soon as we're in position. Last chance, does anyone have any input why we shouldn't do that?"

I expected Paris to begin again. He floated silently beside Shelly.

"I believe all of us are with you, Adrian," said Shelly.

"RJ or Wilson, before we break orbit, would you use the Nasebian FM transmitter and send back a communication explaining everything that happened and that we've lost Doc? It'll still take a long time to get there but at least they'll know as soon as possible. I do not believe he had any remaining family except for his ex-wife, but he had a lot of friends."

"I'll write something up," said Erin.

"Great. Maybe just before we break orbit we can all get together and have a small service for him. I'm not so good at that. Anyone willing to help, I would appreciate it. I'm sorry for what you've all just been through. I think we did everything we knew to do. I don't know what we could have done differently. If there's anything I can do to help any of you through this, please come and see me. I'll do whatever I can. Do your best to focus on what's ahead. I know it's not easy. That's all I have. Does anyone have anything else to add?"

They did not. The air was still heavy with shock and grief. It had been far from a qualified motivational speech but at least it set them to preparing for the next jump. We came around on our loop, and thirty minutes before break-orbit time everyone quietly regrouped in the forward airlock. I put aside my guilt trip and said my best words, all empty, futile expressions of loss. Others made better offerings. Wilson suggested a toast to Doc and there was a discomfited scramble to grab our squeeze bottles. We toasted our lost crewmate and paused for a moment of silence. With no further addresses I changed places with Danica to resume my scheduled shift. She took the copilot seat for the jump as everyone else strapped in. Despite the ceremony, it felt like we were leaving Doc behind. At the designated time we broke orbit and took a position beyond ZY627a, and with a five count the FMC engaged and once again, we became light.

There was one thing I had intentionally left out of my inept little speech: the void. It would mark our departure from the Orion Spiral Arm into the zone that separated the Sagittarius Arm. Ship's computers would record an ingress never before made by humans. I had to hope that we were not going from one bad dream to another. The flight path blue line on the navigation display showed us beginning that deep crossing in less than a week. We would be inside for two. Since the Nasebians provided our charting it was almost certainly accurate. The classified Nasebian Nadir mission documents warned that no stars would be seen once within the void, an isolation that could give the impression the spacecraft was not moving. Pilots would need to maintain a mindset in which they trusted instrumentation completely, and not personal instinct. It was unknown whether there would be any other side effects. Stopping within was not recommended.

In the time we had leading up to trans-void passage, we held discussion sessions in an attempt to prepare mentally. The realization that we were about to fly into an inkwell was certainly not a morale booster, but it did help detract from the solemn attitudes left behind by the loss of Doc. As we closed in on the void we could see a fog of darkness ahead. With each passing day, it grew larger and larger. The rear-facing cameras showed a wall of stars. The forward cameras and windows began to show nothing. In a strange way, the area ahead looked like silence waiting. It was as though the essence of want had claimed this area of space for its own.

We plummeted into it and watched all the monitor cameras suddenly go dark. I happened to be in the pilot seat when it happened. It was exactly as described. All the instruments were still clicking and spinning away. The digital readouts were racing along. The blue line on our navigation displays continued to move and track, but aside from those electronic reassurances there was no sense of time or distance at all. Everyone hung at the portals trying to see something in nowhere. There was nothing to focus on, no depth or dimension. There was more spatial sensation in a sleeper compartment with the lights off than there was outside our portals.

We had been humans existing in the vacuum of space in a tin can. We were now humans existing in a tin can in nothingness. Somehow, we had lost something. We were smart enough to understand, but too human not to feel it.

The daily routines resumed. The habitat table games slowly resurfaced. The exercise equipment in the gym was used even more. The galley jokes returned. But behind it all it felt like we were all looking over our shoulder, because what lay outside did not seem real.

On the fourth day of our exile, RJ's chessboard finally made an appearance. He had several offers, but was still after the bounty on my head. His pieces in the opening game remained symbolic of chickens that had escaped their pen. Toward the middle game he shored things up and settled in, as he always does. We drew an audience.

"This area of space reminds me of the fish story," he said as I pondered sacrificing a pawn, an outlay I always consider significant.

"I don't think I know that one."

"A young goldfish goes up to an old goldfish and says grandfather, what lies beyond our aquarium? The old goldfish says that's a very good question, grandson. We don't have all the answers, but we do know a few things. Some of us have jumped high enough out of the water to look around. Some have even jumped completely out and have miraculously returned. What we know is that the aquarium exists in a gigantic room, so large it could hold a hundred aquariums just like ours. We also know from some of the old ones that our aquarium was once located in a different room altogether, so we know that as large as our room is, there are other rooms besides this one. So, we are in a structure filled with rooms, and the structure is so large it's beyond imagination. In fact, the structure is so large it could hold thousands of aquariums like ours."

"Wow, says the young goldfish. That's amazing!"

"Yes, says the grandfather goldfish. We don't know everything, but at least we know that the structure containing all these rooms is so big that nothing can possibly lie beyond it."

I held one finger on the pawn, studying the consequences of my sacrifice. "And the void reminds you of this?"

"Yes. It looks so final out there. Like there could be nothing beyond it."

"Pawn takes pawn."

"And pawn takes pawn. Doesn't it give you the creeps?"

"I think we're all in agreement on that."

"And since there are no stars to navigate by, we're just holding course per gyros till we're through."

"True."

"There could be a big brick wall ahead and we wouldn't know it."

"No, the CAS would reflect back off it and warn us."

"Well, yes, when we got close enough. But the idea is, we really don't know what's on the other side."

"Bishop takes Knight. But that's true of all space exploration."

"Bishop takes Bishop. I don't know. This feels different." He looked at me with his Nostradamus expression. The gears were turning. Something premonise had called for the analytical RJ to kick in. Even he did not know what it was yet, but some piece of something hadn't fit quite right in the back of his mind and he was now in search mode for the underlying problem. The chess game was providing a distraction from his more elemental psyche. There was a good chance at some point he would come to me with a real problem, or at least a mystery. I could only hope it would be minor.

We played to stalemate. RJ celebrated. I begged off, turned the board over to Wilson, and headed for my sleep cell. I sealed myself inside, called up a Yosemite compartment display with an active sunset, and chomped on a moon pie from my mini refrigerator. From the overhead compartment, I drew out my Nasebian crystal and let it float above me. I hit the button on the wall and the gentle mag force drew me down to the bed cushion. The crystal drifted about. It had become its special ocean-blue passive. As it hung in the zero-G I suddenly had an idea. Gently, I spun it so that it slowly rotated. I wondered, based on the previous message about Paris Denard, if I had just activated some sort of psyche-transmitter. To my surprise, it flashed a brief pulse of red and immediately I knew that meant system off-line, even though a few moments before I had not even known there was a system at all. I captured it, placed it back in its holder and lay back with my eyes closed.

Something woke me. My cell was dark. I called for lights and they slowly came up to dim. It was 3:00A.M. I squinted myself the rest of the way awake and tapped open the sleeper cell door. All the other cells were closed. No one seemed to be up. I made my way to the flight deck and put one hand on Danica's shoulder. She looked up and gave me a tired smile.

"You need a break? I'm your relief."

"In that case, it's all yours, Sir." She rose up and moved backward out of the flight deck. No sooner had I pulled down into the copilot seat than a master power alarm cut in. Phase balance in the OMS power system, the same alarm I had cleared earlier. I did the realignment, canceled it and puzzled over the recurrence.

Danica returned with a coffee dispenser in her hand and jockeyed herself back into the left seat. "Boy, you came to the rescue just in time. The old eyelids were getting heavy. This mocha will do the trick."

"Have you had any power alarms?"

"Just one. An out of phase in the OMS."

"I just had that one for a second time. That makes three. That's too many. We'd better have the systems guys take a serious look at that. When I relieve you in the morning, I'll have one of the engineers take a look at it."

Danica smiled and raised her cup in salute. I floated up and out and headed back to my compartment to finish my assigned rest period. Power phase alarms were fairly common. Nothing to worry about.

Chapter 31

Power systems checkout began at the start of my shift. Wilson and RJ huddled at their engineering stations, running analyses while I sat sideways, watching.

"It's forward of the starboard OMS nacelle, Adrian. It's a wave guide out of alignment," said Wilson.

"An inside job or outside?"

"Inside. Access through the service module. But it's actually propulsion's territory. We'd be stepping on their toes if we went in there."

"Really?"

"Paris has done this in the simulator. I don't think Erin has."

"How big a job?"

"Probably one hour. There's some stuff to move out of the way, and then it has to be put back, of course."

"We need to drop out of light to do this?"

"You guessed it. Don't really want to go climbing around inside that part of the service module with the stellar drives just outside warping space, do we?"

"Crap."

"Yeah. Dead stop in the middle of the void."

"What happens if we don't do it?"

"The phase alarms will get more and more frequent, we could damage the power distribution system, and then we will stop in the void anyway."

"Crap."

"You really don't have choice with this."

"Is Paris out there yet?"

"Nope."

"When he wakes up, would you brief him and ask him to come up front?"

"Will do."

I sat there in the pilot's seat trying to get my head around Paris Denard repairing a critical Griffin system a million miles from rescue. The only reassurance was that his ass was in the sling just as much as ours. There was no way he'd screw around with this. He'd have to do it by the book and correctly. Right?

Paris showed up about a half-hour later more cooperative than usual. "When do you want to do this?" was his only greeting.

"Do you agree with the systems guys that it must be done?"

"Yes, unless you want to deal with more serious failures later on."

"How long do you think?"

"One to two hours."

"What do we have to shut down?"

"All power to the starboard drives, part of the ventilation system, and there's some sensor packages in the way."

"The ventilation system?"

"Yes. A section of duct has to be removed."

"And is this a physical alignment?"

"Yes, but I'll be on a headset with somebody at an engineering station. It's a beam alignment. They'll tell me when we're set right."

"Why'd this happen?"

"You know how many interfaces there are on this ship? Why wouldn't it happen?"

"But there's no dangers in the procedure, right?"

"No. There shouldn't be anything of concern."

"Okay. Would you brief the crew in case they have questions, and when you have your support people set up let me know and we'll begin the dropout?"

"Yes. I'll do that."

He pushed away and headed aft, leaving me feeling off balance. Although he wasn't cordial, he had been reasonably professional. I sat forward in the pilot seat, dreading the shutdown. The stellar drives seemed to be operating perfectly through the void, but what if they did not come back up after stopping? What if they couldn't reform a field from park? We'd be dead in space, but it wouldn't even be space as we knew it. The thought irritated me. I felt like snapping at someone. RJ coasted in.

"Are we almost ready?" I asked with indignation.

"They're setting up tools and equipment."

"Has everybody been told?"

"Just about."

"Here they come. They must be ready."

Paris, Erin, and Wilson regrouped in the flight deck. Wilson took the lead. "We're set up, Adrian. It'll be Paris and Erin in the service module crawlway and RJ and I will man the engineering stations. We need to wake Danica and Shelly up so they can strap in."

I tapped the intercom button and tried not to bark. "All personnel, please report forward."

While waiting for everyone to join us I tapped commands into the flight management computer and told it of our impending stop. A yellow line on the blue flight path appeared, anchored by a red designator showing where we would no longer be moving. The top right hand button next to the crew display indicator lit up with the word 'resume', a button I feared yet looked forward to pushing.

With everyone accounted for and strapped in, Danica and I engaged the flight plan deviation and sat back watching the speed and distance indicators spin down as the darkness outside our windows remained completely unchanged. When deceleration was complete, our status screens lit up with station keeping and we watched the silhouette indicator of our ship sit idly, occasionally firing thrusters for station keeping based on inputs from gyros since there were no stars to orientate by.

Paris and Erin wasted no time. Minutes later, the service module hatch-open indicator flashed on our screen. RJ and Wilson took their place behind us. What I hoped would be a one-hour wait began. RJ switched the intercom to overhead so we could all listen in. The tedious job of removing panels and equipment within the crawlspace of the service module began. Paris' voice sounded calm and collected. Erin sounded impatient.

One half hour into the work things did not appear to be going well. Paris and Erin came forward to explain. There were extra packages in the way, shield and communications interfacing items that had not existed in the sim. They could not give a time estimate. I had to leave my seat and pull out the classified manuals on those items so they could study the removal and installation procedures. They needed some extra tools from the science lab. For some reason, Paris wanted reassurance that the stellar drives were cold. I wanted to know why. He said it was in case they ran into any more unexpected interfacing like weapons systems, for example. He wanted to be sure they weren't live.

I had to pull Danica from the copilot seat and send her back to bed. We couldn't keep her up indefinitely. As I sat drumming my fingers on the armrest, RJ appeared and gazed down at his console.

"It's going okay back there?"

"Except for the surprises. I'm just checking the external nacelle temperatures for Bob."

"For who?"

"Who what?"

"You just said you're checking nacelle temperatures for Bob. Who's Bob?"

"Did not say that."

"Yeah, you did."

"There's no Bob on board. Why would I say such a thing?"

"You're screwing with me. This is not a good time, RJ."

"Would I screw with the guy in the pilot's seat at a time like this?"

"For cripes sake, RJ."

He gave me a bewildered look, shook his head and left.

Hours passed. They had still not resumed work. They had not located some of the tools needed. They were still trying to understand the order of removal. On the science lab camera Paris was pulling up floor panels and removing storage boxes, looking for something he needed. Wilson and RJ were fully into it helping, so at least there was that. When Wilson came forward to check something on the engineering console, I almost slipped and asked him to get Doc to take the pilot seat. I bit my tongue just in time. A short while later Erin showed up, asking me if I had seen her artificer. "What is an artificer?" I asked. Never mind, she could use her pendant instead.

The day of doldrums dragged on. Shelly appeared right on time to start her shift. It allowed me to go back to the aft airlock and stick my head in the door to watch them puzzling over tools and schematics. A three-foot long piece of ventilation duct had been removed from the service module and was fastened to the wall for temporary storage. As much as I detested being stopped in the void, I kept my mouth shut for fear of making things take longer than they already were. I listened for a while, but finally gave up and answered the call of the galley.

With the four of them working aft, Shelly in the pilot's seat, and Danica back in her sleeper, the place was quiet and deserted. It felt even more eerie than usual. Alone in a silent, empty ship with a sinister flat blackness peering in the portals. I could tell it was getting to me. Sometimes there were shadows moving in the corner of my eye, and occasional sounds from the ship seemed more noticeable. I sat alone at the table and ate my muck stew, so named because they make it the consistency of muck so it won't escape the dish in zero-G. As I spooned out the last of it, Shelly suddenly floated by on her way toward the back. That meant Danica was up front and had relieved her.

Bored, I set one of the forward entertainment displays to the aft airlock camera and watched the work. Wilson was climbing in and out of the service module verifying things. Erin was handing tools in and taking things out. RJ was making notes on a tablet. It seemed like he was staring intently at the wall in between notes.

In desperation, I called up the movie list on the second entertainment monitor. I lasted about thirty minutes on a documentary called Ocean Life, clicked it off, and went back to the aft airlock camera where nothing had changed except Danica was up and watching, probably getting in the way more than helping.

Somewhere in the back of my mind a little alarm went off. It took me a minute to get a handle on it. Shelly had left the flight deck more than a half hour ago, but now Danica was back in the aft airlock. I hadn't been paying much attention to the comings and goings. I tensed up and pushed myself out of the seat and into forward airlock, grabbing the flight deck door as soon as it was in reach.

Both pilot seats were empty. All the displays were alive and running. The ship was still obediently maintaining station keeping, but for more than half an hour not a soul had been monitoring flight controls. I hurried into the pilot's seat and quickly went through the hand-off checklist. Everything looked okay. We were still oriented to resume our previous course. I let out a sigh and looked back over my shoulder, then tapped the intercom.

"Danica, would you come up, please?"

Danica showed up with a squeeze-tube of ice cream in one hand. She peered over my shoulder at the readouts. "My shift doesn't start for another few hours, boss. What do you need?"

"Could you check on Shelly, for me?"

"Is she sick or something?"

"All I know is she left the flight deck unmanned for half an hour. I don't know why."

"No!"

"And I'm an idiot. I sat out there thinking you were covering it."

"Wow! I'd better go see."

Off she went. I rubbed my forehead and pinched the bridge of my nose, wondering if empty space was getting to all of us. I kept looking over my shoulder, waiting for someone to report. No one did. Looking back through the open airlock, I could not see anyone in the habitat module. Finally, I used the intercom.

"Danica, would you please report forward?"

A ten-minute wait produced no results.

"Shelly, please report to the flight deck."

Ten minutes. Nothing.

"Would anyone at all please report to the flight deck?"

To my relief, RJ popped his head in. "What might I do for you, Kemosabi?"

"Is Danica back there anywhere?"

"She was working out in the gym, but now she's in the shower."

"Shelly?"

"I think she's sleeping."

"Am I losing my mind?"

"How could we tell?"

"Are they getting anywhere with the wave guide adjustment? Nobody's been up here at the engineering stations."

"I shall go check and come right back."

"Weren't you back there with them?"

"No, actually I've been trying to avoid Bob. I never should have lent him that caliper. It's like he thinks we're BFF's now or something. He's become a real pest. If you see him, please don't say I was here, okay?"

"Bob who?"

"You know. Bob Sulick. Jeez, maybe you are losing your mind. I'll be right back."

"But..."

And he was gone. I waited five minutes and couldn't take any more. Something was way wrong. I checked over systems and reluctantly left the flight deck.

The habitat module was deserted. Someone had screwed with the video wall displays. I was surrounded by a primeval swamp with things slithering by. Crocodiles snapped at me if I floated too close to the wall. I looked around, decided to head for the science lab, and bumped headlong into my high school football coach, Mr. Cunningham. He wore his standard gray sweatshirt with hood, sweat pants and tennis shoes. His hair was streaked gray, as always. His face still had the tanned, chiseled look earned from years as a Marine. He grabbed me by the arm and cast a concerned look. "Mr. Tarn. I've been looking for you. I did not see you on the track with the others. Have you put in any running time at all today?"

It caught me off guard. As best I could remember, I hadn't run in several days. "No, no...Sir. Not yet."

"Well for Christ's sake, Tarn. You're supposed to be a running back. How can you be a running back if you don't run? I saw a treadmill back there. Get your ass on it and give me at least thirty minutes, okay?"

"Yes, Sir. I'm on it."

The flight deck and waveguide procedure would have to wait. I couldn't risk running into him again and not having put in some laps. They wouldn't bench me, but I'd keep hearing about it. I pulled myself back to the gym, strapped in and set up speed. As the treadmill picked up, I went into runner's Zen, kind of glad to have a break from everything else. Occasionally people passed by behind me but fortunately, none of them interrupted.

The thirty minutes was a real pickup. It cleared my head. Now I could get back to the aft airlock and see how the waveguide fix was going. The adrenaline was still pumping. I needed a quick shower first.

Hovering outside my sleeper compartment, I dug into my tiny closet for my shower kit. Something made me stop. I rubbed my temples. What was I doing? Had I just worked out for thirty minutes and left the flight deck unmanned? Did I really see my high school teacher? What was happening? The ship was in trouble. How could I have ignored that?

Reality slapped me in the face, hard. I spun around in time to see RJ passing by. I grabbed him by the arm and stopped him.

"RJ, the waveguide repair, are they working in it?"

His voice sounded jovial. "It's on hold, Adrian. Paris said there's some guy in a black cloak with a hood bothering him. Paris thinks the guy wants revenge or something. He said to tell you he's going into hiding until it blows over. He said not to look for him. You won't find him."

RJ pulled in close to my ear, looked in both directions and whispered, "I know where he's hiding."

"RJ, there's no compartments onboard big enough to hide in. Please tell me where he's gone."

RJ shook his head. "I'm not supposed to tell."

"Please?"

He looked at me with the wrinkled expression of a child making a joke. "Well, if we went there, that wouldn't be telling."

He waved me to follow. He led me to the habitat module. The room's borders had changed in one spot. The habitat area was still surrounded by the swamp, but Paris' hiding place stood out like a newly installed support column.

He had collected several sections of white cardboard that looked like former boxes intended to hold our supplies below deck. It meant that food items and other basic necessities were now floating free about their designated compartments. He had taped the cardboard together into a phone booth-sized cubicle, just large enough for him to fit into. On the outside, in red magic marker, he had written 'High Energy Plasma Conduit. Danger. Do Not Access. The cardboard cubicle was anchored to the ceiling and floor in the far corner, and Paris was hiding within it. The construction was not quite perfect. You could see his zero-G boots through a hole in the bottom.

I pulled myself over to it. "Paris?"

No answer.

"Paris, I know you're in there."

No answer.

"Paris, the ship is stranded until we finish that wave guide procedure. We need you to do that."

No answer.

I turned to ask RJ for help and found him gone. I pushed off the wall toward the flight deck and once again ran into Coach Cunningham.

"Ah, Mr. Tarn. Lucky I found you. Listen, Aikens is out with a hamstring. You'll have to play second string QB. If anything happens, you'll be next in line. Do you have your wrist play list?"

"Yes."

"Where is it?"

"In my locker."

"I need you to get that and let me make a few number changes on it in case you have to go under center. Would you go get it for me?"

"Sure, Coach."

I hurried along to get my play list, but suddenly realized I did not know where my locker was. My sleeper cell. It had to be in my sleeper cell. I swam along, opened my sleeper compartment, and tried to remember where I left it.

What was I doing? I wasn't in high school. I was aboard the Griffin. We were in trouble. Stranded. There was no coach here. As I tried to shake myself back to reality, RJ bumped into me. He was excited.

"Adrian, you're not going to believe what just happened."

"RJ, we're in trouble here."

"Admiral Takuma was here. Did you see him?"

"RJ, you're imagining things. How could Admiral Takuma have gotten on board this spacecraft?"

"He didn't check in with you? He said he was going to."

"RJ, it's a delusion."

"That's strange. I would think he would have come to you with the news first."

"What news."

"I've been promoted to ...Captain!"

"Oh boy."

"Yes, isn't it incredible? Of course, I won't be stepping on your toes. You know me."

"RJ, where is Erin?"

"In the shower, I think. Something about a beauty contest."

"Where's Wilson, then?"

"He's way in the back of the service unit crawlway. He thinks he discovered a secret room back there."

"And Danica?"

"Training in the gym for her upcoming fight. Hey, Adrian. I'm working on a whole new daily routine for the crew. You don't think that's too much too soon, do you?"

"RJ, we're in deep shit here. We need to get this ship going. Do you understand?"

"I'm not the one who isn't working on it."

"Come with me to the flight deck. Let's see if we can tell if they aligned that wave guide or not."

"Okay. That will be my first decision as Captain. We go to the flight deck and check the wave guide alignment readouts."

Before leaving the sleeper section I tapped at Shelly's cell door. There was no answer. As we passed through the habitat module, Paris' cardboard conduit was still in place, and he was still quietly hiding inside.

At the engineering station behind the copilot's seat, RJ tapped a few buttons. "Nope. The crosshairs are in the same place. The calibration beam is running. It's ready for someone to make the adjustment."

I pushed by him, held onto one of his arms so he wouldn't disappear, and looked over the flight control readouts. The Griffin was still holding her position. There were no new alarms. A voice from the habitat area suddenly broke the silence. It was someone softly singing. I moved back through the airlock and froze in disbelief when I spotted the source of the song.

Erin, stark naked, was suspended near the ceiling, her arms outstretched, ivory-blonde hair splayed out in perfect weightless symmetry. Her soft white body seemed to glow. It was possibly the most perfectly proportioned figure I had ever seen. She was smiling a Mona Lisa smile. Hanging there overhead, it was the closest image to an angel I had ever seen. In contrast, the habitat walls had changed again. They were now displaying a perfect imitation of hell. Fires were erupting all around. Molten rock poured through dark crevices. In the middle of it, the naked angel Erin drifted gently.

She smiled and continued to sing, then moved herself around and flew back to the sleeper units, disappearing inside one.

RJ's voice came over the intercom. "All personnel, may I have your attention. As most of you have probably already been informed by Admiral Takuma, I have been promoted to Captain and will be assuming all the duties and privileges thereof beginning immediately. I want you to know how much I appreciate your support in this transition and will make every effort to make this a smooth and seamless handover. I am humbled by this promotion but I believe that together we can create an atmosphere conducive to our mission and personnel. I'll be issuing new daily scheduling later in this period. You will notice the improvements almost immediately, such as group singing every morning, and corn shucking and butter churning classes in the afternoon."

"RJ, hold on a second, will you?"

"What do you need, Adrian?"

"If I sit at the engineering station and monitor the crosshairs, can you do the alignment on the wave guide?"

"Well, yes, but I'm afraid my duties as captain supersede that type of work."

"Okay, but when the ship is in trouble, the Captain will go to any length to save his ship, right?"

"Damn right."

"So at great risk to yourself, and turning away all other distractions, you'd go into that service module crawlway and save the ship, wouldn't you?"

He rose up from the console. "A man has to do what a man has to do."

"Okay then, Captain. I'm standing by for your orders when you reach the wave guide."

"I'm on my way. Don't try to stop me." He charged past me, heading aft.

I turned back to the console, and found Coach Cunningham sitting there. He rose up and put one hand on my shoulder. "You're not going to believe this, Mr. Tarn. Zeke is not working out. We're going to need you to start. We know your running game is up to speed, but we've got to do a little work on the timing patterns, see how your throwing arm is."

He handed me the ball and motioned to a wide receiver on the sidelines. After a few pattern discussions, we began running two-man drills. Some deep passes, some quick cut passes. It went well.

"That's it, Mr. Tarn. You are ready. Now go get some rest until the game starts."

"Thanks, Coach." I headed for my sleeper cell. It was already open. I pulled myself in and as I did, I bumped an overhead compartment and something floated out. It was my Nasebian crystal. It was doing things I had never seen before. The light from it was brilliant. Spokes of white and yellow rays turned like a pinwheel. The crystal's center beamed starlight. I stared, mesmerized.

What was I doing here? Why wasn't I trying to save the ship? It was the void. It was affecting all of us. Something had changed after we stopped.

The crystal pulsed its rays into my eyes. I hung hypnotized and possessed. It was blocking the effect. I grabbed it, stared down into it and began to understand. With it zipped into my breast pocket, I jerked myself out of the cubicle, whacking my head on the ceiling a good one. Ahead in the corridor, Shelly was entering a restroom. As I approached, she stopped and began to look confused. She looked around in a daze, but returned to her delusion. I passed through habitat hell and reached the forward airlock. At the engineering station, RJ was calling me on the intercom.

"Captain Smith to Mr. Tarn, report!"

I hit the com button and held to the console. "Tarn here, go ahead, Captain."

"Where have you been? I've been calling you for five minutes!"

"Sorry, Captain, I was detained."

"You are hereby reduced in rank to ensign, Mr. Tarn. Expect further disciplinary action when I return."

"Yes, Captain. I'm ready for the wave guide alignment."

"Very well. The alignment template is in place. What is the first beam correction radial on your readout?"

"The two hundred and eighty degree is out by seven degrees."

"Correcting the two hundred and eighty. How's that?"

"It's on! That's great, RJ. I mean Captain. Now the zero-nine-zero radial is out two degrees."

"Correcting the zero-nine-zero radial. How's that?"

"We're on, Captain. The waveguide is in alignment. Can you reassemble the interfacing and ducting?"

"I'll need your help back here, Ensign. Get back here on the double."

"On my way, Captain."

After a quick check of the deserted flight deck, I tried to switch on shields but found those power system controls shut down. After closing and sealing the flight deck hatch, I hurried back to the aft airlock where the service module access door was still locked open. I pulled down the section of duct attached to the wall and crawled in. It was a long, tricky crawl inside to reach where RJ was working. Tools were loose and floating around. RJ's stocking feet were sticking out into the isle. I looked into the space he had squeezed himself into. He stopped working and got a confused look on his face.

"What am I doing?" he asked.

"You are saving the ship. Keep going."

Still confused, he continued mating cables on a service box. He closed the cover and went on to the next one. I jockeyed the duct into place where he could reach it and waited. The fear of deluded crewmembers running loose around the ship gripped me. It took another half hour. By then, RJ had been close enough to the crystal that he seemed to be coming out of it, but he was holding on to the captain delusion. We were just about ready to jump to light, except for one thing.

Everyone needed to be strapped in.

Chapter 32

We knew we would not be able to keep the fantasists in their seats. It would be like trying to coral wild mustangs without a high fence. They would have to be lassoed and harnessed one at a time. At least I had Captain Smith to help. He was still pretty looped but as long as he stayed close, he was manageable. We went to the science lab, ran the medical database, and found the strongest sedative in ship's stores. The Captain carried the water bottle.

Paris was the easiest. He was still hiding in his box. I waited outside, not bothering to try to talk to him, and once he knew we were floating nearby he began to get nervous. His false partition began to bump around a bit. RJ dared to ease it aside and look in. The cardboard was quickly yanked back in place. RJ persisted. He pulled it back again, and after a moment, Paris' face peered out the crack.

"Paris, take this. It'll make him go away. That's an order from your Captain."

Withdrawn in shadow he gave us a dubious, fearful stare. He eyed me with complete distrust, but to my surprise snatched the pill rudely from RJ, popped it in his mouth, and accepted the water. To my relief, it was fast acting.

And that was one. As RJ strapped Paris' semiconscious form into a seat, I took a moment to switch hell off the wall displays. From there it became a treasure hunt for crew. One by one we tracked them down and one way or another got the pill into them. With each success we hauled them to a jump seat where they were carefully strapped in and checked over. Fearing she was still naked, I had to override Erin's sleeper cell door. She was inside wearing jeans, a white twill blouse, and a makeshift beauty pageant crown made from paper with pieces of a necklace glued to it. She hung one hand out expecting a bow and kiss, and then allowed us to tow her along as she looked left and right, chin up, nodding and greeting invisible admirers and subjects along the way.

Wilson was the last. He was still deep within the service module crawlspace. I had forgotten him during the waveguide work. RJ could not be left alone, so I begged him along and we followed the snoring. Wilson was at the very end of it. We coaxed him into taking the pill before he was fully awake. He had no idea what he was doing, and went right back to sleep, but even in zero-G, dragging him back by his feet quickly became a task. Clothing kept catching on things. His shoulders were too broad. There was cursing and occasional scrapes and bumps in the process.

With RJ sitting merrily in the copilot seat, I hurried through the pre-jump checklist, saying a prayer of thanks that all systems read nominal. It was one of those occasions where you are reminded you do not give thanks often enough. This time thank-you-God was clearly called for. All of the service module warning lights had extinguished. On command, the power systems lit up and the phase bar graphs all showed aligned systems. RJ was beginning to look embarrassed and humiliated. With a five-second countdown, the flight management system asked for light speed and we felt ourselves sink blissfully back into our seats as the stellar drives formed their fields and pushed us to light.

The medical database said sleep would last for approximately eight to ten hours. RJ became sullen. I could see the gears turning in his head as he tried to compartmentalize what was happening and mitigate the issues one at a time.

"You okay?"

"I'm not Captain, am I?"

"Nobody is. I'm just Mission Commander. The Captain designation is usually reserved for larger spacecraft, or special envoys."

"Well shit, then."

"That's what we've just been through."

"Did I stalemate you in chess?"

"Yep. That really happened."

"Well there, then."

"I am duly put in my place."

"Still, crap."

"You may be forgetting something."

"What's that?"

"You really did save the ship."

"Don't be patronizing."

"I'm not. Even under the influence of the void, your willpower to save the ship overcame everything else. Could I have aligned that wave guide alone?"

"No."

"So who, even under the delusions of the void, crawled into the service module and aligned that wave guide, and then reassembled everything so that we could escape?"

He didn't answer but I could see some color flushing back into his face. He unbuckled and pushed up from his seat.

"Where you going?"

"To check on the others and use the loo."

"I could use some coffee."

"Okay, but remember your place, Ensign."

They began to wake up one at a time. The majority of the void effects had worn off. It was like watching dazed passengers emerge from a train wreck. There was some bargain basement depression and some skyscraper embarrassment. Erin went immediately to her sleeper cell and would not come out. Apparently, they all remembered everything. Paris hurriedly folded up his cardboard cubicle and stowed it somewhere hoping it would quickly be forgotten so his previous illusion of grandeur could again take its rightful place.

Wilson was just fine, having slept through the entire crisis. Danica needed another shower. She had won three title bouts before being sedated into a jump seat. Shelly just looked bewildered.

Seven more days in the void was enough time to dim the edges of memory so that things began to settle into routine again, although the absurdity that had plagued us remained in the back of everyone's mind. On the morning of the eighth day, Shelly's voice came on the intercom from the pilot's seat and exclaimed, "Hey everyone, there are stars ahead!" It caused a mad rush to the forward airlock where eyes high and low struggled to focus through the haze to see the foggy specs of light in the distance. There was an immediate uplifting throughout the ship, as though a secret fear that there would never be stars again finally had been extinguished.

As the celebration around the flight deck began to subside, I quietly asked RJ and Wilson to scan for systems along our route. In less than ten minutes they came back with a doozie. A twin star with satellites too numerous to count not far to starboard. Shelly and Danica both gave me raised eyebrows when I asked for the deviation, but they were more than happy to program it.

We dropped out close enough to see the twin suns. The specs of lights from their satellites were so plentiful and varied they looked like Christmas decorations. A search for class M planets quickly came up with three. We chose the one with the most blue and green. A short jump was required. The mood became quiet anticipation as we strapped back in. The pulse from the stellar drives was so brief it was over before it began. Once again Danica jumped us a bit too close, but I let it go. The view was immediately spectacular, no matter which portal you chose. There wasn't just one planet nearby, there were three, one sand-colored ball slightly smaller than our target, and one larger, its surface concealed by orange and white swirling cloud cover. We moved into a high orbit around the blue and green and the systems guys went to work. The planet seemed to have no oceans. It was heavily covered in green but with large cuts of wide, blue rivers. There were white-capped mountain ranges and canyons.

RJ seemed a little over zealous. "It's safe, Adrian. About 80 percent Earth's gravity, fairly rich oxygen atmosphere. Water and vegetation. We could stock up."

"How can you be so sure it's safe?"

"There is wildlife. Prey animals of some type. Herds of them. Some species appear to be grazing openly. If there were too many predators, they wouldn't be doing that. There are plenty of open areas for landing."

"Anything else?"

"No primates of any kind that I've seen."

"Give Danica your best coordinates. Make it somewhere we can hover and take on water. Continue scanning all the way down. If there's the slightest sign of trouble call out abort. Got it?"

"Got it."

It didn't take him long. Everyone nervously strapped back in. With the navigation computer programmed, Danica let us down through the clean atmosphere and then made a slow spin around to backtrack to RJ's coordinates.

We lowered until we were above rushing water. Fresh water processing systems took a few minutes to give the green light, then evaporator systems kicked in and began sucking up the mist. During the wait, RJ ran low-level scans and once again declared the area safe. When our processing tanks were full, Danica manually side-slipped us to a grassy clearing and let the ship settle on its gears.

Revisiting gravity did not quell the excitement. Once again we stationed Wilson with a weapon by the open forward airlock door. As Danica and Shelly went through their checklists, RJ, Erin, and I stepped down into the green with our own weapons drawn. The place was a tangled, unkempt garden, but it was beautiful. Twin orange suns hung in a blue-white sky. Behind us the two neighboring planets were bright enough to be seen through the haze. We were surrounded by a forest of tall trees that had red flowers draped over them. The river to our right was close enough that the sound of it filled the air. A clearing in the forest ahead opened to a wide plain. A herd of animals was grazing there. They resembled deer with white patches on their brown coats. We could faintly smell them in the warm breeze. They seemed disinterested in our visit.

With Danica and Shelly still at the controls, we let the Griffin idle at ready for half an hour. Our hand scanners were tied into the ship's scanners. It gave us a 360-degree warning of any biology that might try to approach. There was nothing. If there were predators, our landing had apparently frightened them away.

RJ and I began short recon trips. The more we looked, the less threatening the place seemed. Finally satisfied, we let the Griffin wind down and declared the area secured. Wilson and Paris emerged, and with checklists complete, Danica and Shelly followed.

We switched to the gravity medication regiment. In about two hours select neural impulses were being blocked and the correct neurology substituted to give us a chemical approximation of normality. There was strange fruit that was quickly approved in the science lab; a banana-shaped apple that you could peel, and a pear shaped tangerine that did not need to be peeled. RJ was in his element. He had a fire pit dug in the first hour and went about dragging porous white stones from the river to put around it. We explored and photographed in teams of two, taking samples of plant species as we went. Whatever wildlife had been close seemed to be staying away.

Toward the end of the day, RJ's fire was blazing. People were experimenting with food stores to see which could be cooked on an open fire and which could not. Later, someone found marshmallows and there was whooping and hollering and a race to cut sticks quickly followed by the flaming marshmallow and burned tongue ceremony. It was the most social I had ever seen Paris. Whether it was the long spell of zero-G or the phantom man in the black cloak, something had softened him. He joined in around the fire with his marshmallow on a stick, though in keeping with his usual prudence had attached a piece of wire to the end of it as a caliper to indicate the exact distance from the fire a marshmallow should be.

We sat around the fire in long periods of silence, staring at the flames, our minds finally purged of all things despondent. RJ held a marshmallow up to his face and inspected it. He spoke without looking away. "The only thing this campfire is lacking is a guitar and harmonica. I'll bet with all the expensive talent sitting around here, not one of us plays a darn thing."

It worried me. "Oh boy. Look out. Here he goes."

To everyone's amazement, Paris answered. "If you must know, I was a concert pianist in high school, driven there at the whim of my mother who, to my great misfortune, happened to be a music teacher."

Everyone stared in disbelief that Paris had offered something about himself.

Erin said, "I'll bet none of us are even married, are we?"

Danica, who had been testing the combustion limits of marshmallows, blew out the flaming black one on her stick. "We're all too smart for that."

Erin persisted. "How can it be that not one of us is married?"

RJ smirked. "Because we wouldn't have signed on if we were?"

"That's not true. Some people would give anything to get away from their spouse," said Danica.

Erin continued, "Hasn't anyone here been married even a little?"

Wilson laughed. "The little bit part doesn't work there, honey. It's like being pregnant. Either you are or you aren't. There's no halfway."

Once again, Paris' surprised us. He spoke with a distant tone. "I was, once..."

Everyone looked on in disbelief.

"What happened?" asked Erin.

"She was a doctor, but she passed away." He stared deeply into the fire. "That's one mistake I won't ever repeat."

Everyone waited for more. Paris wasn't offering. Wilson's inevitable comic ineptness kicked in. "So Shelly, Danica tells me you really know how to make the shit fly?"

There was another pregnant pause. Shelly glared at him. "That's it, Wilson. You're on probation."

Wilson stuttered, "But I just got off probation."

Laughter erupted.

Erin asked, "Okay then, what about you, Wilson? How come a hunk like you isn't married?"

Somewhere in the back of my mind I had the feeling Erin had been sneaking around to that question from the beginning. Wilson slugged back the last of whatever he was drinking, making me wonder exactly what it was. He held up his empty cup in a lame salute. "Three times I suckered them all the way to the ring, but then they all smartened up and gave it back."

Danica said, "I'm not afraid of marriage. I'd do it in a heartbeat as long as it was someone who could keep up, shut up, give it to me good in the ring, not want children, and loved dogs."

RJ raised his cup to his lips. "Well, that narrows it down."

Shelly laughed. "Give it to you good in the ring, Danica?"

"You know what I mean."

"And you, Adrian? Never a band on the left hand?"

RJ ran interference for me. "Too much of a maverick. He's a desperado. You're wasting your time with that one."

"That's another thing. Adrian, I can't imagine someone like you signing on for a mission like this. What's the deal?"

"It was a debt I owed a friend. That's all."

"Must've been a damn big debt."

Wilson cut in. "So Adrian, one more leg and the hunt begins. Any guess what we'll find?"

"You all pretty much have the whole story. The lost ship was a Nasebian Object Repository. At least that's the closest description of it we have. Just like us they explore the galaxy and gather knowledge, except they do it in a lot bigger way. We will begin searching the cold trail using the signatures and foot-prints they've given us plus any other evidence we can find. Hopefully, we might figure out what happened to that ship and pilot."

Shelly interrupted. "Even after two thousand years? And isn't that a little weird? This deep a mission and they only had one pilot on board? I don't get that."

"It's the way they like it. They prefer solitude, even from each other. Depending on what we find or don't find, phase two is to locate what they are calling the Udjat. They can't seem to explain what it is, or even what it looks like, but we have hand scanner setups that supposedly are guaranteed to identify it. They are more concerned about the Udjat than they are about the missing ship and pilot. So the next time we drop out of light we'll begin looking for clues. We'll do a quick mapping of space, scans, and decide where to begin."

Wilson asked, "Again, why don't they come here and look for themselves?"

"We only know they won't enter this area of space for reasons they cannot or will not discuss. They consider us the best suited for it."

Wilson wrinkled his brow and gestured with one hand. "Another thing I don't get. If these Nasebians are so incredibly advanced, can't they just use their technology to solve every-thing?"

"Uh-oh."

RJ's head snapped up to attention. He raised one finger. "Let me tell you about your so-called omnipotent technology, my good friend."

Someone let out a groan. Shelly rose to her feet. "I need to take a quick look at those tank pressures."

Danica jumped up. "I'll go with you."

Erin stood and brushed herself off. "It's about time for my journal entry."

Paris just stood and left.

Wilson, RJ and I looked at each other. Wilson said, "If you two will excuse me, I need to visit the you-know-where."

RJ made humph sound and threw a stick on the fire. He glanced at me and then poked at the flames. "Lucky for them I'm not still captain."

Despite the gracious welcome given us by the planet, we kept one person on watch all night in three-hour shifts. No one minded. RJ slept in a makeshift sleeping bag by the fire. The rest of us ignored his sissy, city-slicker remarks and took to our temperature-controlled sleeper cells with video, refrigerator, and cushioned bedding.

At breakfast, there was a unanimous vote to stay another day. After extensive monitoring and scanning Erin, Shelly, and Danica ended up swimming in the river in makeshift suits that did not provide the usual detail coverage of normal swimwear. Those of us representing the male half of the species did not take to the water, though some of us seemed to keep finding reasons to pass by there.

Another quiet night around the campfire brought a morning of stowing for departure. RJ had a faraway look in his eye as if he was considering staying. The others went about their duties in quiet reflection.

I downloaded my unusually long flight log to RJ for transmittal. In it, I had designated our adopted planet as CRJS-a. I chose -a because it was number one in a tri-planet orbit. CRJS was for Captain RJ Smith. To my surprise, he didn't pick up on it.

With our water tanks full and fresh oxygen replenishing our environmental systems, we set up a marker beacon and relay station, said a silent thank-you to CRJS-a, and lifted off.

218 | E.R. Mason

Chapter 33

The end of our downward journey brought us to an area of space beyond description. I happened to be pilot in command when we dropped to sublight. The red X on the navigation display flashed on and off, letting us know we'd arrived. The view out the front windows was so profound we had to stare a few minutes just to believe it. Danica sat beside me, speechless for the first time. The crew did not wait for permission to unbuckle. They hung at the portals, stone silent.

Space was so far removed from anything we had ever seen, its unknowns sparked a touch of fear within us. There was an orange and brown nebula to port, a cat's eye nebula to starboard, a red giant far in the distance back dropped by the orange and yellow wisps of an ancient, giant stellar explosion. The place seemed to lack the familiar orderliness to which systems usually adhere. Here, rogue planets were everywhere on our scan screens. Orbiting a large gravitational body was apparently optional rather than compulsory. A multitude of nearby suns were causing a continuous exchange of planetary bodies from one system to another, based on which sun bragged the greatest mass and closest tangent.

RJ came forward. "Adrian, I don't think the outboard cameras are enough for this place. We need to bring out the HQ handhelds and shoot through the windows."

"I agree, but could you ask Erin and Paris to do that so you and Wilson can get setup for scanning. You see how much is out there?"

"It is crowded. It'll take forever to get reflections on everything."

"That's not counting what we can't see. That's why I'm saying you and Wilson need to get on it."

"They should finish snapping pictures about the time we're ready to scan."

"Tell them we'll be rotating on the Y and Z axis so the Nav computer can do its mapping. They should be able to get shots all around. Advise them to tie in with the flight deck on headsets and we'll coordinate with them."

"Wow. This place is really something."

Danica and I went about setting up the Nav computers for mapping, and the ship for incremental rotation. When the rotations began, the Nav computers took longer than normal; extra time needed to plot the movement of so many secondary bodies. It was a two-hour data collection, and when it was done the processing lights on the Nav control panel were whirring like a light show as computers tried to analyze and store all that had been recorded. Wilson and RJ finally took over, and a much longer wait began as they hunted for signs of a Nasebian scan signature.

With maneuvering complete, Danica begged off for her rest period. I twiddled my thumbs and considered the uneventful flight deck shift ahead. Instant popcorn can be a great past time in weightless boredom. When the ventilation fan circulating the flight deck is in its off phase you can hang pieces of popcorn in any multi-dimensioned design that comes to mind. I have created small planetary systems with asteroid belts and constellations more complete than they actually are, a privilege of popcorn artistic license. When the circulation fan inevitably kicks in, it all becomes a wonderful illustration of cosmic chaos. Such artistic endeavors are a serious violation of flight deck protocol, but only if you are caught before you can eat the evidence.

As Erin brought me a fresh bag from the galley, RJ and Wilson were in their engineering seats laughing.

"What's the joke?"

Wilson answered, "Freakin' RJ, Adrian. There's a pulsar way the hell off to our port side. It's too far to be any danger, but it's making one of the other bodies look as if it's emitting an old-fashioned A.M. carrier wave. You know, like 1950's radio. While I was distracted, RJ modulated it with his impression of Jack Benny and for a minute, I actually thought I had picked up Jack Benny. It's a dirty trick, RJ."

RJ gave his best innocent look.

"You guys are seriously working the scans, right? You're not having a void relapse or anything, right?"

"Hey, we're on it. Have no fear."

"But no breadcrumbs yet?"

RJ said, "Breadcrumbs everywhere. It'll be a while."

Several hours later, they came to me with less than I'd hoped for. "We need to make some small jumps," declared Wilson.

"There are so many sources, and so much interference, we just have to look at it from different positions. It's the only way," added RJ.

"Small jumps wouldn't be a problem, would they?" asked Wilson.

I shook my head. "No, but when we ask for a flight path the Nav computer takes quite a bit of time anticipating where everything will be in relation to us. In the post-mapping tests we've run, it sometimes gives us drop out points not exactly where we wanted, but close. It does its best to find us a straight line that approximately gets us there. How much accuracy will you need?"

"No, no," said Wilson. "We don't need any precision. We just need to see things from a complementary angle. Distance and angle are all we need."

With cameras and other loose items stowed, we strapped everyone back in and made the necessary series of jumps to add dimension to our scans. It took most of a day. Later, I emerged from my sleep period to find RJ and Wilson still at it after more than twenty hours. They saw me and floated over, hair askew, beard shadow, wrinkled flight suits. "We're ready to start evaluating hits," said RJ.

"How many targets?" I asked.

"Fifteen to start with," replied Wilson.

"Fifteen? That many?"

"Would we kid you at a time like this?"

"Are they close together?"

"Far apart," replied RJ.

"Does Danica have the coordinates?"

"Yep," said Wilson.

"Then go to bed, both of you."

The first target was a barren rock the size of Jupiter. Synchronous orbit was so far out we could study half the planet at a time without flying over it. Erin and Paris ran the search program left set up by the other two. They were quick studies. Erin gave us the news. "This ball is so mineral-rich it looks like there are composite metals everywhere," she said. "But there's nothing down there artificial at all. No atmosphere. No nothin'."

Fourteen to go. By the third day we had made eight more jumps and crossed off eight more sources from the radio soup around us. RJ and Wilson remained adamant about their target selection. As we waited on orbit around one particularly yellow and green gas giant whose turbulent atmosphere sparkled as though it had tinsel in it, I began to have misgivings. I feared we would find nothing on any of the targets and would be forced to jump deeper along the same heading, a prospect that would lessen our odds significantly. I wondered if the Nasebians would be satisfied if we returned with the news nothing had been found.

Wilson sat drumming his fingers wearing a headset, while RJ diagnosed the latest prospect. Wilson suddenly sat up stiffly, turned, and shoved RJ from behind. RJ rotated around with a mild expression of annoyance.

"Do you really think you're going to get me with the same crap twice? Your nuts, Smith," said Wilson.

RJ made his trademark humph sound. "Excuse me?"

"Come on. Give it up. There's no way."

"To what are you referring might I ask, since you've interrupted this scan which must now be started over?"

"The radio. How could you think I'd fall for that again?"

"Wilson, my dear friend. What are you talking about?"

"Oh come on! The radio. I've got it again. A.M. 1650 on your dial. News at 6:00. You've got to be joking. You think I'm stupid or something?"

RJ was not buying it. "Oh, I see what's going on here. You're setting me up. You're trying to get me back. You're going to hand me the headset with an A.M. radio thing you've created and make me think we really have found some A.M. radio out here. Nice try. Really. It was worth a shot."

"You're trying to say you didn't do this? How gullible do you think I am?" Wilson paused, pulled the headset back over his ears and listened. He spoke too loudly. "This is really good, though. When did you have the time to do all this? It's a good announcer's voice, too."

RJ looked confused. It surprised me. I reached over from the pilot's seat, tapped Wilson on the shoulder, and pointed to the overhead speaker. He nodded and selected it.

It was a fluent, gravelly voice, punctuated by static, fading in and out, broadcasting news.

RJ looked at me wide-eyed. "Holy crap!" He caught himself and gave a distrusting look at Wilson as though the joke was about to break. Wilson sat with his hands on the earphones listening intently.

RJ looked at me again. "Holy crap!"

Except for an occasional word or two, you could not make out the dialogue. It was too weak and buried in noise. The rest of the crew became aware and began gathering outside the flight deck to listen.

RJ fumbled around and grabbed his own headset. He pulled them on and tilted his head forward to listen. His eyes widened. "It's real! My God, it's real! Track it. We need to track it."

Wilson sneered. "Oh come on. This has gone far enough. It's English for Christ's sake. That's impossible. Give me a break."

RJ ignored him and began furiously typing in commands at his station. "It has to be close. It's A.M. Attenuation modulation. Too weak to carry very far. It's breaking up pretty badly but if I can just get a lock long enough..."

Wilson began to look perplexed. RJ twisted at controls while listening intently to the phones.

"That's it! It's target number four, our next target!" RJ waved his hands furiously. "Everybody strap in. Let's go!"

I held up one hand. "Wait a minute. Wait a minute. What's actually going on here? Are we really picking up a radio transmission in English from a planet millions of miles away on the other side of the void, or is this some kind of freak singularity process that's new to us?"

RJ would not calm down. "It's radiating from a planet, Adrian, not a black hole. It's an artificially generated signal. There's no other way."

"It's English, RJ. It's got to be a black hole freak of nature."

"You can only have one or the other, Adrian. The source is coming from a planet, not a black hole."

"So you actually think we've located an inhabited planet with technology using English? Do you see how crazy that sounds?"

"Let's go see!"

"Just hold your horses. If this place actually turns out to be inhabited, and I really doubt that, we can't just go barging in there not knowing what we're doing. We'll make the jump but stay far enough away until we can get an idea of what's going on. It could still be some cosmic anomaly we just don't know about, some kind of time-shifted transmission from Earth that got here by accident. Like a bottle in the ocean or something. So let's just keep our cool and gather data. Then we'll see."

RJ's enthusiasm was not dampened in the least. Wilson continued to look befuddled. The others began preparing for the jump. Danica went back to the sleeper compartments to wake Shelly and Paris and tell them the news. RJ's coordinates appeared on my screen before I could ask.

It was a short jump. I brought the ship out of light an A.U. from the planet. Lots of blue, not so much green and brown. Two moons, opposite sides of the planet, nearly identical orbit. It made me wonder what the tides were like.

The entire crew was up and completely enthralled. With two antenna arrays tuned we could hear the radio transmission fairly clearly. A diversity of space noise still interfered, but we could tell what they were saying. It was indeed English, and after a few minutes of listening it became clear this was not an Earth transmission. Some of the dialogue was foreign to us. There seemed to be slang we had never heard before. Some words were mispronounced. To cap off our confusion, a weatherman closed his forecast by saying, "So it should be another glorious day on Mother Earth," a reference that stunned us all.

Chapter 34

"That's it, Adrian. We've finished scanning both moons. No outposts. Nothing artificial. Same with the planet's orbital corridors. No satellites, no manmade objects, at least down to the sizes we are able to detect at this distance. There are cities, and a lot of them. No frequency modulation, nothing more sophisticated than A.M. radio, low-grade television, and short wave. There is some primitive radar emission. Until we get closer that's the best we can do."

"Radar emissions? How broad?"

"Strictly elementary. Surface scans. Only a few areas. Nothing that could bounce off us on orbit."

"An inhabited planet using the English language. You're still getting hits on the Nasebian materials scans?"

"As strong as ever. All of this has to be related to the Nasebian ship somehow, but we need orbit for a closer look."

"And you're absolutely sure they can't detect us?"

"Absolutely."

I held to the ceiling and stared down at the engineering displays. Danica looked back from the pilot seat, waiting for instructions.

"Dan, go ahead and drop us behind the closest moon. Keep us in shadow."

"With pleasure, Commander. All personnel, strap in for a microburst of stellar in one minute."

I glided into the copilot seat as she set up. She tapped in her coordinates, hit the engage button, and brought us in a little too close, as usual. This time I approved. Someone in back gasped at the crescent of rugged, gray moon surface outside his portal. Using the OMS engines we gently nudged up to the horizon, peering across space at a complex, colorful planet rotating on its axis, transitioning surface into the shadow of terminator, sunlight on the dayside, the incongruous geometry of modest artificial lights on the night side where big oceans left big dark spots.

"My gosh, what have we found here?" said Shelly, appearing over our heads.

It took RJ only a few minutes. "Nothing artificial orbiting. No manmade objects, whatsoever. No space tracking detection radar. We can translate to orbit without being observed."

I let out a sigh of apprehension, and looked back at RJ. "Again, are you sure?"

He nodded.

"Danica, jump us in, then drop to a high orbit, but not synchronous. Let's take a few turns around and see. Remain ready to break away at any time in case things are not what they appear."

Even that close it still required a microburst from the stellar drives. Once there, Danica did not wait for anyone to unbuckle. She switched to OMS and gracefully parked Griffin high enough to avoid the one-in-a-million chance of a telescope picking us up. We aligned on orbit and immediately the entire crew was plastered to the planet side of the spacecraft, staring down with binocs. Too few portals caused occasional grumbling. RJ and Wilson kept working intently at their engineering stations with half a dozen of their displays showing the planet's surface. The view out the front windows was even more captivating: a diverse topography below, a crowded, colorful spacescape all around.

I rubbed my face with both hands and tried to convince myself everything was under control. I tapped the intercom button. "Okay everyone; remember this is not a sightseeing expedition. As you study what's below, begin making mental notes. Use the handheld for areas of special interest. We need to know everything we can about what's down there. We'll complete a couple orbits and then meet around the table and compare what we've learned. Tarn out."

Not one of them came forward or responded. I wondered if they had heard me at all. Even Danica appeared distracted by the secret world scrolling by below us. I had to wave the on-orbit procedures list to get her attention. Her eyes gradually refocused and a smile surfaced. "Wow!" she said. "An undiscovered people down there!"

When the spacecraft was settled in I placed one hand on Danica's shoulder and said, "You have the spacecraft." It was an unnecessary formality except to assure sobriety on the flight deck.

"I have the spacecraft," she replied dutifully.

Back at the engineering stations RJ and Wilson had no less than four of their monitors showing radiological surface scans. The screens looked like weather radar sweeps, but in actuality the beams were searching for specific materials used by Nasebian spacecraft. Half a dozen other displays were showing magnified down-looking camera views.

In the habitat area I couldn't get a window. I pulled myself into a seat at the table and set the wall display screen to the best-magnified view. Gray buildings and skyscrapers passing by. Busy traffic on paved highways. What looked like an open-air stadium.

RJ called out, "There are aircraft! Propeller driven. Nothing above twenty-five thousand that I've seen so far."

Farmland. Populated beaches. As we passed into night, sporadic city and township lights. An airport rotating beacon. Low altitude lightning. A few faint lights over black ocean. Islands with more lights. Back into daylight, steep brown and green snow-capped mountains with trails cut across them. A seaport with large and small vessels at dock.

I had to put the brakes on my mind to stop it from overloading. My contrived expectation of searching some barren celestial rocks for the undisturbed two-thousand year old wreckage of a Nasebian spacecraft, and perhaps with luck finding the priceless Udjat within the wreckage, seemed to have slipped away. Maybe there was still a chance it was not down on this aberrant planet in the middle of dizzying unexplored space, but the odds were against me.

We could not make first contact. If these people believed they were the only-children of the universe as so many naive earthlings had for so long, destroying that security blanket was guaranteed to do widespread harm. Even to this day some groups on Earth refused to accept that any other intelligent species exist, and they adjust their isolation as necessary to preserve their ostrich hole.

We would now have to search a heavily populated planet without calling attention to ourselves. We were probably about to become actors in a strange, real life play: aliens among them. How many times Earth people had laughed and ridiculed that notion. It was as though every Trekker and Trekkie from the past was now staring back in time exclaiming "See!"

Even after the second orbit I had to drag them from the windows. It took a while. We sat around the oval table with pilot Danica piped in on a headset and display screen. Some of them had photos printed on mag-paper plastered to the tabletop. There was too much low-level conversation going on between some of them. Everyone wanted to speak first.

"Okay, let's get started. RJ and Wilson, you guys have the most. Let's start with you."

RJ began. "Well, as we've all seen, black and white television, short wave, A.M. radio. Their only radar is military based. There is a significant military presence, but the radar stations are few and far between. Our scans were interfering with it on every pass, but it was only momentary, nothing that alerted them. There are no computers on the planet that we can see. This is a pre-computer civilization. No smart phones or long-range communicators. No satellites of any kind. No evidence of a space program at all. We do not have a population estimate yet because it is too spread out, but there are metropolis-level cities and large industrial areas. It does not appear they have jet engines, but there's quite a bit of air travel. We have not isolated the Nasebian signature yet, but we're scanning for anything down to the size of a matchbook, so it'll take several days just to cover 80% of the planet. To sum it up, the closest comparison I can make is we are looking at a 1940's, 1950's Earth."

It left a restrained silence. I looked at Wilson. He spoke solemnly. "There has been war. There have been some references to it on the broadcasts. Looking specifically for signs of it you can find some areas that still look bombed out, and just abandoned. In other areas, you can see where they're still rebuilding. It appears it was a big conflict, comparable to WW2. I'd guess it's been over for ten years or so. There's still a lot of military assets down there but no indication of fighting."

Shelly, sitting next to Wilson, cut in. "It seems pretty peaceful down there to me. There are trolleys and streetcars, and steam locomotives. I've been monitoring their broadcasts, mostly. Some of it is pretty funny. It's a post-war kind of starched-shirt mentality, everyone trying to be prim and proper. You can't get too much out of the old fashioned sitcoms they put on. There are advertisements in between for cars and household items. They smoke cigarettes as though it's a healthy thing. But there are subtle things missing."

RJ was engrossed. "Like what?"

"For one thing, there are cowboy style shows but never ever a reference to Indians. I do not believe this planet ever supported Native Americans. On the other hand, I have seen Orientals and other diverse ethnic groups, although some cultures are missing entirely. There are horses here, but they have stubby horns on top of their heads. Dogs look more like wolves than dogs. Most of the animal species are similar to Earth's, only with noticeable differences. People, on the other hand, appear to be identical to us. And, as you've already heard, the language is English. There have been no references to any other languages at all, but many, many words are slang, or simply mispronounced so it's tricky. Since the animal life has differences to what we see on Earth but the people appear to be identical, that begs the question were humans from Earth brought here at some point to seed the planet?"

RJ nodded. "That has to be considered."

Erin said, "I for one, would like to know how this planet came to be called Earth, that's for sure."

"Another good one," remarked Shelly.

Paris leaned forward in his seat to get our attention. "That is the key. Something has happened here we do not yet understand. It is even more intriguing than any of you even realize. Look at these." He slid two eight by ten photos across the table for all to see. On them were extreme close up images of two large pyramids. They looked familiar. "These are on the thirty-degree north latitude near the bank of a large river. The place is forest covered, surrounded by high plateaus. The pyramids are similar in size and design to the Cheops pyramids in Egypt, which also happen to be approximately on the same latitude. They are old. Commander, I want your permission to use the IR cameras to get a look inside these. If the interiors are the same as Earth's, that will tell us something about the history of this planet."

"You can see inside them with infrared?"

"I can with IRAI."

"And what will that tell us?"

"If the interior of the largest one is the same as Earth's Cheops pyramid, it will mean there are parallels between the history of this planet and that of Earth..."

Wilson asked, "Care to elaborate?"

"Earth's Cheops pyramid is complex. There are many ancient pyramids on Earth, but none like Cheops. If the large pyramid we are seeing down there has an interior similar to Cheops, it would suggest that the history of this planet was deliberately made to follow that of Earth, at least in some ways."

RJ raised one hand. "What if the pyramid down there is older than the one on Earth?"

"That's a legitimate possibility. But either way it would not be coincidence. It would be a clue to unraveling what has happened here. It would mean the planet wasn't simply seeded with humans, if that's actually the case. The people here weren't left to develop their own history. A history was provided for them."

"Why would anyone do that?" asked Wilson.

"A dozen possible reasons," said RJ. "If you wanted to experiment with history to see how certain milestones could have gone differently. Or, if you wanted a reenactment of something that happened to understand it better. Or, to test ways of controlling certain types of events. I can think of quite a few reasons to control something in this way."

Shelly added, "In the laboratory we do the same thing with cell growth. We alter the conditions of growth to see what the results will be. This Earth could be a giant laboratory."

Erin raised one hand. "Everyone, we're piling up varia-bles. We do not know that this planet was seeded at all. We do not know if there has actually been manipulation of events. We're theorizing using assumed facts. It's a bad way to make science."

I nodded. "Erin is right. We're getting off the track. Right now, we need to keep gathering information. Anyone else have any actual input for this first discussion?"

No one spoke.

"Well, please proceed with the IR cameras, Paris. Let me know what you find. In the meantime, we need to wait until the Nasebian target scans are in. Everyone keep observing and doc-umenting. We'll do this again at the next shift change, or if something significant comes up."

One by one, they pushed up and headed off in different directions. RJ remained seated, staring at me, tapping one fin-ger on the tabletop. I gave in to his stare. "You left your gears turning."

"You must already be thinking what I'm thinking," he replied.

"You go first."

"Our Nasebian friends give us coordinates to find a lost ship from two thousand years ago. At those very coordinates, in the most crowded part of space I've ever seen, we happen to find a planet called Earth with inhabitants who speak English."

"You're already convinced this is all a result of that ship visiting here?"

"I don't believe in coincidences."

"That's my line."

"So it is."

"Still, it doesn't change what we came here to do...really."

"Unless..."

"Unless what?"

"Unless those people down there have what we want."

"I was hoping not to think about that just yet. Thank you, Mr. Sunshine."

"Sorry. It's what I do."

"And so well, at that."

"You aren't kidding yourself are you? You know you're going to have to go down there eventually."

"Only if you find that ship or pieces thereof."

"Guess I'd better get scanning. I don't want Wilson get-ting all the credit."

"Okay; and I'll get busy fretting about it all."

Chapter 35

They woke me in the middle of my sleep period. They were excited. Something had been found. There was no question. The signature was completely unique and exactly as predicted. I rubbed my eyes hoping the artifact was buried in some distant, seldom-traveled canyon. They informed me it was smack in the center of the second largest city. We hung over Wilson's station staring blankly at the flashing scan circle on his scope. "Gonna hafta go down there. No other way," he said. RJ looked up at me but did not say I told you so.

It was the moment everything had to change. An ominous confirmation that some of us would be forced out of hiding. We would now need to hide in plain sight. Plans had to be made. Stealthy landing sites had to be evaluated. Walking distances kept within reason. Because there was no avoiding the population, inconspicuous clothing had to be tailored. Fake identification and some form of currency would need to be obtained or printed. The first trip would be the most hazardous. Not knowing what would work and what would not made it a dubious undertaking. Little details can kill big plans. I did not ask for volunteers. It would be Wilson and I. If things went sour I wanted the most manpower available for an escape. It would have to be a drop off in the darkness of early morning hours. The Griffin was vulnerable on the ground. Danica would lower us down, make the drop, and then assume a stationary orbit overhead so that we could be tracked. We would not be able to re-board until the next evening's darkness.

Construction worker's clothes seemed to suit us best. There were rough-terrain shoes in the Griffin's stores. We made our jeans look like those on the broadcast advertisements, and came up with gray work shirts to go with them. The science lab had gold, silver, and platinum metal sample kits for analysis comparisons. I appropriated one of each as potential currency. They were using a base denomination called the dinar. You could get a new Meteor convertible automobile for 850 dinars. Erin and Shelly made a chart of the prices of various common items so we could get a feel for what things cost. It was difficult to tell what our metal samples were worth, and it bothered me that we carried no identification. The Griffin's science lab could reproduce anything. The problem was; we did not know what any official documents looked like.

The drop point was five miles from the edge of the city in a patch of forest that bordered a park. No nearby radars. No forest towers. No roads or trails leading in. It would take five miles from there to reach the large gray building that held our object of interest. We would hide out in the park until the city came alive, and then blend in and follow our hand scanners or use guidance from the Griffin to reach the proper coordinates. We would avoid interacting with the locals, if at all possible. The objective was simply to get a look at whatever was triggering the Nasebian scan sweeps. Afterward, we would make our way back to the park, wait for darkness, and call for pickup. Once in orbit, we could reevaluate. It was a very simple plan, with few obvious problems. It made me think back to how many times simple plans had blown up in my face.

There was very little orbital debris around the planet. Man had not been there yet. A few rock or ice fragments dotted the collision avoidance display scope. That allowed Danica to easily move up to a synchronous orbit above the city and follow the planet as it turned into night. Erin and Shelly kept busy learning Earth II's slang. RJ continued scanning, and Paris was fixed in the science lab working his pyramid thesis. Wilson and I made wide belts to wear under our shirts so that a hand scanner, communicator, and weapon could be carried out of sight. We fastened button-cams to our shirt collars, earpiece receivers inside one ear, and mini-mikes inside the cuff of one shirt sleeve so that communications could be discreetly whispered, if necessary.

Wilson buttoned his shirt and spoke without looking up. "I wonder what the women are like?"

"Wilson..."

"I know, I know. But, you got to admit, the thought is..."

"Wilson..."

"Don't worry. Remain as invisible as possible down there, I know."

"As invisible as a Wilson can be, at least."

"You know we're probably going to pass by some sweet-smelling old-time restaurants, too."

"Women and food. Strange, unexplored, dangerous planet...You're thinking women and food."

"Well, it's been a while..."

"If you start getting that dazed look, what should I do?"

"Remind me of our last visit to Heidi's."

"I don't know. That didn't work out all that bad for you, as I heard it."

"Come to think of it, it was worth it. How do I look? Too much bulge?" He patted down his shirt and, and holding to the wall, straightened up.

"It'll pass. Let's hope we don't need any quick-draws."

The Griffin began descent at 3:10 down-there time, no lights inside or out, absolute minimum use of thrusters below one thousand feet. As usual, Danica was at her best. It was artistry in motion. She held us two feet off the ground to avoid making imprints. The airlock outer door made too much rushing air sound as it opened, but there was no one around to hear it. We jumped to the alien grass and looked up to see RJ wave as he closed the hatch. A moment later, the Griffin was a shadow disappearing in the night sky.

Alone in an alien woods at night. One moon low in the western sky, a crescent of the other rising in the east. The air was a touch too cold. There was the smell of damp vegetation. We stood in a shadowy clearing where the grass came up to our knees. My first thought was alien snakes. The surrounding woodland was too cloaked in shadow to make out details. Trees and brush had no color. We both surveyed the place and then stared down at the comforting colored lights on our hand scanners. There did not appear to be an opening of any kind in the direction we wanted to go. We could burn ourselves a way through the brush with our weapons, but that would be too much of a ruckus and would leave too much evidence. I had brought a satchel. I drew out two folded machetes and handed one to Wilson. He seemed unconcerned about reptilian dangers and plowed ahead through the grass. After having once seen his bug-on-your-shoulder semaphore dance, I decided not to mention my own phobias.

The forest offered the strangest of canopies. Sunrise was bringing color to the skyline. We were in the beginning of the fade from darkness to light. It was the end of the day for nocturnals and the beginning for the prey animals that needed the protection of light. The expanding glow from predawn cast a deep eeriness over this never-before seen landscape. There were echoes of alien sounds. Beyond the dense brush I caught up beside Wilson. He had his Marine face on. I would not want to face that expression head on as an enemy. I wondered in earlier years if it had been the last thing some saw.

We marked our trail inconspicuously to save time when the hand scanners would lead us back for pickup. The barriers of underbrush eventually gave way to a thinning forest of trees. The machetes were folded and stored back in the pack. Orange sky revealed a clearing ahead. We had reached the edge of the park.

It was a well-groomed commons. There was a playground not far away with tire swings, a cement slide, a small carousel, and a line of wooden seesaws. A bus stop lean-to stood nearby with strange advertising plastered on the walls. A large pond occupied most of the area on our left. Waterfowl rested on the shoreline and colorful paddleboats were anchored to a dock in a neat row. We stood within the tree line border and appraised our options. There was no one around. Foot trails through the grass lead in every direction.

A spot behind a workshop on the west side concealed us nicely. At one point two uniformed men with guns rode slowly by on horseback. The sun came up a bit smaller than the one we were used to. As it rose people began to appear, mostly adults commuting on foot. A gentleman passed by close to our hiding place. He wore a gray tweed suit frayed around the edges with a tie that seemed too large for the suit. His black wing-tip shoes had too much mileage.

The park rapidly became more and more populated. Children in baggy overalls carrying small rectangular lunch boxes embellished with cartoon characters ran by, followed by other groups in school uniforms with small beanie-style caps. There was no reason to wait any longer.

"Tarn to Griffin."

RJ's voice came back. "With you overhead, Adrian."

"We're ready to step out into the world."

"Your com is good. We have your scanner signatures and collar cam images. We'll be following along as planned. Tell Wilson no stopping off at any bars."

Wilson tilted his head in annoyance.

"We'll check in as opportunities arise. Tarn out."

When it appeared no one was looking our way, we stepped out from behind the shop and began walking the nearest foot trail, then cut across the grass and headed for the bus stop. Behind it a cobblestone street, sidewalks, and factory buildings marked the beginning of the business district.

Our impressions of the park had been easy. It could have been an old-fashioned park anywhere on Earth. There was no time shock there. But as we approached the noise and calligraphy of the city the sights became oddly disorientating. We cut into a red brick alley between two one-story structures and emerged onto a busy sidewalk. In that instant, we suddenly found ourselves back in time. The effect was so overwhelming it took a minute to grasp what was happening. The place was gray and red brick and glass, a combination of modest high-rises punctuating smaller multistory structures alongside them. So many people were crowding the sidewalks there was little chance of being noticed, even with the dumbfounded expressions on our faces. One of Shelly's wooden trolleys was in the middle of the street loading people. A traffic cop stood just beyond it directing old-fashioned cars through an intersection. Someone honked his horn at a distracted driver. A street vendor was selling hot dogs a few feet to our right. I could smell them. Farther down the street a horse drawn carriage was delivering bottles of milk to a business. Directly across from us there was a closed theater, the Ravolo. The movie was Pathfinder, starring Dicana Sprang and Markus Theodore. Cars were parked at various points along the curb. It looked like an antique car show.

The zero-G medication was kicking in, but it hardly mattered. We were so mesmerized the drag was of no concern.

"Holy shit, Adrian."

"Just be cool now..."

"Somehow I wasn't ready for this."

"We'd better get moving. We'll attract attention."

"They look just like us."

"The target is off to our left, up that way."

"I feel like I'm in a Humphrey Bogart movie, for God's sake."

I pulled his arm and we began weaving our way through the fast-moving crowd. It seemed like we were going against traffic.

"Hey you see that place up ahead? It's a pawn shop."

"Swap or Shop? Yeah. I see it."

"We could get money there, I bet."

"It's too soon. Let's stay low-key. Get a feel for the place."

"I'm getting a feel. We should have brought a Tommygun in a violin case."

"I forgot you're a damn movie buff. You probably know this place better than all of us. Be cool, keep moving, that cop over there on the sidewalk is staring at us. I hope to God we're not doing something strange."

"Don't worry. He's looking at the broad in the dress shop window next to us."

"Broad in the dress shop window? You're already starting to talk like them."

"Just playin' the part, amigo. Playin' the part."

There was a four way intersection ahead, busy with more people and a woman traffic cop. I was not sure which way was the best, and we could not pull out a hand scanner. I raised my communicator sleeve and rubbed my chin. "Griffin."

RJ's voice answered. "It's absolutely incredible, Adrian."

"Four way intersection. Which way?"

"When you get to the intersection, take a right. Stay on that street. We'll guide you the rest of the way."

"Tarn out."

We had to wait in a crowd to cross the street. No one was talking. There was some sort of metal-to-metal pounding noise coming from a side street as though a girder was being driven into the ground. Too much exhaust was coming from cars passing by. Wilson and I seemed to be a tad taller than the average Earth II inhabitant. The lady cop noticed us. She let go with her whistle, and waved everyone across. Although it was a five-mile hike, the distractions were so profound we hardly noticed. There were gas station attendants washing windshields, shoeshine stations on the corners, men wearing large advertising billboards front and back, outdoor telephones that had to be cranked, and car hops on roller skates at drive-in diners. We passed by a watch repair shop, a cobbler's shop, and wound around beneath an elevated train rail. There was a telegraph office, the smell of roasted peanuts, and a cigar shop. I had to urge Wilson along from in front of Corley's Old Ale House. The dingy green front doors were wide open and a barmaid in a Swedish short skirt with knee socks tried to beckon him in.

As we walked, RJ interrupted. "Adrian, not far ahead of you on the right is a very large three story structure. Paris just finished looking inside with the IRAI. He believes it's some sort of library. Just beyond that is a second, larger building. That's your target."

I pulled at the collar of my shirt and spoke into my sleeve. "Copy."

As we got closer to the first large building, Paris' intelligence began to pan out. A wide span of white cement steps led up to columns guarding a grand entrance. The large script lettering overhead read, 'Provincial Public Library'. A scattering of people were coming and going.

The next building answered many questions. It was two-story, white stone. The similarly scripted lettering above the entrance proclaimed, 'Provincial Museum of Natural History'.

People were standing outside smoking cigarettes. A billboard nearby assured them that it was the right thing to do. It made me wish we had a pack, it would have transformed our loitering into a smoke break. We lingered across the street from the museum watching people come and go. No tickets appeared to be required, but we could not make out if any entrance requirements were needed inside. We did not want to be asked for identification.

"Griffin."

"That's the place, Adrian," replied RJ.

"Can you see inside well enough to tell if they are stopping people who enter?"

"Stand by."

A few minutes later Paris' voice came over our earpieces. "It's clear, Commander. There is a large desk just inside the main entrance, but only a few visitors stop near it. You should be able to enter without a problem. The target is in the center of the room, approximately one hundred feet past the entrance. It must be an important item."

"Thanks, Tarn out."

"You ready, Wilson?"

"Looks copasetic to me, bro."

"Let's go."

We waited for our chance, jaywalked across to the museum steps and climbed them imitating the casualness of those around us. Beyond the colorful open entrance there was a revolving glass door. One at time, we pushed through.

The main hall was immense: a long marbled chamber with a glass canopy three stories high. Alcove entrances ran along both sides leading to exhibit areas. Balconies protruded above them. In the distance, the end of the hall led to more decorated entrances and balconies. A large information desk was on our right, manned by an attractive young woman dressed in a uniform that looked like old-fashioned flight attendant attire. She smiled at Wilson. He looked at me and I rolled my eyes. Special exhibits were stationed in the middle of the hall at various points along the way. We strolled along, pausing at each exhibit. The first was the skeleton of a woolly mammoth, the next an animal that resembled a saber tooth tiger with its coat intact.

The third display was the one. Two other people had stopped there and were reading the plaque. The object was enclosed in a glass rectangle large enough to cover a small auto. To most onlookers, it appeared to be a slab of something shaped like a shark fin the size of a suitcase. To us, it was clearly a piece of spacecraft appendage. It was bronze colored with a hint of violet when the light hit it just right. As the others moved on, Wilson and I read the inscription.

Capal's Chariot

According to Nasebiana legend, the god Capal descended to Earth from the heavens on a chariot of fire to aid and teach humankind. This fragment has been passed down through the centuries and is said to be a piece of Capal's chariot. It was worshiped by several warring cultures until the Slater occupation of 1640, when it was captured and held by The Church of Dedicated Saints. There, it was eventually put on display beginning in the 1800's. When that province merged with the greater states, the artifact was brought to the museum for safety and further study. In a strange accordance with legend, modern science has not been able to determine the composition or true origin of the artifact. Numerous fraternal organizations continue to subscribe to the legend and pay homage to the fragment through yearly vigils to the museum.

Additional references;
Pauline's Ancient Artifacts: UPBN28743
Archeology and Legend: UPBN76231
Timbres Index of Science In The Laboratory: PATCO 2354

We secretly photographed the fragment from every angle and when an opportunity arose, scanned it. The inscription alone told us we were at the right place. Our initial questions had been answered, giving way to dozens more.

Chapter 36

"It is chaos, Adrian. Pure chaos," said Erin. "There's no way to explain this place."

We sat around the oval table, trying to piece together what we knew. There were a lot of pieces, but they were like pieces from different puzzle boxes.

I tried to offer reason. "Okay, let's back up. Start with what we know. We know that a Nasebian ship came to this area of space, and either crashed or was disabled. We know that because there's a piece of it still down there. And, probably because of that visit, this planet has inherited some of Earth's history. Let's go from there."

RJ held up a photo. "I've seen several religious broadcasts. This is a minister from one of the groups down there reading from a King James Version of the Bible. He referenced both the Old and New Testament."

"So they have a copy of the Bible?"

RJ nodded. "There have been references to a bunch of other religious writings, but all of them sounded original and directly related to this planet's real history. Only their Bible is an exact copy of Earth's."

"So they accidentally got their hands on a Bible, or they were deliberately given one."

"Would someone actually try to manipulate people using another planet's Bible?" asked Wilson.

Shelly answered. "Someone promoting their own religious program. Someone maybe trying to set themselves up as a God."

"The Nasebian race is so far beyond religious denomination we can't even understand them. If they wanted to make themselves appear as gods they wouldn't need a Bible to do that," I said.

RJ added, "There are other reasons to plant something like that in a developing culture. I can think of several. You might try to give a society a common religious root if you were hoping to avoid holy wars."

Wilson said, "Well it looks like that one didn't work out too well down there. They still found a reason to have one hell of a war."

Paris spoke. "If you look back to the beginning, their history is riddled with contradiction. Our long distance scans of the largest pyramid are complete. It is identical in every way to the Cheops pyramid of Egypt, and like Earth, the capstone is missing. It cannot be a coincidence."

RJ added, "Which is even more proof that someone manipulated the development of this society."

Erin said, "It makes you wonder about the races that do exist and the ones that do not. Were they preselected and brought here for a specific reason?"

I raised one hand. "Let's get back to mission objectives. RJ, have there been any other traces of the Nasebian ship?"

"No, but we're not finished with the Polar Regions."

"Could we have missed it?"

"Only if it is buried deep underground."

"Our prime objective is the Udjat. Has there been anything at all on that?"

RJ spoke, "All the answers are available, Adrian."

"What do you mean?"

"You marched right passed them on the way to the museum. The Provincial Public Library. The place is huge. All the answers are in there."

"There are no computers, RJ. That could take forever."

Danica held up one finger. "Not if we work in teams. Erin and I now speak Earth II quite well."

"You guys want to go down there?"

Erin answered, "Are you kidding? Go back in time and feel what the world was like in the 1940's?"

"You're going to give me gray hair. Teams wandering around down there? We still don't even have any fake ID's. You get stopped by someone, they'll drag you into a police station and there will be too many questions. How the hell will we get you out?"

Erin frowned. "There wouldn't be wandering, Adrian. We just want to go to the library."

"And home by eleven or you're grounded for a light year?"

RJ cast a sympathetic look. "What else you going to do, Kemosabi?"

I considered his argument. They all looked at me like puppy dog hopefuls. "Well, shit then, as you would say."

Someone began laughing. Others joined in. It tapered off and we all sat silently exchanging apprehensive glances.

A flurry of wardrobe production broke out. Not to be outdone, Paris had brought along a man's suit and vest that was made to roll up in a tube, the size customarily used for paper towels. He deployed the thing, re-pressed the lapels to enlarge them, sewed extra buttons on the front, and used a chain from the necklace Erin had torn apart to create a pocket watch. He looked so good it almost pissed me off, though I don't know why. Danica and Erin created period dresses that came down well past the knee. Erin had found material in the bedding section, a light brown plaid. Danica used a blue cloth equipment cover. Both outfits were belted in the middle with former equipment strap tie-downs. The makeshift dresses became an amusing example of attire not suited for zero-G space travel. They constantly billowed up so that the two women had to wrestle to preserve their modesty. Zero-G boots were cut, laced, and padded to create footwear. RJ's wardrobe was the easiest. He wore his normal casual clothes and fit right in: baggy brown pants, blue work shirt. Last but not least, the group was carefully networked to communications, collar cameras all.

The teams were Paris and Erin, Danica and RJ. I reluctantly forbid them weapons. If someone got their hands on a communicator or a hand scanner, there was little damage they could do. It would take decades to decode that technology. But, if a weapon was accidentally acquired, a single, experimental push of the trigger could be a very bad thing.

When the time was right Shelly lowered us down to the 500-foot level where we paused to scan for human bios. The coast was clear. We let down and the teams deployed. It surprised me that I did not have more misgivings as I watched them push through the high grass to the woodland. We climbed away and left them back in time.

At first, the expedition became a comedy show. Four collar cams on four monitors showing it all. They did not stalk quietly as they should have. Dresses kept getting caught on brush. There was cursing and sarcastic exchange. They finally settled down and became quiet when they reached the park border. Wilson kept vigil at his engineering station and directed them behind the same shop we had used to hide. Once there, the whispering again became script for any good comedy play. Erin was preoccupied with not getting dirty. Danica kept bumping RJ out of the way so she could see the park.

Once the world came alive, their five-mile hike began. Some of them kept getting separated in the crowd. I had to caution RJ about speaking into his sleeve too much; reminding him we could see most everything he was reporting. His excitement at being immersed in a pre-computer era was a bit overwhelming. Somehow, the undisciplined entourage reached the library with little incident. As they entered, both Wilson and I reminded them to be careful about transmitting in a closed in environment where it could be noticed more easily.

The teams went to work. The place was huge. Similar to the museum, the ceiling was constructed entirely of panels of glass, providing ample light to read. Most of the main room was lined with long tables for just that purpose. The entire east wall of the place was filled with file cardholders and waist high potted plants. There were statutes of famous characters separating some sections. On the left, carved columns divided the wall into alcoves with exhibits in each. Grand portraits lined the highest parts of the chamber. At the far end there was a caged wooden elevator with a man in uniform operating it.

A large circular information desk commanded the room's center with an attractive older woman setting up the counter. Watching on RJ's collar cam I winced when Erin approached her and asked for something. The conversation went on and on, though no one had keyed a mike for the rest of us to hear. The two women laughed. The attendant finally smiled, found a certain folder and handed it to Erin, then turned away to another waiting customer. Integration with the new culture had been successful. Erin seemed to speak the language as well as she had promised. The teams spread out in pursuit of their particular assignments.

The research quickly became mundane for those of us watching, but we made sure at least one of us was always on top of it. I pulled myself away and suddenly realized how empty the Griffin had become. Shelly up front, Wilson at engineering, and me. It had never been this deserted. I did a quick inspection of the other compartments. Some sleeper cells had been left open. Photos were pasted to the walls, magnetic keepsakes in shadowed alcoves. In the gym, a used towel was floating near the ceiling. I pulled it down and shoved it into the laundry hamper. A drawer had been left open in the med section otherwise everything was neatly stowed. The aft airlock felt cold. The hatch to the service module was closed and sealed. The place was neat, clean, and too quiet. Back in the habitat area, Earth II's black and white broadcasts were on the main screens. A cowboy epic was playing. As I took a seat at the table, I choked back a laugh. One of the cowboy extras in the background looked just like a young John Wayne, another example of life's subtle sense of humor.

With Danica on the surface, Shelly and I had to put in twelve-hour shifts. We talked it over and split them into two six's. I used my off time to study more of the broadcasts, hoping to get to know our Earth II brothers and sisters better. I logged onto a tablet and went over the notes made by the others. Images of particular interest from the library were being discretely uplinked to the ship. There were copies of a driver's license, a birth certificate, military discharge, voting registration, and others. Paris' collar cam seemed to show him spending quite a bit of time in front of some kind of old-fashioned display screen that used camera film to show images and printed material.

At the appointed time, we descended into gravitational darkness. The five-hundred foot scans again showed no human biology other than the team. We dropped down and Wilson pulled them back aboard.

They were excited. They had been up for twenty-four hours. They were equally exhausted and hungry. I tried to insist on a rest period before the meeting. They ate, drank, and talked incessantly about what they had seen and learned. Some of it sounded absurd. With hot food in their stomachs, they refused to sleep and gathered at the table for debriefing.

"We can show exactly where false history ends and real history begins," said Erin. The table in front of her was covered with mag-paper printouts, food containers, and drink bottles.

"Okay, okay, but please start from the beginning so you don't lose me," I begged.

"You want the very beginning? Okay, here it is; in the beginning, God created the heavens and the Earth. That's the first sentence in the beginning of these people's history. From there it goes right on up through the Old Testament and then through the New Testament as well, even though none of that actually happened down there. Architects keep searching the deserts for relics and sites described in the bible and they keep finding artifacts and ruins that they try to fit to it. In some cases, they claim to have proven the connection." Erin paused and looked around the table.

RJ picked up the story. "The most interesting things begin showing up around 1500 years ago. From that time back all the forensic records show Neanderthal colonies. Clovis point weapons. No modern humans at all. Only the larger, less developed skulls. Occasional flint tools. It is clear something happened around 1500 years ago, and modern man emerged as suddenly as though he had stepped off a spaceship, if you will forgive the comparison."

"But it's the 1940's, 1950's down there." I said.

RJ was adamant. "Yes. Your confusion is well-founded. What took our Earth's civilization five or ten thousand years to accomplish these people have done in less than fifteen hundred years."

"Are you trying to say that humans from Earth were brought here like Shelly suggested?" I asked.

RJ said, "There are few ways these people could have suddenly shown up here, Adrian."

"And no way they could have advanced that quickly?"

In unison, RJ and Erin replied, "No way."

"So a Nasebian ship brought humans to this planet and helped speed their development along?" I asked.

"Or, if the humans brought here already possessed advanced knowledge, that would also explain the rapid development," said Wilson.

"Except for one thing," said Paris. "These people built pyramids. Why would people with an industrial knowledge base build pyramids? There's more to this. We haven't figured it out."

Erin added, "If the humans that were brought here were already advanced, they would know the Bible they were given was not their history, and that's not the case. The people down there firmly believe that Noah and Moses, and all the other biblical characters and events of our Earth were a part of the history of this planet."

We sat in silent wonder until RJ spoke. "The answer lies in the why of it. If we understood the underlying purpose of all this, our questions would be answered."

I rubbed my eyes and spoke. "Was there anything at all referencing the Udjat? I'm almost afraid to ask that."

"We had luck there at the last minute, Adrian," said Paris. "The very last minute." He slid a tablet with a photo of an Egyptian-styled stone tablet at me. "This was the last microfiche I looked at."

The timeworn stone in the photo was covered with Egyptian carvings. I looked up at him with a questioning stare.

"Do you see the cartouche near the center? It has symbols that are different from those around it. The symbols outside it are standard Egyptian chants and prayer symbols, but the markings inside the cartouche are phonetic references. They tell how to pronounce something. They are the phonetic translation of the word 'Udjat'."

I let out a long sigh of relief. "So what does this tell us?"

He pulled the tablet back. "Only that we've picked up the trail. We have to go back to the library. I can start tracing down these other markings and they will probably lead me to additional info. At least we know the Udjat is somehow related to the pyramids here. At some point, we are probably going to need to get a look at those pyramids first hand. There are probably inscriptions there that are not in the library."

"There's something else, Adrian," said RJ. "While Danica and I were running down the ancient history, I accidentally came across a conspiracy theory section. There's a bunch of stuff making claims of UFO visitations and government cover-ups, just like we used to see on Earth before Disclosure. There are references to Capal's chariot, claims the government actually recovered it buried in a desert somewhere, and that they have it stashed away at a secret facility. The government reports are heavily blacked out, but there was enough to identify the facility and figure out its location. We need to go there and run some scans."

"Why wouldn't we have picked up a footprint already?"

"Because we weren't looking for something that was being hidden."

I sat up and stretched. "Wow, you guys. I'm impressed. Confused, but impressed. I never expected this much. So, the decisions are easy. Back to the library for Paris and Erin. The rest of us will visit this other facility while we're waiting and see what we can see. This time you will have good ID and paperwork. We'll drop you two at the next window. Can you handle the hike again?"

They nodded enthusiastically.

"You all have time to get some sleep now. Does anyone have anything else before we break up? If not, head for your sleepers."

No one spoke. One by one, they pulled up and floated back to the galley or sleeper cells. RJ remained. The two of us sat still mag-locked in our seats.

"Is this making any sense to you?" I asked.

"Are you kidding? It's handwriting on the wall."

"Well clue me in, will you?"

"You ever study Sumerian history?"

"I'm embarrassed to say, not much."

"It's a damned big controversy even to this day. Sumerian history says that a race referred to as the Anunnaki came to Earth to harvest gold. They began mining operations and while they did, they also began genetic manipulation of the primates, the Homo erectus, which inhabited the Earth at that time. They mixed their own DNA with the best of the primates they could find, and over time created modern man. They trained man to mine the gold for them, and when there were enough, they withdrew and let the new species called humans, Homo sapiens, do all the work for them. That is the Sumerian story of creation."

"That's a bit distasteful. I think I'd prefer the special-children version of creation. And, that doesn't quite fit what we're seeing here."

"It doesn't fit yet, only because we don't know the why. Humans were introduced to this planet, and their evolution was accelerated for a reason. As I've said, all we need to know is the why. Then we'll understand."

"Keep thinking, RJ."

He smiled a tired smile and pushed himself up and away, heading for his sleeper compartment.

When everyone had spread out into their personal time, I went looking for Erin. She was alone in the med section of the science lab, mixing herself a medication cocktail.

"What is that?" I asked, suspended over her shoulder.

"Vitamins, anti-inflammatory, and a mild feel-good. The long hike caught up with me a little. The re-G regiment wasn't quite enough."

"You gonna be alright to do it again? We can switch off if you'd like."

"Are you kidding? I wouldn't miss it for the world. It's amazing down there. I doubt I'll ever get a chance to go back in time again."

"Well, you let me know if you have a change of heart. It's no problem to plug someone else in."

"Don't even think about taking any of my field trips, Adrian." She paused and gave me a threatening look no man would argue with.

"I wanted to ask you about Paris."

She turned and drank from the vile of liquid. "I wanted to talk to you about him, too."

"He's been a problem?"

"Just the opposite. He's been super."

"Really?"

"You've seen his work down there. Don't you agree?"

"Yes, and I plan to mention that to him. I just wondered if there was anything going on with him I didn't catch. He's had his problems in the past."

"Funny you should put it just that way. On the way back through the woods to the pickup sight, he and I fell behind a little. We had a chance to talk. I asked him about his wife. He told me. There's some things you should know, I think."

"My ears are open. My lips are sealed."

"It wasn't just a wife he lost. It was a wife and a six-year-old daughter. And, his wife wasn't just a doctor. She was chief of staff at Mt Sinai. There was an incident where some terrorist cell got hold of a new, lethal virus. They secretly exposed a flight attendant to it thinking he'd carry it around the world for them. Fortunately, he became too sick to fly and ended up at the hospital. Doctors there were baffled. Dr. Denard was called in. She contracted the virus without realizing it, and took it home to their daughter. As soon as the problem was identified the CDC was all over it. They contained the outbreak, but those first to come down with it did not survive. Paris' wife and daughter did not make it. Paris was away on assignment and did not get back in time. A year later, he switched to the intelligence department of the space agency. That's where he's been ever since."

"Wow. None of that was in his file. I wish I had known."

"It's as personal as it gets, but I thought you should know."

"Thanks. Guess I'll go track him down."

I found him at the back of the flight deck at an engineering station. He was doing something to a hand scanner. He cleared the display screen and looked up as I entered.

"Anything new?" I asked.

"No, actually I just finished this. It's a present for you."

"For me? Gee, I didn't get you anything."

He did not crack a smile. He handed me the scanner. "There are a couple of rooms in the library with old-fashioned cipher locks. Hand scanners can be programmed to decode any of those old mechanical types. You scan from the front and if it doesn't work scan from each side and you'll get a printout of the numbers in the proper order. It works on dial-type combination locks also." He pointed to the top row of buttons on the scanner. "It's the number six function key. Hit that and you're ready to scan. I made one for myself as well."

I looked up at him. "I'm impressed."

"There's more. The number seven function key will scan for alarm system triggers. That was a bit more complicated. They only use wire types here, so it had to be able to recognize magnetic micro switches, but it does work. It'll tell you if there's an active alarm."

"You thinking of going into some secure library rooms?"

"There's a good chance I won't need to. The stuff I'm looking for they don't understand well enough to classify it."

"Paris, do you mind my asking, how is it you can translate Egyptian and open locks with one hand tied behind your back?"

He looked at me with the same expressionless stare. "No, I don't mind. I started out as a propulsion engineer. You know that. I decided I wanted something more exciting than just shock diamonds and nacelle design. I asked to be transferred to the agency's intelligence group. They won't let quantum physics majors do field work, but they tested me and said I had an aptitude for cryptology. I took their deal to get a foot in the door. Their idea of cryptology amounted to a whole new degree. They used Egyptian, Mayan, Sumerian, and a bunch of other stuff in the training. They even had a German Enigma machine from World War 2 in one of the classes. Locksmith was also part of the curriculum. They figure you can't break an enemy's coded material if you can't open his safe. I did get some fieldwork out of it eventually, but nothing cloak and dagger. Does that answer your question, Commander?"

"Yes, thank you. I'm thinking we're lucky you're here, Paris. It has occurred to me we would probably have failed except for you."

He looked at me and said nothing, but I could see the gears turning. It seemed as though he wanted to say something more, but wasn't ready. I pushed away, nodded, and headed up front to relieve Shelly.

Chapter 37

We made our third team drop at 05:00 Earth II time. I had enough confidence in Erin's interpersonal skills to authorize the trade of an ounce of gold for some Earth II money. If that went well, they could hop the trolley to the library and save five miles of walking. Food from a restaurant was also approved. We held on orbit and watched long enough to make sure those dealings worked out.

Paris had checked the gold exchange price the day before. Gold was going for 25 dinars an ounce. In the pawnshop, Erin's communication skills seemed to work well. The shop owner offered her 15 for the blank coin. I cringed when Erin demanded 20. The shop owner gave in, though he milled around smirking like someone making too good a deal. Erin instructed him to be sure to include change for the trolley. He asked if she wanted a whole dinar's worth of tokens. She agreed, and a few minutes later we watched a smiling Paris help her board the trolley.

Heartened by the success of our first relations, we broke orbit to look for a military base that supposedly did not exist. It was one of those emperor's-clothes military bases. The military insisted it was not there. The rest of the world seemed to know it was. The place was a sprawling airfield on a wide, flat plateau surrounded by mountains. There were big runways, strangely shaped hangers, and miles of fencing and inroads protected by guard shacks and roving security teams. In the center of the complex one large building commanded many other smaller ones sporting busy aircraft hangers. There was testing of some sort going on. A large six-engine propeller aircraft waited on an apron with a lot of personnel fussing over it. The entire base seemed preoccupied with the operation.

We dropped to 50,000 feet above a cloudbank and held. Winds were a brisk one hundred and fifteen knots, but the ship managed it comfortably. Our scans did not find anything. We ran Paris' interior infrared program and mapped out the large building. There did not appear to be anything of interest. RJ rebelled at the idea of forgetting the place and leaving. He insisted nothing was exactly what you were supposed to find at a secret military base. He argued a more personal visit was needed. I countered that it was far too dangerous. To my dismay, he showed me a plan he had already constructed.

It was a nice plan. He had the frequencies of the base radar. We would descend in broad daylight out of sight, and feed back those same frequencies in such a way as to make ourselves invisible. The Griffin would stay on the ground at idle waiting for us, scanning for long-range bio signs so that a quick getaway could be made. While at the library he had located a private company under contract to do the main building's janitorial services. Their cleaning truck arrived daily on the outskirts of the base at approximately 2:00P.M. We would hide by the roadside, stall the truck momentarily with a hand scanner, and climb in the back. Once inside, we would borrow cleaning coveralls if there were any, and become janitors with attitude. We would escape the same way we went in. I said the plan was too iffy. RJ insisted it would work. I said it worried me. He said our job was to learn what happened to the Nasebian's spacecraft and if there was a Nasebian spacecraft the base was where it would be, and did I want to go back and tell the Nasebians we were afraid to check it out. I said, "Oh, damn you."

It took less than an hour to set up. RJ finished making clip-on security badges complete with the company logo. He had no idea what they were supposed to look like, but any badge was better than no badge. I spent the time making up mission abort plans in my head for each stage of the idiocy we were about to attempt. I did not like the plan and I liked my abort strategies even less. Shelly lowered us down into the trees as close as she dared. We ended up in bushes on the side of a dusty unpaved road the color of yellow clay, where if you listened carefully enough you could still faintly hear the Griffin at idle. In the distant sky, the big four-engine plane drew a white chem trail. It released some kind of aircraft which flashed across the blue before gliding powerlessly down and out of sight.

The janitorial truck showed up right on time, but it stalled too slowly and we had to run behind to catch up and climb in. To my relief no one was in the back. I clicked my weapon off stun and held to a strap in the cluttered darkness. The ride was rough and noisy. The truck smelled like every carcinogenic chemical known to man. There were no coveralls to borrow. Our flight suits, badges, and borrowed janitorial accessories would have to do. A long pause at the gate brought friendly voices and laughter. The truck jerked ahead to the clatter of grinding gears. We stopped too quickly. Equipment slid forward and went thud against the floor. RJ quickly peered out the back door. He waved frantically and slipped outside. I tried to keep up.

We were on the most exposed side of the largest building. The gate we had entered was visible in the distance. One guard looked our way, but paid no attention. The only concealment nearby was an office door twenty feet away. We walked briskly to it with a bucket and broom, and found it unlocked. RJ gambled and charged in. No one was inside. It was someone's messy office. We closed and locked the door behind us.

"RJ, I'm now realizing this really was a bad idea."

"We're in, aren't we?"

"Oh yeah, we're in deep."

"It's working perfectly. You'll see."

A paper-cluttered desk in the center of the room boasted a sprung swivel chair that was leaning back too far. A storeroom door behind it was ajar. There was a second door with a glazed window that led into the building. Just at that moment the silhouettes of two people appeared. They were speaking in low tones. RJ and I looked at each other like two kids about to be caught. Bucket and broom in hand, we ducked into the storage room and quietly closed the door. I pulled out my weapon and set it to stun.

The two voices entered. The conversation became clear. "But it wasn't too close, right? You were able to back it off under control."

"No, it was okay, really. We've just got to figure it out."

"And you're sure about the .98?"

"Yeah, I was pretty much paying attention about then."

"This isn't funny, Vance. Control problems are no joke."

"You're preachin' to the preacher, Curt. It was my ass."

"Okay, okay. I'll go see what the lab guys are doin' about it. No reschedule until we have something."

"We're close, Curt. Really close."

There was the sound of a door opening. "Why don't you come down to the lab with me? We'll see what they think."

"Okay. You got it."

The door shut. We waited. Nothing but silence. When I felt sure the coast was clear I put my weapon away, opened the door, and ran face to face into someone no man should have to meet.

Myself. It was me in an old-fashioned wrinkled green flight suit. He was a mirror image. He stood there, one foot away, just as shocked. He was missing a scar that I had on my neck. He had another to make up for it near the front. Everything else about him was identical, a perfect twin.

And it began. He stepped back and raised both hands in defense. I leaned back and half-raised my hands. He grabbed my wrist, planning to twist it around into an open-handed lock, just as I would. I sidestepped alongside him and wrenched my hand free. He countered by trying to wipe a hand over my face to bring me down with a foot behind my legs, just as I would have. I countered by pushing his hand up over my head as it arrived, and spun to face him, bringing a palm heel strike toward his chest. He countered by turning sideways to let the punch sail past, then grabbed the arm and pulled me forward to throw me off balance. I rotated my back to him and used his body to break the pull, then spun to a ready stance. He feigned with the right hand and tried to get me with a left hook. I moved inside and took the forearm from his punch on my right shoulder, then shoved him back into his desk where he reached out to catch himself, wiping everything off the desktop. It crashed to the floor in a heap.

We both moved away and separated. He narrowed his stare in a look of determination that worried me. He opened his mouth to call for help when RJ, staring wide-eyed through the open closet door, finally lurched out and yelled, "Gentlemen!"

The other me looked at RJ and froze. His expression was wide-eyed. "Patrick! What the hell is this? It's impossible! A twin? Can't be... You're too young!" The other me stepped back, placed a hand on the newly cleaned desk for balance, and stared at us. "Who the cruck are you guys? You've got ten seconds before I start screaming security."

I was still breathing heavy from the exchange and had nothing to offer. RJ held up one hand and spoke in earnest. "Wait. We can explain. But it'll take more than ten seconds."

"Of that I'm sure."

"Give us a chance. Can we just calm down a minute? Nobody's here to fight. We're not here to do any harm."

"Two imposters in a high security research facility? I'm not seeing any good answers."

I caught my breath and managed to come up with something stupid. "We're not from around here."

He looked at me with disdain. "Tell me something I don't know, you idiot." He repositioned himself an inch closer to the door.

RJ struggled to maintain the truce. "Thirty minutes in this room. That's all we need and you'll understand."

"You keep telling me nothing. Your ten seconds were up a while ago."

"There's a good explanation for all this. Just give me a second."

"Somebody disguised to look like me? It's too late, you guys. You've screwed up the plan. Give it up." He straightened up and took another inch toward the door.

"No, no. It's not like that. We're the good guys. Just give me a chance to explain," insisted RJ.

"Boy, I'd like to hear that myself," I said.

RJ snapped, "You're not helping."

"I know what this is, guys. You're part of the People's Revolutionary Army. You're trying to infiltrate this base disguised as me and my best friend. You screwed up, though. Patrick Manning died five years ago. Where'd you get your intel? Your plan was blown before you started. There's no way you'll get off this base. Time to turn yourselves in before somebody gets hurt," he said, trying to slide another casual inch in the direction of the door.

RJ persisted. "Who died five years ago?"

"You must know I've got to call for security."

"Please, don't do that. If you turn us in, it'll be messy. What we need is your help."

He hesitated. "You think I'm going to collaborate with you? Man, your Intel really is messed up."

It was then I noticed the weapon in RJ's hand. The other me noticed it, as well.

"What is that?"

"I'm sorry we've put you in this situation. Please believe me, no matter what happens, you won't be harmed." I said.

"And you... I know I don't trust you. Just let me step outside for a moment, that's all. If you're really the good guys, everything will turn out okay. Okay?"

"You should also know that when we're done, nothing bad will have happened here, and there will be no trace of us," I said in a brief moment of insight.

"Look, I'm not the secret agent type. You guys have got to turn yourselves in. Otherwise, there could be shooting and blood and all kinds of unpleasant stuff. Get it?"

"I'm sorry. We just can't allow you to turn us in," I said.

"I'm just going to slowly open this door and bring back someone you can talk to. No need for anyone to get hurt, okay?"

RJ's voice became solemn. "Please don't do that."

"Just take it easy now. Everything will be fine." He began slow, incremental moves toward the door. After seeing RJ's weapon, he had been playing us for time, just as I would have. Out of the corner of my eye I could see RJ's hand shaking a bit holding the weapon. I could also see that the other me had noticed that. The other me was wondering if he could make the door. I was wondering if RJ was fast enough and had it in him, then I remembered the gang leader at Heidi's.

RJ did not wait for him to make his move. Dejected, he hung his head sideways, whispered, "God damn it," and fired a pulse. My duplicate stiffened and fell. I caught him around the shoulders before he hit the floor and lowered him down.

"Nice shot!"

"This is a fine mess you've gotten us into."

"It was stun, right?"

"Of course the hell it was stun!"

"Nice shot, really."

"This man is your identical twin!"

"I noticed."

"This changes everything."

"I'm just glad you shot the right one."

"He said he knew me."

"He seemed to like you, go figure."

"This isn't funny."

"Would you help me get him up? It's the least I can do for me."

We dragged the other me to the desk and set him in the chair slumped over. We leaned on the desk and caught our breath.

"Do you think we made too much noise?"

"No, damn it."

"Do I really look that bad asleep?"

"Worse."

"Well, he should be out for twenty or thirty minutes."

"You know his clothes would fit you perfectly."

"Very funny."

"And his identification could be used by you in any good department store."

"You want me to put on his clothes and ID and see if I can get into the records department."

"What more could we ask for? It's a perfect plan."

"You could have said that before we dragged him over here."

"What, do I have to think of everything?"

We positioned the other me back onto the floor and made the switch. I straightened the unfamiliar green flight suit and stood up straight. "How do I look?"

"Just like Vance Cameron, at least that's what his name tag says. Colonel Vance Cameron, to be exact." RJ clipped the badge to my breast pocket.

"I shall try to remember who I am at all times."

"I, on the other hand, will remain here praying you will be back soon enough that the other you does not wake up and need to be stunned again."

"Oh, that's an ugly thought. And how do we get out of here? Even if we make it, he's onto us. He'll wake up, tell the whole world, and they'll be looking for us at every turn."

"One disaster at a time, Kemosabi. Find out if there's a record of the Nasebian ship anywhere and we'll make the rest up as we go along."

"Well, that puts my mind at ease. You sure you'll be alright here?"

"I will lock the door behind you and take no calls."

"Keep your com open."

"Duh..."

I slowly opened the door to the hall and checked in both directions. No one around. Trying to appear assured, I walked deliberately out and turned right. RJ clicked the lock behind me. There were closed double doors with windows ahead on my left. I did my best to hurry by, hoping to avoid anyone who might be inside. It did not work. A muffled voice immediately called out, "Colonel Cameron! Wait!" A technician or engineer in a white smock stuck his head out and called. "Colonel, wait. We need you to look at this."

There was no avoiding him. I stopped, turned, and waved acknowledgment. As I returned, he became excited. He gestured me into his laboratory where three others in white lab coats were standing at the observation window of a car-sized wind tunnel. I expected them to recognize me as an imposter. They did not.

"We will hit supersonic on the next try. I promise you that. We can beat the control problem. It's just buffeting. Look at this. It's what we think we need." He spread out a drawing of a rocket plane's tail section and tapped one finger on the elevator and horizontal stabilizer. "The control loss only occurs during the buffeting just before Mach one. If we increase the elevator parameters, that might do it. We make the lifting surface larger and you get a finer level of control. There would be structural damage if you overcorrect with this size elevator, but if you're careful it might be enough to overcome the loss of control."

My mind did a back flip. This was a textbook control problem we had all read about during the early days when the sound barrier was being broken. Mach tuck. Just before supersonic, the lift gradient over the tail moves backward because of the buffeting. A guy name Yeager had dealt with the same exact problem.

I shook my head. "Mach tuck."

"What?"

"Oh sorry. It's a phrase I sort of coined. Mach tuck. The lift profile is being moved by the buffeting. It's kind of shock-stalled."

"Yeah, so we enlarge the elevator and that spreads the problem out. You keep control."

"No. The elevator design is okay. You just need to add trim to the stabilizer section, not the elevator, so it can be adjusted to a new neutral. Fine trim. Add fine trim."

He looked astonished. "Trim the horizontal stabilizer? Where did you get that? Trim for the stabilizer… At that speed? It could work. That's it. It's what we've needed all along. Dampening and control all in one." He looked at me with the admiration of a rock fan.

I pointed one thumb over my shoulder. "Records."

"Oh, okay. We'll get on this right now. There won't be time to tunnel it. I'll let you know."

I waved and escaped out the door, breathing a sigh of relief that they let me go. The green-carpeted hallway led to a waiting room with a white reception desk, typewriters, and filing cabinets. Two receptionists were sorting sheets of paper into a cabinet made of wooden dividers. I dared not slow, hoping to plow on by and ignore them. Once again, it did not work.

"Colonel Cameron, should I have your car brought around to your office, or will you be working late?" called one of the women.

In front of me, there were three new corridors to choose from. I paused as though in a hurry. In another rare moment of insight, I turned to her and nodded. "Yes; yes please have it brought around, but I'll drive myself, though."

She looked perplexed. "Yes Sir. I know. You always do."

I raised one hand in awkward acknowledgment, pointed down the nearest hallway and stammered "Records…"

She smiled and pointed at the corridor on my left. "It's that way, Sir."

I slapped myself on my head and turned to go.

"It must have been a wild test flight this morning," she said and laughed.

I smiled, shook my head, and marched on, managing to get past four other closed doors without being stopped. Double doors with safety glass windows at the very end of the hall had a plaque that read, "Blueprint." Unfortunately, several women were milling about inside. It made me wish I had brought Wilson. I pushed my way in.

They were busy everywhere with stacks of documents. A longhaired blond with cherry red lipstick stopped working her machine and came over to the counter.

"Wind tunnel testing?" I asked.

"We're really swamped, Colonel. You'll have to fend for yourself. That would be isle H, on the right. I'm sure you can find it. Please be sure to put everything back in the right spot, please…" She gave me an extra long smile with a wink and returned to her stack.

I pushed through swinging, waist-high doors and found isle H. It was rows of gray filing cabinets stacked to the ceiling. Ladders on rails provided access to the upper drawers. It didn't take long to realize I was wasting my time. As inconspicuously as possible, I moved from isle to isle, trying to map the place in my mind. There was an adjoining room with a keypad lock on the door. Like the others, it had a safety glass window. I managed to get good glimpse inside. There was a very serious looking elevator in there with bright red seals on the keypad and a big threatening sign on its cage. The elevator did not go up. It only went down.

Waving thanks, I left and made it back to Cameron's office. "RJ, open up." The lock clicked and the door opened just enough for me to slip in.

"Someone drove up in a car and knocked on the outside door."

"Yeah. It's our ride out. Did he wake up?"

"No, but he's been stirring. What's the plan?"

"We put him in the trunk and just drive right out the gate. Then, we hide his car in the woods, load him on the ship and keep him until we're done here."

"We're not done here?"

"There's nothing but routine test data in the main records office, but there's a classified elevator in an adjoining room. It only goes down. I'm guessing the good stuff is under us. We need to come back after hours."

"What if someone is waiting for Colonel Cameron at home?"

"Don't be silly. He's me."

"Still..."

"We'll check out his place from orbit, see if there's anyone there. Wanna make any bets? You ready to get out of here?"

"You do the stunning next time, okay?"

"Okay. When we get him on the ship we'll sedate him. He's too devious to take any chances. I know me."

"He's going to be one pissed off you."

"Boy, that's scary."

Chapter 38

I stood outside Colonel Vance Cameron's office surveying the grounds. Several people were working on aircraft in the
distance. One guard still manned the gate. I climbed in Cameron's deep blue sedan to find a strange set of controls. It was
manual transmission with the shifter on the floor. The gas pedal
was round, the brake pedal huge, and the clutch pedal tiny. First
gear was back and to the left, reverse back and to the right. I
carefully backed up to the office door, waited to see if anyone
considered the action suspicious, then opened the trunk. After
pausing suspiciously for another look around, I returned to RJ.

"You ready?"

"Will we make it?"

"I parked the car so the guard's view is blocked. There's
nobody else in range."

"What if he wakes up and starts banging?"

"It'll only take a few seconds to cruise by the guard. After that, there's no one."

"I'll take the feet."

We half dragged, half carried our victim to the door.
Now, with a look of pronounced guilt, I stuck my head out and
checked again. No one around. Getting him into the trunk took
longer and was less graceful than I'd hoped. There was ample
time for someone to show up unexpectedly or notice from afar.
No one did. Like inept criminals, we shut the trunk and stood
with our hands in our pockets trying to appear innocent. It was
agreed RJ would stay down as we drove past the guard. At the
gate, he saluted as I went by.

There were no speed limit signs. The speedometer had
meaningless, ascending numbers. I did my best to drive a normal speed, all the time fearing we'd meet a patrol vehicle and
be stopped. At the turnoff point, we found a path through the
brush and trees and forced that poor sedan through the woods
all the way to the Griffin, warning Wilson, Danica, and Shelly in

advance of what to expect, although they had already seen enough on the collar cams.

There began to be noises from the trunk. We pulled into the clearing a few dozen feet from Griffin, got out and stood behind the car, weapons drawn. Wilson looked on from the Griffin's open hatch.

"If he gets a look at the spacecraft he's going to try for the woods," said RJ.

"That's what I would do," I replied.

"If you get into it with him again, at least it will be a fair fight."

"Very funny. Not my kind of odds."

"It's your turn," he reminded me.

"Regrettable," I mumbled.

RJ took the keys, and inserted them. He clicked the trunk open and quickly stepped back and away. The trunk lid slowly rose open ten or twelve inches. Colonel Cameron's angry, glazed eyes peered out.

RJ said, "We're sorry, Colonel."

I let go with a quick pulse from the pistol and the trunk fell back closed.

With Wilson's help, we dragged the Colonel into the Griffin and fastened him securely to a jump seat by a closed portal. Wilson appeared matter-of-fact about the whole affair. Shelly, on the other hand, had a look of consternation that would have quieted any rambunctious kindergarten class. We lifted off and headed back to monitor Erin and Paris, pausing only to check the Colonel's address from his identification and scan his home to be sure no one would miss him.

RJ sat at his engineering station surveying the inside of the Colonel's modest home. "You were right. There's nobody at his place and no other vehicles in the driveway. It's what they used to call base housing. He has neighbors, though, and they are home."

"Lucky, lucky."

RJ turned to look at me. "You see what's happening here, don't you?"

"Oh no. I hate it when you say that."

"You remember back in the late twentieth century, people complaining that UFOs were spying on them and kidnapping them?"

"Oh boy."

"We've now become them."

"We're on a mission."

"So were they, probably."

"We're only trying to correct some things that went wrong."

"Who's to say that's not what they were doing? What determines unethical imposition from altruistic intervention?"

"I don't understand."

"How important does something have to be before it's okay to do it, no matter what it is?"

"What do you suggest?"

"I don't know. I don't have the answers, either. I sometimes need to grumble about things."

"Really?"

"All I know is we are now the aliens spying in people's homes and abducting them."

A moan from the habitat module interrupted us. RJ said, "The trunk lid absorbed most of the stun. He's coming around. You said you would sedate him. Are you going to blindfold him, as well?"

"RJ..."

"Are you sure we're the good guys?"

"I was only going to say, we don't need to sedate him or blindfold him, for Pete's sake."

"Really?"

With Danica doing the flying, Wilson and RJ at their engineering stations, and Shelly seated at the table, I twisted a jump seat around and sat staring at the Colonel. His eyelids fluttered. Glazed eyes tried to focus, though vision hadn't quite returned. Ambulatory functions were no more than twitches, but it was clear the brain was already at work, racing to adapt and evaluate. Even in semi-consciousness, he had test pilot face. The right hand, the aircraft stick controller, began clenching. This could be a blackout from a fatal dive in an experimental airplane; instantaneous reactions might be needed. He fought his way to awareness and stiffened as he looked around. His gaze met mine.

"Welcome back, Colonel."

"We're very sorry about that, Colonel," RJ called from his station.

He jerked up in his seat, snapping his arms and feet against the restraints, then braced for an incoming assault.

"I'm sorry about those too, Colonel. It's a temporary measure until we work something else out," I said.

"He looked around. "What the..."

"This is my spaceship, the Griffin. We're not going to harm you. When we're done we'll return you to the Base."

He looked down at the restraints holding him and replied sarcastically, "You guys aren't afraid of me, are you?"

"I can't let you up just yet, Colonel. I know you too well. You could try something with the ship or crew. You wouldn't take that chance, if it was you."

RJ called out. "You're confusing me, Adrian."

"RJ..."

"Sorry, just an observation."

The Colonel scanned the ship and looked back at me with contempt. "You've drugged me. I can feel it. This is a set-up. You want information about the sound barrier testing. Why is the PRA interested in Mach 1?"

"Colonel, you have not been drugged. What you're feeling are the effects of weightlessness. We are orbiting your planet at an altitude of approximately 24,000 miles, traveling almost 2 miles per second. I know the term miles probably doesn't mean anything to you. Just take my word we're high and fast."

"Bullshit."

I reached over and tapped the switch by his portal to open it. Below us, patches of white clouds drifted over the continent below. The Colonel strained to look down, then sat back and smirked. "Nice simulation. Where'd you get the color display?"

"You're right. That could be faked. But, how about this?" I reached out and withdrew the pen sticking out of his flight suit pocket. I held it a foot from his face and let go. It drifted gently in front of him.

He paused and wrinkled his brow. He looked at me and then back at his pen, still floating. "Okay, I'll give you that. It's pretty good. But, we get weightless from diving aircraft all the time. I'm guessing in just a minute or so we're going to start getting really heavy as this aircraft is pulled out of a dive."

"Okay Colonel, but while we're waiting for that not to happen, let me try to tell you why you're here."

He looked back at me with a softening expression. "We can't be diving. A dive couldn't last this long."

"You're not space sick at all, are you? Makes sense. I never did get sick."

"Where are we again?" he asked.

"Do you know what geosynchronous orbit is?"

"No."

"It's when you position the spacecraft high enough that the orbit is the same speed as the planet's rotation, so you remain in a fixed point above the planet. Your planet has two moons so we have to continually adjust for their gravitational effects, and there is influence from solar wind and various radiation pressures, but otherwise we're holding position over one of your cities."

RJ pushed out of his seat and floated over to us. The Colonel stared at him hovering next to us. "My God. It's true."

"Colonel, I must apologize for my Commander's lack of manners," said RJ, and he glanced at me like a displeased parent. "This is Commander Adrian Tarn. As he just mentioned, this is his ship, the Griffin. I'm RJ Smith, systems engineer. It is offensive to all of us that you are restrained, but we know we can't trust you. You are too much like our Commander here, and we all know what he's capable of."

I frowned at RJ. "Hey, hold on one minute…"

"Colonel, can I get you something to drink?"

"Not unless I can hold it in my own hands."

"Ah yes, that. I have an idea that I think will allow us to lose the restraints. Give me a few minutes. I'll be right back."

"RJ?"

RJ waved me off and headed aft.

"Why have you brought me here, wherever this really is?"

"We are here about Capal's chariot."

A flash of fear spiked in the Colonel's eye. He tried to appear ignorant. "You're here about what?"

"There's a piece of it on display in the Provincial Museum of Natural History. It's no secret. You've just blown your cover trying to pretend you don't know about it."

"It's only a legend. Nobody knows anything about it."

"We've seen the classified government documents. You just blew your cover again."

"You must know, there are things under the security umbrella that people cannot discuss for fear of repercussions."

"No one has to know. No secrets can escape up here, and we will leave without a trace. "

"Sorry. The government does random security interviews. If they suspect the slightest violation, they use truth serums. The only way to protect yourself is to never have said anything for them to find out about."

I sat back and nodded. "I see. In that case, we must not put you in any jeopardy. You're about to break the damn sound barrier, after all. Wouldn't want to compromise that. We can do what we need to without help from you, but you'll need to tag along until we're done."

RJ returned with a silver band in one hand and several coin-sized remote controls in the other. He handed me one and tucked the rest in his pocket.

He moved behind the Colonel and fastened the band around his neck. "I know this is barbaric." RJ pointed at me. "It's his fault, Colonel. He left the closet too soon."

"I am sorry, Colonel. We couldn't leave you down there or you would have been obligated to give us away. When we're done here, we'll put you back where you belong and hopefully no further harm will be done."

"Oh sure, and I promise not to tell, right?"

"Imagine yourself telling the authorities what has happened to you so far. Then ask yourself if you would rather stay on test flight status."

RJ interrupted. "This collar has a transducer that emits the same stun pulse that we used to knock you out. Everyone on this ship has a control to energize it. I'm going to release these restraints now. I think you know what will happen if you try anything." RJ unlatched the restraints and pushed back. The Colonel began to float upward, grabbing the edge of the portal to steady himself.

"Maybe a tour of the ship will make up a little bit for what we've done to you. I'm sure the cockpit will be of most interest. Follow me, Colonel," I said.

The man took to weightlessness like a fish to water. No unnecessary gyrations of the legs. It was gratifying to see. I was almost proud of myself as idiotic as that was. We coasted through the airlock. He paused to look at the outside hatches.

"You wouldn't want to open those," I said.

He gave me a flat stare. "Right."

I moved aside by the engineering stations so he could pull past for a closer look at the flight deck. Beyond the front windows, the planet was turning with us. Flight controls were in orbital lock, keeping us synched. Danica looked back and up at him. "Hello, Colonel. The terminator is just up ahead. We'll be passing into night shortly."

He looked forward. "My God," was all he said, and when his awe had settled a bit he looked back at me. "All this and a doll in the left seat?"

Danica made a 'tsk' sound.

"Better watch yourself, Colonel. She'll fly circles around you and then beat your ass in the boxing ring, as well."

After formal introductions to the rest of the crew, I guided him through compartment after compartment and could almost see his mind expanding with each new facility. He asked all the right questions. There was enough technical knowledge that he understood things were decades ahead of his time.

When the tour was complete, he and I sat at the oval table in silence for quite a time while RJ and Wilson went back to engineering station work and Shelly began her sleep period. After the long silence, he asked, "What happens now?"

"I need to go back into your facility...as you. That's why I haven't given you your flight suit back. It's stored in my sleeper cell for the time being. I need to take that Blueprint office elevator down. It will be easier now, but I could still use your help."

"It won't be as easy as you might think. I'm not authorized for the lower levels. I'm just a rocket jockey, remember?"

"What's down there?"

"And that brings us to the point, doesn't it? I still can't be sure if you are the good guys or the bad guys?"

"I'm you, aren't I?"

"Are you? How is it you look just like me? I know it's not the surgical thing; too much of you is an exact match. So, how can you be who you are?"

"We don't know. We're working on it. There's all kinds of identical parallels between your planet and ours that we don't understand yet."

"Yeah, you haven't told me a thing about where you come from. Maybe you're here to gather information so your planet can take over and make ours an extension of yours."

"Nope. We're too far away. The distance is almost unimaginable. This was a risky venture for us. I'm sorry, I forgot my manners again. Would you like water, coffee, or something else?"

"Water would be good."

In the galley I set up a squeeze tube for him and filled it with cold water. I pitched it at him through the zero-G and he brought it in like a pro. Back at the table, I sipped at coffee. "The truth is, I understand you perfectly. I'd feel the same way you do. As I said, we can do this without your help. That's probably the way it needs to be so you can live with yourself afterward."

"Nothing personal," he replied.

"Nothing personal."

"When will you go back in?"

"Late tonight when there's less staff there. I sure as hell don't want to stun anybody else."

"Hear, hear..." he raised his squeeze tube.

"One thing's for sure."

"What's that?"

"You'll never laugh at anyone who claims to have been abducted by aliens ever again."

Chapter 39

It was an aggressive schedule. Visit the Colonel's base at 1:00A.M.; be done with it and at the rendezvous to pick up Paris and Erin at 04:00A.M. This time I would go in alone. Erin and Paris seemed to be doing fine. Near midnight they visited a coffee house near the park and were now getting ready to start the hike back. We broke orbit and headed to Colonel Cameron's base. As we set up for descent, he floated up next to me in the airlock and held to the ceiling.

"The elevator will give you three floors down. On the third floor you'll exit into the top-secret documents room. Beyond it, a door will take you to a hallway that leads to a security station with a twenty-four-hour guard. Next to his station is a storage closet with a keypad lock. It's actually a stairwell to the fourth level. That's the one you want. I sure would like to see what's down there."

"Why the change of heart?"

"Because I'm not convinced you're the bad guys, and if you get caught down there I'll be screwed for life."

"I had thought of that. How about alarms?"

"There are no active alarms unless the base is put on alert. The lower levels are visited periodically twenty-four hours a day, so switching the alarm system on and off all the time became a headache. There are a few closed circuit cameras, one on the third level main hallway, others on the fourth. They aren't monitored. They just feed tape twenty-four hours a day. The tapes record over themselves every twenty-four hours. If you are not detected they will never be looked at and your entry will automatically be recorded over."

"How about if RJ sets you up with a communicator so I can talk to you if I need to while I'm in there?"

"Agreed."

"I hope to be quick. If all goes well I'll show you some photos from level four."

"One other thing: in the bottom right-hand drawer of my desk there's a file folder titled Patrick Manning. It's the medical report of what killed Manning, your RJ. I'd take that and study it, if I were you."

It caught me off guard. His RJ had passed away at fifty-five. Mine was not there yet. A spike of fear went through me. I nodded a thank you and got set at the door. "Colonel, that neck collar works even at a distance. If you make a play for the open hatch, you'll be sleeping in the grass."

He gave a sarcastic laugh. "Yeah. I figured."

"Try to enjoy the ship. You won't have it for much longer, then it'll be gone forever."

"Promise?"

We slowed and stopped. Danica's voice came over our coms. "Clear." I popped the hatch and waited for the hiss to die, then tugged it open. A short jump to the grass and I turned to watch Wilson and the Colonel pull it shut behind me. The sedan waited.

Headlights bouncing through woods were a real attention getter. Fortunately, no one was around to notice. As I approached the lighted guard shack, Colonel Cameron's voice came over the com. "Stop at the gate. Show him your badge. It's a gesture of respect."

I did as he said.

"Working extra late, Colonel?"

"Tie up some loose ends."

"What's loose ends?"

"Left over work."

"Okay." He waved me in.

I pulled up to the office door and went in. The desk was still cleared. The lamp on the floor would not light. By the inside door, a wall switch brought on caged lamps overhead. I took a moment to check the hall. There was no one; only a few hallway lights were on. There was no reason to wait.

The secretarial desk at the end of the corridor was deserted and dark. I looked down the passageway that led to Blueprint. All the lights were off. This time the double doors were locked. A quick scan with F6 on the hand scanner gave me the numbers. The place was spooky. The air was cold from lack of human heaters. The door at the back had the same lock. Once again, the hand scanner decoded it. I entered into shadows and searched. No lights, no people. The elevator waited.

The keypad lock was a bit more sophisticated. The scanner took longer. There were red security seals on the cage door. I tore them carefully away and let the pieces hang for a reseal later. Inside the elevator there were three floors, just as the Colonel had promised. I tapped 3 and drew my weapon, checking it for stun. The ride was quick and smooth.

Level 3 was a dark maze of document shelves. One emergency light flickered against a wall. I got lost for a few moments but final caught the dim glow of a windowed door. Beyond it, the long hallway led to the security desk, also just as Colonel Cameron had promised. A guard sat tilted back in his chair, head down staring at a newspaper. I exchanged my weapon for my phony letter of authorization and held it out in front of me as I headed for the guard.

He was snoring. I tucked the letter back in, drew my weapon, said a prayer of forgiveness, and pulsed him with a stun. He jerked in his seat, but remained in the same position. It occurred to me that there were now two of us who hoped the security tapes were never reviewed.

The secure storage door was right where it should have been. The keypad lock was the more complex one, but again the hand scanner broke the code. Spiral stairs led steeply down. At the bottom, pneumatic doors opened automatically. Security doors at uneven intervals lined both sides of a long, shadowy passageway. The white tiled floor was dirty. The white walls had black scars from push-tables bumping against them. There was crumpled up paper and other trash on the floor. There was a faint smell of formaldehyde in the air. It gave me the creeps. One by one I opened and photographed the rooms. Most of it was a tangled mass of unrecognizable junk. Janitorial services seemed to be infrequent here. Every garbage pail was overflowing. Some areas looked heavily used, others abandoned. Several rooms had what looked like old-fashioned x-ray machines. Another room had chemicals, a small furnace, and a tabletop centrifuge.

The fifth door on the right was the one. It had red tape seals, something the others had not. I tore them open as carefully as possible and scanned the keypad. The door pushed open to a room dimly lit by yellow light. On a custom metallic stand in the middle of the room sat a weathered, gold colored, egg-shaped spacecraft. A big window wrapped over the front revealed a single center seat. No engines. Ports for braking rockets. A shark-fin piece missing from the tail section. The spacecraft and everything else in the room were covered with a layer of brown-gray dust. The light from my scanner showed my footprints on the floor. Specially designed consoles sitting around the room were covered with clear plastic tarps. They had either finished testing the spacecraft or given up. I made my pictures and scanned the ship's electronics. To my amazement the scanner showed biological circuits, all long dead. I scanned the surrounding consoles for data and headed back.

The trip up was easier than it should have been. I rejoined the security seals using a clear plastic tape of my own, brought along for just that purpose. The level-three guard was still knocked out. At the door to the Colonel's office there was a note taped to the window I had not noticed when I left. It was a drop time for the next supersonic flight test. Inside the office, I opened the desk file drawers and found the file folder for RJ's duplicate. I left and locked up, and getting into the sedan I noticed bushes sticking out of the front bumper on the driver's side. I pulled them off and headed out. The sleepy gate guard nodded and waved as I went by.

We sat around the oval table in gravity staring at prints of the Nasebian spacecraft. This time Colonel Cameron accepted my peace offering of coffee. We drank and stared in silence.

"It's not actually a spacecraft. It's an escape pod," I said.

RJ added, "No engines."

The Colonel finished his coffee, and looked at me with distrust. "So what now, Commander? You say I have a test flight the day after tomorrow. I do not want to miss it."

I stood, reached over and unbuckled his metal collar, and dropped it on the table.

"Starting to trust me, are you? You shouldn't."

"On your next test flight you'll be the first man to break the sound barrier, Colonel."

"That's not at all guaranteed. There have been control problems."

"I got pulled into your lab while you were passed out in the office. I gave them the answer, or I should say you gave them the answer. A trim system on the horizontal stabilizer. You'll be able to trim out the instability."

"So you're letting me go? I can just walk right out that hatch?"

"Not exactly."

"There are four of you but it would be worth a shot, wouldn't you say? What's to stop me from trying?"

"Six to eight hours."

"What?"

"The coffee. You'll be out six to eight hours."

"Oh shit."

"We'll lock you in your car. Our scans indicate you'll be safe there. When you wake up be careful driving out. You'll still be under the influence a little bit. The six to eight hours will give us enough time to finish what we need to do. You will not see us again. We'll be light years away."

"I guess you don't like long goodbyes."

RJ added, "If you remember this Colonel, invest heavily in silicone doping. It will end the age of vacuum tubes."

His eyes began to glaze, but he shook it off. "Thanks for a look at the future, I guess..."

And he was gone. Carefully, we put him back in his own flight suit, making sure there were no accidental souvenirs in any of the pockets. We dared to use external lights on the Griffin and with a newfound affection, carried him out into the damp, dark night. Seat recline happened to be one of the sedan's few amenities. Shelly covered him with a blanket from the Griffin's linen supply, the only material keepsake to be left behind. We said silent goodbyes, boarded, and lifted off to pick up Erin and Paris.

They were waiting for us with irritated attitudes. There had been a problem. A new kind of flying insect had shown up in droves and attacked. There had been no escaping the bastards. We pulled the two wounded warriors aboard covered with tiny welts on the face and hands. We did not strap in. We went straight to the med lab and worked on the bites while Shelly took us gently up. Fortunately, the topical applications were more than a match. The redness and inflammation faded quickly.

Despite the beating they had taken, they were beside themselves. They had discovered something incredible. They did not want a rest period. They wanted to meet right away. Their excitement was contagious. We raided the galley en masse and gathered around the oval table, completely ignoring the transition to weightlessness. Wilson wasn't prepared; his feet came off the floor and he bicycle-pedaled his way to a seat.

Erin began. "There are duplicates of some of us down there. Once we picked up on the first one we began looking for more and found they were everywhere. They'd been there all along; we just hadn't noticed."

Paris added, "It began with Einstein. Going through newspaper copies on the microfiche machine, his photo was on one of the archeology magazine pages. His name is Alexander Porvios. He's a physicist at a university. No surprise there."

The rest of us looked at each other. I nodded in agreement. "We're with you. We ran into another me at the military base. We had to bring him aboard briefly."

It was probably the only thing that could have stunned the two of them, and it did. There was a long pause and Erin asked, "You made contact? You made first contact?"

I recounted the story. They sat and listened with keen interest. When the story was told Erin looked around the table, then back at me and asked, "What does it mean?"

RJ locked his hands behind his head and said, "It's easy."

We all looked at him and waited.

"What kind of a ship did you say the Nasebian craft was, Adrian?"

"A repository. They use it to document life in the galaxy."

"And how long did you say Nasebians live?"

"At least two thousand years, usually longer. They never die, they just sort of fade in and out over many years, and eventually do not reappear."

"So don't you all see? Shelly's original guess was that humans were brought here to seed the planet. It was a good guess, but not completely accurate. We found an escape pod at the military facility. An escape pod means there was a problem with the Nasebian's ship. The escape pod was used to get to Earth II. The mother ship was a repository, records of the explored galaxy. Records like DNA records. The Nasebian that escaped here brought along everything he would need to rescue himself. He brought the ingredients to create an advanced culture out of the Homo erectus that lived here at the time. They would provide him with the things he needed to survive as well as the industrial manufacturing base to recover and repair his mother ship, and he had two thousand years or more to do it."

We sat stunned. Another long, silent moment and Paris spoke, "That fits the rest of it."

"Rest of it? There's more?" asked Shelly.

Paris nodded. "Earth II's great pyramids were constructed on the banks of the Euros River in the Salara Forest in the Salara Province. Legend has it that is the birthplace of Earth II's culture. The Salara forest is made up of flat, forested plains and high surrounding plateaus. Archeologists have barely scratched the surface exploring caves there. Evidence of modern man first appeared in that area. They do not have carbon dating here yet, or any kind of radio dating for that matter, but they are very good at geological layering. They've dated the oldest evidence of modern man to fifteen or sixteen hundred years ago. That's when the big jump in evolution took place. From Neanderthal to modern man, overnight. What's more, it was an explosion of modern man. Somewhere around eleven hundred to twelve hundred years ago construction of those great pyramids began. They were completed in record time. From there, you know the rest of the history. Those are the archeological facts, but there are legends of the great god Capal who guided man in those times. The same Capal whose chariot descended from the heavens to teach and help mankind."

"Wow!" said Danica over the com.

"Wow!" agreed Wilson.

Shelly asked, "Well, the next question kind of worries me a bit. Where is our Nasebian god Capal right now?"

Paris answered, "That part of the story is incredulous. You will need to be open-minded."

Wilson said, "Compared to what we've already heard? Are you kidding?"

Paris ignored him. "The hieroglyphs are much more complete here than they are on our Earth. Because Earth II's history is so corrupted, they have not been able to translate them with much success. The records here tell how the pyramids were built and what they are used for, something that has been argued on our Earth for thousands of years. The records here say that the great pyramid not a tomb. It is a machine."

Wilson scoffed, "A machine made out of stone?"

Paris remained undeterred. "The interior of our great pyramid has always been a mystery. It does not seem to have been designed for humans to enter and move about in. You enter the pyramid and are immediately confronted with the ascending passage, a smooth, narrow corridor too steep for humans to ascend without a railing or climbing gear. It leads you to the grand galley, another narrow, ascending corridor with an extremely high ceiling and just as difficult to climb without help. When the pyramid was first entered, these passageways were blocked in spots by huge stone slabs nearly impossible to remove. When they were finally extricated, an empty coffer with no lid was found in the King's chamber. There are many small airshafts leading to the surface pointing at different places in the sky. None of this has made much sense, except for some relationships to stars and constellations."

Paris paused to catch his breath. He waited for dissenters, then continued on. "Look at it this way. Imagine a primitive tribe happens to come across a diesel engine the size of a house in the wilderness. The thing is so huge they can enter the exhaust pipes and actually walk around inside the piston shafts, coolant lines, and fuel lines. They would have no idea what those things were for or why they were made. That's exactly what we are doing with the Great Pyramid."

Wilson asked, "Are you actually going to tell us what the thing does?"

Paris nodded. "Like any sophisticated machine, it has several applications. It's a power generator, a communication device, and a transport unit. You fill the empty coffer in the King's Chamber with the proper materials, flood the chambers beneath the pyramid with the correct fluid, replace the capstone with the precise, gigantic polished crystal. Then you wait for the proper alignment and the machine comes to life."

"Wow!" said Wilson.

"That's not all. I'm sure most of you are familiar with the Mayan calendar, the one that predicted the coming of Disclosure, when humans learned we weren't the only intelligent species in the solar system. Well, there is a similar calendar here. It uses the same design, hubs interconnected with larger and smaller wheels that turn to represent time. It's an artifact in the museum, only this one not only tracks Earth II's movement through the heavens, it also has a wheel that tracks something called Capal's star. Capal's star can be only one thing: his spacecraft. He tracked his ship and when he was ready, used the pyramid to transport back to it."

"Talk about science fiction," said Erin.

"A leap of faith to believe," added Wilson.

"So by that reasoning, that's it. He's long gone," said Shelly.

Paris nodded. "Capal is always referred to in the past tense, as though he died or left. But, there is one other thing. The few records relating to the Udjat allude to a story of it being housed in the smaller of the two pyramids. We will need to go there to get more information."

Everyone looked at me. I had to shake off the story I had just heard. The com was open. "Did you get that, Danica?"

"Yes, Adrian. And, I have the coordinates. We may as well just drop to a lower orbit and let Sir Isaac pull us around."

"Make it so."

Chapter 40

The Salara flatlands and surrounding plateaus were beautiful, even from orbit. Jungle canopies bristled with life. The Euros River was wide, snake-like, and deep blue. Canals branched off from it, some appearing manmade and ancient. Northwest of the pyramid complex there was a gigantic, deep hole in the ground; so deep it descended into darkness. The place was remote and wild. It was as though a section of South America had been transported and placed here.

The sprawling pyramid complex seemed odd. The area all around was cleared, leaving a brown carpet with cultivated areas of grass. Crops were being grown on the outskirts. There seemed to be service type buildings located at various points around the complex. Numerous trails led through the woods to nearby settlements populated by single story mud-brick dwellings and other odd structures. There was a lot of activity going on, but none of it appeared to be tourism or commerce. Now that we were overhead our scans could be more detailed. RJ took a seat at an engineering station and began the high-res scanning. For the first time I felt a slight bit of guilt at the intrusiveness of it. He glanced at me as though he agreed.

The rest of us met at the table, waiting for the scan data. As Erin and Paris took their places, I opened the dialogue. "So what do we know about these people? For some reason, I have a bad feeling about secretly dropping in on them."

Erin answered, "That was my end of it, Adrian. Your instincts are right on. I do not know how we will visit their complex. These people are isolationists to a degree; friendly, but not open to outsiders."

"There does not seem to be much technology down there. They are fundamentalists?"

"It's hard to say, actually. They have been described as tribal, cultural, an isolated society, and sometimes religious eccentrics. University groups have requested admittance to learn about them and been summarily turned away. Commerce and trade are erratic. They allow it only when there is something they specifically need, and they seem to require little from the outside world. It is not clear how much technology they actually have or use."

"Aren't there any records of anyone getting in at all?"

"There are. Two or three explorers have gone there over the years and never returned. It is said the cost of admittance is agreeing to never leave."

"Oh brother."

"They have been photographed with only spears, bows, and knives, no weapons more powerful than that but strangely, even through the years of wars, no other society has ever intruded upon them. They have always been left alone."

"How many?"

"Estimates only. Thousands."

"But this is supposedly the birthplace of this planet's population?"

"These people are the descendants of those who built the pyramids. They claim to serve Capal and his teachings to this day."

We sat in silent wonder. I hoped someone else would come up with a good idea, or at least a better question. RJ called out from his engineering station. "Adrian, I'm noticing something peculiar here."

"You? Really?"

"No; seriously. You should come up here and take a look at this."

We all pushed up and pulled through the forward airlock. RJ was turned to face us. He pointed at an overhead monitor. It was a magnified view of the pyramid complex. People were everywhere, working the crops, transporting goods, all the things normally seen in a primitive society's workday.

"Your kind of town," I said.

"That's a photo from the down-facing cameras, taken when we first got here." He paused and then pointed to a second monitor nearby. It was the same shot, but no one was present, no gardeners, no workers, and no commuters. The place was deserted except for several lines of people at various points around the complex. It looked like they were waiting for something, or guarding something.

"That's one I took a few minutes ago," said RJ. "You get it?"

"I'm not sure."

"Our scans. Either by sheer coincidence the whole place shut down when we started hi-res scanning, or somehow they detected our scans."

I held to the ceiling and in exasperation wiped my face with my free hand. "It has to be a coincidence, RJ."

"Who was it that said he didn't believe in coincidences?" he replied.

"But..."

Before I could finish my sentence, Danica called out from the pilot seat. "Oh, if you think that's weird, you're really not going to believe this, Adrian."

RJ added, "I see it too." He pointed down at the main screen on his console. There were coordinates printing out there. He looked at me and shook his head in disbelief. "Those have got to be landing coordinates."

"Right in the center of the complex," confirmed Danica.

"Oh come on, you guys. RJ, trace the source."

RJ hammered a few keys and looked up at me with a wrinkled brow. "The apex of the smaller pyramid. The transmission came straight up from that pyramid."

"Oh, this is just too much."

"It's an invitation, Adrian. What are you going to do?" asked RJ.

"Just hold on one damn minute. Risking a couple lives is bad enough; taking this ship down there is a whole other level." I looked at the rest of them. "Do you guys think we should land there?"

They all started talking at once. I couldn't make out a word of it. They would continuously argue with each other, while the rest were voicing opinions at me. Then they would switch off. Just as suddenly as it had begun, they stopped and stared as though I was now fully informed.

Wilson sounded half-comical. "We have weapons and shields."

"Yeah, Wilson, but what do they have?" I said.

We all stared at Wilson.

"Have there been any other transmissions, RJ?"

"Nope. That was it."

"Paris, you're the expert. Should we leave and drop everyone else off somewhere safe, then return and just you and I make the landing?"

They all began talking at once again. This time I understood. It was not a popular idea. The outburst did not last as long. They all stopped in unison again except this time two words, source unidentifiable, capped it off, "...is bullshit."

"If they have the technology to detect scans, we'd never have a chance at getting in covertly," said Wilson.

"Does anyone have a better idea?" I asked.

In the silence that followed, I felt a tingling sensation against my chest. Putting my hand to it, I felt the bulge of my Nasebian crystal. I drew it out to find it flowing cherry red with spirals of bright white mixed in. It was the first time the crystal had reacted since emerging from the void.

"Ladies and Gentleman, strap in."

I coasted up front and took the copilot seat. "Danica, we'll deploy the landing gear and settle onto it, but keep all systems at idle. At the first sign of trouble, initiate an emergency ascent to orbit whether or not all of us are onboard. Can you make yourself do that?"

She gave me a solemn stare. "Yes."

The ride down became smooth apprehension. It was the kind of gamble wily old Adrian Tarn never takes. No ace in the hole. No plan B. No emergency escape route. You take those kinds of chances; you don't live too long. I had no choice, four words that have been used to explain big mistakes since the spoken word first existed. But down we went, just the same.

The tops of the pyramids came into view in our side windows and rose far above us as we slowed. The ship rocked from contact with the ground as it settled onto its struts. The hum wound down to an idle and remained there. We decided to use the aft airlock door facing the pyramids so the loading ramp could be deployed, a much faster access to the ship if a panicked extraction became necessary. We could eject the ramp and depart said premises with hostility, if so desired.

In the armory closet I pulled out the drawer for hand weapons, intending to take along a small plasma pistol. I was shocked and alarmed when I found not a single weapon with a charge light illuminated. I examined one closely. It was dead; so were all the others. The larger rifles were deactivated as well. There was not a charged weapon in the closet. All had been drained. There would be no armaments coming along on this visit.

RJ came up alongside, looked down and quickly realized what was going on. "Well, it would have been in bad taste anyway."

"So is dying. Plus embarrassment for a moment or two."

"I get the feeling they could have effected our demise already if they really wanted to."

"Well now we know why these people have never been bothered by outside invaders. You don't dare attack them. Your weapons don't work here."

The guinea pigs were to be Paris and me. Erin objected profusely. She had studied some of their customs. She might prevent us from doing something offensive. God knows, I was always capable of that. I said I just didn't think it was a good idea. She insisted it was. I said I was sure it wasn't. She said leaving her behind was not an option and she gave me a narrow-eyed stare that went through me like a plasma beam. I blinked and replied, "Perhaps you're right." She stomped off to get her things.

The guinea pigs were now to be Erin, Paris, and me. I thought about Wilson, but decided we would be too outnumbered for combat. No reason to put him in more risk than he was already in. As the hatch hissed open, a glaring golden portion of the larger pyramid came into view. It was so bright in the afternoon sun I couldn't tell if the structure was encased in gold or the angle of light was just making it seem that way. A marbled pathway led to it. As we bent over to pass out the hatch, two male figures standing twenty or thirty feet away appeared, waiting to greet us. They seemed completely unimpressed that a spacecraft had just landed in the center of their square. They wore gold and white wraps around the waist that came down to the knee, with blue and gold pleated aprons in the front. A pleated white wrap was draped over the right shoulder and fastened at the waist. Their legs and arms were covered with colorful tattoos. They both wore elaborate, jeweled headdresses with a large precious stone centered just above the forehead. Each held a heavily engraved golden staff, curved at the top, reaching from shoulder to ground.

Though usually not one to consider fashion, I suddenly became self-conscious about the garishness of our plain gray flight suits. In one of those idiotic moments of hindsight, I wondered if the blue would have been a better choice. Adrian Tarn, style-advisor for Egyptian dress wear. I had to fight off a sheepish expression as we considered the two greeters staring at us. The world around was so garnished with gold and silver it was breathtaking. There were pathways of colored stone that led to other buildings and the surrounding forest. Some pathways expanded into huge symbols and pictures, then narrowed again. There was no breeze at all, but the air smelled like jasmine. We paused at the bottom of the ship's ramp and tried to absorb it all. There was too much. It was too overpowering.

My best guess was that these two were priests. They waited patiently without a word. I willed myself forward and led the team. We could hear and feel the Griffin humming at idle behind us. As we approached the greeters bowed slightly, turned and took a path that led toward the smaller of the two pyramids. The larger one glistened in its gold but no entrance was visible. At its peak the apex stone was missing, as though someone had taken the key.

At the base of the smaller pyramid a long, shallow ramp trimmed in silver and bronze led up to giant double doors, opened wide. Erin started getting ahead of me, but the slow precession of the two priests kept her at bay. At the top of the ramp, I wanted badly to glance back, but dared only a quick glimpse. There was not a soul in sight, but it felt like thousands were watching.

We passed into the pyramid and a cool, shadowy ante-chamber lit by torches along the walls. We stared in wonderment. A people who had detected our scans from space, using torches to light their temple. RJ would have been beside himself. The antechamber was a vault filled with art and treasure. White polished stone floors, high, flat, intricately painted ceiling. Statues and headdresses everywhere. Gold, silver, bronze. Brightly painted images adorned the walls. This was an ancient structure kept new. The place was pristine.

Our two priest guides led us across the chamber to the far wall, a massive chunk of polished granite covered with hieroglyphs. In the very center a larger cartouche bore animal symbols, deeply engraved. To my surprise, the priests parted and stood on either side. I wondered if we were expected to kneel and pay worship. I looked at Erin. She had no answers. The awkward moment was broken by a loud, echoing boom. To our astonishment, the huge slab began to slide open to the right, the chamber beyond a stadium-sized cathedral heavily decorated with art and light. Intricate, colorful paintings and symbols covered the walls. Three story high statutes were lined against them. Beams of colored sunlight crisscrossed the room. Far in the distance a single figure sat on a throne of white marble, a shaft of light from above spotlighting her.

The priests did not follow. We looked at each other in awe and began the long walk toward the throne. The polished floor was almost slippery. The air smelled like a flower garden.

She was dressed in a sparkling silver robe that ran from neck to floor. It was similar to one I had once seen on the reclusive Nasebian emissary aboard my last ship, the Electra. As we approached, she rose and came down from her pedestal to meet us. Her hair was golden, so golden that the sunlight beaming down from above glistened on it. She was human but had the Nasebian aura; a glow about her that I had only seen once in my life. It formed an egg-shaped illumination, the same one that had surrounded the Nasebian emissary. It was overwhelming. It made you want to get as close as you could. You wanted to immerse yourself in it. It was like meeting someone who was perfectly sin-free, the pure definition of good. Her eyes were deep and blazingly blue, and also like the Nasebian emissary it was difficult to look into them for more than a moment at a time. She had a tiny nose and child-like skin-tone, ears hidden beneath the shimmering fall of long hair.

"Thank you for coming. I foresaw your arrival," she said, but her mouth never opened, her lips never moved. We all heard her.

I wanted to ask how she should be addressed, but before I could speak, there was an answer.

"Amoura."

Paris and Erin stood dumbfounded, a flood of astonishment filling their minds.

Amoura thought to us, "You have many questions but require few answers. Let me offer them." She clasped her delicate hands within her sleeves and continued. "My father was Capal. He descended to Earth long ago. He was not well. He organized those living here and eventually one of my ancestors became his protégé and helped him recover. Nasebians proliferate differently than your species. Although there was absence of physical contact, my ancestor eventually found she was with child, a conception caused by prolonged close contact with a Nasebian host. She gave birth to a daughter and a new life cycle began. When he was able and had those resources necessary, Capal returned to the heavens. I am a continuation of the hereditary line graced to this world by Capal. Someday I will give birth to a daughter and I will begin the euphorisis. Evolution to higher dimensions is a gradual one. My daughter will remain and continue the line, as I have."

"I am the Udjat you seek. All that the Udjat is, am I. In recent times a distant species has begun visiting this Earth. They have become aware of my presence. When I leave, there will be nothing of interest for them here. My people, the others of this world, and the visitors, will again be safe. My people have been preparing for this coming for many years. Nothing you see around you will change. They will make provisions for me to travel with you. I will remain in stasis for the duration of the journey. Arrangements will be made to receive me when we arrive. Have I answered your many questions?"

Apparently she had, because we all stood there with blank stares on our faces.

She began again, "If you will go now and prepare your craft and people, I will be brought to you."

I bowed. I do not know exactly why. All vanity had escaped me, no small accomplishment for Adrian Tarn. I did not see how the other two reacted, but there was no doubt we all sufficiently expressed our awe before turning and silently walking back to the ship. It occurred to me I had not said a word, and had barely even managed a single question. Nor had the others. I had the feeling we were all wondering what had just happened. We were now heading back to the ship to await the arrival of a hybrid Human-Nasebian, a prospect that left me feeling inadequate and exhilarated.

Chapter 41

We kept the ship at idle as we waited. I sat in the nuisance of gravity at the oval table, swept away by yet another turn of fate. Erin briefed the rest of the crew, leaving them in the same near-catatonic state trying to grasp what was happening. I looked up from my seat in search of a blast of daylight and found Paris standing next to me.

"Adrian, we need to talk."

"Sure, what's up?"

"It needs to be private. Can we use the science lab? No one's back there."

We walked heavily back to the lab. Paris pulled the connecting door shut but did not close it all the way. Light from the open door in the adjoining airlock beamed in.

"There's some things I need to clear the air on," he said, and he had never looked so intent.

"Paris, this may not be necessary. I know things haven't always been exactly good between us. I've always known I was a bad judge of character. I should have done better with you. I was wrong about you from the start."

"Forget it, Adrian. You weren't so wrong about me. Part of what I need to tell you is pretty ugly. I might as well get right to the point. If you take down the little overhead night light in my sleeper cell, you'll find a memory module. It contains all the information I've gathered on the stellar drives, the weapons systems, and the shields. There are two people within the agency who are dealing illegally with off-worlders. They want the Nasebian technology badly. Their names are there. I kept them on the module for insurance. The reason we had an antenna fail on the way in was because I was secretly trying to force XYK band transmissions through the antenna amplifier to send the classified data out. No one would have seen those transmissions."

"Why? Why would you do that?"

"Are you kidding? There are off-worlders who can offer you part of a populated planet as your own if you'll do their bidding; live the rest of your life as a God, almost."

"And you wanted that?"

"No. A quantum physics doctorate like me? Hell no. They were going to give me the names of the people who caused the death of my family. I would have done most anything to get those names."

"Well, at least I'd have to say I can understand that part. I might feel the same way in your position. Tell me something, was Bernard Porre one of the names on your bad-guys list?"

"Are you kidding? No. Porre is so infatuated with his own sense of perfection the mere suggestion of him breaking the law would probably make him faint. I guess at this point I'm not in a position to be judging anyone, though."

"Why this sudden change of heart?"

"This trip has changed a lot of things. It's been more than a wakeup call, it's been the best thing that ever happened to me. The man in the black cloak was my recent past come to call. I knew that all along."

"Paris, this is kind of a strange time to pick to come clean, isn't it?"

"There's a reason for that. Besides, it's never too late to confess your sins, don't you agree?"

"Maybe this can all be worked out. This mission would not have succeeded without you. Seems to me that balances things out pretty well. Back on Earth, they can still get the bad guys. I don't see you as really being one of them. When we get back I believe I can manage this. I'll see that it's taken care of and that you're left out of it. When we return I think I can arrange it so that you'll be free and clear."

"That's the other thing, Adrian. I'm not going back. I'm staying."

"What? Are you out of your mind?"

"Something else I haven't told you. My wife is here. She's an exact copy in every way. She's three or four years younger than she would have been had she lived, but it's her."

"How do you know this?"

"In the library, when we discovered the duplicates, I fished around just on the outside chance. I found a recent picture of her at a hospital fundraiser. I nearly passed out from the shock. It's the largest hospital in New Province City, not that far from the library. I went AWOL and took a trolley there while you guys were still away. I promised Erin I would tell you when the time was right. I got a look at the hospital staff schedule when the front desk was left unattended, and hung around until my wife came on duty supporting the ER. Then I cut myself to get admitted. She walked by my treatment room door and I called her by her new name, Maretta. She stopped and stared at me for the longest time. She came into the room and I hit her with the same lines I used on my wife. She came back with some of the same answers. She waved off the intern and treated me herself. There was an instant thing between us. I picked a subject that I knew was dear to my wife's heart and asked her if she'd meet me over lunch to discuss it. She agreed. I need to get back there."

"Holy crap, Paris!"

"I really need to get back there."

"This isn't your world, Paris."

"It is now."

We stared at each other in a long, silent, telling moment. I did not need to measure his determination. That old saying that the eyes are windows to the soul was more than fitting. Everything Paris Denard had lived through was there, impressed upon me.

"You could have disappeared from us right from the hospital, couldn't you? We would have played hell trying to find you."

He looked at me but did not speak.

"You came back to finish the mission, even though you knew I might not let you stay. You knew we might not have been able to do this without you."

We stared at each other in a moment of understanding.

"My God, Paris. What are you getting into?"

"I will marry her and I will get my wife and daughter back."

"What if it goes bad? What if it doesn't work out? She dumps you a few weeks into the relationship?"

"I know that woman better than I know myself. I'll give her all the things she wants before she even knows she wants them. It's a test I already have all the answers to."

"After we leave, there won't be any Earth ships coming by this way any time soon."

"If any do, tell them not to bother dropping by. I won't need them."

"You're that sure?"

"Absolutely."

"My God, Paris."

"You going to let me do this?"

"What if there's another you out there somewhere?"

"I'll change my appearance just enough. No one Erin and I ran into knew me. No one at the hospital knew me. I doubt there's another me anywhere in that part of the world."

"Wow, still, you're asking a lot."

"You can just leave me right here. I'll work my way back to the city."

"Family and friends on Earth?"

"No family left. I've been pretty reclusive. I'll barely be missed."

"Paris..."

"I know this is a bitch for you. There will be red tape when you get back. You could get called on the carpet for leaving me."

"Not too concerned about that part. I get in trouble better than anybody I know. If they want to call me on the carpet they'll probably have to get in line. You could say I have post graduate work in breaking all the rules."

"There could even be legal ramifications."

"I'm usually on the beach with a fishing pole when those happen."

"So will you do it? Will you risk your career for me?"

"Stay on board, but be ready to be dropped off."

"Please don't trick me on this, Adrian. It's everything to me."

"I'll call you to the forward airlock when it's time."

A tap at the door interrupted us. RJ called out, "Adrian, you'd better come see this."

We returned to the habitat area and found everyone glued to the portals. We squeezed in to see. There was an ocean of people surrounding the ship. Thousands. Colorful clothing, signs and banners, the name Amoura held high in every direction. It was becoming noisy. Tambourines, cymbals, horns, and drums began going off everywhere. There did not appear to be any kind of security personnel, but somehow a wide pathway on our right remained open. We strained to look and spotted a procession in the distance headed our way. Lavish wardrobes, large golden medallions hanging from necks, tall staffs, sacred relics held high.

The parade slowly passed by. It was a long one. Twenty minutes of marchers before the heart of the ceremony came into view. Our guest of honor was inside a sarcophagus woven from strands of gold. It was shaped in her form and the spaces within the weave made her sparkling silver gown partially visible. Six bearers carried her on a litter covered in bright red cloth. They paused in front of the ship and slowly turned to face our ramp. The crowd quieted. There seemed to be no verbal coordination required. At the base of the ramp they stepped up in unison. Near the top a reorganization of positioning began, but the litter remained absolutely motionless and protected. At the airlock entrance two bearers entered and received the litter. Their motions were fluid and calculated. They seemed to require no guidance whatsoever. They brought the sarcophagus in, never touching a wall or door, and turned it for entry into our sleeper section. I stood at the door near the galley. They ignored me.

We had left the sleeper cell across from mine open to receive her. The lead bearers backed into the corridor and aligned the litter. They cautiously slid litter and sarcophagus into place and secured it with heavily embroidered ties. From satchels they withdrew items that looked like incense, alms, and other items of worship and turned to look at me with expressions of patient entreat. I understood and backed away to the habitat area. The crew looked on stone silent as the Griffin continued to hum at idle. The ceremony took less than ten minutes. The bearers slowly departed single file out the airlock and down the ramp without speaking a word. The sleeper cell compartment door had been closed. Amoura was in her stasis travel state.

The crowds persisted outside the ship, though they became quiet. I made my way to the flight deck and asked Danica to make the ascent as slow and as gentle as possible. A pause at fifty feet seemed called for. Wilson and I cast a last look at the somber faces in the crowd, retracted the ramp, and slowly closed and sealed the hatch. Danica brought the engines up gradually, causing the masses to back away. We slowly lifted off, paused at fifty feet and brought the gear up, then drifted upward away from the assembly.

Back on the flight deck I stood behind Danica and said, "One more stop to make." She looked up at me inquisitively.

"We have to drop Paris off. He's staying."

"You can't be serious."

"He has his reasons, and I agree with them."

"But we're not coming back."

"He knows."

"But why?"

"Hold on orbit until darkness, then take us down to the same drop off point."

She looked at me with an endearing expression I had not seen before. I nodded but could not think of anything appropriate to say.

"Setting course to the geosynchronous Provincial City drop point, Commander."

Paris began saying goodbyes as we readied ourselves for descent into the planet's early evening darkness. I met him in the airlock without having to call. I handed him every bit of gold, silver, and platinum from the science lab. We opened the hatch together at fifty feet and watched the shadows of Earth II's forest slowly come into view. Danica brought us to a hover two feet off the ground. Without hesitation Paris jumped to the grass and turned to look back. I nodded and he reciprocated. I yelled clear to Danica and we slowly began to rise, but I could not bring myself to shut the hatch. Paris and I locked eyes. It was as though a new man was staring back at me. It was also a new friendship, one I suddenly regretted leaving behind. The moment was so intense I stood bent over holding the hatch, unable to close and break our gaze. At one hundred feet, he was a silhouette too far for eye contact. I reached out and waved, and saw him wave back. He looked away and ducked into the brush, a man heading back in time in more ways than one. I twisted the hatch shut, stood and held on, then considered the value of love and what both men and women were sometimes willing to do for it. It occurred to me there was nothing exempt, nothing at all. A time-tested proof that if you loved your family enough, there was absolutely nothing you wouldn't do to protect them or find your way back to them. Paris was on his way back, and way down deep inside in a place usually avoided there was a voice telling me he would make it.

Danica brought us to orbit and when we came into position, kicked in the OMS engines to drive us away from Earth II's stronger influence. She put us in station keeping so we could prepare for the jump. Amoura's bearers already had secured her sarcophagus within the cell. All that remained was last minute stowage and strapping in. The jump position put Earth II outside our starboard portals. We all took a moment to float there and stare out at the blue and green orb slowly rotating in the sunlight. The vision was so different from when we had first arrived. We knew who lived there. It was a sibling race of humans. It would be difficult not to consider them family. They were getting ready to enter the dirty nuclear age, the age where you learn by hurting yourself. There was a quantum physicist from the future down there now. Maybe he would help make that transition less painful. Maybe no Hiroshimas would be necessary on Earth II.

Strapped in and waiting for the jump, we watched the last of the Earth II's broadcasts on the forward monitors. RJ, sitting next to me, said, "I'm going to miss these black and white 2Ds."

"You can always shut the color off your screens."

"It's not the same. The intent isn't there. The honestness of gray scale is missing."

"Then there are the uncolored versions of the classics."

"Yes. The only saving grace."

A banner suddenly popped up on the screen announcing 'Breaking News'. A news broadcaster appeared with a headline behind him reading 'Sound Barrier Broken'. A military spokesperson had confirmed that today at 09:50 standard time, test pilot Colonel Vance Cameron had piloted the rocket aircraft Flair 1 past the sound barrier at an undisclosed military facility. No further details were available at this time. An image of a pilot climbing down from a rocket plane appeared on the screen. The

Colonel was seen walking away still wearing his helmet, his oxygen mask hanging down against his chest. As he past the camera, he paused for a moment and stared directly into it. It felt like he was looking at us. The Griffin kicked forward to light. The image faded into snow.

Wilson called back from his station, "By God, he did it!"

RJ looked over at me, "I have a feeling our secrets are safe."

Danica and Shelly settled us to our first leg. As we pulled away, I realized we were on a different spacecraft. From the moment Amoura had been brought aboard the ship had become a very different place. I thought perhaps the effect would wear off once we settled into routine, but the aura persisted. There was a golden tint in the air. Golden sparkles out of the corner of your eye made you stop and look, though they seemed to disappear when you searched for them. The corridor between the sleeper cells had a visibly golden glow to it, as well. I felt both apprehension and entrancement at the thought of sleeping within that strange ambiance. Somehow, I seemed to feel it was more than I deserved.

We were affected in other ways even more personal. There was a subtle joyousness between us. It was the night before Christmas, the morning of leaving for Disney World, or the day of the family camping trip. It was all of those and it did not wane or ebb. The crew consciously had to stop themselves from smiling at each other, often unable to do so. Everyone came to understand it was the Amoura effect, though we did not speak of it. Everyone's jokes were especially funny. When someone told a story, it was totally captivating. The poker games were intensely entertaining. You found yourself just as happy for the winners as you were dejected by losing. Everyone was always on his best behavior. It wasn't actually euphoria, it was more like euphoria was coming.

Time became a luxury, though not in the conventional sense. Every minute of every day was too good to miss. We plunged into the void without a second thought and realized it had seemed like days not weeks getting there. There would be no stopping this time. No high school coaches, beauty contests, professional kick boxing events, and no figures in black cloaks looming.

Something unexpected waited for us on the other side. We burst into stars hardly noticing, still at top warp, until Shelly in the pilot seat called out "Adrian," on the com system and the tone of her voice made everyone stop what they were doing and pay attention.

Out the front flight deck windows the largest spacecraft I had ever seen was leading us. It was pancake-shaped but had appendages here and there and nacelle-like structures aft. It looked like the thing was riveted together with tiny beads of light all over it. As I gawked from behind Shelly, someone called out, "Adrian, you'd better get back here."

"Not now," I answered.

"Yes, now," replied RJ.

I went back to find there was another identical ship alongside us to port, and a third ship flanking us to starboard.

Wilson, at an engineering station, called out next. "Adrian, check your monitors."

I looked up at the nearest display in time to see a message slowly spelling out one letter at a time.

'Commander Tarn, permission to transfer your passenger and mission logs? –Mellenia.'

I am not one prone to goose bumps, but when I saw the name Mellinia, I had them. My heart skipped a beat. The Nasebian emissary I had shared so much with on my last fateful mission was aboard one of these ships. I wanted to see her in the worst way, and I knew she was already sensing that. I realized I was holding my breath. My Nasebian crystal was vibrating in my breast pocket. I hurried over to the engineering station next to Wilson and typed the message myself.

'Permission granted. Our warmest regards.'

There was a faint hum as we became enveloped in a white glow. It lasted no more than thirty seconds. Suddenly the Griffin seemed to have less color. We were weightless, but the weightlessness seemed to be slightly heavier. Things did not look quite as good as they had. I discovered I was hungry. I looked at the others. They were experiencing the same feelings. I went to the sleeper section and tapped open Amoura's compartment. It was empty. Wilson called me once more.

"They didn't just copy the logs. They cut them, Adrian. We have no mission logs left whatsoever, and no personal logs. There is not one reference to Earth II left on this ship."

"I believe we can infer that all mission information is now classified," I replied.

Wilson nodded. Before he could speak, Shelly called out. "Adrian, you better get up here and look at this."

RJ hung behind me. As I pulled forward he remarked, "Busy day..."

The Nasebian ships were gone. Shelly was pointing one red fingernail to the navigation display. "Two days," she said.

I looked at the display and tried to get my mind to believe. On the blue flight path line our ship designator was now located two days from Earth. In the time the Nasebian ships had accompanied us we had traveled in minutes what should have taken weeks. We were two days from home, just the right amount of time to organize and get ready for reentry and mission resolution.

When we had regained our composure and begun to adapt to reality without Amoura, I took a seat at the table with RJ and helped him capture escaped solitaire cards. He seemed moody in a delighted way. He needed the ace of hearts to go up top, but the deck left in his hand was too small. He wasn't going to get it. He spoke as he counted cards out. "You see what has happened here, don't you?"

"Oh boy, here you go again, coming up with some brilliant insight, making me feel like an idiot."

"Well do you want to know or not?"

"Go ahead,"

"The Nasebian escape pod had a combination of machine and biological circuitry, according to your scans."

"Yep."

"So bio-systems are why the Nasebians can't go through the void, and that's why the first Nasebian ship got into trouble, causing Earth II to happen."

"I would have thought of that, eventually."

"Add to that, something in that area of space is incompatible with them, though Capal seems to have overcome it. I'm guessing this sort of thing is as close as you can come to a Nasebian embarrassment. That's why they cut all our Earth II data and will dispense it only as required."

"Pretty messy affair. A whole planet."

"And the question remains, where is Capal?"

"My guess would be, probably anywhere he feels like being."

"There's something else perhaps I should not mention."

"Oh, for Pete's sake! The embarrassing insights are bad enough."

"Well do you want to know or not?"

"Go ahead, dignity lost in any case."

"The Nasebians have been careful to guide our Earth along in its development of deep space travel. It's what they do. And, the Nasebians are responsible for Earth II. They're not going to just let the place run amok. They're going to want to make adjustments. The void, and the space beyond it, is a problem even for them. They're going to need someone to go back there eventually, someone who knows the score."

"Oh my God."

"Well, it's just a guess."

Chapter 42

We put down on the very same launch apron used for departure so many months before. It had rained during the night and there were patches of water on the tarmac. The buildings and greenery glistened in the morning light. The air was cool without wind. With the rear airlock hatch open and the loading ramp deployed, the whine of the Griffin's engines wound down. I secretly had a touch of regret in knowing they would not restart any time soon.

It was 06:10 EST. There was much more of a reception than any of us expected. Dignitaries in formal wear, Genesis people in great numbers, a few family members who had traveled long distances to be there. A surprisingly large crowd behind them even topped by a few welcome back banners. It was such a boisterous ceremony, I was grateful they had not hired a band. We had to stand on the tarmac and endure unnecessary people at the portable podium. We were quietly taken aside and told how the Akuma crew had been placed in induced comas in a cryogenics facility while doctors perfected their recovery treatment. In a curious coincidence, the last of them had been awakened in just the past month. They had recovered completely. Captain Mako Hayashi had also made a full recovery, her memory more intact than the others as a result of her self-imposed isolation in an Akuma cold-storage locker. Recovery of the Akuma crew had dominated the news for the past several weeks. Between approvals of our mission from the Nasebian ambassador and delayed accolades related to the Akuma, our return was too much of a political wildcard for politicians to ignore.

When the torture of it finally whimpered to a close, there were no shuttles to take us home. There were limousines. The most expensive floater limos I had ever seen. No tires, no suspension, gravity repulse ride. The crew fled each other like fleas off a sprayed dog. In my limo was a bottle of champagne in a bucket of ice with a card attached.

'I'll give you a day or two in gravity, but be ready. I'm coming, -Nira.'

There was to be no debriefing. The Nasebians would provide any debriefing information required. We were quietly told never to mention Earth II or anything related to it. At the time, I could have cared less. My primary thought was for a hot whirlpool soak and a stiff drink. The rest of the crew did not disclose their destinations. We did not even say goodbye. That's not what it was. Most of them planned to head out of state immediately. It's not so much that you actually want to be that far away from your former crewmates. It's more that you wish to prove to yourself that you can get that far away from your former crewmates.

The cover on the Vette had such a layer of dust I had to roll it up slowly. She glistened black at me and dared me to the open road. I patted the glass top and resigned myself to a beer and bed.

The next afternoon I drove to Genesis to pick up a few things left behind. At the gate a different guard waved me in. To my surprise, RJ sat in the corner of my office, his feet propped up on a chair drinking steaming black coffee, staring at a tablet magazine article about the Akuma.

"You wouldn't believe what just happened to me," he said, without looking up.

"RJ, you're a sight for sore eyes."

"You don't know the half of it."

"Aren't you planning on living in the woods or something for a while?"

"Yep. Forever Florida. Gonna do some volunteer work there with the animals. Get some dirt under my fingernails. Eat wild radishes. Probably catch a cold. Chase naturalist women, sit around a campfire and tell tall tales."

"So why are you here?"

"Thought I'd stop in on my way back from the doctor's."

"Which doctor is that?"

"The medical report you brought back from the place we never were. I took it to my primary care guy. He had a lot of trouble with the strange terminology. I told him it was a bad translation from a foreign language. He called in his associates. They gradually deciphered it. They became alarmed. Brain scans needed to be run right away. They were probably misinterpreting the data. They ran the scans right there in the MD's office. They became even more alarmed. The patient began to be concerned. It was a tiny aneurysm waiting to happen in the worst possible place. A beam treatment needed to be done immediately. They made the patient take an ambulance. Hundreds of light years out and back and I wasn't allowed to drive five miles to the hospital. The treatment took forty-five minutes including the undressing and dressing. A routine procedure. The area in question could have ruptured at any time. The hi-res scans showed no other problems. The doctors celebrated their intervention and went to lunch with several of the female scanner technicians. They forgot to tell me I could leave, but, here I am. So, how's your day been going?"

"Jesus, RJ."

"Played a part in all of that, I have no doubt. What about you? Any life changing events scheduled?"

"Nira is on her way."

"Well, that answers that. There's something else I probably shouldn't tell you."

"Oh no. There's more?"

"Well, do you want to know or not?"

"Go ahead. It's too late now."

"Mr. Bernard Porre is in Julia's office."

"Oh shit! Do I have time to sneak out?"

"Nope. He's here to see you. He'd just follow you like a stray dog."

"I'd prefer the dog."

Just then, there was a timid tap at my door. It was Bernard. He opened and slid inside, forcing his briefcase through as the door tried to close, then brushing off his too-blue Nehru suit jacket, becoming completely distracted with it when it was not to his liking, and finally looking up at us.

"Mr. Tarn. Mr. Smith."

"Mr. Porre. How is it we are graced with your presence?"

He began to say something but became distracted with his suit jacket again. Finally, he refocused. "Gentleman, greetings and salutations. I require just a few moments of your time, Mr. Tarn, if you have that much available. Mr. Smith, you are welcome to remain."

"Bernard, on your last visit you promised you would leave forever."

"Mr. Tarn, the humiliation is mine. Not only must I endure the aberrance of your presence yet again, to make my indignation complete I must also present you with a reward. Can there be a crueler fate for anyone? I ask you that."

"Reward me? You're here to reward me? How can your being here in any way be considered a reward?"

"I wish only to take my leave of you. To be rid of me, you need only to sign this receipt." He pulled out a stack of printouts stapled together and dropped them onto the desk in front of me.

"Just the last page, please."

"Paper? You're using paper for this? You're asking me to sign a paper document?"

"Bravo!" piped RJ.

"Bernard, there must be two dozen pages here."

"Twenty-seven to be exact. They just say that you accept delivery and will comply with all appropriate conditions."

"I have to read all twenty-seven pages of this?"

"Only if you wish me to remain with you for that long. If you simply sign it, I shall depart with vigor."

"God, you're good at getting people to do things they don't want to, Bernard."

"It is a gift, I think."

I grumbled and signed. Bernard said nothing. He drew a small box from his briefcase and slid it across my desk. It looked like a gift box for a watch. This had to be the gold watch ceremony. I popped it open and stared inquisitively. "There's been some mistake here, I think. These are the flight deck keys to the Griffin. Oh, I get it. This is a souvenir. But why all the paperwork, Bernard? Is this classified technology or something?"

"Oh, the indignation of it. It is a gift from our grateful Nasebian friends, Mr. Tarn. Like you, they made us an offer we could not refuse. We have a set of stellar drives in Washington now to study as we please, though we are not allowed to use the technology until such time as we can reproduce it. The condition was that the Griffin be transferred to you, with ground support as needed. An old hanger near the VAB has been set aside. Though it pains me greatly to say it, the Griffin is there, at your disposal."

"Are you saying I own the Griffin?"

"Please, I can barely tolerate the thought."

"And I can go wherever I want?"

"Beyond the current Earth star charts, you will be required to file with a Nasebian agency for approval."

"This is another joke. Like when you took the Vette's lug nut key."

"I do not know how you managed to recover that. The asteroid field I chose should have been dense enough to destroy that probe completely. It is yet another injurious neuron set in my mind that will fund my confusion about your undeserved successes for years to come."

"I own the Griffin?"

"The agency may request your assistance from time to time. You are not obligated to accept, God forbid. The Nasebians have also instructed that you bring the Griffin to their Enuro service port some time within the next six months for installation of artificial gravity. They were not perfectly happy with the constraints you had to endure without it. They also may ask you for special assistance in the future and again you are not obligated to accept."

"I own the Griffin?"

"It reminds me of something my wife once said."

RJ interjected, "You have a wife?"

"It was when my youngest daughter returned from her fourteenth driver's test, holding the signed certificate out for all to see. Can you imagine what my wife's comment was, Mr. Tarn?"

"Bernard, I cannot imagine anything about your wife."

She said, and I quote, *"Oh my God, the airways will never be the same."*

He began to add something but paused to brush an errant ant off his trousers. "I now understand fully what she meant, Mr. Tarn. Handing you those spacecraft administrator keys, I can only think the galaxy will never be the same."

I looked at RJ. He was staring wide-eyed, his coffee cup tipped, a small flow of coffee streaming down the side.

Bernard gathered up the documents from my desk and headed for the door. "Mr. Smith, how's the Corvair?" He turned at the door to add something, thought better of it, waved the two of us off, and disappeared out.

RJ looked at me with coffee still dripping from the side of his cup. "Holy crap!"

My visit to Genesis was supposed to have been a quick stop, barely a footnote to the day. I headed back home with my mind in state of numbness. I could not process what had just happened. I parked the Vette in the garage and for no reason stood and watched the big door roll shut. Inside, I grabbed a bottle of bourbon, scooped ice into a glass and poured myself a stiff one, my hand shaking a small bit, overpowered by visions of the Griffin sitting in a hanger at KSC waiting for me. In my living room I snapped on a light and froze from a completely new kind of disbelief. There sitting on a recliner was Reeves 'Doc' Walker. He was smiling.

I had to brace myself against the arm of the couch. I tipped my drink and some of it ran onto the carpet. I rubbed my eyes with one hand and refocused, expecting him to disappear. He did not. He held up one hand and spoke, "You're okay. It really is me."

"What the hell?"

"I'll explain. You'll want to sit first."

I took a belt of the bourbon and slowly sat without taking my eyes off him for fear he'd disappear.

"I'm not really here. I'm sitting in a control seat in the center of a humongous pyramid on Nasebia. Incredible, isn't it?"

There was still a chance this was a hallucination. I sat with my glass still held near my mouth and tried to think of a way to test reality.

"I've got about thirty minutes before the Earth rotates outside the transmission window. But that's plenty of time."

"You weren't killed on ZY627a?"

"Nope."

"But I saw that thing capture you. You were submerged in slime and then you were gone. There was nothing we could do."

"Yep. One second I was immersed in green crap, the next second I was standing on some kind of Nasebian transport pad, clean as a whistle."

"A Nasebian ship? A Nasebian ship rescued you at the last minute?"

"More like the last second. The Nasebians secretly escorted you in stealth mode all the way to the void. If you don't know they are there, you do not think about them and that's less of an intrusion to them. The void was as far as they could go. It was the best they could do. They were monitoring our landing when the giant grasshopper showed up. Here's the deal. When the Nasebians asked you to take this mission, to them that was like meddling in someone's destiny. It's very unusual for them to make that kind of request of a lower species like us. They could not allow my death or they would be responsible for a major screw up in my life's timeline. When a human dies a whole bunch of complex science happens on levels we do not understand yet, and to interrupt that particular timeline is a really big deal, but that's a whole other story. When the big grasshopper decided I was lunch, they pulled me out and brought me back to Nasebia. They could not return me to the Griffin or to Earth because that would be another violation of their rules. After all, the grasshopper won fair and square, right? To put me back on the Griffin would have conflicted with what naturally happened and they don't do that. So, I get to live the rest of my life on Nasebia with the Nasebians. This place is one step away from heaven, by the way."

"My God, Doc. That whole affair was a hurtful damned thing."

"Yeah, sorry to put you through that, but it's what happens sometimes when humans go exploring, eh?"

"But don't Nasebians abhor being near humans?"

"Pretty much. Truth is they don't like being next to each other all that much, either. The thing is, their auras, if I can use that term, have expanded so much over the centuries that they are in each other's space even when they're not in the same room. So all of us here on Nasebia sense each other all the time. Actual personal presence just makes it that much stronger. In a way, you are never alone on Nasebia. The other thing is, there's a feeling of euphoria here all the time. So for me, it's like living in a heavenly euphoria with a bunch of ghosts. But after experiencing that, nobody would want to leave. I sure don't."

"But how will you live?"

"I will be a new kind of emissary for them. I can provide them with a better way to communicate with humans. It's not so much them needing to understand us, it's us needing to understand them. Contacting you is my first official job. Otherwise, I'm here learning at my own pace, enjoying the hell out of myself. I can experience things here you cannot imagine."

"Can I tell the rest of the crew about this?"

"Please do. Their life cycles were affected by my untimely demise. Knowing I'm more than okay is important for them."

"Can I contact you if I need to?"

"Yes, as a matter of fact you can. Go through the agency's Extraglobal Affairs group. You and the rest of the crew will be warmly received. Tell them you are requesting a contact. I'll pop up somewhere convenient as soon as I'm able."

I realized I was still holding the bourbon near my mouth. I took a drink and lowered my hand. "We did okay with the Akuma, didn't we?"

"Yes. We did. A really good mark in time, as they would say. Another thing, the Earth II mission turned out to be a really big deal here. The Nasebians did not know about Amoura. When they got wind of a half-Human half-Nasebian hybrid coming it was the first time I've seen them show excitement. She will take over Earth's galactic management. It will be a big status boost for Earth."

"What about Earth II?"

"It's being sorted out. It's so far away it's a challenge, and that area of space is a bit incompatible with Nasebian spiritual biology. They are compelled to oversee it, though. It's Amoura's home. There will be a plan. They don't consider anything to be an accident, but they seem to still be trying to fit this into the scheme of life. There is also the matter of Capal. I have not been able to understand their feelings about him. Sometimes I get the impression he's a rebel, but that doesn't really fit."

"Doc, there's one thing I'd like to know. Do the Nasebians believe in God?"

"Ah, such a good question, Adrian. You sure wouldn't want to ask them that and have the answer directly downloaded into your brain, would you? It's not a question of belief with the Nasebians. God is a fact to them. God is defined as the basic laws of the universe or cosmos. God is everything that existed the instant before the Big Bang took place. They contend that all humans believe in God, too. If you believe you are real and alive, then by default you must believe that the universe and everything around you is real, therefore you believe in God. They also concede some humans do not believe God is intelligent, that God is just some natural laws at work. I've struggled to get a handle on their discourse about that. It's a mind-bender. In studying it I am reminded of something I once read in a very old science fiction B-novel. It went like this: can a desert completely void of water give birth to a garden, and can a universe completely void of intelligence give birth to billions of intellects?"

"Doc, I'm glad I didn't lose you."

"I'm just about out of time here. One thing, Adrian. I'm not afraid of people anymore. I understand now that the mix of immature souls and mature souls is the fastest way for both to learn. Remember to keep an eye on the airspeed indicator, buddy. I'll see you around."

And he was gone. The room suddenly felt empty. My glass of bourbon was almost empty, most having run out onto the floor, the ice nearly melted. I walked dazed back into the kitchen and made a new drink, deciding I needed it even more now.

In the days that followed, I turned Paris' memory module over to the Office of Extraglobal Affairs. Three weeks after our landing text messages began flying around about a one-month reunion for the Griffin crew. Wilson had taken an apartment in Satellite Beach, as near as he could get to Heidi's. Shelly bought a condo on Merritt Island. Erin returned home to her cat and parents, apparently in that order. Danica flew herself home in a borrowed antique T38 trainer jet. RJ was still camping out at Forever Florida.

On the day of our reunion, Nira and I cruised south on A1A until the turnoff for Heidi's came into view. The place was busy. I had to park in the rear to find a safe spot for the Vette's paint job. As I locked the car, RJ's faded blue Corvair pulled in and parked next to us. He got out wearing baggy jeans, worn work shoes, and a T-shirt that read 'Back To Analog'. It made me feel like my white dress shirt, tan sports jacket, and black slacks were overdress. Nira just laughed. A bouncer greeted us at the door, a man who looked like he could handle himself. No cover charge for the Griffin crew.

They had set up a big table in a far corner. Danica and Erin had come in on the same connecting flight. They were already seated and saw us through the noisy crowd. They held up wine glasses as we approached and clinked them. Danica was in jeans with a white cotton blouse covered by an open gray cardigan sweater. Shelly had chosen a light tan business-styled suit with a ruffled white blouse. Erin wore a turtle-necked blue and black flowered dress that stopped above the knee. We arrived at the table as Wilson emerged from the crowd holding two amber beer bottles. He craned his neck against the collar of his black turtleneck and worked his way back into his seat where he raised a bottle to us. "Captain Nemo and the Farmer In The Dell, escorted by the Princess of Mars, glad you could join us." Jeannie, in her server outfit, pushed in and plunked drinks down in front of us, then stood behind Wilson resting her hands on his shoulders.

We took seats and our table quieted. We looked at each other with silent affection that can only be understood after months of exotic confinement together. It is a combination of family and friendship, and when danger has been a strong part of the experience, that friendship becomes tempered like the heated, folded blade of a tuned Excalibur. It will not break.

RJ raised his glass. "Ladies and Gentleman, let us begin with a toast to Doc, a good friend not with us today."

They quietly raised their drinks, called out in agreement, but before they could seal the toast, I held up one hand and said, "Wait!"

They paused and looked at me with questioning stares. I motioned them to put their drinks back down. I leaned forward, and as best I could, told them the epilog of Reeves 'Doc' Walker, the man who had so unexpectedly greeted me just days before in my living room. As the story unfolded, they became speechless. Erin wiped a tear away. Wilson sat with his head cocked to one side fearing it was all a bad joke. Danica looked at me with threatening eyes as if to warn it had better not be. RJ remained expressionless. Shelly, eyes wide, held one hand over her mouth. I finished up by telling them if anyone had any doubts they too could get in touch through the agency's Extraglobal Affairs office.

The silence remained heavy. They continued to stare as if there might be more. RJ broke the spell. He raised his glass and said, "Ladies and Gentlemen, to friends not lost."

One by one they joined the toast. We clinked our drinks and sat back, relaxing from the effects of surprise.

Erin was next. "I would like to propose one for Mr. Paris Denard. A man who traveled farther than anyone ever has to get back home."

We toasted in agreement once more. The celebration broke up into smaller conversations that spread around the table. As the night wore on, the stigma of having been cooped up together for too long gradually faded away. We became a fresh crew again. Some of us were enjoying the drinks too much. RJ and I remained respectable. At one point, the owner came in a back door and waved. I grabbed Jeannie and told her I wanted to speak to him to be sure things were okay between us. She escorted RJ and I over and introduced us over the crowd noise.

It turned out he was an avid Griffin fan. There were no hard feelings from our last visit. No credits were needed. There was one thing we could do for him however: a picture of the Griffin crew together, signed by each of us. I explained we'd be glad to do that but no such picture existed. He said tonight was the perfect time to take one. He could hang the only photo of the Griffin crew, signed by all of them. It would be a treasure. We agreed. We shook hands. He lifted the bar to go find his camera, but was suddenly stopped by the sound of glass breaking, followed by Wilson's booming voice above the crowd noise.

"Now I don't want any trouble!"